FRONTIER AMERICA

This Large Print Book carries the
Seal of Approval of N.A.V.H.

A PREACHER & MACCALLISTER WESTERN

FRONTIER AMERICA

WILLIAM W. JOHNSTONE
AND J. A. JOHNSTONE

THORNDIKE PRESS
A part of Gale, a Cengage Company

GALE
A Cengage Company

Copyright © 2019 by J. A. Johnstone.
WWJ steer head logo is a Reg. U.S. Pat. & TM Off.
Thorndike Press, a part of Gale, a Cengage Company.

ALL RIGHTS RESERVED
Following the death of William W. Johnstone, the Johnstone family is working with a carefully selected writer to organize and complete Mr. Johnstone's outlines and many unfinished manuscripts to create additional novels in all of his series like The Last Gunfighter, Mountain Man, and Eagles, among others. This novel was inspired by Mr. Johnstone's superb storytelling.
Thorndike Press® Large Print Western.
The text of this Large Print edition is unabridged.
Other aspects of the book may vary from the original edition.
Set in 16 pt. Plantin.

LIBRARY OF CONGRESS CIP DATA ON FILE.
CATALOGUING IN PUBLICATION FOR THIS BOOK
IS AVAILABLE FROM THE LIBRARY OF CONGRESS

ISBN-13: 978-1-4328-7215-1 (hardcover alk. paper)

Published in 2019 by arrangement with Pinnacle Books, an imprint of Kensington Publishing Corp.

Printed in Mexico
1 2 3 4 5 6 7 23 22 21 20 19

FRONTIER AMERICA

CHAPTER 1

Preacher nestled his cheek against the smooth wood of the Sharps rifle's stock and peered over the barrel. He stood behind the thick trunk of a pine tree, aiming back along the valley through which he'd been traveling all day.

For a while now, he had felt a tingling on the back of his neck that told him he was being followed. Whoever was on his trail was about to be in his gunsights . . . and that wasn't a good place to be.

Preacher had been roaming these mountains for almost forty years now, although most folks wouldn't guess by looking at him that he was in his early fifties. His hair was still thick and dark, as was the mustache that drooped over his wide, expressive mouth. He stood straight and tall and muscular, with his broad shoulders stretching the fringed buckskin shirt he wore.

His brown canvas trousers were tucked

into high-topped boots of a darker brown shade. His broad-brimmed hat was also dark brown, as were the crossed gunbelts he wore. In earlier days, from the time when Preacher had first come to the Rockies not long after the beginning of the fur-trapping era, he had carried a long-barreled flintlock rifle and a brace of flintlock pistols, but in recent years he had taken to using the .52 caliber Sharps, and a .44 caliber Colt Dragoon revolver was holstered on each hip. Attached to one of the gunbelts was a squarish leather pouch holding a couple of already loaded extra cylinders for the Dragoons.

To someone who had spent many years using muzzle-loading weapons, the Dragoons seemed like an incredible amount of firepower to have at his disposal. Preacher had spent a lot of time practicing with the revolvers until he could handle them swiftly and skillfully. The Sharps was a single-shot weapon like his old flintlock rifle had been, but it was extremely accurate, reloaded quickly, and packed enough punch to bring down a grizzly bear or a buffalo with one shot, if placed correctly.

One thing that hadn't changed was the heavy-bladed hunting knife Preacher carried in a sheath strapped to the gunbelt behind the left-hand Colt.

Farther back in the trees, the rangy gray stallion Preacher called Horse waited, reins tied to a sapling. Preacher had told the big wolf-like cur known as Dog to stay there with Horse until he found out who was trailing them. They were not the first Horse and Dog to travel the frontier trails with him, but as always with the animals that seemed to find their way to him, they were good companions.

He breathed easily and calmly as he sighted along the rifle's barrel toward a cluster of boulders that filled a gap between two hogback ridges. He expected whoever was following him to emerge from the cover of those boulders momentarily. He had no way of knowing that for sure, but his instincts had seldom been wrong over the long years of surviving on the frontier . . .

They weren't wrong now, either. A huge figure in buckskins rounded one of the boulders, striding confidently into Preacher's view. The Indian was even bigger than Preacher, with broader shoulders. He looked almost powerful enough to pick up one of those boulders and toss it around like a toy, although in reality, of course, such a thing was impossible.

The sight of the man caused Preacher to

relax. A grin spread across the mountain man's rugged face. He lowered the Sharps and was about to call out to the Indian when movement from the top of one of the boulders caught his eye. A tawny, muscular mountain lion was crouched there, tail twitching as it got ready to spring.

Instantly, Preacher snapped the rifle back to his shoulder and then fired in a continuation of the same movement. He hadn't taken the time to aim, but instinct and keen reflexes guided his shot. The heavy slug intercepted the mountain lion in midair as it leaped from the boulder. The big cat yowled and twisted as the .52 caliber round tore through its sleekly furred body, but the momentum of its attack caused it to crash into the big Indian anyway. The man went down under the mountain lion's weight.

Preacher lowered the Sharps and ran forward, drawing the right-hand Colt Dragoon as he approached. The mountain lion might still be alive, which meant that its intended target was still in danger.

However, as Preacher came closer, he saw that the big cat had gone limp in death. The Indian lifted the carcass and shoved it aside, then looked up at Preacher with a surprised expression on his broad, copper-hued face.

"Preacher!" he said.

10

"Howdy, Big Thunder," the mountain man replied. He holstered the Dragoon and extended a hand to the Indian.

Big Thunder reached up. His ham-like hand enveloped Preacher's and closed in a crushing grip. Instead of letting Preacher help him up, though, Big Thunder yanked and pulled Preacher down. Preacher yelled and dropped the Sharps as he sprawled on top of the Crow warrior. Big Thunder's arms, as thick as young trees, closed around him and squeezed hard enough to make Preacher's ribs groan.

Grimacing, Preacher got both hands under Big Thunder's chin and shoved up, forcing the warrior's head back. The bear hug didn't ease, so Preacher slammed a punch against Big Thunder's slab-like jaw. That did about as much good as punching one of those boulders would have. Preacher rammed a knee into Big Thunder's midsection, but the Indian's belly was hard as a rock, too.

Big Thunder's lone weakness was his nose, Preacher recalled. He drew back his head and then butted the middle of the warrior's face. Big Thunder grunted, and finally the terrible pressure of his arms diminished. Preacher bucked and heaved his body up, breaking Big Thunder's grip. He shot another punch to Big Thunder's nose to keep him paralyzed with pain for a moment, then rolled away quickly.

Chest heaving as he tried to recover the breath Big Thunder had squeezed out of him, Preacher surged to his feet. A couple of yards away, Big Thunder lumbered upright and shook his head, causing fat drops of blood to fly from his nose. He stood there swaying a little, as if undecided what to do next.

Preacher held up his left hand, palm out, and rasped, "Now just hold it right there, Big Thunder! Dang it, you're gettin' too old to be actin' like this. Every time I come around, you try to fight me!"

He spoke in the Crow tongue, Big Thunder's native language. Preacher knew that Big Thunder had learned a little English over the years, but he had the mind of a child, and if there was something important to communicate to him, it was better to use Big Thunder's own tongue.

"But Preacher is the only one who can give Big Thunder a good fight," the massive warrior said. He dragged the back of his hand across his face, leaving a crimson smear from his nose on the back of it. "We always do battle when you visit Big Thunder's village."

12

"You mean you try to start a ruckus. I usually manage to talk you out of it, but you took me by surprise this time."

"Oh." Big Thunder frowned and then flinched, as if he were thinking and the process was a little painful for him. "Big Thunder sometimes forgets things."

"That's all right, old son, all of us do." Preacher picked up his hat, which had fallen off during the brief scrap, and batted it against his thigh to get the dust off. He put the hat on, then picked up the Sharps and checked to make sure dirt hadn't fouled its action.

"You shot that cat?" asked Big Thunder as he waved a hand at the mountain lion's carcass.

"That's right. I spotted him just as he was about to jump you. I'm glad I was able to shoot him in time."

"Big Thunder would have killed him if you did not."

Big Thunder sounded mighty confident about that, but Preacher wasn't so sure. If the mountain lion had landed on Big Thunder's back as it intended, it probably would have been able to rip out the Indian's throat before Big Thunder could do anything about it. Preacher figured he had just saved Big Thunder's life . . . but that wouldn't be the first time, and for that matter, Big Thunder had saved him on occasion, too. The two of them were old friends, even though Big Thunder's roughhousing might have made it seem that that wasn't the case.

Ten years had passed since Preacher had first met Big Thunder during an adventure that involved battling both a gang of ruthless fur thieves and a war party of bloodthirsty Blackfeet. Since then, Preacher had visited the Crow village where Big Thunder lived numerous times. He had a very good reason for that, in addition to renewing old friendships.

His son Hawk That Soars lived there, along with Hawk's wife Butterfly and their children, a boy known as Eagle Feather and a girl named Bright Moon.

It had been a while since Preacher had been there, and he was looking forward to seeing Hawk and his family again.

"What are you doing out here this far from the village by yourself, Big Thunder?" he asked.

"Hunting." Big Thunder scowled. "You have been gone for a long time, Preacher. Our hunting grounds are not as good as they used to be. We have to go out farther and farther to find enough game to feed our people. Waugghh! The white people and their houses on wheels drive away all the animals. Big Thunder wishes they would all go away and leave us alone."

Preacher knew the warrior was talking about the wagon trains full of immigrants headed west along the Oregon Trail, which ran some miles south of where he and Big Thunder were at the moment. Over the past decade, thousands and thousands of those settlers had made the long, arduous journey, hoping that a new life in the Pacific Northwest would be better.

But to get there, they had to pass through hundreds of miles of territory where many different Indian tribes roamed, including the Crow. Naturally, there had been trouble. As Big Thunder had just indicated, the Indians didn't like it when the whites — whom they regarded as invaders — encroached on their hunting grounds. As someone who had always been dubious of so-called civilization, Preacher understood that feeling quite well.

It was true that sometimes the immigrants killed buffalo, deer, elk, and antelope for food on the way west. They had thinned the herds to a certain extent. But those herds were vast, and Preacher thought it would be many more years before the advance of civilization had a significant effect on the

Indians' food supply.

Maybe he was wrong about that, he told himself now. Big Thunder was in a better position to know about such things than he was.

"You are going to our village?" Big Thunder asked now.

"That's right."

"I will come with you. Let me take this cat with us. I will use its hide, and there will be meat for the pots from it."

Big Thunder picked up the carcass, not even grunting from the effort of lifting more than a hundred pounds, and draped it over his shoulders. He walked easily with it. When they got back to the village, the women would dress it out, then scrape the hide and stake it out to dry.

Preacher retrieved Horse and Dog from the woods, then led the stallion as he walked with Big Thunder. He had never minded traveling by himself except for his four-legged trail partners, but it was nice having a human companion on this trek through the mountains toward the river where the Crow village lay in a bend of the stream. Big Thunder was talkative, filling Preacher in on all the gossip from the village. Preacher chuckled more than once at the stories. Whites tended to believe that Indians

16

were stoic and emotionless, but in truth they led lives just as full of romance, comedy, and tragedy as anyone else.

It was dusk before the two men reached the village. Cooking fires were already visible in the twilight as they approached. Several curs caught their scent and ran out to bark in greeting. Dog growled at them, and that sent them scurrying back toward the lodges, but the commotion had already alerted the village's inhabitants.

A group of warriors, some with bows and quivers of arrows, others carrying tomahawks, strode forward to see who was coming. The Crow were not as warlike a people as the Blackfeet, but they were still fierce fighters and not likely to be taken unawares by enemies.

The warrior in the lead was a stern-faced, medium-sized man in his thirties. He smiled slightly, though, as he recognized the white man accompanying Big Thunder.

"Preacher!" he said. "It is good to see you again."

"Broken Pine," Preacher replied. The two men clasped wrists. Broken Pine had been a young warrior the first time Preacher had met this band of Crow. Now he was their chief.

"Did this one try to fight you as soon as

he saw you?" Broken Pine asked with a nod toward Big Thunder.

Preacher laughed and said, "He did more than try. We had ourselves a good tussle, didn't we, Big Thunder?"

The massive warrior lifted a hand to his nose, which had stopped bleeding. He touched it gingerly and winced.

"Big Thunder's nose bled!" he announced. "It was a very good fight, but not long enough."

Broken Pine sighed and shook his head, but he didn't actually seem upset. He said, "I have spoken with you about this, Big Thunder. If you keep fighting with Preacher, he will stop coming to visit us."

"No, he will not! Not as long as Hawk That Soars lives among us."

That was true. Preacher might have numerous children among the various tribes in the mountains and plains; he had wintered often enough with them and had always had a woman to warm his blankets at night. But Hawk was the only one he was *certain* was his son, the product of a winter spent with the Absaroka woman Bird in a Tree. The Absaroka and the Crow were close cousins — some went so far as to say they were the same tribe — and the Crow in this band had not hesitated to accept

Hawk as one of them, since he was married to a Crow woman, in a way, at least.

Preacher said hello to several other warriors with whom he was acquainted from previous visits, then asked, "Where *is* Hawk? I'm a mite surprised he wasn't part of this greeting party."

"He went out to hunt today, too," Broken Pine said. The chief's face grew even more solemn than usual. "The game is not plentiful as it once was. We have given thought to moving our hunting grounds. But where can we go?"

"There's bound to be someplace that's better."

"Where?" Broken Pine waved to indicate the territory to the east and south. "The white men and their wagons come closer every year, and they are as many as the ants that swarm from a mound. Their hunters range farther out from the trail the wagons follow. And there has been talk that the soldiers will come, too. They have not ventured close to us yet, but the time will come when they do."

Preacher didn't say anything. He knew that Broken Pine was right. Preacher had seen for himself how the army was building forts farther and farther west. They had a ways to go before reaching the mountains, but if they kept coming in this direction, it was inevitable.

"But worrying about the future can wait for another time," Broken Pine went on. "For now, we are glad to see you. You are always welcome among the Crow, Preacher. Would you wait in the lodge of Hawk That Soars?"

"Butterfly and the young'uns are there?"

"They are," Broken Pine nodded.

"Then that's where I'll be," Preacher told him. "It's in the same place?"

"Yes. Big Thunder, go with him . . . but no more fighting!"

Big Thunder sighed in disappointment but agreed.

"Our men will tend to Horse and put him with our ponies," Broken Pine went on.

"I'm obliged to you. But don't get Horse too close to those ponies," Preacher warned. "He can get a mite proddy and obnoxious . . . like me."

Broken Pine smiled again and nodded.

Preacher started across the village, with Big Thunder falling in beside him. He didn't really need the guide, but he supposed that with evening coming on and shadows gathering, Broken Pine thought he might get turned around. Instead, Preacher walked unerringly through the large village to the hide lodge where Hawk and his wife and children lived.

As he approached, he saw the woman hunkered next to a cooking fire. She was no longer the girl she had been when they first met. Instead she was a beautiful woman in the prime of life. Her long black hair was done into two braids that hung over her shoulders and down across the rounded bosom of her buckskin dress. She was stirring something in an iron pot over the flames, but she glanced up as Preacher and Big Thunder drew near, then looked again and leaped to her feet as she recognized the mountain man.

"Preacher!" she said as she flung her arms around his neck and embraced him. The two children who threw back the hide cover over the lodge's entrance and scrambled out must have heard that exclamation. In their eagerness to greet the visitor, they ran up behind the woman, but then their natural shyness got the better of them and they stopped to hide behind her with their eyes cast down to the ground. The boy appeared to be around eight years old, the girl a couple of years younger.

Preacher returned the woman's hug, patted her on the back, and then stepped back to rest his hands on her shoulders as he smiled at her.

"Let me look at you," he said. "I reckon you're as beautiful as ever . . . Caroline."

CHAPTER 2

*Fort Kearny, on the Platte River, unorganized
territory*

The man riding toward the fort appeared
mighty big at first glance, but anyone looking at him might think that was because he
was riding a tall, very sturdy horse.

They would have been wrong. Jamie Ian
MacCallister looked like that because he
was mighty big.

Unlike military posts back east, Fort
Kearny had no stockade fence around it; in
fact, no fortifications of any kind. It con-
sisted of a four-acre parade ground with
cottonwood trees planted at regular intervals
along its edges, surrounded by sod and
adobe buildings, with the exception of one
frame building that housed the post commander's home and office.

This was Unorganized Territory, so called
because the recent Compromise of 1850,
worked out by politicians squabbling over

23

slave and free states, hadn't settled what to do with vast stretches of the Great Plains. A short distance to the north of the fort ran the Platte River, divided by sandbars into many channels. Some wag had once described the stream as a mile wide and an inch deep, and while that was an exaggeration, the Platte was definitely broad and shallow. It might not be navigable, but despite that it was an important waterway for the settlers headed west in their wagon trains. Fort Kearny was the last spot on the trail west where those immigrants could stock up on supplies.

The last place they could truly feel safe from Indian attack, too. Out here on the Great Plains, the Pawnee and the Cheyenne were constant dangers. Farther west, in the mountains that could be seen dimly on the horizon, the Crow, the Blackfeet, and the Shoshone lurked, ready to slaughter the settlers who just wanted a new and better life than they could have in the crowded squalor of the cities back east.

That was the way all those greenhorns saw it, anyway, Jamie Ian MacCallister mused as he rode slowly along the edge of the parade ground, past the flagpole, toward the sprawling adobe building where the sutler's store was located.

Manifest Destiny, they called it. Some newspaper scribbler back east had come up with the term, and the politicians in Washington City had been quick to latch on to it as an excuse for their schemes to "civilize" the entire continent — and make themselves rich in the process. Maybe they weren't all that way, but Jamie had been around enough of them to know that most were.

But regardless of their motivations, the politicians and the journalists kept filling folks' heads with the dream of the West, and they kept streaming out here to try to capture it.

He hadn't ought to be so damn cynical, Jamie told himself as he reined the big horse to a stop in front of the store. He had been part of that westward expansion himself, after escaping from the Shawnee raiders who had massacred his family and made him a captive and slave for several years when he was just a boy. A lot had happened since then. Jamie had roamed the West and had all sorts of adventures. He had married the beautiful Kate and sired several children. Kate and their youngsters were back in Colorado, at the ranch he had established in MacCallister's Valley. He knew he should have been there himself, but from time to time the wanderlust seized him, and this was one of those times. He had been drifting for a while and figured that soon he would turn around and head for home, but not yet. Not just yet.

He swung down from the saddle and looped the horse's reins around the hitch rail in front of the store, where several other horses were tied. Although some men were old by the time they reached their early forties, Jamie still appeared to be in the prime of life. He stood well over six feet, which meant he towered above many men, and had the broad shoulders to go with his height. No one would call him handsome, except maybe Kate, but his craggy face had a definite power to it. A few strands of gray ran through the thick fair hair under his broad-brimmed brown hat and could be seen in his mustache as well. He wore a faded blue shirt, a brown vest, and buckskin trousers. A heavy Walker Colt rode in a holster on his right hip.

A group of dragoons had been drilling on the parade ground as Jamie rode past, and other soldiers hurried here and there around the fort, bound on mysterious errands that kept them busy. The four soldiers on the porch of the sutler's store must have been off duty, though, because they were taking their ease and passing a jug back and forth.

"Look here," the man currently holding the jug said as he waved a hand toward Jamie. "It's one of them mountain men." He took a swig and then laughed. "Where's your squaw, mister? Didn't want to bring her along where decent white men could see her?"

Jamie's eyes narrowed as he looked at the soldier, who was a big, redheaded bull of an Irishman. For a second, Jamie considered not wasting the breath it would take to respond to the man's taunt. But then, with all the dignity he could muster, which was considerable, he said, "I'm not married to an Indian woman. I have a wife over in Colorado Territory, but she's white. However, I've met some fine Indian ladies I'd be proud to be wed to, if circumstances had been different."

The Irishman, who had a sergeant's three stripes on the sleeve of his blue jacket, pushed his stiff-billed black cap back on his head and guffawed.

"Fine Indian ladies!" he repeated. "You mean filthy heathen squaws stinkin' of bear grease and fit only for warmin' a man's belly at night, don't ye?"

"Sergeant," said one of the other soldiers, who looked a little nervous, "you know what the cap'n told you about fightin'. He said

27

next time you'd wind up in the guard-house."

"And you know what I think about the cap'n! He can kiss my hairy Irish a—"

The sergeant stopped short as Jamie shouldered past, intending on going on into the store. Jamie needed some coffee. He'd been out of it for the past couple of days and felt the lack.

"Wait just a damn minute, squawman!" The sergeant's hand came down hard on Jamie's shoulder. Even though Jamie had his back to the man now, he could still smell the whiskey fumes on his breath.

Without turning around, Jamie said, "Get your hand off of me, mister."

"You'd better call me sergeant," the Irishman said without letting go.

"I'm not in the army."

"Doesn't matter. You'll show me some respect, squawman, or I'll —"

Jamie shrugged off the hand and said, "Respect has to be earned. You haven't earned the time and energy it would take to spit on you."

He took another step toward the door.

"O'Connor, no!"

That shout from one of the other soldiers was enough warning for Jamie. He turned swiftly and leaned back so that the fist the

28

big Irish noncom swung at him passed harmlessly in front of his face, missing by several inches. The sergeant had had too much to drink, so he wasn't very steady on his feet and stumbled forward, thrown off balance by the blow that hadn't landed.

That brought him within easy reach of the left fist that Jamie hooked into his midsection. The punch had so much power behind it that Jamie's hand sank into the man's belly to the wrist. More whiskey stink gusted from the Irishman's mouth. Jamie hit that mouth with a straight right that made blood spurt from O'Connor's lips and sent him flying backward off the store's porch.

The ground was dry and dusty in front of the store. A pale cloud flew up around O'Connor when he landed hard. He rolled onto his side, retched, doubled up, and spewed out the rotgut he'd been guzzling. The smell in the air got even worse.

Jamie shook his head in disgust and turned toward the door again. The last thing he'd wanted when he rode in here was to get into a fight.

On the other hand, this hadn't been much of a fight.

Unfortunately, it wasn't over. He heard big feet slap the ground and started to whirl around again. Getting hit like that and then emptying his stomach of all the booze must have sobered up the sergeant, because he was moving fast now. He plowed into Jamie from the side like a runaway freight train.

The collision drove Jamie against the door. The latch splintered under the impact of the combined weight, which had to be close to five hundred pounds. The door flew open and spilled both men onto the floor just inside the store.

O'Conner yelled in fury and hammered punches against Jamie's body. He rammed a knee at Jamie's groin. Jamie twisted aside from that just in time to take the blow on his left thigh. It was powerful enough to make that leg go numb for a moment. Jamie would have been incapacitated completely if the sergeant's knee had landed where it was aimed.

Jamie shoved the heel of his left hand up under O'Connor's chin and forced the sergeant's head back. He brought his right fist around in a pile-driver blow that caught O'Connor on the side of the head and knocked him to the side. Jamie rolled the other way to put a little distance between them and came up on one knee.

He'd been vaguely aware of shouting around them. Now he saw that the store was crowded with soldiers in light blue trousers, darker blue jackets, and black caps, as well as a number of civilians including roughly dressed bullwhackers who handled the teams of oxen hitched to freight wagons, buckskin-clad fur trappers trying to scrape a living out of that fading enterprise, and dapper gamblers in frock coats and beaver hats.

At the moment, all of them were excited about the battle that had broken out in their midst. They had drawn back to give the combatants some room. Bets began to be made back and forth, even though Jamie and O'Connor were both catching their breath.

Jamie's hat had been knocked off when the Irishman tackled him. He pushed back the hair that threatened to fall across his eyes and said, "Let it alone, O'Connor. I don't want to fight you."

O'Connor had pushed himself up on an elbow. He shook his head groggily, glared at Jamie, and said, "Too late for that, squaw-man. I'm gonna beat you to death with me bare hands!"

He scrambled onto hands and knees and then surged to his feet. Jamie got up at the same time and barely had a chance to get his boots planted on the puncheon floor

31

before O'Connor charged him, swinging wildly. Jamie took a step back but bumped against a barrel of flour or sugar, he wasn't sure which. Several such barrels were lined up behind him, so he didn't have anywhere to go.

Not that he believed in running, anyway. If O'Connor wanted a fight, then he had come to the right man, by God!

Jamie met the sergeant's ferocious attack with one of his own. Fists flew back and forth. The thuds and cracks of flesh and bone colliding violently punctuated the chorus of shouted encouragement from the onlookers. Jamie blocked as many of O'Connor's punches as possible, but he couldn't turn all of them aside. With some of them, he just had to absorb the punishment they dealt out.

But he was dealing plenty of punishment himself as he and O'Connor stood toe to toe, slugging away at each other. Blood smeared O'Connor's mouth, and the area around his left eye was starting to swell. Jamie's jaw ached where one of the sergeant's blows had caught him, and he tasted blood in his mouth, as well. O'Conner was a few inches shorter than Jamie but probably outweighed him by ten or fifteen pounds. Their reach was practically the same. They were about as evenly matched as two men could be.

That meant the outcome of the fight would probably come down to pure luck. One of them would slip or drop his guard just a hair too much, at just the wrong second, and that would be the end of it.

Jamie figured he just had to hold on for a little while longer. He could tell that O'Connor was tiring. O'Connor might not be drunk now, but all the whiskey he had consumed earlier was taking a toll on him anyway. Big beads of sweat rolled down his face and mixed with the blood leaking from his mouth.

O'Connor must have realized he was on the verge of being defeated and was willing to go to any lengths to prevent that. He swayed backward to avoid one of Jamie's punches and reached out to close his right hand around an ax handle lying with a number of others in an open crate on a shelf beside him.

Jamie had to throw himself backward desperately to avoid the ax handle as O'Conner swung it at him. O'Conner bored in, slashing back and forth with the makeshift weapon. Jamie knew that if it connected, it might crack his skull wide open.

He couldn't allow that, so he ducked and

dived forward, wrapping his arms around O'Connor's waist. From this position, O'Connor could whack at his back with the ax handle but couldn't get a lot of strength behind the blows. Jamie drove hard with his feet and heaved, forcing O'Conner backward. O'Connor yelled in alarm as Jamie literally lifted him from the floor and dumped him on his back.

O'Conner came down on those barrels that had blocked Jamie's path earlier. He knocked a couple of them over, and one dumped its contents onto him: flour that turned his uniform white and covered his face in a choking, clinging cloud. Jamie stepped closer and swung his right leg in a kick that sent the ax handle flying from O'Connor's hand.

Then he reached down, caught hold of the front of O'Connor's jacket with both hands, and hauled the sputtering, disoriented sergeant to his feet. Jamie hung on to O'Connor's jacket with his left hand, drew his right arm back, and cocked that fist, then delivered a punch to O'Connor's jaw that was perfectly timed and aimed. The devastating blow slewed the man's head around and knocked him off his feet again.

This time when O'Connor landed on the puncheons, he didn't move, other than his chest rising and falling. He was out cold.

An awed silence fell over the inside of the sutler's store. Most of the men in here had lived rough-and-tumble lives and had witnessed and participated in countless brawls. But seldom had any of them seen such a knockout punch.

Jamie shook his hand a little as he stood there. It would be sore the next morning, he knew, but as he flexed his fingers, he could tell that no bones were broken. It took a great deal of skill to land a bare-knuckles punch like that and not do any damage to his own hand. Jamie Ian MacCallister was skillful in fighting and many other things, as well.

One of the bullwhackers broke the hush with a stream of colorful, inventive profanity, the sort of thing he would have bellowed at his oxen as he cracked a long whip over their heads. Short, black-bearded, and almost as broad as he was tall, he stepped up to Jamie and fetched him a resounding slap on the back.

"That was almost pretty enough to make me cry, mister," the bullwhacker said.

Some of the other civilians crowded around Jamie and began congratulating him, too. The soldiers hung back, though. Most of them cast surly glares in Jamie's direction, but a few kept their expressions carefully neutral. Jamie noted that and figured that Sergeant O'Connor had made some enemies among his fellow Dragoons, in addition to rubbing the civilians at the fort the wrong way. As obnoxious as the sergeant had acted, that wouldn't be surprising.

The sutler came out from behind the counter at the back of the store and stomped toward Jamie, causing the crowd around him to scatter. The man was short and wiry, and what he lacked in size, he made up for with the fierce expression on his face as he glared up at Jamie. He had gray hair that stuck up wildly, a bad, milky left eye with a permanent squint because of the scars around it, and a stubby black cigar clenched between his teeth.

"Who's gonna pay for the damages?" he demanded around the cigar.

Jamie stuck a thumb at O'Connor's still senseless shape and said, "You'd better talk to him. He's the one who wouldn't let it go."

"But you were right in the thick of it with him."

"He didn't give me any choice in the matter," Jamie protested.

The sutler waved a hand disgustedly and

36

said, "O'Connor don't have any money. Everybody knows that. He gambles and drinks it all away."

"Take it up with his commanding officer, then."

"That's just what I intend to do." The sutler looked past Jamie and went on, "Lieutenant Davidson, this big galoot bulled in here, started a fight, and caused all this damage, and now he won't pay for it!"

"That's a blasted lie!" Jamie said. He turned to see who the sutler was talking to —

And found himself looking down the barrel of a gun pointed at his face.

CHAPTER 3

The man holding the gun had a red sash tied around the waist of his blue jacket, and a white sash angled diagonally from his right shoulder to his left hip, where a scabbarded saber hung. The flap holster that had held the revolver rode high on his right hip.

"Stand still there, you," he ordered Jamie.

"I'm not moving," Jamie said. "You just be careful with that hogleg. Neither of us want it going off accidentally."

"I'll have you know that I'm an expert when it comes to handling weapons and a crack shot," the officer informed him. "If this gun goes off, it will be because I intend for it to do so."

The prissy accent was straight out of New England somewhere, Jamie thought. The man was in his mid-twenties, with curly, sand-colored hair under his black cap, and bushy side whiskers that dominated his slender face. His upper lip curled in what

38

appeared to be a natural sneer.

"You better arrest him, Lieutenant," the sutler said. "Otherwise he's liable to take off for the high country without payin' me what he owes. Fellas like him are half-wild, not much better than red savages."

The bullwhacker who had been the first to congratulate Jamie scowled and rumbled, "This ain't right. The big fella didn't do nothin' but defend hisself agin that bully of a sergeant. Liam O'Connor's been ridin' roughshod over ever'body at this post for months now, Lieutenant, and you can't see it 'cause he's always suckin' up to you!"

"That'll be quite enough out of you, Fincher," snapped the lieutenant. "I hardly need advice from a civilian, especially not from an unlettered lout such as yourself."

The bullwhacker's hands clenched into fists. He took a step forward and said, "Nobody talks to me like that, you —"

Jamie lifted a hand just a little to stop him.

"You can take up your argument with the lieutenant later, friend," he said. "Right now, I'd like to settle this little dispute."

"Ain't nothin' to dispute," the sutler said. "I got a barrel of flour that's ruined and a busted latch on the door. That's . . . uh . . . five dollars' worth of damage, I reckon."

"That's more than a barrel of flour ought

to cost," said Jamie. "Nearly twice as much. And you can fix that latch without much trouble."

"Well, I ain't even said nothin' about the sugar that got spilled and all the cleanin' up I'll have to do! That's worth somethin', too, ain't it?" The sutler nodded curtly and decisively. "Five dollars, that's what I want to call it square."

"Oh, hell, it's not worth the argument," Jamie muttered. Although no one could tell it to look at him, his ranch in Colorado was quite lucrative and had made him a wealthy man, especially for this time and place. He dug in a pocket, came up with a five-dollar gold piece, and tossed the Liberty Head half eagle to the sutler, who caught it with ease despite having only one good eye.

Jamie turned back to the lieutenant and went on, "There, I've settled the damages. Now put that gun away."

The officer didn't lower the revolver. Instead, he said, "There's still the matter of you assaulting a noncommissioned officer of the United States Army."

"For hell's sake!" the bullwhacker called Fincher burst out. "Didn't you hear me say that O'Connor jumped this fella, not the other way around?"

"Brawling on an army post is against the

40

regulations."

"I'm not a soldier," Jamie said.

"It doesn't matter. By being on this post, you have placed yourself under the jurisdiction of the army, and as a duly commissioned officer of that army, I am within my rights to place you in custody, which I hereby —"

"Lieutenant Davidson." A new voice came sharply from the open door of the sutler's store. "What's going on here? I heard the commotion all the way at the other end of the parade ground."

The lieutenant finally lowered the revolver. He shoved it back into the holster, hastily closed the flap, and saluted as he came to attention.

"Captain Croxton," he said. "Begging your pardon, sir, but there's no need for you to spend your valuable time pursuing this unfortunate matter. I'm handling it —"

The captain returned the salute and said, "I'll be the judge of how I should best spend my time, Lieutenant."

"Of course, sir. I didn't mean to suggest otherwise, just that the matter is under control —"

"Son, any time you're waving a gun around in the direction of Jamie Ian Mac-Callister, the matter definitely is *not* under

41

control. In fact, I'd say you're pretty close to all hell breaking loose." A smile appeared on Captain Croxton's ruddy face as he strode forward and extended his hand. "Jamie, I didn't know you were anywhere around these parts, but it's mighty good to see you again anyway."

Lieutenant Davidson stood there with his mouth hanging open as Jamie shook hands with the stockily built, clean-shaven officer and said, "Good to see you, too, Cap'n."

"You're not here on business, are you?" asked Croxton, suddenly looking a little concerned. "Hunting for someone? Looking to settle a score?"

Jamie laughed and shook his head.

"Not hardly. I just had one of my spells where I wanted to get out and roam around for a while. You know how I get. And this is where the wind brought me."

"Well, I'm glad it did. Come on over to my office and have a drink with me."

"Don't mind if I do."

Davidson finally found his tongue again, saying, "Begging your pardon, Captain, am I to understand that you know this . . . this man?"

"Indeed, I do," Croxton replied. "He served as a scout for me in a campaign against the Pawnee last year, before you ever came out here, and he's well known across the frontier." The captain frowned and nodded toward O'Connor. "The sergeant should have come to by now. You'd better make sure he doesn't require some medical attention."

Fincher said, "Hell, Cap'n, as hard as MacCallister hit him, O'Connor may not wake up until next week!"

"Get him cleaned up, anyway," Croxton went on, "and then have him thrown in the guardhouse overnight. He knows how I feel about brawling." He turned away. "Come on, Jamie."

Lieutenant Davidson stood there, gaping, red-faced with barely suppressed anger, as Jamie and Captain Croxton left the store. Then Fincher jostled him with an elbow in the side, grinned, and said, "You didn't know it was Jamie Ian MacCallister you were tryin' to lord it over, did you, Lieutenant? He's a cross betwixt a grizzl' bear and a lobo wolf, and you're lucky he didn't chew you up and spit out the bones!"

"Sorry all I have are tin cups," Captain Croxton said as he poured brandy for himself and Jamie. "This far west, the finer things of life haven't really caught up to us yet."

43

Jamie took the cup the captain handed him, clinked it against Croxton's, and sipped the brandy.

"I'd say this brandy is pretty much one of the finer things," he commented.

Croxton smiled in pleasure at the compliment and said, "I've been saving it for a special occasion, and I'd say that you paying us a visit qualifies, Jamie." He grew more serious as he went on, "I appreciate you not making that young lieutenant *eat* that gun he pointed at you, even though he probably had it coming."

"I thought about it," Jamie admitted with a smile of his own, "but it didn't hardly seem like it would be worth the trouble. Your Lieutenant Davidson seems to have a pretty high opinion of himself, doesn't he?"

"Edgar Davidson is an arrogant prig who's not one-tenth as smart as he thinks he is," snapped Croxton. "I really shouldn't be talking about one of my junior officers that way, especially to a civilian. The worst part about it is that he was sent out here to be my second-in-command and eventually take over as the commanding officer of this post."

Jamie winced and asked, "He's never been on the frontier before?"

"No . . . but that doesn't stop him from believing that he's learned everything there is to know about it in the three months he's been here."

Jamie shook his head slowly and said, "I'm sorry, Captain. You're going to have your hands full with that one. He might make a decent officer someday . . . if he can manage not to get himself killed before then."

"I'm more worried about him getting some of my soldiers killed." Croxton tossed back the rest of the brandy in his cup. "But that's not a concern for today. I'm just glad to see you. How long do you plan to stay?"

"Probably not more than a day or two. I just rode in to stock up on provisions. I ought to be heading back to Colorado before too much longer."

"Keep an eye on Tom Corcoran, the sutler," Croxton advised. "He'll overcharge you if you're not careful, especially now that he has a grudge against you."

"I paid him what he asked for," Jamie pointed out.

"That won't stop him from being resentful. He and Liam O'Connor are friends."

"O'Connor's a regular troublemaker, isn't he?"

Croxton sighed and reached for the bottle of brandy, but he stopped himself before he poured another drink and replaced the cork instead with a stern look.

"He's an Irish noncom used to getting his own way and running things," the captain said. "There are a lot like that in the army. Sometimes I think we couldn't function without them. O'Connor's more obnoxious and brutal than most, however. He has a few cronies who flock around him. Some of the men hate him. Most just try to steer clear of him as much as possible."

"And somehow he managed to get on Lieutenant Davidson's good side."

"No mystery about it. He simply tells Davidson that he's a brilliant officer. That's all it takes."

Jamie finished his brandy and set the empty cup on Croxton's desk.

"I wish you the best of luck dealing with them, Captain," he said. "And I'm mighty glad it's not me who has to do it!"

Croxton smiled and said, "There's an empty officer's cabin, if you'd like to use it tonight, Jamie. The War Department is supposed to send me another second lieutenant to go with the four I have, but they haven't gotten around to it yet."

"Letting a civilian use officers' housing is bound to be against the regulations."

"I'm the commanding officer here, so I decide how to allocate the fort's resources."

"You said Davidson's slated to take over

this post eventually. He might decide to hurry things along by writing to the War Department and reporting any breaches of army protocol you might make. He struck me as the ambitious sort."

"Ambitious beyond anything his capabilities justify," Croxton said. "But you let me worry about that, Jamie."

With a shrug of his broad shoulders, Jamie nodded. He shook hands with the captain again and asked, "Where's that cabin you mentioned? I'm obliged to you for your hospitality."

Jamie took his horse to the stable and turned it over to the grizzled old corporal working there. A mixture of army and civilian mounts were kept in the stable. As the old-timer explained, "There's talk of a town startin' up not far from here. In fact, a fella with a wagon full o' whores showed up a while back and built hisself a soddy so's he could put them doves to work and sell the Who-hit-John he brews up." The hostler slapped his thigh and cackled with laughter. "Them's always the first two signs of civilization, ain't they? Whores and whiskey!"

"I suppose if there gets to be a town, civilians will have to take their horses to a stable there," Jamie said.

"Yep. For now, though, the cap'n don't mind folks keepin' their mounts here, so long as they pay for the grain the critters eat."

Jamie took that hint and handed over a coin, then went to look for the cabin Croxton had told him he could use.

The officers' quarters at Fort Kearny were half a dozen small, single-room adobe structures lined up on one side of the parade ground. The cabin at the western end of the line was empty since only five lieutenants were currently assigned to the post: one first lieutenant, Edgar Davidson, and four second lieutenants.

One of those second lieutenants was sitting on a three-legged stool in front of the cabin next door, cleaning a revolver. The parts were spread out on a cloth he had placed on a small table in front of him. He looked up and nodded as Jamie approached.

"You're the fellow who tangled with Sergeant O'Connor, aren't you?" he said by way of greeting.

"Guilty as charged," Jamie replied, then chuckled. "Although I wasn't actually charged with anything. Lieutenant Davidson would have liked to throw me in the guardhouse, though."

The young officer set down the revolver's

cylinder, wiped his hand on the cloth to get rid of the gun oil, and stood up to extend that hand to Jamie.

"I'm Hayden Tyler," he said.

"Jamie Ian MacCallister." Jamie gripped Tyler's hand.

"I've heard Captain Croxton speak of you, Mr. MacCallister, and others as well. You seem to be quite well known on the frontier."

"That's not always a good thing," Jamie said with a grin. "Usually not, if what a fella wants is peace and quiet."

"Is that what you want?"

"Sometimes. But if I'm being honest . . . only sometimes."

Tyler laughed. He was a tall, well-built young man with close-cut dark hair and a neatly trimmed mustache.

"I know what you mean. If life is too tame, it gets boring."

"Don't reckon you'll have to worry too much about that out here," said Jamie. "Trouble's bound to come along, probably sooner rather than later. How long have you been at Fort Kearny, Lieutenant?"

"Three months."

"You were assigned here at the same time as Lieutenant Davidson?"

"That's right." A trace of curtness in Tyler's tone made Jamie wonder if the young man resented being outranked by Davidson.

"Where are you from?"

"My family is in Ohio. I had a hankering to see the West, though, and the army seemed like a good way to accomplish that. Plus it's something of a tradition. My father was a colonel before he resigned his commission to go into business, and my older brother served in the Mexican War."

"Is that so?"

Tyler nodded and said, "Yes, he was at Veracruz. He . . . didn't make it back."

"I'm sorry, son," Jamie said.

"He knew the risks, and so do I. I'd like to think he would be proud of me for following in his footsteps . . . while encouraging me not to follow *too* closely."

Jamie felt an instinctive liking for this young officer. Hayden Tyler seemed to be level-headed and clear-eyed about what he was doing on the frontier, and the hint of self-deprecation in his manner told Jamie that he wasn't full of himself like Edgar Davidson was.

Leaning his head toward the next cabin, Jamie said, "I'm going to be your neighbor for the night, Lieutenant. Maybe I'll see you at this evening's mess."

"Only for the night?" Tyler asked with a

slight frown. "I thought that maybe you were going to —"

"Going to what?" Jamie asked when Tyler stopped short.

"Never mind, sir. I was about to speak out of turn. I need to finish cleaning this sidearm."

Jamie was curious, but he didn't press the issue. He just nodded and went on to the cabin he'd be using.

He couldn't help wondering, though, if something more than was readily apparent was going on at Fort Kearny.

CHAPTER 4

The Crow village

The eyes that gazed back at Preacher from Butterfly's beautiful face were startlingly blue. She said, "It has been many moons since anyone has called me by my white name, Preacher. You are the only one who does."

"I can stop doin' that if you want," he told her.

She shook her head and said, "No, it is good for me to remember that once I was white. My life is here, with Hawk That Soars and my children and the Crow, and it always will be, but that is part of who I am as well."

When Preacher and Hawk had first met Butterfly, having rescued her from the fur thieves who had taken her prisoner, they had had no reason to believe she was anything other than the young Crow maiden she appeared to be. However, it hadn't been long before Preacher noticed her blue eyes

52

and realized that she wasn't what she seemed.

Gradually, he had dug enough old, painful memories out of her brain to establish that she was the daughter of a minister and his wife who had come to the frontier, only to be attacked and killed by a war party from some unknown tribe.

The girl named Caroline, a small child at the time, had wandered away from the scene of the massacre and been found by a band of Crow Indians. They had taken her in and raised her as one of them, until the day they were attacked by the Blackfeet and the young woman now known as Butterfly was taken away as a slave.

Fate, in the persons of Preacher, Hawk, the old Absaroka called White Buffalo, and two young trappers, Aaron Buckley and Charlie Todd, eventually had freed her and brought her to this satisfying life with Hawk and a different band of Crow. But as she said, everything she had been in the past had gone into making her the person she was now, and she didn't want to turn her back on any of it.

Preacher leaned to the side to look around Butterfly and grinned at his grandson and granddaughter.

"How are these two young'uns doin'?" he

asked. "They're growin' like weeds, ain't they?"

"Eagle Feather, Bright Moon, say hello to your grandfather," Butterfly told the children.

"Hello, Grandfather," Eagle Feather greeted Preacher. The boy stood up straighter, still maybe a little bit nervous about talking to the old mountain man but determined not to show it. His little sister remained shy, though, and clutched at Butterfly's buckskin dress as she peeked around her mother's hip.

"Does Hawk That Soars ever take you huntin' with him?" Preacher asked his grandson.

"Sometimes. But only close to the village. He said he might have to go far today."

Worry lurked in Butterfly's eyes as she said, "Our hunters must go farther and farther away to find enough game."

"Big Thunder told me about that, and so did Broken Pine," Preacher said with a nod. "They blamed it on the white wagon trains." He rubbed his chin. "I ain't so sure about that, though. Huntin' grounds get played out from time to time. That's just the nature of things."

"Broken Pine says the village may have to move." Butterfly shook her head. "I would

54

not like that. I have been here longer than anywhere else in my life. But what is best for our people is what we must do."

Preacher couldn't argue with that. He let Butterfly get back to preparing her family's supper while he talked with his grandson Eagle Feather. Bright Moon stayed close to her mother, but as Eagle Feather relaxed, he began to chatter more and eagerly showed Preacher the bow Hawk had made for him.

"Are you a good shot with it?" Preacher asked.

"Very good," Eagle Feather boasted. "Would you like to see?"

"Sure."

"Come with me," the boy said. He led Preacher to a meadow at the edge of the village. It was bordered by trees, and Eagle Feather pointed at one of them and went on, "See the knot on that tree trunk? I will put an arrow right below it."

"Are you sure? That's a pretty good ways."

"I can do it," the youngster said confidently. He had slung a quiver of arrows on his back before he and Preacher walked out here. Made to use with the smaller bow, they were shorter and lighter than the arrows a full-grown warrior would use. Eagle Feather reached up and back to select one

55

of them and nocked it to the bow.

Preacher nodded in approval of the crafts-manship that had gone into the arrow. He asked, "Did you make those yourself?"

"My father and I made them. He showed me how, and I did most of the work."

"Good. That's how you learn."

Eagle Feather raised the bow and pulled back the string. He aimed for a moment, then let the arrow fly. It zipped across the distance between him and the tree and smacked solidly in the trunk about six inches below the knot he had pointed out.

Preacher whistled in admiration and said, "That's some pretty good shootin'."

"I can do better," Eagle Feather said eagerly. "Let me try again."

Before the boy could draw another arrow from the quiver, though, someone called Preacher's name. When he turned, he saw Hawk That Soars striding toward him. Hawk was trying to look serious and digni-fied, as he always did, but Preacher could tell that his son was glad to see him.

They embraced and slapped each other on the back. Hawk asked, "What are you doing here, Preacher?"

"Can't a fella come and visit his family? I was driftin' in this direction anyway, and then when I ran into Big Thunder, I decided not to wait any longer."

"Did you and Big Thunder fight?"

Preacher grinned and said, "Shoot, of course we did. That boy wouldn't have it any other way."

Eagle Feather looked up at his father and asked, "Did you find any game?"

"I brought us a deer," Hawk replied with a solemn nod. "It was a good day, and for that we must thank the spirits of our ancestors."

Eagle Feather pointed at Preacher and said, "He is our ancestor."

"But I ain't a spirit just yet." Preacher grinned. "So I can't take no credit for your pa's good luck."

"Come," Hawk said as he put one hand on his father's shoulder and the other on his son's shoulder. "Let us return to the lodge and talk of many things."

"Hunting?" Eagle Feather asked.

"That," said Hawk, "and more."

The children were asleep in their buffalo robes. The cooking fire outside had been put out, but a small fire burned inside a ring of rocks in the center of the lodge and beneath the smoke opening at the top. Preacher and Hawk sat next to the flames while Butterfly was beside the children but

57

still attentive to what the men were saying.

"Some of our scouts were in the foothills last week and were able to look far out onto the plains," Hawk said, gesturing fluidly to illustrate what he was telling Preacher. "They saw wagons to the south and east."

"The pass that most of the immigrants use is a ways farther south of here," said Preacher. "I ain't sure what a wagon train would be doin' this far north unless the fellas guidin' it were searchin' for a new route."

"A path that would get them to their destination faster than the others traveling west would be a good thing for them, would it not?"

Preacher considered that and nodded.

"Folks are just naturally competitive, especially ones who are bold enough to set out across hundreds of miles of untamed land in hopes of makin' a new start somewhere else."

Hawk grunted and repeated, "Untamed land. White men are strange. I do not see how land can be tamed or untamed. It just *is.*" He paused, then added, "I do not mean to insult you by calling white men strange, Preacher."

The mountain man chuckled and said, "Don't worry about that. I reckon you could say that most folks are strange, though, in one way or another. But you're right: if a wagon train guide could promise to get the folks who hired him to Oregon sooner than some other guide would, that'd be a mighty valuable thing for him. The settlers would be fine with gettin' there ahead of the others, too. They'd feel like they had a better chance of claimin' the best land and water."

"And along the way they will kill the game and foul the streams and attack our people out of fear or the sheer viciousness they feel toward us," Hawk stated with more than a trace of bitterness in his voice.

"Maybe not," Preacher said, but in truth, he knew that more than likely Hawk was right. The history of the Indians' encounters with the white men as they pushed the frontier farther and farther west was filled with hard feelings at best — and bloody violence at worst.

Hawk knew that, too. He said, "We could fight them. Try to make them go a different way through the mountains."

"You could," Preacher said, nodding slowly and solemnly. "You might be able to turn back a couple of wagon trains, too. But then word would get around about what happened and the pilgrims who come along later would just hire more men with more guns to escort them . . . and some of them would start yellin' to Washington for help from the army, too." He paused, then added heavily, "You don't want that."

Hawk sighed and said, "The Crow have always gotten along with the white men. They are more inclined to work with the whites rather than to fight them."

"That's a good thing, ain't it?"

"It is . . . until the children begin to cry in the night because their bellies are empty."

"It hasn't come to that, has it?"

"Not yet," said Hawk. "But if the hunting continues to get worse, it may, and not very far in the future, at that."

Preacher seemed to be staring into the fire, but actually his eyes were directed elsewhere in the lodge. One of the first things he had learned after coming to the mountains all those years ago was not to impair his vision by looking directly into flames. That was a good way to be taken by surprise . . . and being taken by surprise on the frontier usually meant winding up dead.

"So if you don't want to have a fight on your hands . . . a fight you'd have a hard time winnin', in the long run . . . the best thing to do is move."

"Indians never stay in one place for too long," Hawk pointed out. "This band of

Crow has been here in this village for more years than most remain without moving."

Butterfly spoke up, saying, "It is a good place for a village, the best I have ever seen. The river protects us and gives us good water that never runs out. The mountains to the north and west shelter us from the worst of the wind and storms during the winter. The buffalo herds graze near to the foothills in the east so our men can ride out and hunt them, and many elk and antelope roam the high country."

"They do," said Hawk, "but for how long?"

"How long?" repeated Butterfly as she impatiently flung out a hand. "How long will anything last in this world? We do not know. We *cannot* know such things. All we can do is have faith in the spirits of those who came before us, and faith in those we love in this world."

"You can't argue with that," Preacher said.

"A wise man does not argue with his wife," Hawk said with a hint of a smile. "Now that you know the problems we are facing, will you think on them and talk with me and Broken Pine and the elders tomorrow?"

"You reckon they'll put any stock in what a white man has to say?"

"I believe you are the *only* white man they will truly listen to, Preacher," Hawk said.

CHAPTER 5

The council took place in the middle of the next day, in Broken Pine's lodge. Broken Pine was there, of course, along with Preacher and Hawk That Soars.

In addition, half a dozen other Crow warriors sat around the fire in the center of the lodge. Preacher knew all of them from previous visits to the village or had at least met them. A couple of the men glanced at him and frowned when he came in with Hawk, as if they weren't sure about the wisdom of having a white man sit in on the council with them, but no one voiced any objection. Everyone knew that Hawk was Preacher's son and that Preacher had fought side by side with Broken Pine in the past. The mountain man had always been a good friend to the Crow.

But he was white, and sometimes it was hard to put that fact aside.

Broken Pine began by talking about something they all knew already: the white settlers bound for the Pacific Northwest, along with their wagons pulled by teams of massive oxen or rawboned mules, had been spotted coming closer and closer to this river valley where the village was located. Most Indians never used one word when ten could be made to express the same idea, and Broken Pine was no different. His opening oration was lengthy and eloquent.

Then he launched into a recitation of how it was becoming more and more difficult to find game within reasonably close confines to the village. Preacher wanted to speak up in response to that, but he held his tongue. When dealing with Indians, everything had to run its natural course and proceed at its own pace.

Finally, Broken Pine brought his opening statement to a close by saying, "It has been suggested that the wisest course of action we might follow is to move our village and search for a new, more suitable location for it. I would hear what all of you think about this idea."

That led to more lengthy speeches. As one who had come from somewhere other than this village, Hawk waited until all the other warriors had gone before him. Then he said, "I have fought many white men in my time.

They cannot be trusted. You never know what to expect from them. As evil as the Blackfeet are, when you do battle with them, you know what they will do and what they will not do. There are things not even a Blackfoot will stoop to." Hawk shook his head solemnly. "The same cannot be said of a white man. If he wants to win badly enough, he will do *anything.*" Hawk leaned back and crossed his arms. "For this reason, I say that we should fight the whites if we must in order to protect our hunting grounds . . . but if we can find better hunting grounds, we should go there instead of fighting."

Several of the other men had expressed that same sentiment during the council. The rest were violently opposed to the idea, though, including a warrior named Many Pelts who was the most passionate about it. He leaned forward now as he sat cross-legged beside the fire and slammed a fist against his thigh.

"The Crow do not run away and hide like frightened children," he said. "Those of you who have suggested such a thing should be ashamed!"

Hawk bristled at that, and he wasn't the only one. Several men muttered angrily and looked like they were about to get to their feet.

"Hold," Broken Pine said sharply. "All are free to say what they wish in this council. If you wish to take issue with Many Pelts, do it outside this lodge." The chief looked at Preacher. "You have not spoken."

"Bad enough we must listen to one who is half-white," declared Many Pelts as he sneered toward Hawk. "Nothing a white man could say holds any interest for me!"

"Preacher is an elder among his people and has long been a friend to the Crow," Broken Pine said. "And he is *my* friend, Many Pelts. You will speak of him with respect."

Many Pelts scowled and didn't say anything, as if he would rather keep quiet than show any deference toward Preacher.

Broken Pine nodded to the mountain man and went on, "I would hear your thoughts, Preacher."

"And I'll be happy to share 'em with you," Preacher said, "but you may not like some of them."

Broken Pine gestured for him to continue.

"First of all, I have a question. I don't doubt that the wagon trains have been comin' closer. I trust the eyes of your scouts. But what makes you believe they're

66

responsible for the problems you've been having with huntin' in this area?"

One of the men asked, "What else could be the cause?"

"Nothing else has changed," said another. "The land goes on as it always has, and that means the game should be as abundant as ever. But then the white men came, and a hunter can go all day without ever seeing a deer or an elk. It is because of the white men. It must be."

Preacher wasn't sure how to argue with that logic. What the warrior had said made perfect sense to him. Preacher knew he had to try to make the men understand, though.

"Did it rain in the spring?" he asked.

"Of course, it did," Many Pelts said. "It always rains in the spring."

"As much as it usually does?"

Broken Pine said, "There was an entire moon when no rain fell. The wildflowers did not bloom until much later than they usually do."

"And the grass didn't grow as tall or as thick, I'm guessin'," Preacher said.

"The flowers bloomed and the grass grew," Many Pelts burst out. "What difference does it make?"

"The grazin' isn't as good when it's been dry like that. Animals know that. They

67

wander on, lookin' for someplace where there's more to eat. And then that carries on over to you folks. You have to look for a better place, too."

"Bah! The grass is there! The game left because of the white men, not because it did not rain for a time."

Broken Pine said, "It seems to me that Preacher may be right. All of us" — his expansive gesture took in the other members of the council — "have either heard about such things, or seen them with our own eyes. A bad winter, a bad spring, these can cause much hardship among animals and people alike."

"That is why all the tribes never stay in one place forever," said Hawk. "It is in our nature to move."

"And it is in our nature to fight when we are threatened!" Many Pelts insisted. "I will not be driven away before my enemies. I will stand, and if I have to, I will *die* where I stand!"

What it came down to, thought Preacher, was that Many Pelts wanted a fight and was bound and determined to get one, no matter what it took. But Broken Pine was a smart chief, and he would be aware of the same thing.

"We have talked much," Broken Pine said.

"Now we will think about what has been spoken."

"There is no need," Many Pelts insisted. "I say we decide now, and my decision is that we place scouts in the foothills and wait for the next wagon train to come near our land. When it does, we will ride out and attack it and drive the white men away!"

"Our land!" Broken Pine repeated sharply and scornfully. "The land is not ours, Many Pelts. It belongs to the Maker of All Things. We only live on it and make use of it."

Many Pelts let out a disdainful snort that made Broken Pine stiffen with anger.

"Ask the white men if they believe that. You know they do not! They believe that everything in the world belongs to them." Many Pelts jerked a hand toward Preacher. "Ask that white man if he believes that he and his kind should own all the land between the great waters on both sides that we have heard about."

"Manifest Destiny," Preacher muttered in English.

"What?"

"Never mind. I'll tell you what I own, Many Pelts. The clothes I'm wearin'. The gear I carry. These two guns." Preacher rested his hands on the butts of the Colt Dragoons. "A Sharps rifle, a knife that's served me well for more than twenty years, a good tomahawk. The same sort of things *you* own. I've never set foot on ground that belonged to me and don't care if I ever do. And I'm the only white man I speak for."

"A good answer," Broken Pine said with a nod. He looked hard at Many Pelts and went on, "We will make no decision today. Go to your lodges and think on what has been said. We will talk again."

Many Pelts didn't like that, as his glare made clear. But he didn't argue anymore, as even those other warriors who leaned toward agreeing with him didn't want unnecessary trouble with Broken Pine. A chief could be overruled or even removed from a position of power, but neither of those things was ever done lightly or hastily.

The men stood up to leave. As Broken Pine came to his feet, he said, "Preacher, Hawk That Soars, wait a moment."

The two of them stood there while the others filed out. Many Pelts cast a sullen glance over his shoulder as he left the lodge. If the place had had a door, Many Pelts would have slammed it, thought Preacher . . . but it was hard to do that with a buffalo hide flap.

When the rest of the warriors were gone, Broken Pine said, "Many Pelts may try to cause trouble for you, Preacher. He is very proud . . . proud to the point of sometimes being rash."

"I'll keep my eyes open," said Preacher. "He won't sneak up on me."

Broken Pine smiled faintly, an uncommon expression on his usually so solemn face, and said, "I was more worried that you might kill him. He is a good man, no matter how stubborn he can be at times, and I would not see him hurt if that can be avoided."

Preacher nodded and said, "I'll remember that. I'll try to take it easy on him . . . if he'll let me."

"I cannot ask for more." Broken Pine paused, then went on, "Do you really believe that the white men from the wagon trains have nothing to do with the lack of game being so bad around here now?"

"I'm sure they send out huntin' parties to bring in fresh meat, but think about it. How many wagon trains have there actually been, and how many elk and antelope and deer would their hunters have had to kill in order to affect the huntin' around here? Seems like it would have to be an awful lot."

"So you think we have blamed this on the white men even though they are innocent?"

Preacher snorted and said, "I wouldn't

71

start throwin' around words like *innocent* too freely. But I think it's easier to blame somebody else than to blame pure bad luck. If it's the white men's fault, you can run them off and things'll go back to bein' like they were. That's what Many Pelts and the others who feel like he do believe will happen. But if it's bad luck that's to blame, there's really no way to fight that. And bein' helpless frustrates the hell outta folks."

"As usual, you are wise, Preacher," Broken Pine said as he nodded slowly. "I do not want to go to war with the white men. But I do not want their wagon trains coming closer and closer to our hunting grounds, either."

"I reckon that's a reasonable way to feel." Preacher rubbed his chin as he frowned in thought for a moment, then he said, "The next time a wagon train comes along, would you like me to ride out and have a talk with the fellas leadin' it? Maybe find out what they intend on doin' and why they're this far north?"

"That was my hope. Do you mind staying here until such an opportunity comes along?"

"Do I mind?" Preacher grinned. "You've just given me a good excuse to hang around and spend more time with my son and daughter-in-law and grandkids. I'd be mighty happy to do that, and if I can help you folks out at the same time, I sure can't argue with that."

CHAPTER 6

Fort Kearny

Jamie Ian MacCallister was getting dressed
the next morning when a knock sounded
on the door of the borrowed officer's cabin.
He finished pulling the faded blue shirt over
his head, then went to the door.

Second Lieutenant Hayden Tyler stood
outside in full uniform. The pistol he had
been cleaning the previous evening was holstered on his right hip. He straightened as if
he were about to salute, then caught himself, obviously remembering that Jamie
wasn't an officer or even a member of the
army. Jamie was such a big, impressive
figure that he often had that effect on folks.

"Good morning, sir," Tyler said. "I trust
you slept well?"

"Well enough for a man my age," Jamie
said. "What can I do for you, Lieutenant?"

"Captain Croxton asked me to let you
know that he'd like to see you in his office

once you've had breakfast. In fact, I'd be happy to walk over to the mess hall with you and then accompany you to see the captain."

Jamie's eyes narrowed slightly as he regarded the young man.

"Lieutenant, if I didn't know better, it would sound to me like the captain *ordered* you to bring me to him and told you to keep a close eye on me until we got there."

Tyler looked and sounded a little flustered as he said, "Oh, no, sir, that's not . . . I mean . . ."

Jamie stopped him by grinning.

"It's all right, I was planning on stopping in to see Captain Croxton again this morning before I ride out," Jamie said. "Let me get my hat, and we'll go see about that breakfast."

The flapjacks, salt pork, and coffee in the officer's mess weren't very good, but Jamie had found that to be true of army grub just about everywhere.

He couldn't say much for the company, either, other than Lieutenant Tyler, who remained friendly, although a little reserved. Two other second lieutenants were there, but they studiously avoided looking at Jamie.

Not so First Lieutenant Edgar Davidson, who sat at the far end of the table and glared at Jamie throughout the meal.

Jamie acted like Davidson wasn't there. He wasn't looking for trouble . . . and anyway, he figured being ignored would bother the arrogant young officer as much as anything short of a bust in the snoot.

When they had finished the meal, Jamie and Tyler left the mess hall and walked toward the frame building where Captain Croxton's office and quarters were located. Lieutenant Davidson had gone out ahead of them, leaving some of his breakfast uneaten, with an expression on his narrow face like he had a bad taste in his mouth. Jamie looked around for Davidson as he and Tyler walked beside the parade ground, but he didn't see the lieutenant.

"You don't happen to know why the captain wants to see me, do you?" Jamie asked casually.

"I'm afraid not, sir. He didn't confide in me."

Jamie nodded. That was the answer he expected, even if Tyler *did* know what it was about. Jamie still had the sense that something unusual was going on at Fort Kearny. He also had a hunch that he was about to find out what it was.

76

One thing he noticed on the way to the captain's office was that over by the quartermaster's storehouse, dragoons were loading what looked like crates of supplies into a couple of wagons, under the watchful eye of a sergeant. It didn't seem likely they would be doing that unless some of the command was about to go somewhere.

Was the army preparing to mount an expedition of some sort from Fort Kearny? That seemed likely to Jamie. The real question was whether the soldiers would be setting out on a campaign of exploration . . . or war.

The chunky corporal who was Croxton's adjutant ushered them into the captain's office. Croxton stood up, returned Tyler's salute, and said, "That'll be all here, Lieutenant. You can go attend to that other assignment I gave you."

"Yes, sir," Tyler responded with what Jamie thought was a noticeable lack of eagerness, then turned and left the room.

Croxton waved his visitor into the chair in front of the desk and asked, "How are you doing this morning, Jamie?"

"Fine, I reckon," Jamie said as he lowered his big figure onto the chair. "But I've got a feeling you're about to say something to me that may change that."

"Not at all, not at all," Croxton said with an unconvincing wave of his hand. He resumed his seat and reached for a wooden box on the desk. "Cigar?"

"No thanks. Whatever it is, Captain, just spit it out."

Croxton sighed and then slowly nodded.

"You're right. Nobody could ever put anything over on you, Jamie. You're just too sharp for that."

Jamie squinted and said, "I don't cotton much to somebody paying me compliments in order to get me to do something, either."

Croxton laughed and held up his hands in surrender.

"All right. Straight talk it is, then. I need your help, Jamie."

"That's more like it. I'm not promising I'll do it, but what is it you want from me?"

"You're familiar with the Crow Indians, aren't you?" asked Croxton.

"Sure. I've spent time in a few of their villages."

"What do you think of them?"

"I've always gotten along just fine with them," Jamie said. "Most folks do. They've had a few skirmishes with the whites over the years, but by and large, they'd rather talk things over and try to reach an understanding, instead of fighting." Jamie paused.

"But don't let that fool you. When they have to fight, they're mighty good at it. You can ask the Blackfeet. They're the Crows' natural enemies, and those two bunches have been at war for farther back than I can remember. I'd go into battle with the Crow on my side anytime."

Croxton nodded and said, "That's the impression I have of them, too. But you and I are out here on the frontier, Jamie, and the men who make the actual decisions about policy . . . men in the War Department and the Bureau of Indian Affairs . . . well, they're sitting in offices back in Washington. They believe in pieces of paper more than they do in the opinions of fellows like you and me."

"You're talking about treaties?"

"That's right."

Jamie grimaced and made a slashing, dismissive motion with his hand.

"Those fellas in Washington believe in treaties only when it suits their own ends to do so," he declared. "If there's something they want and a treaty stands in the way, they just ignore the treaty."

Croxton sighed and said, "Unfortunately, that's true at times. Perhaps most of the time. But even so, when they send out orders saying that I'm to begin treaty

79

negotiations with the Crow who live in the mountains a week's ride northwest of here, I have no choice but to carry out those orders."

"What sort of treaty are they after? Do they want to take the Crows' land?"

Jamie knew that Indians, for the most part, didn't believe land could be owned, but that was one of the bedrock principles for the whites so it was a waste of time *not* to think in those terms.

"No, not at all," Croxton replied. "There's talk of opening a new wagon train route that will pass through that area and cut a week or more off the journey to the Pacific Northwest."

Jamie frowned and said, "I'm not sure there *is* a route through those parts that will do that. It's been a while since I've been through there, so I'd have to take a look with my own eyes to be certain."

"All I know is what my orders say," Croxton said as he spread his hands. "Washington wants a treaty guaranteeing safe passage to any wagon trains that travel through the area, and it's my job to get the process started. I'm supposed to send a detail to the Crow village and invite their chief to come here to the fort to discuss a treaty with representatives from Washington."

"Why don't those representatives just go to the Crow, instead of making the chief come here?"

"I suspect they believe the negotiations are more likely to go in our favor if they take place here," said Croxton as he shrugged his shoulders. "But again, the only thing I know for sure is what my orders require of me."

"I don't see how any of this involves me," Jamie said, although that wasn't really true. He believed he had a pretty good inkling of what the captain had in mind.

Croxton clasped his hands together in front of him and leaned forward to look intently over the desk at Jamie.

"I want to hire you as a civilian scout. You've done work like that for the army in the past."

"Quite a few times," Jamie said, nodding.

"You and I have even been part of the same command in the past. There's no one who knows the frontier better than you do, Jamie, and even though I'm not expecting any trouble, I'd like to have a good, experienced man going along on this trip. Most of the dragoons assigned here are pretty green, I have to admit. And unfortunately, the same thing is true of the officers."

Jamie toyed with his hat, which he had

taken off and placed on his knee when he sat down. He said, "I was fixing to head back home pretty soon, Captain. I've been gone for a while. I get too fiddlefooted to stay in one place for too long, but then once I'm away from home, I start to missing my wife and kids."

"Of course, you do. I'm sorry to have to put you in this position. But the whole prospect of sending that detail to the Crow village has been bothering me, and when you showed up yesterday, it seemed like fate had sent me an answer to my problem."

"I don't know about that. I'm not exactly what anybody would think of as an instrument of fate."

"Anyone can be, at one time or another," Croxton said. "I don't want to pressure you for a decision, Jamie, but I really need to get that detail started on its way."

Jamie nodded and said, "I saw supplies being loaded on a couple of wagons. I reckon they're going along?"

"That's right. Provisions and ammunition and everything else the men should need. Plus there are a few gifts in there for the Indians." Croxton smiled. "Something to sweeten the pot, I suppose you could say."

"And bribe them into doing what the politicians and the bureaucrats want."

Croxton frowned and looked uncomfortable but didn't respond to Jamie's caustic comment. Jamie told himself to take it easy on the captain. The man was a soldier and had to follow orders like any other soldier.

Something important occurred to Jamie, though, and he asked, "Just who's going to be in charge of this detail? Are you going along, Captain?"

"No, I'm to stay here. This fort is an important supply point for the wagon trains heading west. A jumping-off spot, you could say. I have to make sure it continues to function in that respect. So one of my junior officers will be commanding the delegation to the Crow village."

Jamie scowled and said, "You're not talking about —" A deferential knock on the office door interrupted him, and the pudgy adjutant stuck his head in to say,

"Lieutenants Davidson and Tyler are here, sir."

"Send them in," Croxton said, even as Jamie leaned back in his chair and thought, *Hell, no . . .*

CHAPTER 7

Edgar Davidson stepped into the office, came to attention, and saluted. Behind him, Hayden Tyler did the same.

Captain Croxton stood up, returned the salutes, and said, "At ease, both of you."

Despite that, Davidson remained standing as stiffly as ever as he said, "You wanted to see me, sir?"

His eyes flicked toward Jamie, who kept his seat in front of the desk. Dislike filled the lieutenant's glance.

"I have new orders for both of you," said Croxton as he settled down in his chair again. "But before we get to that, there's some business with Mr. MacCallister that I need to finish."

"It's finished," Jamie said flatly. "I refuse, Captain. You're going to have to find somebody else for the job."

"There *isn't* anyone else," Croxton argued. "This is an important mission, Jamie, not just for me but for the Crow as well. Don't you think peace means as much to them as it does to us?"

"I know it does. But I can't help you."

Davidson cleared his throat and said, "Begging the captain's pardon, but perhaps Lieutenant Tyler and I should come back later . . . ?"

"Stay right where you are," Croxton snapped. "Jamie, I had the feeling you were leaning toward accepting my proposition —"

"Maybe I was," Jamie broke in, "but that was before I knew who was going to be in command."

That made Davidson's eyes open a little wider. He might be as obnoxious as all get-out, but apparently he wasn't stupid. As the second-highest ranking officer at Fort Kearny, if someone was going to be given command of something, he was likely the one. He couldn't stop himself from saying, "Captain —"

Croxton cut him off with a stern look. The captain turned back to Jamie and said, "If it's a matter of money . . ."

"You know better than that," Jamie said. "I'm just not going to go along and wet-nurse this green lieutenant."

Davidson's lip curled as he said, "If you're

referring to me, MacCallister, I hardly need any assistance from the likes of you, no matter what the mission under discussion may be."

"That's where you're wrong, Lieutenant," Croxton said. "Jamie Ian MacCallister is one of the best scouts and most experienced frontiersmen you'll find anywhere west of the Mississippi!" The captain came to his feet again. "Not only that, but I consider him a personal friend of mine, and I won't have him insulted."

"I don't feel insulted," drawled Jamie. "For that to be true, I'd have to give a damn what this shavetail thinks of me."

Davidson turned toward him and exclaimed, "By God, I won't stand for —"

"As you were, Lieutenant!" Croxton's voice lashed out at the young officer.

Davidson stood up straight again, and his lips were a tight, thin line as he said, "I beg the captain's pardon, sir, and I apologize to Mr. MacCallister as well. I meant no offense."

Well, that was a blatant lie, thought Jamie. Offending him was exactly what Davidson had intended. But as he had indicated, he didn't care what Davidson thought of him.

The breath that Croxton blew out eloquently expressed his disgust and frustration. He said, "I suppose it's all moot anyway, if you absolutely refuse to go along, Jamie. Lieutenants Davidson and Tyler will have to do the best they can without you."

Davidson lifted his chin, preened like a peacock, and said, "I assure you, sir, you have nothing to worry about. I'll see to it that this mission proceeds smoothly and effectively, whatever it may be."

Jamie looked at Hayden Tyler, who had stood behind Davidson without saying anything. Jamie asked him, "You're part of this, Lieutenant?"

"That's right, sir. I understand that I'll be Lieutenant Davidson's second-in-command."

Davidson cocked an eyebrow and then frowned again. He had to realize that Tyler actually knew more about what was going on than he did, and he didn't like that.

Tyler's involvement changed things a little, Jamie thought. He had just met Tyler the day before, but he felt an instinctive liking for the second lieutenant. Even though the mission sounded like a fairly simple one, the way Captain Croxton had described it, if there was a way to foul things up and put the soldiers in danger, more than likely Edgar Davidson would find it. Jamie didn't want anything bad happening to Tyler or any of the other dragoons assigned to the detail, if it could be avoided.

Besides, if he refused to go along, he would be handing Davidson exactly what he wanted. That idea didn't sit well with Jamie.

The thought crossed his mind that maybe Croxton had slyly maneuvered him into this position, knowing that he wouldn't be able to stand it if Davidson came out on top. Jamie didn't know if Croxton was that cunning, but he wouldn't put it past the man.

"If there's nothing else, Captain . . . ?" Davidson began.

Jamie held up a hand and said, "Hold on a minute. Maybe I was a mite too hasty."

Croxton sank back into his chair, and Jamie could tell that he was trying not to grin in triumph.

Davidson turned sharply toward Jamie and demanded, "What are you talking about? You've already stated that you have no intention of coming along."

"And maybe I ought to think about that some more." Jamie nodded across the desk toward Croxton. "The captain and I are old friends, and I wouldn't want to let him down."

Davidson's mouth began opening and closing slightly, as if he desperately wanted to say something but couldn't come up with the words.

"Besides," Jamie went on, "there could be a lot riding on this treaty with the Crow. I wouldn't want to see a war break out with those folks. The less violence and bloodshed there is on the frontier, the sooner the whole place gets civilized."

In truth, Jamie wasn't so sure he thought the spread of civilization across the West was a good idea. He had seen much of this country the way it was originally, or at least the way it had been before the white men started crowding in.

But there was no stopping the so-called march of progress, and so the best thing to do was try to hold down the damage on both sides. Maybe he *could* help by going along with the detail Captain Croxton was sending out, Jamie told himself.

Looking pleased with himself — the sly dog — Croxton said, "I'm very pleased that you've changed your mind, Jamie. I'll add you to the post's roster as a civilian scout. I'm afraid I won't be able to issue you any wages until you get back . . ."

"So if I don't come back, the army's not out any extra money. Sounds like a good deal." Jamie glanced at Davidson, who was still standing there looking dumbfounded.

"A really good deal."

Croxton got to his feet again and said in a brisk tone, "Now that that's settled, we need to go over some details. If you'll come over here, gentlemen . . ."

Croxton moved to a large map on the office wall and rested a fingertip on the parchment, in an area on the eastern slope of a mountain range angling down from the main body of the Rockies.

"This stream is called Bishop's River on the map, after the trapper who first explored it," the captain said as his finger traced a winding line on the map. "I'm sure the Crow have some other name for it. There's a large village here" — he tapped a spot on the map where the river made a large bend — "and other villages scattered throughout the area to the north. This main village is the one we're interested in, because of rumors of a nearby pass that might allow wagons to get through the mountains."

Jamie shook his head and said, "There's no such pass, Captain. The more I think about it, the more sure I am of that. There are trails through the mountains, and maybe with some work one of them could be fixed up to where wagons could use it, but it would be a big job."

Davidson said, "And I'm sure the army

surveyors and cartographers responsible for this map know more than you do about this subject, MacCallister. Pardon me, *Mister* MacCallister."

The correction managed to be even more insulting than the original statement.

"I trust your judgment and knowledge, Jamie," said Croxton, "but again, that doesn't affect the orders I'm supposed to carry out. It's the treaty we're concerned with, not whether there's actually a viable wagon train route through the mountains in that area."

Jamie's broad shoulders rose and fell as he said, "Fair enough."

"So my assignment is to negotiate a treaty with the savages?" Davidson asked.

"Your assignment is to bring the Crow chief back here to the fort so that representatives from Washington can negotiate a treaty with him," Croxton said.

The eager expression fell off of Davidson's face. He must have been thinking that this mission would result in him having a place in history, minor though it might have been. He said, "Oh," then recovered from his disappointment with a visible effort and went on, "Very well, sir. Rest assured that I will deliver the redskin here as ordered, whatever it takes."

Jamie said, "I think you're supposed to convince him to come to the fort, not take him prisoner and drag him back here. He won't be in much of a mood to sign a treaty if you do that."

Davidson looked to Captain Croxton for clarification. The captain cleared his throat and said, "We don't want to spark a war with the Crow, Lieutenant. Keep that in mind at all times. But I believe if you explain the situation in a satisfactory manner, the chief will come with you."

That dodged the question, thought Jamie. He asked, "Do you know anything about this chief?"

Croxton shook his head and said, "Very little, only what some of the trappers who have worked in that region told us. His name is Broken Pine. He's supposed to be a relatively young man, which leads me to hope he might be more reasonable and open to discussion than some of the elders in the tribe."

The captain was wrong about that, and Jamie knew it. It was the young warriors who were the firebrands, the ones with unshakable opinions that often led to conflict and even war. The old men had already seen their share of violence and destruction and were more likely to want to avoid such

92

things in the future.

But that was why he was going along, Jamie supposed, to put such knowledge to good use, and serve as a wise, experienced advisor to Lieutenant Davidson.

Who wasn't likely to listen to a damned thing he had to say, Jamie thought grimly.

"Now, it should take you a week to ten days to reach the Crow village," Croxton went on. "It'll probably take a day or two of discussions with the chief before he agrees to accompany you back here. So I'll expect you to return in approximately three weeks."

Lieutenant Tyler spoke up, asking, "The wagon train that left here more than a week ago, was it headed in the same direction?"

"I believe the wagonmaster intended to cross the mountains somewhat to the south of your destination," said Croxton. "It's not likely that you'll overtake them, but I suppose it's possible if anything happened to delay them. That wagon train doesn't really have anything to do with your assignment, though, Lieutenant."

"Understood, sir," Tyler said with a nod.

Davidson asked, "Am I to have the ability to pick the men I want to form this detail, Captain?"

"You're taking B Troop, Lieutenant Tyler's troop," Croxton replied with a nod toward Tyler.

Jamie could tell that Davidson didn't like having that decision made for him, but after a moment, Davidson nodded in acceptance of it. Then he said, "In that case, sir, I request that Sergeant O'Connor be reassigned to B Troop so that he can come along."

"O'Connor?" Croxton raised an eyebrow in surprise.

"He's an experienced man, sir, and you yourself spoke to the need for experienced men on this mission. Besides, I've worked well with Sergeant O'Connor in the past and have found him to be an exemplary noncommissioned officer."

"But the man's been locked up for fighting!"

Davidson looked coolly at Jamie and said, "For fighting with Mr. MacCallister, who *is* coming along on this mission, I believe."

"He's got you there, Captain," Jamie said dryly. "If you think I might object, don't worry about that. It doesn't matter to me who comes along. I intend to do my job, and as long as everybody else does their jobs, I won't have a problem with them."

Croxton thought it over for a moment, then nodded.

"All right," he said. "But I'm holding you

94

responsible for O'Connor's behavior, Lieutenant."

"If I'm to be in command, sir, won't I be responsible for the behavior of everyone in the detail?"

"That's right, you will be. And don't forget, Lieutenant, you're also responsible for helping to keep the peace here on the frontier."

"Of course, sir," Davidson replied with a smirk, and Jamie thought, *God help us all . . .*

CHAPTER 8

The Crow village

A couple of very enjoyable days passed for Preacher as he continued his visit with his son's family. He and Hawk roamed the forests, sometimes just the two of them and sometimes in company with Broken Pine, Big Thunder, and other old friends.

During those jaunts, Preacher saw that what he had been told was true: game was surprisingly scarce. Preacher didn't believe there was any way that could honestly be blamed on the wagon trains coming increasingly closer, but he didn't see any point in stirring up arguments, so he kept his mouth shut about that.

He also spent quite a bit of time with Eagle Feather, telling the boy tall tales about his adventures that occasionally had Butterfly frowning in disapproval when the stories became too lurid.

He even got his extremely shy granddaughter, Bright Moon, to be more comfortable around him and actually talk to him, telling him about her friends and the games they played and all the things Butterfly had been teaching her about the work a woman of the tribe had to do.

Preacher was having a good time here and was in no hurry to leave, but then Broken Pine sought him out and said, "Three of our men ventured out onto the plains yesterday in search of buffalo, and they saw many of the white men's wagons traveling toward the mountains."

"The wagons are headed this direction?"

"South of here," Broken Pine replied, "but well north of the river white men call the Sweetwater."

Preacher knew the Sweetwater River very well. He had trapped up and down its length many times and also traveled along it when he was on his way to the annual rendezvous fur trappers held on the Green River, a ways farther west. The stream rose near the broad, level valley known as South Pass, where most of the wagon trains had been crossing the Rockies in recent years. A wagon train moving north of there had to be aiming for a different route.

That was the way some folks were — never content to follow the established trails, to walk in the footsteps of those who had gone before them. They had to break out of the established routine and find their own path . . . even though sometimes those paths led straight to disaster.

"I'll go talk to them and find out what their plans are," Preacher told Broken Pine. "I really doubt that they're much of a threat to you and your people, though."

"When Many Pelts and those who believe as he does hear about this, they will want to confront the wagon train and make the whites go another way."

"It'll be your job to keep them from doing that, Broken Pine."

"And they will do as I say. I am still chief here."

But for how much longer, if Many Pelts continued stirring up trouble, Preacher asked himself.

Maybe he could help the situation by finding out why the wagon trains kept pushing farther and farther in the direction of the Crow village and hunting grounds.

"I will come with you, Preacher," Hawk said.

The mountain man frowned and said, "I don't know if that's necessary —"

"It would be a good thing," Broken Pine said. "Hawk That Soars is one of us. Some of our people will be more likely to listen to him than to you, Preacher, even though he is half white."

Preacher supposed that made sense. Hawk had won over the Crow, despite his status as a half-breed, because he was such a fine warrior and good man. When it came to convincing somebody like Many Pelts to be reasonable, Hawk would have an advantage because of the Indian blood that flowed in his veins.

"All right, fine," Preacher said. "I'm always glad to have you ridin' with me, Hawk."

"I will tell Butterfly, and we will leave now."

Preacher nodded.

"I'll go get Horse saddled up."

They set out less than ten minutes later, with Butterfly and the two children standing in front of the lodge and solemnly watching them go. Preacher and Hawk might be back that night, but they were taking supplies with them in case they weren't able to return until the next day.

They followed the river, which gradually curved until it flowed eastward through the foothills at the base of the great peaks. Preacher knew that once the stream reached the prairie, it would make another bend, southward this time, and eventually flow into the Sweetwater, which in turn merged with the North Platte far out on the Great Plains.

As they rode, Hawk said, "I remember what St. Louis was like when you and I went there, Preacher. Will there be cities like that out here someday? Cities with so many buildings that you can no longer even see the earth? Places where the air stinks of too many people?"

"I reckon there's a good chance of it," Preacher admitted. "It's already like that all over, back east. You might find a little piece of wilderness here and there, but before you know it, you're surrounded again."

"I would never want to go there."

"I don't plan on goin' back, unless somethin' mighty important comes up." Preacher paused, then said, "The good part about the whole thing is, by the time it gets that bad out here and the frontier is gone, I will be, too. Dead and gone for a long time."

"But what about the children," Hawk asked, "and the children's children?"

Preacher shook his head and said, "I reckon they'll have to find their own ways of dealin' with it. Folks always do, because things never stay the same. There just ain't no gettin' around that."

The conversation made both of them a little melancholy, and so they rode in silence for quite a while.

It was the middle of the afternoon before Preacher and Hawk spotted the long line of wagons up ahead. The arching canvas covers over the backs of the large vehicles gleamed in the sunlight. Preacher and Hawk urged their mounts to a faster pace, and Dog bounded ahead.

Someone with the wagon train must have seen them coming. Four men on horseback broke away from the caravan and rode out to meet them.

Preacher had the Sharps with him, of course, as well as the brace of Colt Dragoons. He reached down to the guns and made sure each revolver slid smoothly in its holster.

Hawk noticed that and asked, "Do you expect trouble from these men, Preacher?"

"Nope, not at all," the mountain man replied. "But it's always a good idea to be ready for it, whether you expect it or not."

Hawk didn't say anything in response to that, but he touched the knife and tomahawk stuck behind the belt at his waist.

One of the men approaching them wore buckskins and a coonskin cap. Two had on rough work clothes. All three of those riders carried rifles across their saddles in front of them.

The fourth man, who led the little group, was dressed in a sober black suit and hat and collarless white shirt. He looked more like a minister than a wagonmaster, but he rode with an unmistakable air of command about him. At first glance he didn't appear to be armed, but as they came closer, Preacher spotted the handle of a big knife, probably an Arkansas Toothpick, sticking out from under the man's coat.

The leader of the welcoming party reined in and raised a hand in a signal for the others to stop. Preacher and Hawk slowed their mounts and walked them forward until only fifteen feet separated the two groups. Dog had come to a halt, as well, and stood there stiff-legged, with the fur on the back of his neck ruffled up a little.

"I'm guessing that's not actually a wolf, since he seems to be traveling with you two fellows," the man in the black suit greeted them.

"Oh, he's probably part wolf," Preacher drawled, "but I reckon he's mostly dog. That's what I call him, in fact. Dog."

"We won't shoot him, then," the man said.

"Best you don't," Preacher said.

The man in the black suit was burly, with

a barrel chest and powerful-looking shoulders. A thatch of white hair stuck out from under his hat, and a thick white mustache bristled under his prominent nose. Bushy side whiskers framed the deeply tanned face of a man who had spent most of his life outdoors.

"I'm Major Frank Powell," he introduced himself, "the wagonmaster of this here immigrant train. My scouts" — he inclined his head toward the other three men — "Jethro Haines, Tom Nolan, and George Ogden."

Each of the men nodded in turn as Powell said his name. Gray-bearded Jethro Haines was the one in buckskins. Preacher thought he looked vaguely familiar and figured they had crossed trails sometime in the past. Haines hadn't made any threatening moves with the flintlock rifle he held, though, so Preacher didn't reach for his guns.

Haines had something to say, though. He drawled, "A white man and a Injun travelin' together . . . That ain't somethin' you see ever'day. That redskin your slave, mister?"

Hawk bristled, but Preacher gave him a glance that told him to control the reaction. Then the mountain man said, "This *man* is my son, Hawk That Soars. And folks call me Preacher."

Haines knew the name, and so did the

other two scouts, Nolan and Ogden. Preacher could tell that by looking at them. Powell seemed to recognize the name, too. He confirmed that by saying, "I've heard a lot about you, sir. I didn't know if you were still alive."

"And kickin'," said Preacher. "What are you folks doin' this far north of South Pass?"

"Why, we're headed for the Oregon Territory, of course. Those intrepid pioneers in the wagons behind us have engaged my services to lead them there."

"Then they won't be happy when they have to backtrack for a week or more because you've taken them astray."

Powell sat up straighter in the saddle and glared at Preacher as he said, "I don't appreciate that comment, sir. I know what I'm doing here."

"You couldn't prove it by me. You need to turn around now and head back to South Pass. It'll save you some time in the long run."

"You're wrong," Powell insisted. "We plan to cross the mountains by way of Churchill Pass." The man pointed to the peaks visible in the distance. "There."

"Churchill Pass?" Preacher repeated with a frown. "I never heard tell of it."

"That's probably because Edward Churchill, who discovered the pass and laid out the new route, didn't do so until this past year. It's been the talk of St. Louis and Independence, Missouri, in recent months, especially since Mr. Churchill's book has come out —"

"Hold on just a minute," Preacher broke in. "You say this fella Churchill wrote a book?"

"Yes, about his explorations of the Rocky Mountains. It not only details his discovery of the pass, it also mentions that there are a whole series of passes to the north, some more rugged than others, but all of them capable of having wagons travel through them. The area needs more extensive mapping . . ." Powell's voice trailed off as he saw the grin spreading across Preacher's rugged face. "What do you find so amusing, sir?"

"A fella writes a book and makes all these wild claims, and folks just *believe* him without ever settin' eyes on what he's talkin' about?"

"I don't see why Mr. Churchill would lie about such things," Powell said stiffly.

"He's a writer, ain't he? A fella who'll write a book will do damn near *anything* to get folks to buy it, even if it means spewin' out a pack of lies!"

Powell stared angrily at Preacher. The three scouts didn't look happy, either, but they weren't as visibly upset as their boss. They had just been following Powell's orders; their reputation as scouts and frontiersmen wasn't at stake.

Preacher figured it wouldn't hurt anything to try to soothe Powell's ruffled feathers. He asked, "How many wagon trains have you led west . . . Major, was it?"

"That's right."

"You're in the army now?"

"Well . . . no. I served in the Mexican War and retained my rank."

In other words, he just called himself a major, thought Preacher.

"And to answer your other question, I've led four immigrant trains from Independence to the Oregon Territory, and before that I took charge of more than a dozen such caravans from my home state of Pennsylvania out to Missouri. I have an excellent reputation, and frankly, I'm surprised you haven't heard of me."

"Well, I don't get back east that often," Preacher said. "Listen, Major, I don't mean to put a burr under your saddle, but I know these mountains, and I don't care what some fancy pants book writer says, there ain't no good passes in the direction you're goin'."

"But why —" Powell stopped short. "Never mind. You've already given me your answer to that question. And I suppose there's a faint possibility you may be right about Mr. Edward Churchill. But there's also a chance you're wrong. You can't know every foot of this country."

Jethro Haines drawled, "I wouldn't be so sure about that if I was you, Major. This is *Preacher* we're talkin' about. He's been out here longer than just about anybody, and there can't be many places west of the Mississipp' where he *ain't* set foot."

The other two scouts muttered their agreement with Haines. Powell didn't like hearing it, but there was nothing he could do except swallow it.

"We're near the foothills," he said. "We'll push on that far and make camp for the night, and then we can discuss this further. I'll need to talk to Mr. Dawlish and get his opinion on the matter."

Preacher asked, "Who's this fella Dawlish?"

"The settlers elected him the captain of the wagon train," Powell explained. "I'm in charge, but I need to consult him before any decisions are made."

"I'd be glad to talk to him, tell him what I know about the mountains west of here."

Powell jerked his head in a curt nod and said, "Of course. You and your, ah, son are welcome to spend the night in our camp, as late in the day as it is."

"We're obliged to you for your hospitality."

Powell wheeled his horse around and barked orders at the scouts. All four men rode back toward the wagons, which had come to a halt by now while the conference was going on.

Preacher crossed his hands on the saddlehorn, leaned forward, and said to Hawk, "At least we know now why the wagon trains have been comin' farther and farther in this direction. They're all lookin' for a pass that ain't there."

"How can we stop them?" Hawk asked.

"I don't know, short of goin' back east and writin' a book about how this fella Churchill is a windbag who don't have any idea what he's talkin' about." Preacher laughed. "And I don't reckon that's gonna happen. But once enough wagon trains have to turn around and go back down to South Pass, word will get back to Independence sooner or later and folks will stop puttin' any stock in Churchill's lies. Many Pelts and

108

the rest of the Crow who agree with him will just have to put up with things the way they are for a while."

"That will not be easy to do as long as the hunting is bad."

"I'll have a talk with Haines," Preacher said. "He seems to have a pretty good idea what's goin' on. If he can keep any huntin' parties close to the wagons and not let them go too far into the foothills, it shouldn't be a problem. Of course, the best thing would be if those wagons turn around in the mornin' and head back the other way. Maybe I can help get that idea through Powell's head."

He lifted Horse's reins and nudged the stallion into an easy lope. Hawk rode beside him as they headed toward the slowly rolling wagons.

CHAPTER 9

The foothills

The man with the long, ragged beard lowered the spyglass from his eye and turned his head to look at the others gathered on the back side of the ridge.

"The wagons are movin' again," he reported. "Looks like they're comin' on in this direction like they were before those two fellas rode up. The parley with the old gent and the redskin didn't change their minds."

A tall, slender figure with a ruddy face and hawk nose moved closer and asked in a husky voice, "What could you tell about the two riders?"

The bearded man shook his head as he collapsed the spyglass and stowed it away in a beaded, fringed pouch slung over his right shoulder so that the strap angled down to the left across his chest.

"Not much, really," he said, "except that

110

one was white and t'other was an Injun. I said the white man was old, but I don't even know that for sure. I just saw some gray in his hair and mustache. Some fellas turn gray before others." He grinned as he ran the knobby-knuckled fingers of his left hand through his long, tangled beard. "Reckon I'm livin' proof of that."

One of the others, a gangling man with straw-colored hair under his pushed-back felt hat, laughed and said, "You was born old, Appleseed."

"And born mean, too," said the man called Appleseed. "You best remember that, Charlie." He looked at the lean figure who had spoken first to him. "Plan still the same, Winter?"

"Why would it not be?"

"Well, those two who came ridin' up look like they're throwin' in with the pilgrims, at least for now. That'd be two more guns on their side."

Winter made a curt, dismissive gesture.

"It doesn't matter. We will take them by surprise, and many will die before they even know what's happening. Just like the other times."

Some of the men nodded and muttered agreement. There were twenty-five of them in all, each man a hardened, experienced thief and killer. It had taken Winter years to put together this gang, and now they were ready to loot the steady stream of wagon trains heading west through this country.

They had attacked three such trains so far without losing a man, taking all the money the immigrants had saved up to start their new lives in the Pacific Northwest, as well as plenty of goods that they had sold at trading posts where the unscrupulous proprietors never gave a thought to where the loot came from and wouldn't care if they had known.

Sure, there were some risks, but they didn't really amount to much, and the scheme was going to make them all rich in the long run. A lot of blood would be spilled along the way . . . but that didn't matter to any of these men.

"All right," Winter went on. "For now we stay out of sight. Appleseed, you and Harkness follow those wagons. Once they've made camp for the night, one of you stay there to watch them while the other comes back to fetch us. Understand?"

"You bet," Appleseed replied. "Come on up here and belly down beside me so we can keep an eye on 'em, Charlie."

Charlie Harkness moved up to the ridge crest and stretched out beside Appleseed.

He took off his hat so there would be less chance of being spotted as he peered over the top, but at this distance, that wasn't really much of a worry. And the sun was behind them, so Appleseed could use the spyglass without having to worry about the light reflecting from its lens.

Winter motioned for the other men to withdraw. They moved back down the hill and along a brushy gully until they came to a circular depression in the rocks where a spring trickled out and formed a small pool. It was a good campsite, with water and enough grass for the horses and rugged terrain around it that kept anybody from stumbling into it accidentally.

Winter had searched for a long time for such a suitable spot. A Crow village was located about ten miles away, but the Indians seldom ventured in this direction. Winter had nothing but disdain for the Crow, anyway.

One of the men poked around at the embers of the fire until flames began to leap up again. He put a pot of water on to boil for coffee.

Winter stood next to the fire, a compelling figure in a flat-crowned black hat with a tight chin strap, high-topped boots, black leather trousers, and a beaded poncho taken

113

from the body of a dead Mexican down around Santa Fe several years earlier. A sweep of a copper-colored hand was all that was needed to brush the poncho back and reveal a black gunbelt and holster in which rode a Colt Dragoon. Hundreds of hours of practice had made Winter an expert in the revolver's use.

One of the men stepped up to the fire and said, "It's still a couple of hours until dark, Winter. We're gonna be waitin' here for a while. I got an idea about how you and me could spend that time."

Winter glanced over and said, "You've got an idea, do you, Porter?"

The man had a rust-colored goatee and bushy eyebrows the same shade. He wore a black frock coat but had a coonskin cap on his head with the tail hanging straight down his back. He nodded in answer to Winter's question and said, "That's right. I figured you and me could go over yonder in those trees and have us a sportin' good time."

He reached down to rub his crotch with his left hand and leered.

Winter's right arm came up in a vicious backhanded blow almost too swift for the eye to follow. Knuckles cracked against Porter's cheekbone. Caught by surprise, he took a half-step back. The toe of Winter's right boot hooked behind his left ankle and jerked. Porter yelped as he went over backward and landed hard on his butt. The coonskin cap fell off his head. Instinctively, he started to reach under his coat for the gun or the knife he carried there.

Winter was faster, by a large margin. The poncho swung back, strong, slender fingers closed around the Dragoon's grips, and the gun whispered out of leather. Winter stuck the muzzle under Porter's bearded chin and roughly forced the man's head back. Porter's hand froze where it was, halfway under the coat's lapel. His eyes were wide.

"You haven't been riding with us for long, but you've been a good man so far, Porter," Winter grated. "You follow orders, you keep a cool head under fire, and killing doesn't bother you. But what the hell ever possessed you to make you think you could say such a thing to me?"

With the gun muzzle shoved so hard into his throat like that, Porter couldn't get any words out. He grunted a couple of times, but that was all he could manage.

Without moving the gun, Winter reached up with the other hand, loosened the chin strap, and pulled the black hat off. Long, straight hair as black as a raven's wing tumbled out. A shake of the head let the hair fall halfway down the back of the poncho. The late afternoon sunlight shone on a few strands of pure white in the midnight dark hair.

"Your mistake, Porter," Winter went on as she held the hat in her left hand, "was thinking that just because I'm a woman, I'd be interested in a handsome, silver-tongued devil like you. Is that what you think?"

She moved the gun a little, enough for him to gasp, "Not . . . not anymore. I'm sorry, Winter."

She had eared back the Dragoon's hammer when she shoved the barrel under his chin. She lowered the hammer carefully now, moved the gun, and patted its barrel lightly against the side of his head a couple of times.

"That's all right. You're not the first man I've had to teach that lesson to in the last ten years. And you're still alive, so it turned out better for you than it did for a lot of them." Her husky voice hardened. "Just don't do it again."

"I won't. You . . . you can count on that."

Winter stepped back and holstered the Dragoon. She put the hat on again but pushed it back so that it hung behind her head by the chin strap and her hair still fell loose. She looked around at the rest of the men and asked, "Anybody else have a suggestion about how we can spend the time while we're waiting for that wagon train to make camp?"

Nobody spoke up, and after a moment, Winter nodded. She extended a hand to Porter. After a second's hesitation, he reached up and clasped wrists with her. She helped him to his feet, displaying the strength in her lean, muscular body.

"This never happened," she said to him.

He shook his head and agreed, "No, ma'am, it sure didn't."

"Don't ma'am me," she snapped. "I'm not some white schoolmarm. My name is Winter Wind, warrior of the Blackfoot people, and do not ever forget it."

The wagon train camp
Major Frank Powell had halted the wagons on a broad, level stretch between two of the first foothills. By this time in the journey, the immigrants were quite experienced and efficient in setting up camp. They pulled the wagons into a circle, unhitched the teams of oxen, and herded the massive, stolid beasts into an enclosure set up with stakes and ropes inside the circle.

Cooking fires were built using firewood and buffalo chips diligently gathered along the way. The plains these wagons had crossed were largely treeless. Now that the foothills and mountains were in sight, the settlers could see more trees than they had laid eyes on in weeks.

Preacher and Hawk rode up to the camp-site, dismounted, and led their horses through a gap between two of the wagons. Saddle mounts were corralled in a different part of the circle from the ox teams. Preacher and Hawk headed that way, and as they did, Preacher spotted Major Powell talking to a medium-sized man with thinning gray hair and a sober demeanor. Preacher figured that was Dawlish, the man Powell had mentioned who'd been elected by the immigrants as their captain.

Powell saw them and waved them over. Still leading their horses, Preacher and Hawk joined the wagonmaster.

"Mr. Dawlish, these are the two men I was telling you about," said Powell. "Preacher and his son, Hawk That Soars. Fellows, this is Jason Dawlish, the captain of this wagon train."

Dawlish nodded and said, "Preacher, is it? No last name?"

"Oh, I've got one," Preacher said, "but it's been so long since I used it that I don't hardly remember what it is. And it don't

118

matter. Preacher will do."

"Major Powell tells me that you doubt the existence of Churchill Pass."

Preacher noticed that the man hadn't acknowledged being introduced to Hawk, and that irritated him. But he put that feeling aside for the moment and said, "It ain't a matter of doubt. I *know* there ain't any good passes in the direction you're goin'. None that you can take a whole passel of wagons over, that's for sure."

"Mr. Churchill's book was very specific —"

"He was wrong, or he was lyin'," Preacher broke in. "More'n likely lyin', since accordin' to Major Powell this fella Churchill is a book writer."

Dawlish frowned and said, "That's a very cynical attitude."

"I don't know about that, but I do know the mountains. You folks are wastin' your time tryin' to go any way other than through South Pass."

"But without someone taking a chance and exploring, new routes are never discovered," Dawlish argued. "You sound like all the naysayers who told Christopher Columbus that he couldn't reach the east by sailing west."

"And you sound like a teacher."

"I was the headmaster of a school back in Pennsylvania. I hope to set up a similar institution of higher learning once we reach the Oregon territory."

Preacher nodded and said, "That'd be a fine thing. It's good for folks to learn. Most of my schoolin' came from livin' out here" — he swept a hand at their surroundings — "and that's taught me where you can go and where you can't. But that ain't my decision. I reckon it's up to you and Major Powell where this wagon train goes, so we'll leave you to figurin' it out."

Preacher started to turn away, with Hawk following suit, when Dawlish said, "You really are convinced there's no passable route the way we're going?"

"That's right."

Dawlish sighed and looked at Powell.

"We'll have to take that into account, then, Major," he said. "If we've already gone astray, we don't want to make the situation worse."

Powell said, "That all depends on how much stock you place in Mr. Churchill's book. A lot of folks believe it's true."

The two men were still discussing matters earnestly as Preacher and Hawk walked away. The young warrior said quietly, "What do you think they will decide?"

120

"Don't know, and it ain't any of my business. Let's put these horses up."

One of the settlers, a gray-bearded old-timer, was taking care of the saddle mounts. He introduced himself to Preacher and Hawk as Simeon Warren and explained that he had owned a livery stable in the small town in Ohio where he had lived until he headed west.

"This here wagon train come through, and all of a sudden my feet commenced to itch," Warren explained. "Don't know where the feelin' come from, since I never had much of a restless nature before. But my wife had passed away a while back and all my kids is grown and gone, so I thought, shoot, might as well have myself a little adventure whilst I still can. So I sold my place, bought a wagon and some supplies, and joined right up."

"I wish you luck when you get where you're goin', Mr. Warren," Preacher told him.

The old man chuckled and said, "It ain't so much the gettin' there as it is the goin'."

"I know that feelin', sure enough," Preacher agreed with a smile and a nod.

He and Hawk walked around the campsite as darkness settled down over the landscape, a vast sweep of black relieved only by the garish orange glow of the fires. Some of those fires were good-sized, but they looked small anyway against the seemingly endless night.

Women cooked, men tended to livestock or wagons, kids ran around and played. It was like any such collection of folks anywhere, thought Preacher. They had formed their own community centered around this wagon train. When they reached Oregon, would they stay together, claim land and settle in the same area, establish a town?

Preacher didn't know and honestly didn't care to find out, because he was a totally different sort, a man who would never be content to remain still for very long. These immigrants were on the move now, but that would come to an end. For Preacher, it never would, until the day he crossed the divide for the last time.

"You're the two men who rode up a little while ago, aren't you?"

A woman's voice made Preacher pause and look around. The woman stood beside a big iron pot hung over a cookfire, stirring the contents with a long wooden spoon. She was around forty, Preacher thought, and the fire struck reddish highlights in her fair hair.

"That's right," Preacher replied. "I'm called Preacher, and this is Hawk."

"I have plenty of stew here, and I'd be happy for both of you to join me for supper. My name is Margaret Lewis."

"Pleased to meet you, Miz Lewis, and we're obliged to you for the invite. You reckon your husband will be all right with us eatin' with you?"

"I'm a widow," the woman said, "so that won't be a problem."

"Oh." Preacher wasn't too surprised. Since he'd started getting some years on him, any time he was around any widow women they seemed to notice him right off. Some were just looking for companionship, others were on the hunt for a new husband to replace the old one. Either way, in the end Preacher's restless nature always proved to be a disappointment to them.

But the aroma coming from the pot was an appetizing one, and he and Hawk had to eat something for supper. Margaret Lewis was a right handsome woman, too, and he had a hunch she'd be pleasant company. So he smiled, nodded, and said, "We'd be happy to join you, then."

Margaret returned the smile, turned to the nearby wagon, and fetched a wooden bowl and spoon from it. She used the big spoon to fill the bowl with stew from the pot and then stepped toward Preacher, holding it out to him.

"I'll get you some next, Hawk —" she began.

A gun boomed somewhere outside the circle of wagons, and the bullet it fired struck the woman in the side of the head, blowing away a chunk of her skull and dropping her dead at Preacher's feet as the fallen bowl of stew splashed on the ground along with Margaret Lewis's blood.

CHAPTER 10

Preacher's swift reflexes and uncanny instincts had saved his life many times in the past, and the same was true of Hawk. Both of them dived forward on the ground and rolled as more gunfire roared somewhere close by. Bullets scythed through the air above them. Preacher heard a couple of slugs strike the iron stewpot and ricochet off with wicked whines.

Around the wagon train camp, women and children screamed in fear while men shouted curses and questions that did no good. The immigrants were under attack, and they had to fight back or have the camp overrun.

Preacher wound up on his belly. The two Colt Dragoons had already leaped into his hands as if by magic. A few feet away, Hawk pushed himself up onto one knee and lifted his flintlock rifle as he searched for a target.

A shouting figure leaped through one of

the nearby gaps between wagons. He carried a double-barreled shotgun that he swung up toward a woman hustling along with several children in front of her as she tried to get them to safety.

The leering, evil grin on the shotgunner's face disappeared in a red smear as a round from Preacher's right-hand gun smashed his jaw. An instant later, Preacher's left-hand gun spewed fire and sent a bullet coring through the shotgunner's brain. The would-be murderer dropped to the ground bonelessly.

Next to Preacher, Hawk drew a bead on another man who had invaded the camp and planted a heavy lead ball in the center of the attacker's chest. The impact slapped the man off his feet like a giant hand.

Preacher shoved up onto his knees and saw a woman running toward him with her face twisted in lines of terror. Preacher would have tried to protect her, but he never got the chance. She stumbled suddenly, caught herself, and gazed down in horror at the bloody arrowhead protruding several inches from her chest. The arrow had struck her in the back and gone all the way through her body. She made a sad, sighing sound that was probably just the exhalation of her dying breath and toppled forward.

Preacher looked past the woman and spotted the man who had fired the arrow. The raider was already nocking another shaft on his bowstring. He was an Indian, but he was dressed mostly in white man's clothing. That told Preacher the gang attacking the wagon train was a mixture of red renegades and white outlaws.

Didn't really matter. They were all murderous bastards as far as Preacher was concerned. He fired both Dragoons at the same time and blew a pair of fist-sized holes through the man's belly as he drew back the bow. The arrow he loosed as he doubled over, dying, plowed into the ground.

It was pretty clear what had happened. The raiders had sneaked up in the darkness, fired a couple of volleys from outside the circle of wagons with the intent of killing as many of the immigrants as possible, then had charged into the camp to mop up and slaughter the rest of the defenders.

Preacher wasn't going to let that happen. He surged to his feet and dashed through the camp, one of his revolvers booming every time he spotted a man he was certain belonged to the gang. His instincts never betrayed him, and neither did his aim. His deadly accurate fire took a surprising toll among the raiders.

Hawk had dropped his empty rifle and pulled the pair of flintlock pistols he carried from behind his belt. These weapons would fire only once, as well, but he had picked up the habit from Preacher of double-shotting them with a heavy powder charge. That made them even more deadly, although somewhat riskier for the man wielding them.

The pistols roared and cut down three men among a group of attackers clambering over a wagon tongue to try to get into the camp. Then Hawk dropped the pistols and flung himself among the stunned survivors. By the time he reached them, he had his knife in one hand and his tomahawk in the other. Those weapons flashed back and forth, blood flying in the air every time they landed a blow.

Preacher and Hawk weren't the only ones mustering a surprisingly stout defense. Major Powell might have kept referring to himself by his rank because of vanity, but he *had* served in the Mexican War and evidently hadn't forgotten what he knew about commanding men in battle. His stentorian voice boomed out, rallying the immigrants. Several of them formed a ring of riflemen and protected each other as they fired back at the attackers.

When Preacher's Dragoons were empty,

he pouched the irons and drew his knife. However, before he could throw himself back into the fray, a shrill whistle sounded and the raiders who were still on their feet broke and ran. It was more of a rout than a retreat. Several men were wounded and stumbling, but they managed to stay on their feet and make it out of the wagon train camp.

Preacher let them go. He figured the outlaws hadn't expected the immigrants to put up such a fight. They had decided to cut their losses and get out of here while they could.

But the possibility that they might double back and try another attack, thinking the immigrants wouldn't expect it, couldn't be ruled out. For that reason, Preacher said to Hawk, "Grab your guns and get 'em reloaded."

He proceeded to do the same with the Dragoons, replacing the empty cylinders with loaded ones from the leather pouch attached to his belt. While he was doing that, he asked Hawk, "You get hit by any of that lead flyin' around?"

"No. What about you?"

"Dodged it all, I reckon." Preacher thought about Margaret Lewis and the way the widow had been struck down without warning, mere moments after he'd met her, as well as the woman who had been killed by the arrow. "I was a heap luckier than some."

Hawk just grunted as he poured powder from his powderhorn down the barrel of his rifle.

Preacher snapped the reloaded revolver closed and looked around for Major Powell. He spotted the wagonmaster not too far away and strode over to him. Blood dripped down Powell's cheek from a cut opened up by a bullet grazing him.

"Do you know how many folks you lost yet?" Preacher asked.

Powell shook his head. He was pale in the firelight and looked shaken to his core, but he glared furiously at the same time.

"No, but too many, you can be damned sure of that," he said. Wearily, he scrubbed a hand over his face and smeared the blood on his cheek. "What happened? Who were those men?"

"Desperadoes, I reckon. I've heard of gangs who trail wagon trains and jump 'em when the time's right. There's never any shortage of sorry sons o' bitches who'd rather steal and kill than work for an honest livin'."

"That's certainly the truth," Powell said.

130

"I know of such atrocities happening, of course, but I never ran into anything like this before. Honestly, I didn't believe anyone would attack such a large, well-armed group, even the savages. Speaking of which . . . I think I saw some Indians among that bunch."

"You did," Preacher confirmed for him. "I spotted one myself." The mountain man pointed with a thumb. "He's layin' over yonder somewhere with a couple of well-deserved holes in his belly." Preacher went on briskly, "You need to round up some good men who weren't hurt, or not too bad, anyway."

"So we can go after those marauders?"

"So you can post guards in case those varmints come back." Preacher managed to keep his tone neutral as he answered Powell's question. "I know you're mad and I don't blame you a bit, but you don't want to go chasin' after that bunch in the dark, in unfamiliar territory. They'd just ambush you and wipe you out."

"But we have to avenge the people we lost! Why, Jason Dawlish himself is dead, cut down by a bullet fired by one of those outlaws."

"Folks will have to elect themselves a new captain, then. I'm sorry about Dawlish. He

131

seemed like a good man, the few minutes I knew him." Preacher shook his head. "But gettin' more fellas killed won't avenge nobody. To be honest, Major, the best thing you can do right now is bury the dead, tend to the wounded, then turn around and head on back down to South Pass. I'm assumin' most of these folks will want to go on to where they were headed, and the safest way of doin' that is by stickin' to the regular trail."

Powell sighed heavily and said, "To be honest, I was thinking the same thing. I don't know whether Churchill Pass exists or not, but South Pass does, there's no doubt about that. We can make it through there without too much risk."

"I'm glad to hear that's the way you're leanin'."

"Preacher . . . I saw what you and Hawk did during the battle. I had my own hands full, of course, but the way you whirled among those raiders with your guns spitting fire . . . I've never seen such a thing. And Hawk fought magnificently, too. I don't think we could have driven them off without the two of you. I would have been honored to have both of you under my command during the war."

"I'm obliged to you for those sentiments,

Major. Now, let's see what we can do for the folks who are hurt . . ."

Appleseed Higgs was cussing a blue streak as he limped across the hidden clearing where the outlaw camp was located. A bullet had gouged a chunk out of his upper left thigh, and it hurt like blazes.

A short time earlier, when they got back to camp, Charlie Harkness had poured some whiskey onto the wound — after first giving Appleseed a good swig from the jug, of course — and bound a rag around the leg to serve as a bandage. Appleseed had been shot enough times to know that the injury wasn't really serious, as long as he didn't get blood poisoning, but it was annoying as all hell. Appleseed should have been sitting down somewhere with his leg propped up, taking it easy.

He wanted to talk to Winter, though. The Blackfoot woman stood at the edge of the firelight, a smoldering cheroot clamped between her teeth, looking mad enough to chew nails instead of that smoke.

She glanced at Appleseed as he came up to her, and the expression in her dark eyes was as cold as the season she was named after. She asked around the cheroot, "How many did we lose?"

133

"Five dead, their bodies left behind," Appleseed reported. "And another fella died on the way back here. Plus we got four or five hurt bad enough they ain't gonna be any use for a while, and damn near ever'body picked up some sort of nick. Like me with this leg o' mine. I can get around, but I ain't very spry." He cocked his head a little to one side. "You may be the only one who came through the fight without a scratch, Winter."

Her gaze got even colder, although he wouldn't have thought that was possible.

"What are you saying, Appleseed?" she demanded.

Hastily, he held up his hands and said, "Not a thing, not a damn thing. I wouldn't say nothin' bad about you, Winter. Hell, I wouldn't even *think* it. I been ridin' with you for a good long spell. You know how I feel about you."

That was true. Appleseed had thrown in with Winter back in Missouri, when she was first starting to recruit a gang of cutthroats and thieves. Not many men believed that a woman could lead such a band, but Appleseed had sensed right away just how smart and dangerous she was. They had robbed stores and banks and held up stagecoaches, and they had never come close to getting caught. Any man who decided he wanted to take over the gang — or just take unwanted liberties with Winter herself — she killed swiftly, mercilessly. The fellas who stayed with her learned quickly not to cross her.

Just because she was a woman didn't mean she was weak or soft. Appleseed wasn't sure he had ever been around anyone more dangerous.

Winter never let her guard down, even with him, but now and then she had made a few comments that led him to believe she'd always been that way. Back in the mountains, growing up with the Blackfeet, before she had ever seen any white men, she had longed to be a warrior.

The men in her tribe weren't having any of that. Eventually, she had become an outcast, and that led to her heading east and finding her way among the whites. She dressed like a white man, carried herself like a white man, and in that poncho she wore, with her hair tucked under her hat, it was difficult even to tell that she was a woman. Her copper skin and her features gave away her Indian heritage, but a lot of people took her for a half-breed. Most even figured she'd been raised white.

It was a remarkable transformation, Appleseed had thought more than once. And that was because Winter Wind was a remarkable woman.

"See to it that the wounded men are cared for," she said now around the cheroot. "I want them to recover as quickly as possible. Also, I want you to visit the trading posts. Find men to replace the ones we lost. More, if you can get them. We need a bigger gang."

"To go after other wagon trains later, right? I mean, you ain't thinkin' about tryin' to jump this particular bunch of pilgrims again, are you? Sure, we hurt 'em, probably pretty bad, but we'd be outnumbered even worse now, and they'll be on their guard. I reckon we couldn't take 'em by surprise again." Appleseed ran his fingers through his beard. "They'll probably turn around and light a shuck for South Pass, anyway."

Winter said, "I care nothing about those immigrants. It is the two men who joined forces with them yesterday I want."

Appleseed's leg was paining him worse. He wished he could sit down on the log they used for a bench, not far from the fire. But Winter was still standing, so he supposed he ought to stay on his feet, too.

"You mean the old mountain man lookin' fella and the redskin?" He let out a low whistle of grudging admiration. "Yeah, them two were holy terrors, wasn't they? Never

136

seen anybody move quite that fast or shoot quite that good. I reckon things might've turned out different if those two hadn't come along yesterday and thrown in with that wagon train. Just our bad luck, I suppose."

Winter puffed on the cheroot for a moment, blew out a cloud of smoke, and said, "Not bad luck. The white man was Preacher."

Appleseed's eyebrows crawled up his forehead in surprise.

"Preacher!" he said. "Dang, I've heard plenty of stories about that varmint. Are you sure it was him?"

"I got a good look at him in the firelight. It was Preacher. I will never forget him."

"You've met him before?"

A faraway look came into Winter's eyes as she said, "It was ten years ago, perhaps a little more. Preacher had long waged war on the Blackfoot people, but this time he set out to destroy an entire village, to kill all the warriors who lived there and leave the women and children defenseless. They fought him, of course. Preacher had the help of his bastard son, an Absaroka youth called Hawk That Soars. But still, it was just the two of them against many, many Blackfoot warriors." The note of bitterness in her voice was plain to hear as she went on, "Even so, they triumphed. They brought bloodshed and destruction to my people. I fought them. No one believed I could be a warrior because I am a woman, but I fought Preacher and Hawk That Soars and almost defeated them. In the end, though . . ."

Her face might have been carved out of wood as she sighed, but the bleak iciness of her soul sparkled in her eyes and made it clear how that previous clash had turned out.

"I vowed that I would make myself even more of a warrior," she went on after a moment. "And I swore that someday, I would find Preacher and Hawk and kill them. Now that time has come. Fate has delivered them into my hands."

Appleseed frowned and responded, "I thought you said we weren't goin' after that wagon train."

"We are not . . . unless Preacher and Hawk accompany it. But they rode up from a different direction and may have business here in the foothills or the mountains. I intend to watch and follow them, whether they go with the wagons or not, and when the time is right, I will return here, gather everyone together, and strike for vengeance long overdue."

Appleseed scratched at his beard again and slowly nodded. He was about to say something, but then he got distracted by something he picked out of the tangled growth hanging down over his chest. He studied it for a second, crushed it between his fingers, and then wiped them on his greasy buckskin trousers.

"You need to be careful," he told Winter. "Preacher's supposed to be half mountain lion, half grizzly bear, and half whirlwind. Although . . ." He chuckled. "Come to think of it, a fella could say pretty much the same thing about you. Don't worry, Winter. I'll take care of ever'thing else so you can track them varmints to their lair. Can't think of but one problem with this deal."

"Problem?" Winter repeated with a frown.

"Them fellas." Appleseed inclined his head toward the rest of the gang. "Helpin' you settle your score agin Preacher ain't gonna put no money in their pockets. I don't know how they're gonna feel about that."

"They will do as I say," snapped Winter.

"Well, sure, sure, you're the boss, but they figure on gettin' a good payoff for anything they do."

Winter considered that for a moment and then said, "I will not take a share of the money from our next two . . . no, our next three jobs. What would have been my share will be divided among those who ride with me on this quest."

"Now that's a deal I can sell," Appleseed said with a nod. "And after Preacher and Hawk are dead?"

"We will loot the frontier from one end to the other," said Winter Wind.

CHAPTER 11

Fort Kearny

Once Jamie had agreed to accompany the expedition to the Crow village, Captain Croxton didn't waste any time getting the mission underway. He might have been worried that if he delayed too long, Jamie would change his mind.

The soldiers loading the supply wagons finished with the task by nine o'clock that morning. B Troop saddled their horses and mustered on the parade ground. Lieutenant Hayden Tyler had the dragoons looking good. Jamie had to admit that as he led his horse out to join them. Their uniforms were clean, their boots were polished, and they wore their black caps at precisely the correct angle.

They might *look* like soldiers, Jamie mused, but that didn't mean they would act like them. These weren't veteran troops, blooded and hardened by battle.

Of course, the mission on which they were setting out shouldn't be a particularly dangerous one, either. They weren't riding to wage war. It was more of a diplomatic detail.

The frontier was an unpredictable place, though. Just because they shouldn't run into trouble . . . didn't mean that they wouldn't.

And the possibility of that happening increased because of who Croxton had placed in command, Jamie thought as he watched Lieutenant Edgar Davidson strut out to the parade ground with Sergeant Liam O'Connor lumbering along behind him like a trained Irish bear.

A soldier was waiting for Davidson, holding mounts for him and O'Connor. Davidson took the reins from the trooper without thanking him, barely acknowledging the man's presence. Then he turned to the approximately sixty members of B Troop who stood beside their horses, waiting for orders.

"Sergeant," Davidson said to O'Connor.

"Mount up!" the sergeant bellowed, his harsh voice carrying easily across the parade ground in the morning air.

The dragoons swung into their saddles, their movements crisp and efficient. Jamie waited a moment to observe what they were doing.

Lieutenant Tyler mounted easily. Davidson struggled more getting into the saddle. Jamie told himself not to let that color his opinion of the young officer too much. There was more to being a soldier than just horsemanship, although that was certainly important.

With that thought in his mind, he mounted up, too, and nudged his horse forward to join Davidson and Tyler.

"Got any particular orders for me, Lieutenant?" he asked Davidson.

"Captain Croxton said that you've served as a scout in the past."

"That's right."

"Well, then, just do whatever it is you'd normally do," Davidson snapped peevishly. "Or do I have to do *all* the thinking for this expedition?"

Having somebody so young and arrogant talk to him like that rankled, but Jamie nodded and said, "I'll ride on ahead a ways. You can follow me. You won't get lost if I'm out of sight, though. We'll be following the river for several days before we swing more to the north."

"Yes, I studied the map in the captain's office as well."

"I'm not really basing that on the map." Jamie couldn't resist adding, "I've been

143

through the country where we're going. More than once, in fact. So I know how to get to that Crow village."

Davidson's lips tightened. He nodded and said, "Let's get on with it, then." He turned his head to look at O'Connor. "Give the order to move out, Sergeant."

O'Connor lifted his right hand above his head and waved his arm forward.

"Mooove out!"

The troop rode across the parade ground. Some of the soldiers who weren't going along on this mission had turned out to watch B Troop depart. The faces of those staying behind were a mixture of envy — because life on a frontier fort was pretty monotonous and B Troop was getting to break that routine — and relief . . . because they weren't setting out into what could be a dangerous unknown land.

Captain Croxton stood on the porch of the headquarters building and watched B Troop ride away, as well. Jamie lifted a hand in farewell to him, not as a salute but in a casual wave. Croxton nodded. The captain's reputation — and future promotions — might be riding on the outcome of this mission, Jamie knew, and the tenseness of Croxton's stance indicated that.

The dragoons moved away from the fort,

keeping their horses at a walk, but Jamie put his mount into a trot that carried him a couple of hundred yards ahead. He was glad to be away from Lieutenant Davidson and Sergeant O'Connor.

Might be a good idea for him to keep his distance from those two as much as possible, he told himself.

The troop rode steadily that morning, with Jamie usually a quarter of a mile or so in the lead, riding by himself. That solitude didn't bother him; he was as comfortable with his own company as he was surrounded by his large family back home in Colorado.

He didn't mind, though, when he heard hoofbeats coming up behind him and turned in the saddle to see Lieutenant Hayden Tyler approaching.

"Lieutenant," Jamie greeted him as the young officer came alongside.

"Mr. MacCallister. Lieutenant Davidson sent me to find out when he should call a midday halt."

"He could have sent the bugler or one of the other troopers to ask about that."

"I suppose," Tyler said.

"But he didn't want anybody else to know that he was asking for advice, did he?" asked Jamie. "He'd rather make it look like he sent you up here to tell me his orders."

"I wouldn't know about that, sir," Tyler replied, but Jamie could tell that Tyler *did* know. He had figured it out just like Jamie had. Davidson didn't want anything to indicate that he wasn't completely in command and didn't know exactly what he was doing.

"Then tell me this, Lieutenant . . . Has Davidson led any patrols since he's been here?"

"I don't believe *Lieutenant* Davidson has done that, no, sir."

Tyler was reinforcing military protocol and wanted Jamie to respect Davidson, or at least make a show of doing so. That wasn't likely to happen, since Jamie didn't demonstrate respect for anybody who hadn't earned it.

"So he's been just a desk soldier so far."

Tyler didn't say anything.

"Take a look around, Lieutenant," Jamie suggested. "What do you see?"

Tyler sounded puzzled as he replied, "Grassland, sir. And the river, of course."

"Yep, that's all there is to see, all right. This prairie stretches for miles and miles. No trees, no real hills, maybe a little ridge or pile of rock now and then. So it's not a matter of finding a good place to stop. It's all the same. What you have to know is how your men and their horses are holding up. On a long journey like this, you don't want to push them too hard. If you do, you'll wear them out and break them down before you get back."

"How can you tell?" asked Tyler. He seemed genuinely interested now.

"Watch the men's shoulders. When they start to slump, straighten them up again. You don't want to take it *too* easy on them. But when it happens again, stop and let them take a short rest. If the men need it, chances are the horses do, too." Jamie gestured toward the fiery orb overhead. "And watch the sun. When it's directly above us, that'll be the time to stop for a longer rest. Let the men eat something and let the horses drink. Not too much, though. They'll still have a whole afternoon's ride to get through. Can't have them bloating up."

"Yes, sir," Tyler said with a nod. "I'll remember those things."

Judging by the intent look on the young man's face, Jamie had a hunch Tyler actually would remember. He was eager to learn and willing to listen to those who had the knowledge he needed. That was a good combination for an army officer or anybody else.

"What do I tell Lieutenant Davidson, though?" Tyler went on.

"Tell him I said you should decide when to call the halts."

Tyler frowned and said, "I don't think he'd like that."

"You're both lieutenants. Shouldn't you have some responsibility?"

"He's a first lieutenant, though. I'm only a second. And he's in command of this detail."

"Tell him what you want," Jamie said. "But don't let him push the men or the horses too hard. It's up to you."

Tyler looked like he didn't care for that at all. He started to turn his horse, but Jamie added, "Lieutenant."

"Yes, Mr. MacCallister?"

"What happened to the sergeant who was assigned to B Troop?"

"Captain Croxton reassigned him to D Troop, Sergeant O'Connor's old post."

"Your sergeant knew the men in this troop."

Tyler sighed and said, "Sergeant Flaherty was very experienced. Very competent."

"And O'Connor's a loudmouthed bully. That trade couldn't have set very well with you."

"It was . . . an unconventional move."

"And Croxton just did it to placate David-son."

Tyler's frown deepened as he said, "Are you trying to stir up trouble, Mr. MacCallister?"

"No, son, I'm just trying to make sure I understand everything that's going on here. Might come a time when my life depends on it." Jamie paused. "All our lives. I'm thinking maybe I can count on you."

"I certainly hope so," Tyler said.

"So do I," Jamie said.

Despite putting the burden of deciding when to call halts on Lieutenant Tyler's shoulders, Jamie kept an eye on the troop as best he could from his position in front, just in case he needed to step in.

That proved not to be necessary. Whoever made the decisions, Tyler or Davidson, the stops during that day were spaced out well, and by the time they made camp late that afternoon, men and horses alike were tired but not exhausted. With Tyler giving most of the orders, camp was set up quickly and efficiently.

A small group of soldiers gathered buffalo chips for the fire. As they came back into camp carrying baskets full of the dried dung, Jamie grinned and said to them, "You

149

boys got yourselves some plains oak, I see."

One of the young soldiers returned the smile and said, "After all the years she spent yellin' at me and my pa and my brothers to wipe our boots off before we came in the house, my ma would have a conniption fit if she saw what I was doin' now!"

Corporal Mackey, one of the teamsters who had been driving the supply wagons all day, also served as the cook. He had put a big pot of beans on to soak before leaving the fort that morning, and he soon had them heating over a fire. He had biscuit dough ready to go into the Dutch ovens as well, and several pots of coffee were soon boiling, too. The smell of cooking food and the light from the fires created a peaceful atmosphere as the men settled down for the evening after tending to their mounts.

Jamie stood at the edge of camp, peering out into the gathering dusk. He was searching for any signs of trouble, but except for him and the soldiers and the horses, the prairie seemed to be deserted.

He knew better than to trust in appearances, though. Danger could be lurking unseen in the shadows.

A footstep sounded behind him. Lieutenant Tyler said, "Is there a problem, Mr. MacCallister?"

"Nope," Jamie replied. "Just havin' a look around. Have you posted sentries?"

"Yes, there's a man on each side of the camp."

"I'd double that if I was you. Two-hour shifts."

Tyler considered that suggestion, then nodded and said, "I can do that."

"Do you need to ask Lieutenant Davidson about it?"

"Lieutenant Davidson has discovered that he doesn't mind delegating some of the details to me."

Jamie chuckled and said, "It's easier on him that way, I reckon." He grew more serious as he went on, "It would be a good idea if you passed the word to the men not to spend too much time looking into the fires. That'll ruin a man's night vision for a while, and if any trouble crops up, he won't be able to see what he's shooting at."

"But you're not expecting trouble."

"Nope. Still . . . after everybody's eaten, might be a good idea to let those fires die down. There haven't been any Pawnee raiding parties in this area lately, as far as I've heard, but you never know when they might take it in their heads to start roaming around, looking for mischief to get into."

"Mischief," Tyler repeated. "Like scalping

151

American soldiers."

"Well . . . they see it as great sport."

Tyler shook his head and said, "I'll double the guard, and I'll warn the men about not looking into the fire."

"Once it gets good and dark, I plan on going out to have a better look around. Make sure the sentries know that, and tell them not to get trigger-happy and shoot me when I'm on my way back in."

"You're going out alone?"

"It's best that way," Jamie said.

Truth be told, there wasn't one of these dragoons he would trust to accompany him on a nighttime scout. He could move through the shadows without being seen or heard, but he was convinced none of the soldiers could.

Jamie went back to the fires and got himself a cup of coffee and a couple of biscuits to gnaw on while he waited for full dark to fall. He was hunkered on his heels when something struck the back of his right shoulder. The impact made him lurch forward, spill his coffee, and drop the second biscuit as he caught himself by putting a hand on the ground.

He recovered his balance almost instantly and surged to his feet. He knew that someone had bumped heavily into him, and when he turned to see who was responsible, he wasn't the least bit surprised to see Sergeant Liam O'Connor giving him an ugly grin.

"You should pay attention to what's going on around you, MacCallister," O'Connor said. "You might get in the way of a soldier on army business."

"What sort of army business were you bound on, O'Connor?" Jamie demanded.

"Got to take a leak. Now, you can get out of the way . . . or I can piss all over your boots, if that's what you want."

The troopers who had gathered around the fire to eat supper turned eager eyes toward the two big men who stood there in confrontational attitudes. Most of them probably hoped a fight would break out. That would be a good evening's entertainment.

Instead, Lieutenant Davidson stepped up with his hands clasped behind his back and asked, "What's going on here?"

"MacCallister got in my way," O'Connor said.

"More like you ran into me," Jamie shot back.

O'Connor's shoulders rose and fell.

"I bumped into him," the sergeant said. "It didn't amount to anything."

"Made me spill my coffee and drop a biscuit."

"There's more coffee. And a little dirt getting on one of those biscuits isn't going to hurt it." O'Connor laughed. "Hell, that might give it a little more flavor. Those are some of the worst biscuits I ever ate!"

He sneered at Corporal Mackey as he made that last comment. The corporal's broad, red face flushed even darker with a mixture of embarrassment and anger.

"That's enough," Davidson said. "It was an accident, anyone can see that. Everyone just go on about your business."

"Sure, Lieutenant," O'Connor said. "I was just waiting for MacCallister to get out of my way so I can do that."

Davidson looked at Jamie and said curtly, "Well?"

Jamie was more accustomed to people getting out of his way. Not that he ever demanded such a thing . . . well, he might every now and then . . . but he was such a big, impressive-looking fella, folks just naturally stood aside from him.

On this occasion, though, he decided that he didn't want to have a brawl with Sergeant O'Connor on their first night out here, so he said, "I was fixing to go get more coffee anyway."

"That's right, MacCallister," O'Connor practically jeered. "If that's what ye want us to believe so you can salvage a little of your wounded pride, that's fine. I don't mind bein' the bigger man here."

He mockingly waved a hand toward the fire where the coffeepot was staying warm. But as Jamie started to step past him, he added under his breath, "This ain't over."

"It sure as hell ain't," Jamie agreed.

CHAPTER 12

Over the next several days, as the expedition followed the North Platte River and then began to curve away from the stream toward the northwest, O'Connor kept his distance from Jamie. At times it seemed as if he actually went out of his way to do so.

Jamie wondered if Lieutenant Davidson had given the sergeant orders to avoid trouble. Even if that turned out to be the case, Jamie knew it couldn't last. O'Connor was too belligerent, too full of unreasoning hatred, to keep it bottled up indefinitely.

One day while Jamie was scouting fully three-quarters of a mile ahead of the others, he spotted a dozen pronghorn antelope grazing several hundred yards ahead of him. The wind was in his face at the moment, carrying his scent away from them, but that could change without much warning. He swung down from his horse and left the reins dangling, knowing that the well-trained animal wasn't going to wander off.

Before indulging his restless nature and setting off on this trip from home, he had bought a new Sharps rifle and fired it just enough to sight it in and get used to it. He pulled the rifle from its saddle scabbard now and started toward the herd of antelope on foot. He couldn't risk getting too close, because the pronghorns had excellent eyesight to go along with their keen senses of hearing and smell. Those senses, along with their incredible ability to go from standing still to eye-blurring speed in almost no time at all, kept them alive.

Luckily, with the Sharps in his hands, Jamie didn't have to get too close.

He stopped when he was still two hundred yards from the herd. The animals were grazing peacefully, unaware that a human being was so close by. That would be a shame for one of them . . . but the troopers would appreciate the fresh meat.

Slowly and carefully, Jamie went to one knee and raised the Sharps. A lot of men would need a stand of some sort to hold the heavy rifle steady, but Jamie was strong enough to manage just fine without one. He drew the hammer back, taking pains to keep it from clicking too loudly, and picked out a good-sized buck. As he settled the sights on the target, just behind the pronghorn's right foreleg, the buck's ears twitched. Some instinct had warned him, Jamie thought, so there was no time to waste. If this buck bolted, the whole herd would follow.

He squeezed the trigger. The boom from the Sharps rolled across the prairie like thunder.

At almost the same instant, the pronghorn buck sprang forward, but although that reflexive muscle action carried the animal a good dozen feet, when the buck's hooves hit the ground again, his legs went out from under him and he rolled sprawling on the grass and didn't move again. Jamie knew the buck was dead when he landed.

By this time, the rest of the herd was almost fifty yards away and still putting on speed. Jamie let them go. He'd done what he set out to do.

And now the next thing he did was reload the Sharps. He didn't believe anyone was close enough to have heard that shot except the dragoons coming up behind him, but just in case that wasn't true, he planned to be ready for more trouble.

Once the Sharps had a fresh round in it, he got his horse and led it closer to the fallen antelope. He pulled his knife and set to work gutting and skinning the animal. By the time he'd done that, Lieutenant Tyler was visible in the distance, riding quickly toward him.

Jamie stood up and waved to let the lieutenant know that everything was all right. Tyler pounded up to him and reined in.

"We heard a shot, Mr. MacCallister. Lieutenant Davidson sent me to find out what happened."

"He should have sent a couple of troopers with you, anyway," Jamie said. "In case I was lying up here dead with a bunch of Pawnee arrows in me and a war party waiting to ambush whoever came to check on me."

Tyler frowned and said, "You mean he ordered me, alone, into a situation that could have been dangerous."

"Yeah, but he probably didn't *intend* to get you killed. He just didn't think."

Tyler didn't look like that was much comfort. He said, "That possibility should have occurred to me, too."

"More than likely," Jamie agreed. "But lucky for both of us, I'm not dead and neither are you. Ride on back and tell the others to come on up as quick as they can. And tell Corporal Mackey there's fresh meat for supper. It's late enough in the day

159

to go ahead and stop, and I'll have antelope steaks ready for him to start frying by the time he gets here."

The prospect of that put a smile of anticipation on Lieutenant Tyler's face as he wheeled his mount and rode at a fast lope back toward the rest of B Troop.

An almost festive air filled the camp that evening. It was amazing how much some fresh meat could lift the men's spirits, Jamie thought as he sat on the lowered tailgate of a supply wagon and used his knife to cut off and spear another hunk of steak seared black on the outside and oozing blood in the center, just the way he liked it.

Soldiers sat around the campfires talking and laughing, except for the ones who had eaten first and then gone on guard duty. Everyone seemed to be in a good mood . . . except for Lieutenant Davidson and Sergeant O'Connor. They were eating, too, but they did so in silence, O'Connor scowling and Davidson with a cold, disdainful look on his face.

When Davidson had finished his meal, he carried his plate and cup over to the wagon and dumped them in the bucket where one of the troopers would wash them later. He stopped in front of Jamie, clasped his hands behind his back as he was in the habit of doing, and asked, "How many more days will it be before we reach the Crow village?"

"We still have about a week to go, I'd say," Jamie replied. "Maybe a day or two less if everything goes well. A day or two longer if we run into trouble."

"What sort of trouble? Savages?"

"We've talked about that. You never know when the Pawnee will decide to act up. But there are other things that could happen. One of the wagons could break an axle. Not likely, but it's possible." Jamie glanced at the sky, where the vast sweep of stars scattered against the ebony ended abruptly over toward the western horizon. "There are some clouds moving in. This time of year, out here on the plains, some pretty bad storms can crop up."

Davidson frowned and asked, "Do you believe that's likely?"

Jamie spotted a faint flicker of lightning in the distance.

"I wouldn't be surprised," he said. "Depending on how much it rains, there could be enough mud to bog down the wagons. We might have to wait a day or two to let the ground dry out."

"I don't want to wait," Davidson snapped. "Whether the ground is muddy or not, we'll be moving on in the morning."

Obviously, the lieutenant had never seen a wagon bogged down to its wheel hubs. When that happened, a man could give orders until he was blue in the face and it wouldn't do a damned bit of good.

Jamie sipped what was left of the coffee in his cup and said, "Reckon we'll just have to wait and see."

Davidson looked like he wanted to argue, but then he nodded and turned away. He went back to the other side of the camp to talk to Sergeant O'Connor.

Jamie looked to the west again, saw the glow from more lightning. It was too far away for him to see the actual streaks of electrical fire ripping through the heavens, but the flashes were visible as they reflected from the clouds. Jamie thought he heard a faraway rumble of thunder, too, but he wasn't sure about that.

Every night, after the soldiers had settled down, Jamie ranged out about two hundred yards and made a circle around the camp, just to reassure himself that nothing unusual was going on. He did the same thing tonight. As he moved soundlessly through the dark, the wind picked up, blowing out of the west. It held a hint of coolness, and he smelled rain, as well. When he looked at the sky, he saw the clouds swiftly blotting out the stars as if those glowing pinpricks were being swallowed up by the gaping maw of some huge beast.

A storm was on the way, all right. Jamie had no doubt about that now.

He turned and headed back toward camp. He wanted to alert the guards and warn them that they'd need to hunker low to the ground as the lightning approached. Out here on these flat plains, a man standing straight and tall might be a tempting target for one of those deadly bolts. The rest of the men would need to get the horses to lie down, to keep them from being struck.

If the storm was as bad as Jamie was beginning to think it might be, those young troopers were in for a display of nature's fury unlike anything they had ever seen before.

The wind was at his back, blowing hard with a rising moan as his long-legged strides carried him toward the camp. He saw the embers of the fires glowing faintly ahead of him. He was still about fifty yards from the wagons when a large, dark shape suddenly appeared out of the night and lunged at him. In the split second when he realized he was under attack, Jamie also knew the wind had kept him from noticing any sounds the lurker might have made.

The attacker grunted with effort. Jamie dived forward, figuring the man was swinging some sort of weapon at his head. That was pure instinct, rather than conscious thought, but it was correct. Something swished through the air and knocked the broad-brimmed brown hat from Jamie's head.

The next instant, Jamie's right shoulder rammed against the man's thighs. He closed his arms around the man's knees as the collision's impact knocked the attacker over backward.

Jamie dug his knees against the ground and pushed himself forward. His right fist rose and slammed down into the man's midsection. Then something clipped the side of Jamie's head — the bludgeon, swung in a backhand, maybe — and sent him rolling away. The blow had enough power behind it to make bells toll loudly inside Jamie's brain.

He came to a stop on his belly, raised his head and shook it for a second to get the cobwebs out of it, and pushed up onto hands and knees. A couple of yards away, the attacker was trying to get up, too. Lightning flashed, closer now, and the instant of stark glare revealed Liam O'Connor's hate-twisted visage as he struggled to his feet. He had an ax handle gripped in his right hand. No ax-head was attached to the handle, but the sturdy wooden shaft was dangerous enough by itself. It could crush Jamie's skull.

Darkness closed in again as O'Conner rushed toward Jamie, swinging the ax handle. Jamie took a fast step back to avoid it, and then lightning flickered again, showing him that O'Connor was slashing back and forth with the ax handle as he continued his charge.

Sometimes a strategic retreat was the smart thing to do, but the Good Lord had put only so much backup in Jamie Ian MacCallister. He was damned if he was going to turn and run from O'Connor. The lightning came a third time, and as it did, Jamie lunged forward and reached up to intercept the ax handle with his left hand. His fingers closed around the wood, and the muscles in his back and shoulders bunched as he stopped its swing and jerked O'Connor toward him.

Jamie's right first shot out and landed in the middle of O'Connor's face. With Jamie's weight behind it, and the sergeant's own momentum adding to the force, the impact jolted O'Connor's head back so far it seemed that his neck might unhinge. The bottom half of his body continued moving forward, but his legs got tangled with each other and he went down.

Jamie had the ax handle now. After that stunning blow, O'Connor hadn't been able to hang on to it. Instead of using it as a weapon himself, Jamie flung it aside into the darkness.

Lightning flashed. Thunder boomed. The bolts were closer now as the storm moved in rapidly. In the now almost constant glare, Jamie saw O'Connor climb onto hands and knees and pause there, shaking his head groggily. Jamie was a little surprised the sergeant was still conscious after that devastating punch.

"Stay down, O'Connor," Jamie said over the rumbling echoes of the thunder. "Crawl back to the wagons."

O'Connor pushed up, although he was still on his knees. His chest heaved as he said, "I don't . . . crawl for anybody . . . you bastard!"

"You damned fool! That storm's not far off, and sometimes lightning strikes out ahead of one like that. We all need to get down and stay down until it passes!"

"You can . . . go to hell!"

With that roared curse, O'Connor came

to his feet and charged Jamie again. His fists were his only weapons now, but Jamie knew they could be deadly, too. Despite the threat of the approaching storm, he had to deal with O'Connor.

The lightning continued to flash. For long moments, its stark glare washed over the prairie and the two men battling like titans of ancient times. Then the lightning would stop, and for a second or two, impenetrable blackness fell over the world like a shroud, only to be rent asunder again by the next flash.

The heavy thud of fists landing on flesh and bone competed with the thunder. Jamie stood there, feet braced wide apart, trading punch for punch with O'Connor, absorbing the punishment the brutal sergeant dealt out in order to deliver some thunder and lightning of his own. The battle swayed back and forth, one man knocked on his heels only to recover and throw more punches.

This clash didn't go unnoticed. Some of the troopers spotted them in the flickering glare and ran out from the camp, shouting. Jamie couldn't make out any of the words, didn't know if the soldiers were yelling encouragement or warnings. All his attention was focused on O'Connor.

Both of them were experienced bare-knuckles brawlers. There was nothing fancy about the way they fought. This was a battle of sheer strength and willpower . . . and endurance. Jamie sensed that O'Connor was moving a little slower now. The sergeant's punches didn't have as much snap and speed.

Jamie's own stamina was waning, too, though. If he didn't wrap up this fight soon, O'Connor might get lucky and land a decisive blow . . .

Instead, an eye-searing flash washed over them, and a blast louder than the roar of any cannon slammed into Jamie's ears. He felt himself flying through the air, then he crashed into the ground with bone-jarring force. A sharp electrical stink stung his nostrils.

His brain was stunned, but the part of it still functioning knew that a lightning bolt had struck somewhere very close by. It hadn't actually hit him, he supposed, or else he'd be dead now or at least unconscious. He looked around, halfway expecting to see Liam O'Connor's charred corpse, but instead the sergeant was sprawled on his belly a few yards away, shaking his head. The bolt had missed him, too, but obviously not by much.

O'Connor's mouth was open, but Jamie

couldn't hear anything. The tremendous blast had deafened him. Not permanently, he hoped. O'Connor looked like he was groaning. That made sense, since Jamie felt like doing the same thing.

A strong hand grasped his arm and lifted him to a sitting position. He looked up and saw Lieutenant Hayden Tyler silhouetted against the near-constant flickering that lit up the night sky. Tyler leaned over him and shouted something. Jamie caught only the last couple of words: "— all right?"

That was enough to tell Jamie that his hearing was coming back. He nodded. Tyler helped him to his feet. While the lieutenant was doing that, a couple of the dragoons lifted O'Connor from the ground.

"— back to the wagons?"

Jamie nodded again in response to that half-heard question from Tyler. He raised his voice and said, "Hurry, but stay low! Crouch over while you run!"

They started for the camp. O'Connor stumbled some, but the troopers helped him. More lightning bolts slammed into the prairie around them, but all the strikes were at least a hundred yards away. That luck might not last.

When they reached the wagons, Jamie was glad to see that the men had forced the horses to lie down and were stretched out on the ground with them, holding their headstalls. The horses were badly spooked but appeared to be under control so far. Someone in the troop must have had experience with lightning storms in the past and had known what to do, more than likely Corporal Mackey or the other teamster.

Lieutenant Davidson was waiting beside one of the wagons. He screeched at Jamie, "Why were you and O'Connor fighting?"

"He jumped me when I was on my way in," Jamie replied. "You'd have to ask him why."

He could hear fine again, which was a relief — even though it meant he had to listen to Davidson.

"You've caused enough trouble, MacCallister —" the first lieutenant began.

"Save it for later," Jamie told him. "Right now, you'd better get under this wagon until the storm passes."

"You can't give me orders —"

That was all Davidson got out before the rain hit. It was like someone had upended a giant bucket over their heads. The rain poured down, hitting them with staggering force and instantly drenching all the men to the skin. Jamie dropped to his knees and crawled underneath the wagon. Tyler followed him. Jamie didn't know what happened to Davidson, and at that moment, he didn't really care.

Lightning slashed down, thunder shook the earth, and rain mercilessly lashed everything in sight.

It was like the end of the world.

CHAPTER 13

Before morning, the storm moved off, grumbling, to the southeast. Stars appeared again overhead. A three-quarter moon even sailed into view, lighting up the prairie and revealing the men who staggered around looking like half-drowned rats.

Despite the troopers' efforts, some of the horses had broken loose during the deluge and vanished. When a soldier reported this to Lieutenant Davidson, who slumped on a wagon tailgate, he wailed, "We'll have to go back to the fort! We can't possibly continue without enough horses."

Jamie was standing nearby, looking around at the huge pools of shallow, standing water that covered much of the landscape and glimmered in the moonlight. The storm had dumped an incredible amount of rain on the prairie, and in this flat terrain, there was no place for it to run off. It would have to soak in.

Luckily, it had been a fairly dry season until now, so that might not take a very long time.

"Those horses won't have gone far, Lieutenant," he said. "They probably scattered hell-west and crosswise, as panicky as they were, and that'll be the hardest part of rounding them up. But we still have plenty of mounts to do that while we're waiting for the ground to dry up enough for the wagons to move."

"I told you, we can't afford to wait —"

"Try to drive the wagons in this mess, even if you're turning around and going back to Fort Kearny, and you won't make it a hundred yards."

Lieutenant Tyler asked, "What's your suggestion, Mr. MacCallister?"

That drew a glare from Davidson, but Tyler ignored it. So did Jamie, who said, "The sun will come up in a couple of hours and start drying the mud. While it's doing that, I'll take a few men with me and we'll start looking for the horses that ran off. I don't know if we'll find all of them, but we brought extra mounts with us from the fort. My hunch is that we'll be able to round up enough to keep going."

"You can't just ride off on your own," snapped Davidson. "I'm in command of this mission."

"And I'm telling you what I believe is our best course of action," Jamie said. "I reckon it's up to you to decide if you agree, Lieutenant."

Davidson frowned and gnawed at his lower lip. Jamie's plan was sensible, and Davidson had to be smart enough to realize that. The question was whether his pride would allow him to go along with it.

Finally, Davidson nodded and said, "All right, MacCallister. How many men do you need?"

"Oh, four ought to do it, I'd say. Lieutenant Tyler and three troopers."

"Me?" Tyler said.

"That's right. I've seen you ride, Lieutenant. I reckon you can handle the job. And you know the men, so you pick the three to come with us."

"Well . . ." Tyler looked at Davidson, who wearily flipped a hand in a gesture for him to go ahead. "All right. When do you want to leave?"

"As soon as it's light enough for us to see what we're looking for."

With that settled, Jamie was about to go check on his horse, but then Davidson straightened from his beaten-down stance and said, "There's another matter that

174

needs to be settled."

"What's that?"

"Once again, you've attacked a man under my command, MacCallister."

Jamie stared at Davidson for a long couple of seconds, then said, "Who told you that?"

"It doesn't matter who. Do you deny it?"

"I damn sure do!" Jamie burst out. "I was on my way back to camp just before the storm hit when O'Connor jumped me! He tried to bust my head open with an ax handle."

"Then you admit that the two of you fought?"

Jamie waved a hand toward the area of the prairie where the battle had taken place and said, "Hell, the whole camp saw us whaling away at each other. But it was O'Connor who started it."

"*Sergeant* O'Connor has informed me that his encounter with you took him by surprise and that *you* attacked *him.*"

"Well, that's a lie, and I'll tell him as much to his face." Jamie looked around. "Where is he?"

"Resting in the other wagon, trying to recover from the beating you gave him." Davidson was much more animated now. He pointed a finger at Jamie as he went on, "You seem to be under the mistaken impression that you are indispensable to this mission, MacCallister! Nothing could be further from the truth. I studied the map in Captain Croxton's office and even drew a map of my own to bring with us. I can lead us to our destination every bit as well as you can. If you continue fomenting trouble and attacking my men, I'll have no choice but to remove you from your position as scout and press on without you!"

Tyler cleared his throat and said, "Lieutenant, I, uh, I'm not so sure —"

Davidson whirled on him and demanded, "What are you trying to say, *Second* Lieutenant Tyler? That you disagree with the stance I've taken? That you believe it's your place to give advice to an officer who outranks you?"

"No, sir," Tyler responded stiffly.

Jamie couldn't contain a snort of disgust. As far as he was concerned, the difference between a first lieutenant and a second lieutenant didn't amount to a gobbet of spit. But the army put stock in such things, and he couldn't blame Tyler for answering the way he had.

Jamie, however, was bound by no such formality. He said, "Any time you want me to leave, Davidson, you just say the word. But whatever happens after that will be completely on your head. You just remember that. As for O'Connor, he started it, and that lightning bolt ended it . . . for now. Tell him he'd better steer clear of me, though. Next time he comes at me, I'm liable to put a stop to it permanently."

"How dare you!" Davidson flared. "If you think you can threaten a noncommissioned officer of the United States Army and get away with it —"

"I'm done here. You go on blustering as long as you want to." Jamie turned away, adding over his shoulder, "Pick those three troopers and be ready to ride when the sun comes up, Lieutenant Tyler. With any luck, this expedition won't be stuck here for too long."

Lieutenant Davidson didn't continue the argument, but he stood so stiffly as he watched Jamie and the others get ready to leave camp that the fury he felt was visible in every line of his body.

Jamie saw that but ignored it. He had things to do that were actually important and worthwhile, rather than worrying about what some annoying, stiff-necked little martinet thought of him.

The clouds were gone and the sky was completely clear as dawn approached. A curtain of golden light formed an arch in the east as Lieutenant Tyler and three troopers approached Jamie, leading their horses.

Jamie's mount, steady and cool-headed as always, hadn't bolted during the storm. Jamie had saddled the big stallion and now snugged the Sharps rifle down in its leather sheath.

"Are you ready, Mr. MacCallister?" Tyler asked.

Jamie nodded and said, "I reckon it's light enough. Did anybody happen to see which way those horses went when they stampeded last night?"

"From what the men told me, they all took off in different directions."

"We'll make a big circle, then. Might as well head north to start."

"I need to tell Lieutenant Davidson that we're leaving, and then we can go."

Jamie nodded toward the wagon where Davidson was standing and said, "I expect he can see that."

"I'm going to tell him anyway."

"Do what you need to do, son," Jamie said with a wave of his hand.

He swung up into the saddle while Tyler went over to speak to Davidson. Davidson spoke sharply to him. Jamie could tell from the way Tyler stiffened that he didn't like what the other officer was saying to him. But after a moment, Tyler jerked his head in a nod and saluted.

Arrogantly, Davidson took his time about returning the salute. When he finally did, Tyler turned and came back over to rejoin the detail. He mounted his horse and said to Jamie, "The lieutenant has given me until ten o'clock this morning to return with these troopers. He says that he's leaving then, and if we're not back, we'll be considered deserters."

The eyes of all three soldiers widened when they heard that. One of them asked nervously, "He can't do that, can he, Lieutenant?"

"Lieutenant Davidson is in command of this expedition, private. He can do whatever he wants."

Jamie scratched his jaw and asked, "What did he say about me?"

Tyler hesitated before answering, "He said you can come back by then or go to hell, whatever you want. He doesn't care."

"Sounds like he and I feel the same way about each other," Jamie said with a chuckle. He grew more serious as he lifted his reins. "He can give the order to pull out at ten o'clock if he wants to, but it won't do him any good. The ground won't be dry enough by then. Those wagons will get stuck as soon they try to move. Then it'll be even longer before they can get started again." Jamie shrugged. "We'll try to be back. If we're not, don't worry too much, boys. Davidson can accuse you of desertion, but Captain Croxton isn't going to believe him. You'll just have to tell him what really happened."

"No offense, sir, but you won't be facing a court-martial if you're wrong," Tyler pointed out.

Jamie grunted in acknowledgment of that point and turned his horse. He rode north with Tyler beside him and the three dragoons following. The thick mud sucked at their horses' hooves, so they couldn't move very fast.

For the next few hours, as the sun peeked above the horizon and then climbed into the sky, Jamie and his companions rode in large circles around the camp, moving farther out each time. They began spotting the strayed horses fairly early in the search. The animals had gotten over the fright that caused them to bolt and had stopped to graze, as horses will do. The four soldiers were all good riders. They were able to gather up the horses and drive them along in a steadily growing group.

After a while, Jamie asked Lieutenant Tyler, "Do you know how many of those varmints got away last night?"

"Fourteen, according to the count we made this morning."

"We've rounded up eleven of them so far. If we don't come across the others pretty soon, we'll head back."

Tyler pulled a turnip watch from his pocket and opened it. He sighed and said, "That's good, because we're almost out of the time Lieutenant Davidson allotted to us."

A few minutes later, one of the dragoons spotted another of the army mounts off to their right. Jamie told him to go get it and bring it back. The trooper did so, and when he had returned, Jamie said, "That's an even dozen. That's enough." He turned his horse back toward the camp. "Come on."

The terrain was flat enough that even though they were pretty far out, it didn't take long for the wagons to come into sight. Jamie saw the men of B Troop moving around. His eyes narrowed as he realized that the mule teams had been hitched to the wagons.

"Looks like Davidson's getting ready to leave," he said.

"But he can't be," Lieutenant Tyler objected. "It's still at least a quarter-hour until ten o'clock. He told me we had until then. And surely the sentries will spot us pretty soon and let him know we're on our way in."

"Could be he decided he didn't want to wait that long. I've got a hunch he can be a mite impulsive sometimes."

Tyler swallowed hard, and that was enough to tell Jamie that his hunch was correct.

"He'd better not try to say that we deserted," the young lieutenant muttered.

"Don't worry. He's not going anywhere."

The horses' hooves still frequently sloshed through standing water as the detail rode toward the camp. Jamie knew the ground was too soft and muddy for the wagon wheels. So when he heard whips cracking and the drivers shouting at their teams, he wasn't surprised to see the vehicles lurch forward for a few yards and then come to abrupt halts.

Lieutenant Tyler saw the same thing and asked, "Are they stuck?"

"That'd be my guess," said Jamie.

As they came closer, he saw that was exactly what had happened. Both wagons sat there with their wheels sunk deeply in the mud. The sticky stuff wasn't quite up to

182

the wheel hubs, but it was close.

Sergeant O'Connor stood next to the lead wagon, which was being driven by Corporal Mackey. O'Connor lashed the teamster with blistering curses. Mackey sat on the driver's box and took the abuse stolidly, as if he knew what had happened was not his fault but also knew there was nothing he could do to turn aside O'Connor's wrath.

O'Connor broke off his tirade as Jamie and his companions approached with the horses they had recovered. The sergeant's face was purple with rage, and also from the bruises that mottled his features.

"Look what this damn numbskull of a corporal did, Lieutenant," O'Connor said as he waved a hand at Mackey's wagon.

Tyler didn't respond to O'Connor's blaming of Mackey. Instead, with a puzzled frown on his face, he said, "I don't see Lieutenant Davidson, Sergeant. Where is he?"

"He took two men and rode on ahead a ways. To scout, he said." O'Connor sneered at Jamie as he answered Tyler's question.

"Then who gave the order to move these wagons?"

"I did." O'Connor's slab-like jaw jutted forward defiantly. "He told me to bring 'em on when they were ready to roll."

Tyler glanced over at Jamie and said, "He ignored everything you told him."

Jamie shrugged, as if to ask Tyler if he had expected anything different from Davidson.

"Well, they're stuck now," Tyler went on. "You might as well have the teams unhitched again, Sergeant."

"I'll bet we can get 'em loose, sir. If Mackey'll just whip those damn jugheads, instead of babyin' 'em —"

"By God, a twenty-mule team couldn't pull this wagon loose!" Mackey interrupted, unable to contain his anger and frustration any longer. "Even after the ground dries out some more, we're gonna have to hitch both teams to one wagon and take off some sideboards to use as leverage to pry 'em out of that mud."

"Watch your tongue, trooper!" O'Connor roared. "I'll have you in the guardhouse when we get back to the fort!"

The sergeant was about to unleash more curses when Jamie suddenly held up a hand and said, "Be quiet!"

Something about the big frontiersman's attitude alarmed Lieutenant Tyler. He said, "What is it, Mr. MacCallister?"

"Listen," Jamie said.

There wasn't much wind, but there was enough to carry some faint popping sounds to their ears.

"Is that —" Tyler began as his eyes got big.

"Gunshots!" Jamie said. He pulled his horse around and sent it galloping to the west, mud flying from the animal's hooves as it pounded across the wet ground.

CHAPTER 14

Jamie had heard the shots well enough to know the direction they came from, so he rode that way as fast as he could, without looking back to see if Tyler or any of the other soldiers were following him. After a few minutes, he began seeing puffs of powdersmoke in the air ahead of him and knew he was headed the right way.

Spotting movement from the corner of his eye, he glanced over and saw Lieutenant Hayden Tyler drawing even with him. Tyler leaned far forward in the saddle as he coaxed all the speed he could get out of his mount. Jamie had been right: Tyler was an excellent rider.

Jamie turned his attention back to the scene in front of him. Lithe, coppery figures on speedy ponies dashed around a small, grassy hummock. The gunshots and powdersmoke came from that little mound. The mounted Indians raced in to fire arrows at the defenders, then pulled back quickly because those forays brought them within rifle range.

Jamie didn't see any army horses, but he supposed they had run off after Lieutenant Davidson and the dragoons with him took cover behind the hummock. Either that, or the horses were down, killed by Pawnee arrows.

That the attackers were Pawnee, Jamie didn't doubt. They roamed this part of the country more than any other tribe. And as he and Tyler came closer, he was able to make out the distinctive roached head-dresses Pawnee warriors usually wore.

There hadn't been any Indian trouble in these parts recently, at least as far as Jamie knew, but it wasn't unusual for young bucks to go out looking for trouble even when most of the tribe was peaceful. The sight of white soldiers riding along had been too much temptation to resist.

Jamie hauled back on his reins and motioned for Tyler to do likewise. As Jamie's mount skidded to a halt, he swung a leg over the saddle and dropped to the ground. He pulled the Sharps from its scabbard and turned his horse so he could rest the barrel across the saddle.

They were still several hundred yards

away, and the Pawnee didn't appear to have noticed them. The warriors realized they were under attack from another direction a moment later, though, when the big Sharps boomed and one of them flung out his arms and toppled off his pony. The heavy-caliber round had blown a fist-sized hole clean through his torso.

"Good Lord!" exclaimed Tyler. "What a shot!"

"Better get ready," Jamie advised as he started reloading the Sharps. "They know we're here now, and they'll be coming our way."

Tyler hastily dismounted and readied his rifle. The warriors had broken off their attack on the hummock and were already galloping toward Jamie and the lieutenant. Shrill cries of rage came from their throats.

Jamie didn't rush his reloading. He knew he had time. His fingers performed the task in smooth, efficient motions. He glanced over at Tyler and saw that the young officer had followed his example and turned his horse so he could rest his rifle's barrel across the saddle.

"Which one are you aiming at, Lieutenant?" asked Jamie, his tone as casual as if he'd been inquiring about a Sunday picnic.

"The . . . the one on the right," Tyler

answered. "My right. With that black stripe painted across his face."

"All right. Make your shot count." Jamie nestled his cheek against the smooth wood of the rifle's stock as he aimed. "I'll take one of the others."

A couple of seconds ticked by as the two men steadied their aim. Jamie's Sharps boomed first, followed an instant later by Tyler's rifle. The Indian Jamie had targeted flew backward off his pony, drilled through the chest. Tyler's shot wasn't quite as accurate, but the bullet shattered the black-painted Pawnee warrior's right shoulder. The impact twisted the man around, but he didn't fall off his pony. Instead he hauled the animal around and rode back the other way.

That left three of the hostiles mounted and charging at Jamie and Tyler. There wouldn't be time to reload the rifles again. Jamie shoved his Sharps back in its sheath and dropped his hand to the Walker Colt on his hip.

Tyler carried a Colt Dragoon pistol in a flapped holster on his right hip. Jamie figured between the two revolvers, they had enough firepower to make a good stand against the three Pawnee warriors.

The problem was that the Pawnee bows

had a longer range than the handguns. Arrows began whipping through the air around Jamie and Tyler. One of them grazed the rump of Tyler's horse and made the animal whinny shrilly in pain.

A rifle boomed again, this time from the hummock. One of the remaining Indians slumped forward over his pony's neck, struck from behind by the bullet. He slid off the galloping pony, and the warrior riding beside him had to jerk his mount away to avoid getting tangled up with the fallen man.

That disrupted the attack, and the two Pawnee who were still mounted must have decided it wouldn't be a good idea to remain in this crossfire. One waved an arm and yelled at the other, and then both turned their ponies and rode hard to the north, away from the scene of battle.

"They're giving up?" Tyler asked in amazement as he stared at the dwindling figures.

"No Indian will keep fighting once the price for winning gets too high," said Jamie. "They're hardheaded that way. So they'll just light a shuck and figure on fighting again some other day."

He peered toward the hummock where a figure was now visible, standing on top of the mound and holding a rifle. That was the man who had picked off one of the remaining Pawnee and convinced them to abandon their attack. Jamie grunted in surprise. He was pretty sure the rifleman was Lieutenant Edgar Davidson.

"We'd better go check on those fellas," Jamie said.

He and Tyler mounted up and rode toward the hummock. As they came closer, Jamie saw he was right. Davidson was the man standing there. The lieutenant was reloading his rifle as they rode up.

"A timely arrival, Lieutenant Tyler," Davidson said.

"We had just gotten back to camp when Mr. MacCallister heard the shots," Tyler said. "I'm glad we were able to get here in time to help."

"Yes, the situation looked a bit dicey when those savages attacked us. This was the only cover we could find."

Davidson's voice was calm, and his fingers didn't seem to be shaking as he finished reloading the rifle, but all the color was washed out of his face and his eyes were a little bigger than normal.

"Are any of you hurt?"

"I'm afraid Private Hodgson is dead."

"No!" Tyler said.

191

"He was struck in the throat by an arrow as we dismounted. There was nothing Private Thomas or I could do for him."

"Where are your horses?" Jamie asked.

Davidson had been ignoring him so far, but the lieutenant answered that direct question.

"They ran off while Thomas and I were taking cover. As far as I know, none of them were injured by arrows, so you should be able to find them."

"Yeah, I'll do that," Jamie said.

He had started to turn his horse away when Davidson said to Tyler, "I assume the wagons are on their way, Lieutenant?"

"The wagons are stuck in the mud," replied Tyler. "They didn't get very far when Sergeant O'Connor gave the order to move out."

Davidson blew out a breath in obvious disgust. He looked at Jamie, who had paused, and said, "I suppose you're going to gloat now."

"Nope. I'm just going to find those horses so we can get you fellas back to the wagons. Private Hodgson will need to be laid to rest."

"Yes," Davidson said, nodding slowly. "Yes, he will. Did you find the other horses that ran away during the storm?"

"All but two of them," Tyler said.

Davidson nodded again.

"Enough that we can push on, then," he said. "Once we get the wagons free."

Jamie rode out to look for the horses. Davidson seemed a little subdued, even humbled, by what had happened, he mused.

But Jamie had a hunch that wouldn't last.

Jamie found all three of the horses, so they were able to load Private Hodgson's body onto one of the mounts and take it back to the spot where the wagons were stuck. Sergeant O'Connor hadn't made any progress in getting the vehicles loose from the mud, and the attempts were abandoned as the grim news of Hodgson's death spread.

Lieutenant Davidson placed Hayden Tyler in command of the burial detail. Jamie knew that finding a spot dry enough for a grave to be dug would be difficult, so he gave the young officer a hand. They had to go about half a mile to a slightly higher stretch of ground. Even there, when the two dragoons who'd been assigned to dig the grave were about a foot down, water began to trickle into the hole. As the water deepened, Tyler told two more men to fetch buckets and bail.

It was miserable, frustrating work. If there

had been any trees around, Jamie might have suggested that they build an elevated scaffold and lay Private Hodgson to rest Indian fashion, but that wasn't an option, either. So the men kept digging, and by the middle of the afternoon, they had a muddy pit into which Hodgson's blanket-wrapped body was lowered. One of the troopers who served as a chaplain of sorts had a Bible with him, and he read Scripture in a short burial service.

Then, while a couple of men shoveled dirt back into the grave, the rest returned to the chore of trying to free the wagons from the mud. Even though it was too late in the day for the detail to resume its trek toward the mountains, it would be best to get the wagons loose before the mud hardened around the wheels.

That took both teams, boards for leverage, and a number of men putting their shoulders to the wagons and pushing. Jamie found himself on one rear corner and looked over to see Sergeant Liam O'Connor at the other corner. O'Connor scowled at him, but both of them threw themselves into the work of grunting, straining, and heaving against the mud's stubborn grip. More men tugged on the mules' harnesses and urged the beasts to put their strength into it.

Finally, with loud sucking sounds, the wheels came loose and the wagons rolled forward a few feet. Corporal Mackey bellowed for everyone to stop before the wheels had a chance to dig in again. They all moved to the other wagon and worked it loose as well, just as the sun was going down.

Jamie went to Lieutenant Tyler and said, "I don't think there's much of a chance those Pawnee who got away will come back, but just in case, you'd better put on some extra sentries tonight and make sure they know to keep their eyes and ears open."

"I was just thinking the same thing," Tyler replied with a nod.

That precaution proved to be unnecessary, as the night passed peacefully. The next morning, Jamie stomped the ground to test its firmness and decided it might be dry enough to try moving the wagons again.

"Once they're going, keep 'em rolling," Jamie told Corporal Mackey. "There's a little slope up to the west, so gradual you can't really see it, but the farther we go in that direction, the better it should be."

Mackey nodded his understanding and said quietly, "I never would have tried it yesterday if Sergeant O'Connor hadn't ordered me to, Mr. MacCallister."

"I know that."

"And Hodgson wouldn't be dead if —" Mackey stopped short and took a deep breath. "Reckon I've said enough. Almost more than I should."

"You weren't about to say anything the rest of us haven't thought, Corporal," Jamie told him.

Mackey shrugged and went to see about getting the mule teams hitched up. Jamie looked around for Lieutenant Tyler and saw him talking to Davidson. Somewhat to his surprise, Davidson motioned for him to come over and join them.

When he did, Davidson traded salutes with Tyler, who walked off to see to whatever task Davidson had given him. Then Davidson clasped his hands behind his back and said to Jamie, "You haven't said anything to me about what happened yesterday, Mac-Callister. I'm sure you have an opinion on the matter."

"Not really," said Jamie. "We ran into some pure bad luck, that's all. Private Hodgson had the worst luck of all."

"You don't blame me for his death?"

"He probably wouldn't be dead if you hadn't taken him with you," Jamie admitted. "That's just the plain truth of what happened. But I don't know that you did anything wrong."

Davidson cocked an eyebrow and said, "Oh?"

"That's right. As the officer in command of this detail, you had every right to ride ahead and do some scouting. Had I been here, instead of being out rounding up those horses, I probably would have done the same thing."

"The difference is that the savages wouldn't have taken you by surprise."

Jamie shrugged and said, "Likely not. But I might've wound up in a fight with the Pawnee anyway. Things like that happen out here on the plains." Jamie shook his head. "If you're waiting for me to condemn you, Lieutenant, I'm not going to. Not for what happened yesterday."

"I did manage to kill one of the hostiles," Davidson said with a sniff.

"You did, and it was a good shot. I'll give you credit for that."

"But not respect."

"Lieutenant," Jamie said, "why do you give a damn whether I respect you or not?"

Davidson stared at him, and for a second, Jamie saw something in the young officer's eyes he hadn't seen before: fear. For all his arrogance and seeming self-confidence, despite the fact that he was surrounded by soldiers at the moment, Davidson was scared. Whether it was the idea of failing in his mission that frightened him, or just that he was scared of being killed, he was terrified — and he didn't like it.

Then, almost instantly, Davidson controlled that emotion and shoved it down deep inside him where it had come from. Jamie saw that as well, in the thinning of the young man's lips, the jut of his jaw, and the stiffening of his backbone.

"That will be all, MacCallister," he said. "You can go on about your job now."

"Yeah." Jamie rubbed his beard-stubbled chin. "I'll do that."

He turned and walked back to his horse. Corporal Mackey was on the driver's box of the lead wagon, the other teamster held the reins of the second vehicle's team, and the dragoons were waiting for Sergeant O'Connor's order to mount up. Within minutes, the little column was on its way again, and although the wagon wheels left deep ruts in the soft ground, this time they didn't bog down.

CHAPTER 15

The Crow village

Following the battle with the outlaws who had attacked the wagon train, Preacher and Hawk had returned to the village the next day. They were lucky enough along the way to run into a small herd of deer, so they brought quite a bit of fresh meat back with them. The Crow ate well that night, well enough that it seemed like a celebration of sorts.

Preacher and Hawk also sat down with Broken Pine and the other leading warriors, including Many Pelts, and told them everything that had happened.

"Those settlers won't cause any trouble for you," Preacher assured the warriors sitting around the fire in Broken Pine's lodge. "They've turned around and headed back down to the Sweetwater, and from there they'll go on through South Pass. They won't come anywhere close to your village."

"But other white men will come," Many Pelts insisted. "You said they all believe there is a good way up here to cross the mountains with their *wagons.*"

Disdain practically dripped from Many Pelts' voice. Several men nodded in agreement with him. As so often happened, these Indians couldn't even begin to comprehend how white men thought and felt about things. Of course, Preacher told himself, the same thing was true when it was turned around and pointed back the other direction.

"Over time, folks will realize that fella who wrote the book didn't know what he was talkin' about. When that happens, the wagon trains will stop driftin' in this direction and you won't have to worry about them anymore."

"How long?" Many Pelts demanded. "And how much will they ruin our hunting grounds before this thing you promise happens?"

"Your huntin' grounds will be fine," Preacher said, trying to restrain the impatience he felt at Many Pelts' stubborn attitude, an attitude obviously shared by several more of the Crow warriors. "As long as it starts rainin' again, like it's bound to, the game will come back and be as plentiful as ever."

Broken Pine said, "There is no way to be sure this will happen, Preacher. If it does not, our people will starve."

"I guess we can never be sure somethin's gonna happen until it does," Preacher said.

"Another thing worries me," Broken Pine went on. "These men who raided the wagon train . . . what are the chances they will come here and attack our people?"

Preacher shook his head and said, "I don't see any reason why they would. There were some renegade Indians among 'em, but most of 'em were white, from what I could tell, and that means they were after loot. The Crow lead happy, peaceful lives here, but no offense, Broken Pine, you folks don't have anything that'd interest a bunch of greedy, no-account varmints like that."

"Preacher is right," said Hawk. "Those evil white men are no threat to us."

Many Pelts scoffed and said, "Of course you agree with your white father. I say the best way, the only way, for our people to be safe is to fight any white men we see and make them want to stay far away from here."

"You talk like a Blackfoot," Hawk snapped back at him.

Many Pelts snarled, leaned forward, and reached for the knife at his waist.

"We do not fight each other," Broken Pine said sharply. "Especially in my lodge."

"You heard what he said!" Many Pelts exclaimed.

"My apologies, Many Pelts," said Hawk. "My words were unwise. But I do not want our people to seek trouble when it is not necessary."

Broken Pine said, "There is wisdom to be found in *those* words. We will not fight among ourselves, and we will not go to war against the whites. Perhaps the spirits will smile upon us and no more wagon trains will come near our hunting grounds."

"That's a good thing to hope for," Preacher agreed with a nod.

For the next week, it appeared that those spirits *were* smiling, just as Broken Pine suggested. Hunting parties found more game, which led Preacher to hope that animals were already starting to return to the area in greater numbers. No more wagon trains were spotted out on the plains.

Preacher spent his days with Hawk, Butterfly, Eagle Feather, and Bright Moon. This was probably the longest stretch he had ever visited with his son, daughter-in-law, and grandchildren. He thoroughly enjoyed this time.

But even while he was doing that, he

began to feel restlessness growing stronger inside him. Going to sleep and waking up in the same place, day after day, was something to which he had never become accustomed. Pretty soon now, he was going to have to be on the move again.

Before that happened, though, he wanted to spend time with his other friends in the village, so he suggested to Hawk that they go hunting again, but on this occasion, they would take Broken Pine, Big Thunder, and several other warriors Preacher had befriended with them.

"This is good!" Big Thunder enthused when Preacher told him about the hunting trip. "And when we get back, we will fight again?"

"Why is it you're so bound and determined to tussle with me?" asked Preacher. "I'm gettin' old, son. I can't be much competition anymore."

Big Thunder shook his head and said, "Preacher will never be too old to fight! That is what you do."

"Sometimes, it seems like that's all too true. It ain't like I go lookin' for trouble, though. Somehow it just finds me."

There were ten men in their party when they set out from the village. They planned to be out for two or possibly even three days

203

but took the bare minimum of provisions needed for a trip like that. They were counting on finding game to feed them.

Dog ranged far ahead of them, but Preacher didn't worry about the big cur scaring off any deer or antelope. If Dog spotted any worthwhile game, he would come back and lead them to it. The only things he would go after for himself were rabbits and grouse.

The men took their time, not pushing the ponies they rode. As they loafed along, they talked about many things, from women they had known to great battles they had fought in the past to their hopes for what they would find in the world beyond this one. Preacher reflected that there wasn't much difference between a hunting trip with this bunch of fellas and one he might have taken with a group of white friends. When you got right down to it, folks were folks . . . mostly.

They didn't find any game the first day, so they pushed out farther into the foothills the second day. A lone deer provided enough meat for the hunters to have a good meal, but not enough to make traveling back to the village worthwhile. On the third day, one of the warriors suggested that they venture out onto the plains, where they might find a herd of buffalo.

The others were willing to go along with that, especially Big Thunder, who said that he needed a new buffalo robe.

"You are so large, it may take *two* buffalo to make a robe for your lodge," one of the other men joked.

Big Thunder crossed his arms over his massive chest, scowled, and said solemnly, "You should not make sport with Big Thunder, Swift Water."

"I mean no insult," Swift Water assured him, grinning. "But they call you *Big* Thunder for a reason, my friend."

The hunting party moved on, leaving the foothills and riding out onto the grassy plains. They scared up some prairie chickens, which took awkward flight and fled, but no buffalo. When the middle of the day had passed, Broken Pine brought his pony to a halt and the others did likewise. The Crow chief said, "We should start thinking about turning back."

"But we have found hardly any game!" a warrior protested.

"We have enjoyed our friendship," Broken Pine said with a shrug. He looked over at the mountain man and added, "I believe this is what Preacher really sought to find."

"You're right about that, Broken Pine," Preacher said, nodding. "But I've got a hunch we might find something else after all." He raised a hand and pointed. "Look over yonder."

A yellow haze hung in the air in the direction Preacher indicated.

"Dust," Hawk said, recognizing the sign.

"Yep. Somethin's on the move over there, and to kick up that much dust, it must be a mess of buffalo."

"We will go and see," Broken Pine decided. He heeled his pony into motion again, and the others followed suit as they all rode toward the rising dust.

Several days had passed, and there had been no sign of the Pawnee or any other hostiles as the party of U.S. army dragoons continued their journey toward the mountains. The weather had been good, and the sun shining brightly each day had dried the ground and made it easy for the wagons to travel along in the wake of the riders.

If anybody thought about Private Clarence Hodgson, lying now beneath the sod in a lonely grave miles behind them, they kept those musings to themselves.

Jamie rode at least half a mile ahead of the troop most of the time and avoided Lieutenant Edgar Davidson except to report to him a couple of times a day. Jamie took advantage of any opportunity to talk to Hayden Tyler, though. The young second lieutenant impressed Jamie with his intelligence and level-headedness. Tyler had the makings of an excellent officer. He just needed experience, and he was getting that on this trip.

One evening at supper, Jamie was hunkered on his heels, drinking coffee and chatting with Lieutenant Tyler, when Corporal Mackey came over to him and said, "Can I talk to you for a minute, Mr. MacCallister?"

"Sure, Corporal. Is there a problem?"

"No, sir, not really. It's just that we haven't had any fresh meat for several days, and I was thinking the men might really like some."

Jamie smiled and said, "I reckon they would. Nothing perks up a fella quite like a good steak."

"I know. That's why I asked Lieutenant Davidson if he could send out a hunting party tomorrow."

"And you figured maybe I ought to take charge of that hunting party," Jamie guessed.

Mackey grinned and said, "You're the famous frontiersman, sir, not any of us. You'd know what you were doing."

"You don't have to flatter me, Corporal. I

think it's a good idea, and I'll be ranging out away from the wagons, anyway. I don't mind taking a few fellas along with me so they can haul back some meat if we run across any game."

"I'm glad to hear it, sir, and I have just one more question for you." Mackey paused. "Is it all right if I come along with you?"

Tyler spoke up for the first time, saying, "I didn't think anybody could pry you away from that wagon, Mackey."

"That's just it, sir. My rear end's spent every day for a week planted on that hard wagon seat. It's getting a little tired!"

Tyler laughed and said, "All right, Corporal. If Mr. MacCallister is agreeable, I don't see why you couldn't go. One of the other men can drive that wagon for a day."

"It's fine with me, Corporal," Jamie said. "I'll be happy to have you along."

"Should I ask Lieutenant Davidson, too, sir?" Mackey asked Tyler.

"B Troop is still my troop," Tyler responded, his voice hardening slightly. "I think I can make decisions as to who should handle which job. If Lieutenant Davidson doesn't agree, I'm sure he'll let me know about it."

"I reckon you can count on that," Jamie drawled.

The next morning, as Jamie was getting his horse ready to ride, Lieutenant Davidson came over to him and said, "I know that you're taking several men with you today to form a hunting party, MacCallister."

"That's right."

"It was my idea, you know. Something to improve the men's morale."

That absolutely wasn't true — the hunting party had been Corporal Mackey's suggestion — but Jamie didn't point out that he knew better. If Davidson wanted to be that petty, he could go right ahead.

Davidson continued, "I'm sending along Sergeant O'Connor as well."

Jamie straightened from tightening the cinch on his saddle and frowned as he turned to face Davidson. He said, "I'm not sure that's a good idea, Lieutenant."

"I can't order men under my command away from the column and into potential danger without at least a noncommissioned officer along to take charge of the detail."

"What about Corporal Mackey?"

"A cook and a wagon driver." Davidson's dismissive wave of his hand matched the tone of his voice. "He has no command experience."

"Anyway, I sort of figured the troopers would do what I told them."

"You're not an officer." Davidson's voice made it sound like Jamie was a lunatic for even suggesting such a thing. "You're not even a soldier."

"But I know what I'm doing out here. I reckon that ought to count for something."

"Nevertheless, my decision is that Sergeant O'Connor *is* going along," Davidson insisted, "and I expect that you'll treat him with the appropriate respect a civilian should display to a noncommissioned officer."

"The fella's tried more than once to stove my head in," Jamie said tightly.

"According to the sergeant, he was simply protecting himself from your aggressive actions."

"And you believe him."

Jamie's words weren't a question, but Davidson responded to it as one, anyway, saying, "That's right. I'll take the word of a soldier over that of a civilian any day."

Jamie didn't like the idea, not one little bit, but he could tell by the expression on Davidson's face that the lieutenant was going to be stubborn about it. So he nodded and said, "All right. But if O'Connor does something foolish and gets himself in trouble, I'm not going to be responsible for it."

"Just do your job," Davidson snapped. He turned on his heel and stalked away.

Jamie scowled but finished getting his horse ready. When he was done, he led the mount over to where Corporal Mackey and three more troopers stood waiting with their horses.

"I saw you talking to the lieutenant, Mr. MacCallister," said Mackey. "Is there some problem?"

"You could say that," Jamie muttered, but before he could explain, Sergeant Liam O'Connor strode up with the usual sneer on his rugged face. He was leading a horse of his own.

"Mount up," O'Conner snapped at the men. Their faces fell as they realized what this development meant.

"You're coming with us, Sergeant?" asked Mackey.

"That's right. Lieutenant Davidson knows he can't trust a bunch of numbskulls like you to do what you're supposed to. Hell, if it was up to me, I wouldn't let *you* get anywhere near a rifle, Mackey. You're not fit for any job that doesn't involve jackasses or pots and pans!"

Mackey looked like he wanted to take a

swing at O'Connor. Jamie caught the corporal's eye and gave a little shake of his head to let Mackey know he shouldn't lose his temper. That wouldn't accomplish anything and would just get Mackey in trouble.

Anyway, O'Connor had moved on to another target for his wrath. He swung toward Jamie and said, "As for you, MacCallister, don't try giving me any orders out there. As a matter of fact, *I'm* in command of this hunting party. The lieutenant said so. So you'll do what *I* tell you, not the other way around, understand?"

"Don't push your luck, O'Connor," Jamie said in a flat, hard voice. "Let's just go out there and see if we can find some game."

"You didn't agree to obey my orders."

"That's right," Jamie said. "I didn't."

O'Connor glared at him for a moment longer, then swung up into his saddle and jerked his horse around.

"Come on," he barked at Mackey and the other troopers. "MacCallister, you can come with us or go to hell, I don't care either way."

As O'Connor rode off, Corporal Mackey said quietly, but with a note of desperation in his voice, "Mr. MacCallister, you're still coming with us, aren't you?"

"I reckon I'd better," Jamie said.

Otherwise, he thought, this hunting party might not ever come back.

Otherwise, he thought, this hunting party
might not even come back.

CHAPTER 16

Jamie rode with Corporal Mackey beside
him. Sergeant O'Connor was off to the right
of them about twenty yards, and the other
three troopers — Privates Albright, Jenkins,
and Stallworth — trailed behind. Jamie had
advised the men not to talk too much and
to keep their voices down when they did.
Voices carried out here on the prairie, and
Jamie didn't want to spook any game they
might come across.

O'Connor hadn't looked happy about
that. Not because he disagreed, necessarily,
thought Jamie, but rather because the
sergeant didn't like the idea of anyone else
giving orders. O'Connor had gone along
with it, though, and stayed relatively quiet
during the morning.

So far they hadn't come across any wildlife
except rabbits and prairie chickens, and as
Jamie explained to the others, such small
game wasn't worth messing with when they

were after fresh meat for a whole troop of hungry dragoons.

"Yeah, I reckon you'd have to kill a bunch of rabbits to satisfy those appetites," Mackey commented with a smile. "Nobody can eat like soldiers."

"I don't know about that," Jamie said. "I've known some fur trappers and bull-whackers and keelboaters who can really put away the grub."

They rode on mostly in silence. At midday they paused to make a skimpy meal on some salt pork and biscuits they had brought with them. Then, to let the horses rest and graze some, the men sprawled on the ground and took it easy themselves for a while.

"I wish we'd brought along some coffee and a pot," Private Albright said. The Platte River was still in sight, about a quarter of a mile to the south, so they could have gotten water there.

Jamie sat there with his knees drawn up and his forearms resting easily on them. His eyes narrowed as he gazed to the northwest.

Corporal Mackey noticed the big frontiersman's intent look and asked, "Is something wrong, Mr. MacCallister?"

"Nope. Maybe something right." Jamie lifted an arm and pointed. "Look yonder."

O'Connor was lying on his back, a ways apart from the other men just as he had ridden during the morning. He sat up now, looked in the direction Jamie was indicating, and said, "I don't see a damned thing."

"Look closer," Jamie advised.

O'Connor's frown deepened as he peered toward the northwest. All the troopers were sitting up and looking now. After a moment, O'Connor shook his head and said, "I still don't see it."

Jamie stood up, slapped dirt and grass off the seat of his trousers, and said, "There's dust in the air, a good-sized cloud of it. It's a little thin, and that makes it hard to see, but it's there."

Corporal Mackey scrambled to his feet as well and asked, "What's causing it, Mr. MacCallister?"

"Only thing I know of that would kick up that much dust is a herd of buffalo."

That brought excited exclamations from the other three troopers. O'Connor didn't look as impressed. He said, "We've heard all about how these plains are supposed to be covered with buffalo, and we haven't seen any of them yet. I'm starting to think they're not really out here."

"Oh, they're here, all right," said Jamie. "During the winter, the herds drift pretty far to the south, where the grazing is better and the weather's not as bad, and then during the spring they start meandering back up this way. What you've got to remember about a buffalo is that he hardly ever gets in a hurry." Jamie grunted. "Of course, when he *does* get upset about something and starts to run, you don't want to be in his way."

"Are we going to try to find that herd?" Mackey asked.

"Buffalo's pretty good eating. And if we bring down a few of them, we can skin them and have plenty of meat ready to roast by the time the wagons and the rest of the troop catch up with us."

"What if they stampede?" Private Jenkins asked nervously.

"We'll try to make sure they don't come in our direction," Jamie replied with a faint smile. "Let's get ready to ride."

"Hold on a minute," O'Connor snapped. "I haven't said we were going after any damn buffalo."

"I am," Jamie told him bluntly. "You can make up your own mind."

O'Connor looked like he wanted to argue, but after a couple of seconds, he jerked his head toward the horses and told the troopers, "Get mounted."

The five men rode toward the area where Jamie had spotted the dust. As they came closer, the grayish-yellow cloud became easier to see.

"Are they stampeding?" Corporal Mackey asked.

"No, if they were running, they'd be kicking up a heap more dust than that," Jamie replied. "You wouldn't have had any trouble spotting it. I think they're just ambling along, looking for a good place to graze."

"Are our rifles powerful enough to kill a buffalo?" asked Private Stallworth. "I've heard that they're enormous creatures."

"Twelve feet tall at the shoulder, that's what I heard," Private Albright added. "And their heads are so big, you need a wagon to haul one in."

Jamie couldn't stop himself from laughing. He said, "Buffs are big, all right, but not that size. A middling big one would run about half that." He grew more serious as he went on, "But don't let that make you take them lightly. Like I said, you don't want to get in their way. They'll hit you like a runaway locomotive on one of those railroad lines back east."

"What about the rifles, though?" Corporal Mackey pressed. "Can we use them to kill buffalo?"

"Just don't shoot the varmints in the head," Jamie advised. "Their skulls are thick enough that most bullets will just bounce off. They're like any other kind of game animal. You want to target your shots so you take 'em in the heart or lungs. Heart's better." He paused. "That's a quicker kill. I'd just as soon not see any creature suffer any more than necessary."

O'Connor let out a harsh laugh and said, "I wouldn't think a big, bold frontiersman like you would care about such a thing, MacCallister. They're just dumb animals."

"That's right," Jamie said. "That means they hadn't done anything to deserve to suffer. Not like some two-legged critters I've come across, who had whatever they got coming to them."

O'Connor drew in a sharp breath and scowled. He asked, "You're talkin' about me, are you?"

"I didn't say that."

But Jamie didn't deny it, either.

O'Connor subsided into a sullen silence as the hunting party rode on. After several minutes, Jamie pointed again and went on, "Look how the dust cloud is thinning and breaking up. That means the herd has stopped moving. They'll be grazing for a while now. If nothing disturbed them, they'd probably settle down for the night right where they are."

"But we're going to disturb them, aren't we?" said Corporal Mackey.

"That's the plan," Jamie agreed.

More time went by, and a large, dark mass came into view up ahead, unmoving and low to the ground.

"That can't be the herd," Mackey said. "It's too big."

"That's it, all right," Jamie said, nodding. "Some of those herds have millions and millions of buffalo in them. I've heard men talking about sitting on a hill and watching a herd go by all day and all night, and it still hasn't all passed by the next morning."

"There can't be that many buffalo in the whole world," Private Albright said in awe.

Jamie looked over his shoulder with a smile on his rugged face and said, "That's just *one* herd I'm talking about, son. There are a lot of different bunches out here, scattered from up in Canada almost all the way down to Mexico. All the Indian tribes live on them, using the meat, the hides, the bones, the guts, everything about them."

"Then we should get rid of the buffalo," said Sergeant O'Connor, "because that'd make it easier to get rid of the filthy redskins, once and for all."

"I don't reckon the buffalo will ever be gone," Jamie said, "but if that ever happens, it'll be a sad day."

And the same was true of the Indians, he thought.

As the riders came closer to the herd, Jamie motioned to the others and said quietly, "All right, it's more important than ever not to make much noise now. Buffalo can't see very well, but they've got good senses of hearing and smell. The wind's blowing toward us, so they shouldn't catch our scent, but we don't want them to hear us sneaking up on them, either. Let's get down and go ahead on foot."

For a second, he thought about telling O'Connor to stay there and hold the horses. But he knew the sergeant would never go along with that, so instead, when he had swung down from the saddle, he said, "Private Jenkins, you stay here and hang on to these mounts for us. I'll let you know when to bring them on up."

"Yes, sir, Mr. MacCallister," the trooper responded.

O'Connor snorted disgustedly and said, "Jenkins, you ought to show that much respect to Lieutenant Davidson when you talk to him."

"Yes, Sergeant O'Connor," Jenkins said.

"I'll try to remember that." He didn't sound very sincere about that.

O'Conner glared at him for a second, then turned to Jamie and said, "What do we do now?"

"Your rifles should be loaded and primed. We'll walk ahead until we're in range, then stop and pick out our targets. We'll probably only have time for one volley. We might be able to reload and get off a second shot before the rest of the herd spooks and takes off. But most likely not, so make that first shot count."

Mackey, Albright, and Stallworth nodded. O'Connor just looked vaguely hostile.

Side by side, the five men started forward at a deliberate pace.

Jamie was at the right end of the line, with Mackey next to him on his left, then Stallworth, then Albright, and finally O'Connor at the left end. Jamie didn't care how they were arranged as long as they all did what he told them to do.

Soon they were close enough that instead of a large, amorphous dark blob, they were able to see individual buffalo and make out some details in the animals nearest to them. The huge, shaggy beasts stood with their heads down as they grazed contentedly. Jamie and his companions approached until they were a hundred yards away from the edge of the herd.

"Good Lord," Albright breathed. "There are so *many* of them. If they ever *did* stampede in this direction, there's no way we could escape. We'd be goners."

"They're not coming this way," Jamie said. "They'll run away from the sound of the shots." He raised the heavy Sharps. "Draw your beads, and make sure none of you are aiming at the same buff."

The troopers lifted their rifles and pressed their cheeks to the stocks. Jamie aimed his Sharps at a massive bull that might weigh close to a ton.

"Wait for me to give the word," he whispered.

Before that could happen, however, quick movement came from the other end of the line. Jamie saw it from the corner of his eye and looked in that direction in time to see O'Connor swinging his rifle to the south.

"Indians!" the sergeant yelled. "They're attacking us!"

"No!" Jamie said. "Don't —"

It was too late. O'Connor pressed the trigger, and his rifle went off with a loud blast that echoed across the plains.

CHAPTER 17

Preacher knew his Sharps could bring down a buffalo at a distance of several hundred yards, but his Crow friends didn't have that luxury. They had to get a lot closer than that for their arrows to be effective. Back in the village, there were a few old muskets, but they were even less suitable for hunting buffalo than bows and arrows.

So as they approached the vast herd, Broken Pine said, "I ask that you not shoot, Preacher. Allow us to go among them."

Preacher nodded in both agreement and understanding. The Crow were good horsemen. Not as good as the Sioux, the Pawnee, the Cheyenne, and the other tribes that spent most of their time on the Great Plains, carrying out all their hunts from horseback. But the Crow were capable of riding among the buffalo, dashing alongside as the shaggy beasts stampeded, and driving arrows through their thick hides until the buffalo collapsed.

"You go ahead," Preacher said from atop the slight rise where the Crow hunting party had come to a halt to study the buffalo herd. The mountain man chuckled. "I'll wait here and enjoy the show."

Preacher dismounted and called Dog to him. The big cur sat beside him. Preacher laughed again when he heard Dog whine quietly.

"Yeah, I know you'd like to go out there and chase them buffs around. Hawk and his friends don't need you spookin' 'em, though. Just stay here with me, and I'll make sure you get a bloody haunch later on."

Preacher and his friends had ridden quite a distance to the south, then swung back to the northeast to approach the herd. That way the Crow hunters wouldn't be coming in with the wind at their backs. That would have carried their scent to the buffalo. The big beasts were a mite stupid, but they still had a survival instinct and knew to run away when they smelled humans.

Broken Pine and Hawk That Soars rode in front of the others. As chief, Broken Pine would have the honor of leading, and he must have told Hawk to come with him. The others were close behind and would be ready to dash into the herd as soon as the time came.

There was considerable danger in this method of hunting. The buffalo were lumbering creatures, but once they had built up some speed, they could move fairly fast. If a pony placed a hoof wrong and fell, horse and rider both were almost certainly doomed. The shaggy brown tide would roll over them, and what was left would barely resemble anything that had ever been alive. Preacher had witnessed such grim, deadly accidents before.

It was thrilling, though, no doubt about that. Watching the nimble-footed ponies darting and weaving among the leviathans, guided unerringly by the slightest touch of a knee or a moccasin-shod foot . . . that was enough to make any man's heart pound with excitement, even one as experienced in life on the frontier as Preacher.

Hawk and Broken Pine were moving faster now as they urged their ponies toward the herd. Behind them, Big Thunder and the others did likewise. The warriors drew arrows and nocked them on their bows.

Preacher frowned suddenly as he caught sight of something on the prairie beyond the hunting party. They were just dark shapes at first, but as Preacher's keen eyes narrowed, he realized he was looking at men standing there, and even farther away, several horses. Another bunch of hunters after the buffalo . . . ?

He saw a spurt of grayish-white smoke and a second later heard the flat boom of a rifle shot. Preacher stiffened, and his hand tightened on the Sharps he carried.

Somebody else was out there on the plains, all right, and they were shooting at Preacher's son and friends!

As Preacher watched, one of the warriors jerked but didn't fall off his pony. Preacher figured the man had been hit and could only hope the warrior wasn't wounded too badly. And he was human enough to be glad that it wasn't Hawk who was hurt.

More shots boomed in the distance, accompanied by puffs of powdersmoke. Dog barked in alarm. Preacher said, "I know," and turned quickly toward Horse. "All hell's breakin' loose out there."

He vaulted into the saddle with a grace and agility that belied his age. A touch of his heels sent Horse bursting forward into a gallop. Preacher saw that Hawk, Broken Pine, and the other warriors had wheeled around and were riding hard back toward the little swell from which the mountain man had been watching the buffalo hunt.

But now the men who had attacked them were mounted and charging after them.

Preacher hauled Horse to a halt and lifted the Sharps. He aimed at the attackers, who had to be close to half a mile away. The Sharps would carry that far. While hunting, Preacher had knocked down mountain goats at that range. He hadn't been aiming from horseback, though, at moving targets.

He pulled in a deep breath and held it as he drew a bead on one of the riders. He might not score a hit, but he figured he would come close enough to spook them and break up their charge. As his eyes narrowed slightly, he stroked the trigger.

The Sharps boomed like thunder and kicked hard against his shoulder. In the distance, one of the riders slewed around in his saddle and toppled off his horse. Preacher smiled grimly as he lowered the rifle.

One of the other riders slowed and turned his horse to see about the fallen man. But the others continued pursuing Hawk, Broken Pine, and the other warriors. One of the men — Big Thunder, judging by the size of him — rode close to the wounded warrior and held on to his arm to support him.

Preacher reloaded the Sharps as his son and friends galloped toward him. He waved them on, and they swept past him and disappeared over the rise. Preacher wheeled Horse and followed them, with Dog running and barking beside him.

That little swell of ground would give them some cover, thought Preacher. They could fort up there . . . and then those varmints would discover that they had bitten off a lot bigger chunk than they could chew!

"Damn it, no!" Jamie shouted even though he knew it wasn't going to do any good. Not at this point. O'Connor had already made a terrible mistake.

Jamie could only hope that it wasn't going to get all of them killed.

The mounted Indians were too far away for Jamie to make out many details about them. He couldn't tell what tribe they belonged to, although he didn't think they were Pawnee. He wasn't even sure exactly how many there were, since the shot had caused them to mill around a little.

"Open fire!" O'Connor bellowed. "Shoot those savages!"

"Don't —" Jamie began, but Privates Albright and Stallworth ignored him. They had lowered their rifles in surprise when O'Connor fired, but now they jerked the weapons to their shoulders, pointed them roughly in the direction of the Indians, and pulled the triggers. Jamie didn't think they were going to hit anything, but just the fact that they were shooting at those warriors was going to make the situation worse.

Hoofbeats thudded behind them. Jamie looked around and saw Private Jenkins hurrying toward them, bringing the horses with him in response to urgent arm waves from O'Connor.

"Mount up!" the sergeant yelled. "We're going after those redskins!"

"Blast it, stop this!" Jamie said. "You don't have any reason to pursue those men."

"They attacked us!" insisted O'Connor. "They had their bows and arrows ready to shoot us!"

Jamie knew then that the Indians must have been after some of those buffalo, too. They were a peaceful hunting party, ready to dash among the herd, start the buffs running, and pepper some of them with arrows until the beasts collapsed. He had witnessed such things many times.

O'Connor, in his ignorance and inexperience and arrogance, had mistaken that for an attack on them and had responded violently, without thinking. Now he was trying to aggravate the problem even more.

"Mount up!" the sergeant shouted again. The troopers started to climb onto their horses.

"Mackey!" Jamie snapped. "Don't do this."

The corporal had a miserable expression on his round face as he hesitated and turned to Jamie.

"The sergeant gave us a direct order, Mr. MacCallister," he said. "We can't just ignore it."

"I'll have you in irons, Mackey!" roared O'Connor.

Mackey just glanced at Jamie again, shook his head, and stepped up into the saddle. The others, including O'Connor, were mounted by now, and with the sergeant in the lead, they thundered after the Indians, who appeared to be heading for a small rise not far away. Jamie figured they intended to take cover there and put up a fight.

If they did that, O'Connor was liable to lead those soldiers blindly to their deaths.

Grimacing, Jamie swung up into his saddle and galloped after them, hoping he could still do something to head off this disaster.

Before he could catch up, he heard a boom from somewhere up ahead. One of the troopers jerked in the saddle and then fell off his horse. Jamie couldn't tell which

231

of the soldiers had been hit, but none of them deserved it. This was all O'Connor's doing. Chances were, the Indians would have left them alone if O'Connor hadn't shot one of them.

The gunshot puzzled Jamie, though. From the sound of it, he thought the shot might have been fired from a Sharps like the one he carried. Some Indians had firearms, although such a thing was rare and usually the guns were old and not that effective. The Sharps was a fairly new design, though.

The man who had been shot off his horse was lying on the ground, writhing in pain. At least he wasn't dead . . . yet . . . thought Jamie. One of the other soldiers turned back, probably to aid the wounded man.

As Jamie rode closer, he recognized the man on the ground as Private Jenkins. The one who'd turned back was Corporal Mackey, which came as no surprise to Jamie. The corporal was conscientious and would want to know how badly his comrade was hurt.

O'Connor, Albright, and Stallworth continued to pursue the Indians.

Jamie and Mackey reached Jenkins at the same time. Jamie was out of the saddle and on the ground before his horse even stopped moving. He dropped to a knee beside the wounded private.

The upper left arm of Jenkins' uniform tunic had a dark stain on it. Jamie didn't see blood anywhere else. He put a hand on Jenkins' shoulder to stop him from jerking around.

"Take it easy, son," Jamie said. "I don't think you're hurt too bad."

Mackey had dismounted, too. He knelt on Jenkins' other side and asked, "Where was he hit?"

"Left arm, looks like." Jamie felt around on Jenkins' torso. "Doesn't seem to be any other wounds. Let's see how bad this one is."

Jenkins had subsided a little now. He had been writhing around in panic as much as pain, Jamie thought. Now the young soldier lay there on his back, face pale and eyes wide as he panted.

Jamie pulled out his knife, cut through the sleeve of Jenkins' tunic, and then ripped a piece of it downward to reveal the wound. There was quite a bit of blood, but Jamie could tell that the bullet had just plowed a shallow furrow in the outside of Jenkins' upper arm.

"You're going to be fine, Private," Jamie assured him. "We just need to clean that wound and bandage it up some. Your arm will be a mite stiff and sore for a while, but there shouldn't be any lasting damage."

Jenkins gulped and asked, "You mean I . . . I'm not going to die?"

"Not from this." Jamie glanced after O'Connor and the others. "Although I don't make any promises about what other stupid thing that sergeant of yours might do."

Corporal Mackey got to his feet and said, "If Jenkins is going to be all right, I have to go after Sergeant O'Connor and Albright and Stallworth."

"You'd better not," Jamie said in all seriousness. "They're going to get themselves killed, charging after those Indians like that." A note of anger came into his voice as he added, "That was just a harmless hunting party. They would have left us alone. Now, because of O'Connor, their blood's up and there's no telling what they might do."

Mackey swallowed hard and said, "All the more reason for me to do my duty, Mr. MacCallister."

"Do what you have to, son," Jamie said as he jerked his head in a curt nod. "I'll look after Jenkins here."

Mackey started to turn away and reach for his mount's dangling reins. As he did so, he paused and said, "Wait a minute. It looks like they're coming back."

Jamie lifted his gaze and saw that the corporal was right. O'Connor, Albright, and Stallworth had turned their horses and were headed this way at a hard run. A few arrows flew around them. Other shafts fell just short, burying their heads in the ground right behind the flashing hooves. That Sharps boomed again, and Jamie grunted as he saw dirt geyser into the air about ten feet to O'Connor's left.

Jamie closed a hand around Jenkins' uninjured arm and hauled the private to his feet. That made Jenkins gasp.

"Come on," Jamie said to his companions. "We'd better pull back some, or else whoever has that Sharps is gonna be taking potshots at *us* before you know it!"

CHAPTER 18

Preacher rode over the rise, dropped out of the saddle, and swatted Horse on the rump so the gray stallion would run off for a ways and be out of the line of fire. Carrying the Sharps, the mountain man turned back to his friends.

The warriors had dismounted and sent their ponies running on to safety, as well. As Preacher hurried to join them, he saw that Swift Water was the one who had been wounded. The sturdy warrior lay there, breathing hard as one of the men held a handful of grass to a bloody patch on his side, trying to slow down the bleeding.

"I . . . I am ready to fight!" Swift Water managed to say. "Let me . . . fight!"

Broken Pine knelt beside him and touched his shoulder, saying, "Rest, my friend. You will fight another day. Today, we will deal with our enemies."

Hawk stepped up beside Preacher and

said in a low voice, "Preacher, those are white men. They wear blue and white clothes, like the soldiers we saw in St. Louis. And you shot one of them."

"I know," said Preacher, his voice hard and grim. "I saw that, too, just about the time I was squeezin' the trigger. But they were comin' after you and these other boys, so I wasn't gonna worry too much about what they was wearin'."

"The white man's law may come after you for shooting a soldier."

"Right now, I don't give a damn about that," Preacher declared. "Those sorry sons o' bitches might've killed you or Broken Pine or Big Thunder, instead of just woundin' Swift Water. For that matter, we ain't sure yet how bad he's hurt, and he's a mighty good fella, too. So I don't care. Somebody shoots at me and my friends, he's gettin' some lead comin' back his way."

Broken Pine said, "Big Thunder, hold this grass against Swift Water's wound. The rest of you, come with me."

Like the other warriors, once the shooting started Broken Pine had put the arrow he'd had nocked back into the quiver of shafts slung over his shoulder. He drew one now and readied it as he eased up to the crest of the little rise. The rest of the hunting party, including Hawk, joined their chief. Preacher stretched out on his belly beside them to watch the soldiers riding closer.

"There are only three of them now," Broken Pine said, "and yet they pursue and intend to do battle with us. They are foolish, like most white men."

He came up on his knees, drew back the bow, and loosed the arrow toward the soldiers. The other warriors followed his example. The flint-tipped missiles arched through the air and came down around the white men, narrowly missing.

Before those arrows even landed, another volley was on the way. These came even closer, although none of them struck any of the riders.

Frantically, the white soldiers yanked their mounts to a stop, wheeled the animals around, and began riding back the other way. That didn't stop Broken Pine, Hawk, and the others from firing yet another flight of arrows after them.

Preacher figured it might be a good idea to hurry them on their way even more, so he lined up the Sharps and fired again, deliberately pulling his shot a little wide. The soldiers leaned forward in their saddles and urged their horses on faster.

"Look at them run!" said one of the warriors. "They are full of fear!"

"We should go after them and kill them all!" another man urged.

"Many Pelts was right," said a third warrior. "No white men can be trusted! They should all be driven far away — or killed!"

Hawk glanced over at Preacher. Neither of them liked to hear talk like this. It could only stir up more trouble. And these warriors, like most Indians, really didn't understand just how *many* white men there were. Hawk had seen the teeming swarms in St. Louis, and Preacher had been to some of the even larger cities back east. If it ever came down to an outright war between white men and red men, it probably wasn't going to end well for the vastly outnumbered Indians.

Preacher knew he couldn't say that to them, though. The mood they were in right now, they wouldn't listen to such a warning if it came from a white man. He couldn't blame them for feeling that way, either. They hadn't attacked the soldiers, probably hadn't even noticed them yet, when they had come under attack themselves.

Being half-Indian, though, Hawk could risk speaking up. He said, "The best thing for us to do is to leave them alone and let them go on their way. One of their men is wounded, as was one of ours. Let there be an end to fighting."

At one time, Hawk would have found it difficult to advise such a thing. He'd been as hotheaded and ready to fight as any of his friends. He had grown wiser in the past ten years, reflected Preacher . . . although some of the Crow warriors doubtless would say that he had become too timid.

"We cannot allow this to go unavenged," one of the men argued. "And it was Preacher who wounded the white man, not one of us! We must have vengeance for Swift Water!"

That brought mutters of agreement from most of the other warriors.

Preacher couldn't stay silent. He said, "Swift Water ain't dead. But if you keep up this fight, there's a mighty good chance some of you will wind up that way."

"No true warrior fears death in a cause that is right!"

Preacher couldn't argue with that sentiment. He felt the same way. But he had already thought of something that hadn't occurred to his Crow friends: that small group of soldiers hadn't come 'way out here on the plains by themselves. Somewhere, probably not too far away, was a bigger bunch.

Maybe a whole heap bigger.

He might have pointed that out to the Crow and made that argument, but before he could do so, a rattle of gunfire sounded. Something hummed past Preacher's head. He had been shot at enough times, and experienced enough near misses, to recognize the wind-rip of a bullet when he heard one.

"Get your heads down!" he barked. "They're shootin' at us."

As he and the Indians stretched out just below the swell of earth, more shots crackled. Preacher took his hat off and eased his head up for a better look. He couldn't see any men or horses out there, but he saw clouds of powdersmoke hanging in the air. The soldiers had gone to ground, found some cover of their own, and opened fire.

They didn't want this fight to be over with, either.

Corporal Mackey led the three horses while Jamie helped the wounded Private Jenkins retreat. Jamie had spotted a couple of old buffalo wallows that would be better shelter than nothing. He lowered Jenkins to the ground in one of them and waved Mackey on.

"Go back yonder at least a hundred yards

and then picket those horses," he told the corporal. "They won't be out of range of that Sharps, but at least it'll take a longer shot to hit any of them. Then come back here and bring your rifle."

"I . . . I dropped my rifle when I got shot," Jenkins said.

"I know, son. That's all right. You're not in any shape to be shooting, anyway."

Jamie knelt beside the wounded man, pulled a bandanna from his pocket, and knotted it around Jenkins' arm. The wound would still need to be cleaned as soon as there was a chance, but at least that makeshift bandage would slow down and maybe stop the bleeding from it.

Then he stood up and waved his hat over his head to get the attention of O'Connor, Albright, and Stallworth. The three men swerved toward him as they slowed their mounts.

"I sent Mackey back yonder with the other horses," Jamie told them. "Take your horses and picket them, too, then come back to these buffalo wallows. The Indians have gone to ground on the other side of that little rise, so we're out of arrow range here."

"Why don't we just go back to the wagons?" Stallworth asked.

"Because that fella with the Sharps is liable to pick off one or two of us if we try. But if we hunker down here, we can wait for the wagons and the rest of the troop to come to us, and those Indians will light a shuck when they see a force that size coming toward them."

Judging by the expression on his face, Sergeant O'Connor didn't like Jamie making decisions and giving orders that way. For the time being, though, he kept any response to himself.

Within a few minutes, the horses were all picketed to the rear and the six men were stretched out in the small depressions, three in each of the buffalo wallows. Jamie was in the one with Mackey and Jenkins. O'Connor called to them, "Keep up a steady fire on that rise! I want those redskins to stay pinned down!"

Mackey looked inquiringly at Jamie, who said, "Go ahead and do what he says, Corporal. I don't think you're going to hit anybody over there, but all it costs you to try is a little powder and shot." Jamie chuckled, but there wasn't much humor in the sound. "O'Connor's wrong about them being pinned down, though. If they pull back away from that rise, we can't do a thing to stop them."

"Do you think there's a chance they might

do that?" Mackey asked with a note of hope in his voice.

Jamie shook his head and said, "It's not very likely as long as they've got us outnumbered even a little bit, and from what little I saw of them, I'm convinced they do. O'Connor shot one of them. We don't know how bad he was hit. If he's dead, or hurt bad, his friends won't just forget that. They'll want to settle the score for him. If there were more of them, they probably would have overrun us by now, even though we would've killed a few of them, more than likely."

"Sergeant O'Connor shouldn't have shot at them and started this fight in the first place."

"You're right about that, Corporal."

"It wouldn't do any good to tell Lieutenant Davidson about it, though," Mackey said. "He wouldn't believe the sergeant did anything wrong. He'd just find a way to make it all *your* fault, Mr. MacCallister."

"More than likely," Jamie agreed, smiling ruefully.

Shots began ringing out from the other buffalo wallow. Mackey joined in, firing slowly and deliberately and not rushing his reloading between rounds.

Jamie didn't fire. He had something else

244

in mind.

After a while, when he had given both sides a chance to settle in to this standoff, he said to Mackey, "I'm going to see if I can circle around and get behind them, Corporal. I want to take a better look at that bunch."

"Why, Mr. MacCallister? So you can see which tribe they belong to?"

"That, and I'm curious about that Sharps rifle they've got. I wouldn't have expected any Indians to have one yet."

"They probably took it off some white man they killed, didn't they?" Mackey asked with a frown.

"That's the most likely explanation, I reckon, but I'd like to see for myself." Jamie rubbed his chin. "Could be there's a white man traveling with them, and the Sharps belongs to him."

Private Jenkins asked, "What sort of *traitor* would do that, sir?"

"Plenty of white men feel some sympathy, even liking, for the Indians," said Jamie. "I do myself . . . although it's a little hard for me to do that since the Shawnee wiped out my family when I was a boy and carried me off to make me a slave for years."

Jenkins' eyes widened. He said, "Seems to me like you'd want to kill all of them, no matter what tribe."

Jamie shook his head.

"This bunch didn't have anything to do with that. I've read that in some parts of the world, folks still hold grudges against other kinds of folks because of things their ancestors did hundreds of years ago. That never made a lick of sense to me."

Staying low in the grass, Jamie began to back away from the other two. Corporal Mackey called after him, "Be careful, Mr. MacCallister!"

Over in the other buffalo wallow, Sergeant O'Connor lowered his rifle as he noticed what Jamie was doing.

"MacCallister!" he yelled. "MacCallister, what are you doin'? Are you runnin' out on us, you son of a —"

"He's going to circle around and get behind the Indians, Sergeant," Mackey interrupted. He started to make a gesture to describe what Jamie was doing, then evidently thought better of it. The Indians wouldn't be able to hear much of what was said, but they might see Mackey's motions and figure them out. So the corporal just went on, "He's not deserting us."

Jamie heard that exchange. It annoyed him that O'Connor would think he would run out on them and try to save his own

246

skin. It didn't particularly surprise him, though. Somebody like O'Connor would always think the worst.

He stayed low until he had moved back several hundred yards and could no longer see the rise where the Indians had taken cover. Then he began trotting to the west and didn't curve back to the north until he had gone at least half a mile.

It took Jamie a good while to make the big circle that was going to take him behind the Indians. As he did that, he continued to hear the troopers' rifles going off.

Not the Sharps, though. The distinctive boom of that high-caliber weapon was significantly missing. Whoever owned it was holding his fire.

Or else he was trying to flank the soldiers and get behind *them* so that he could pick them off . . .

That thought made Jamie move a little faster.

The grass was fairly high and waved back and forth some as a breeze blew across the prairie. Jamie crouched as he approached the rise. As big as he was, he would have to get down on his belly and crawl if he wanted to be completely hidden, and he wasn't going to do that. But at least he tried to make himself less conspicuous.

He came to the spot where the Indian ponies were grazing. They shied away from him, and one of them nickered. Jamie dropped to a knee as up ahead on the rise, one of the warriors heard the sound and turned to look. Jamie froze. After a moment, the Indian turned back around. Jamie waited longer, just to be sure the man wasn't trying to be tricky and pretending not to have seen him. Finally, he resumed his approach.

The warriors definitely weren't Pawnee. He could see them well enough now to know that. Could they be part of the Crow band with the village on the smaller stream above the Sweetwater? The village that was the army detail's destination?

That would be ironic if it was true, thought Jamie. If that was a Crow hunting party, they were quite a distance from home, but it was certainly possible they had ventured out onto the plains in search of a buffalo herd.

He saw now that his speculation about a white man being with the Indians was correct. The man wore a buckskin shirt, as well as brown trousers, boots, and hat. That broad-brimmed hat really identified him as a white man, as well as the crossed gun-belts supporting a pair of holstered revolvers. Jamie had never known an Indian to dress like that. However, the man was clearly an ally to the Crow, if that's what they were.

The white man turned his head to say something to one of the Indians, giving Jamie a better look at him. Something about the craggy face with the dark, drooping mustache immediately struck Jamie as familiar. He had seen that man somewhere before . . .

Recognition hit Jamie like a punch in the gut. It made his memories go back more than twenty years to a place hundreds of miles away, to a time when he and Kate were young, newly married, and on their way to Texas intending to settle there.

But there were enemies on their trail, and they might not have survived the journey if they hadn't encountered a mountain man who helped them. Jamie had run into that same mountain man a few times since then. The frontier, for all its vastness, seemed like a small place at times.

One thing was for sure, he told himself now. If he was right about who that man was, then O'Connor touching off a fight with this bunch was even dumber than Jamie had thought it was.

Feeling certain that he was correct, Jamie

straightened to his full height and strode forward, no longer trying to conceal himself or sneak up on the Indians. One of them, a great big fella who was tending to the wounded man, saw him coming and shouted a warning. Jamie didn't understand all the words, but he recognized the language as the Crow tongue, meaning he'd been right about that, too.

The warriors whirled around, nocking arrows and drawing back bowstrings. But before they could loose the arrows at Jamie, the white man with them called out sharply, telling them to hold their fire. He got to his feet and looked at Jamie with a slight frown on his rugged face.

Jamie walked right up to him, nodded, and said, "It's good to see you again, Preacher. Been a long time."

CHAPTER 19

It took a lot to surprise Preacher, but having this big fella appear seemingly out of nowhere, then walk up and greet him like that almost did the job. The reaction lasted only a heartbeat, though, before Preacher recognized him.

The mountain man stuck out his hand and exclaimed, "Jamie Ian MacCallister! Never expected to run into you out here."

"I don't see why not," Jamie said with a grin as he clasped Preacher's hand in what would have been a bone-crushing grip for most men. The two of them were pretty evenly matched when it came to strength, though. "We sort of travel in the same circles."

Preacher chuckled and said, "Yeah, I reckon that's true."

The Crow warriors still had their bows drawn back. Their faces made it clear that they would like nothing better than to fill

Jamie full of arrows.

Preacher went on, "These fellas are honin' after turning you into a pincushion, Jamie. Walkin' up here like this probably ain't the smartest thing you ever done."

"I figured if they're your friends, they'll likely listen to reason."

"Maybe. Maybe not." Preacher's eyes narrowed as he glanced at the Sharps Jamie held, then at Swift Water. "You're the one who winged my friend there."

"I'm afraid so."

At least some of the Crow spoke enough English to understand that. They drew back on their bows even more, and the rest followed suit.

"But *you're* the one who shot that young dragoon who's with me," continued Jamie, "so I reckon we're sort of square on that score." He looked at Swift Water. "How bad is that fella's wound?"

"From what I've seen, I reckon he'll probably be all right." Preacher paused, then asked, "How about the soldier?"

"Just a graze on his arm. He'll be fine."

Preacher nodded curtly and said, "That's good to know."

"So how about we call a truce?" Jamie suggested. "Nobody's been killed so far, and I'm hankering to keep it that way."

"How many more soldiers are in the bunch those came from?"

"A whole troop, and two supply wagons," Jamie said. "They're probably less than a mile away by now. They may have heard some of those shots earlier, so there's a chance a patrol could show up anytime."

"That's about what I figured," said Preacher as he nodded slowly. He turned to the warriors and went on in Crow, "It would be a good idea for you fellas to put down those bows. There are a lot of white soldiers not far away, and they all have rifles."

"We can fight them!" one of the men said.

"And you can all die." Preacher's tone was grim. "But right now, this is all just a big misunderstandin'. And it was the soldiers who opened fire on us, not the other way around. If we explain that to their commandin' officer —"

Preacher saw the face Jamie made at that. Switching back to English, he said, "You savvy enough Crow to know what I was tellin' them?"

"Yeah. And that commanding officer you were talking about . . . well, he's not the most understanding sort in the world. However, I reckon I can make him see what actually happened here, and *maybe* he won't lose his head. His orders are to go to the village of Chief Broken Pine —"

"I am Broken Pine." The declaration came from Preacher's old friend in English.

Jamie looked a little surprised, but he nodded and said, "It's good to meet you, Chief. I wasn't expecting to run into you this far away from your village."

"The huntin's been bad in these parts," Preacher explained. "We were after those buffalo." He added with a touch of wry humor in his voice, "And those critters must've heard the shootin' and smelled the powdersmoke, because they've all done run off."

Broken Pine said to Jamie, "You and those soldiers are on your way to my village?"

"That's right," Jamie replied.

"Why do you go there?"

"Well . . . I don't know if that's for me to say. My government . . . the leaders of my people . . . they have business with you, Broken Pine. They want to talk to you."

"About a treaty?" Preacher guessed.

"That's about the size of it," Jamie admitted.

Broken Pine looked at Preacher and asked, "What is this . . . treaty?"

"An agreement," the mountain man explained. "A promise that folks make to each other not to fight."

"The Crow do not wish to fight with anyone. Except the Blackfeet, of course."

Preacher had to chuckle at that. He understood the sentiment completely, having been at war with the Blackfeet for many years himself.

While Preacher, Jamie, and Broken Pine were talking, the other Crow warriors had relaxed slightly. The continuing rifle fire from the soldiers kept the tension from going away entirely, though. Preacher said, "You reckon you can do anything about those varmints who keep shootin' at us, Jamie?"

"I can sure try." Jamie looked at Broken Pine. "That is, if the fight's really over for now."

Broken Pine nodded and said in Crow to the others, "Put away your arrows. We will talk instead of fight."

Several of the warriors didn't look happy about that, but Broken Pine was chief and they obeyed his order. Jamie took off his hat, put it on the end of the Sharps' barrel, and moved just below the top of the rise. He raised the hat on the rifle enough that the soldiers couldn't help but see it, then waved it back and forth to make sure he had their attention.

Then he shouted, "Hold your fire! Sergeant O'Connor! Corporal Mackey! Hold your fire! The fight's over!"

The shots had stopped already when Jamie raised his hat. They didn't resume. After a minute or so, Jamie called to the soldiers, "I'm going to stand up now. Don't shoot!"

He got to his feet, took the hat off the rifle barrel, and put it on again. Then he waved his hand to reassure them that everything was all right and turned back to say, "Why don't you come with me, Preacher, and we'll go talk to them?"

"I reckon I can do that," Preacher said. He told Hawk, "Stay here."

"You trust this white man, Preacher?" asked Hawk.

"I sure do. We've known each other a long time. Jamie, this is my son, Hawk That Soars. Hawk, meet Jamie Ian MacCallister. You've heard me talk about him before."

"Yes," said Hawk. "Yes, I have." He still didn't seem too friendly, though, and he didn't acknowledge the introduction other than giving Jamie a curt nod.

"Your son, eh?" Jamie said as he and Preacher walked down the rise and started across the prairie.

"That's right. I've probably got more kids than that scattered around the frontier,"

256

Preacher admitted, "but Hawk's one that I know about for sure. You and Kate have young'uns, Jamie?"

"A whole passel of 'em," Jamie replied with a definite note of pride in his voice.

"And Kate's doing well?"

"Still as beautiful and feisty as ever."

"I'm glad to hear it," Preacher said. "You two always seemed like a mighty good couple, right from the first time I met you down yonder in what they call Indian Territory now."

They walked on for a few moments in silence, then Jamie said, "I'm sure sorry about shooting that fella."

"Swift Water," Preacher supplied the name.

"Swift Water. I hope he's going to be all right. When it happened, I didn't know who those warriors were, only that they were coming after us."

"Because you started shootin' at them."

Jamie shook his head and said, "Not me. That was a fella named O'Connor. Sergeant Liam O'Connor."

"From the sound of your voice, you ain't over fond of this varmint," Preacher commented.

"Not by a long shot," Jamie said. "But I'd appreciate it, just on general principles, if you didn't kill him."

"I'm ain't promisin' nothin'," Preacher said.

The soldiers stood up in the buffalo wallows as Preacher and Jamie came closer. Jamie led the way toward one of the circular depressions where a trooper was on his feet and another sat up on the ground. The soldier who was standing held a rifle, but it was pointed downward.

"This is Corporal Mackey," Jamie introduced the stocky soldier. "Fella sitting there with the wounded arm is Private Jenkins. Boys, this is an old friend of mine who goes by the name of Preacher."

The mountain man nodded and said, "Good to meet you, Corporal." To Jenkins, he went on, "Son, I'm the one who put that graze on your arm. I'd say I'm sorry for doin' that, but it looked like you and the rest of your bunch were tryin' to hurt some friends of mine, so it seemed like the thing to do at the time. I'm glad I didn't kill you, though."

"I . . . I'm glad you didn't, too," Private Jenkins said, clearly nervous.

One of the men from the other buffalo wallow came out of it and stalked toward Preacher and Jamie, holding his rifle as if he were ready to raise it and fire at any moment. His face was flushed, his jaw thrust out defiantly.

"I reckon that must be Sergeant O'Connor," Preacher said. "I don't even need to see the stripes on his sleeve to know that."

"That's him," Jamie confirmed. "He's itching for a fight. He always is."

As O'Connor came closer, he yelled, "Hold it right there, mister!"

"If you're talking to me, I don't appear to be goin' anywhere," drawled Preacher.

O'Connor's face reddened even more as he said, "You're under arrest!"

"What the hell for?"

"Attempted murder of a United States Army dragoon and aidin' those red savages!" O'Connor snapped the rifle to his shoulder and aimed at Preacher. "Drop those guns or I'll blow a hole through you!"

Preacher's right hand itched to claw out the revolver on his hip and commence to work with it. He restrained himself only with an effort.

Jamie must have felt the same way. He said, "O'Connor, you pull that trigger and you'll be dead half a second later. I'll put a bullet through your brain myself. There are plenty of witnesses here to testify that Preacher's not doing anything threatening."

"Preacher?" blustered O'Connor. "What

preacher?"

"That's what they call me," the mountain man said. "I ain't a real sky-pilot, though, if that's what you're thinkin'." Preacher shook his head. "And I don't cotton to bein' put under arrest, so I don't reckon I will be."

Coolly, he turned his back on O'Connor and spoke to Private Jenkins again.

"Like I was sayin', son, I'm glad you're gonna be all right. Hope you'll forgive me for nearly ventilatin' you permanent-like."

Big-eyed, Jenkins gulped and said, "That . . . that's all right, sir. I know it was just . . . uh . . . a misunderstanding, like you said."

"You see, Sergeant," Jamie said, "there's no hard feelings on Private Jenkins' part. And since the Crow have forgiven me for wounding one of their warriors, it seems to me like we can just call the whole thing square."

Preacher wasn't sure the Crow had exactly forgiven Jamie for shooting Swift Water — not all of them, anyway — but he wanted this situation settled down and so did Jamie. For one thing, the rest of the troop would be here soon, and Broken Pine and the other warriors wouldn't stand much of a chance against them.

Sergeant O'Connor continued glaring

over the barrel of his rifle for several more seconds, but finally he lowered the weapon, with obvious reluctance, and said, "Somebody better tell me what the hell's goin' on here. Who are you, mister, and what are you doin' with a bunch of red heathens?"

"They're my friends," Preacher said, "and they ain't heathens. They're Crow. A fine, spiritual bunch of folks."

"And the Indians we're looking for," said Jamie. "In fact, their chief Broken Pine is in that bunch, and he's the one we were sent specifically to find."

O'Connor looked a little confused as he said, "I thought that village was supposed to be up in the foothills."

"It is. Preacher, Broken Pine, and the others are out here on the plains hunting . . . just like us."

Corporal Mackey said, "Somebody's coming!"

They all turned to look. Half a dozen men on horseback galloped toward them. All wore the white trousers, blue tunics, and black caps of army dragoons. One of the riders pulled out in front of the others.

"That's Lieutenant Tyler," Jamie said. "I reckon they heard the shots, and Lieutenant Davidson sent him and a patrol to check them out, just like I expected."

The young officer leading the patrol brought his mount to a skidding, dust-raising stop and quickly dismounted. He looked around, frowning at the sight of the buckskin-clad stranger, and demanded, "Sergeant O'Connor, what's going on here?"

"We had a run-in with some damned savages —" O'Connor began.

"Not exactly," Jamie interrupted him. He waved a hand toward the rise, where Hawk, Broken Pine, and the other warriors were visible, standing with their bows in hand, ready for trouble if it broke out again. "The Indians are members of a Crow hunting party from Broken Pine's village. Broken Pine himself is with them, Lieutenant. In other words . . . we found who we're looking for."

"They attacked us," O'Connor insisted with a surly look on his face.

Preacher said, "You fired the first shot, mister. Don't reckon any of the rest of it would've happened if you hadn't done that."

O'Connor snarled and started to move toward Preacher. The officer, who Jamie had said was Lieutenant Tyler, lifted a hand to stop him and said sharply, "That'll be enough, Sergeant. It appears there's some sort of truce going on here, and I don't see

262

any reason to break it."

Jamie said, "Lieutenant, this is an old friend of mine. Folks call him Preacher. He's part of the Crow hunting party. Preacher, this is Lieutenant Hayden Tyler."

Preacher's eyes narrowed slightly as he asked, "Is this the lieutenant fella you were tellin' me about?"

"No, that's Lieutenant Edgar Davidson. He's the commanding officer of this little expedition."

"In that case . . ." Preacher extended his hand to Tyler. "Pleasure to meet you, Lieutenant."

Tyler coughed a little and shook Preacher's hand.

"How do you do, Mister . . . Preacher, was it?"

"Just Preacher. No mister. That's for fellas who ain't spent their whole lives out here on the frontier."

"I see that Private Jenkins appears to be wounded," Tyler said to Jamie. "Is it serious?"

"Probably hurts like blazes, but he'll be all right."

"That's right, Lieutenant," Jenkins put in. "It hurts like blazes."

"Any other casualties?" asked Tyler.

Jamie shook his head and said, "One of

263

the Crow was wounded, too. We're hoping it's not too bad."

"I hope so, too." Tyler glanced back in the direction he and the dragoons had come from. "The wagons and the rest of the troop will be here soon. I suppose I should go meet this Chief Broken Pine, so I can introduce him to Lieutenant Davidson when they get here."

"Come on with me," Preacher said. "You can leave your horse here. And it'd be better if just you and Jamie came with me to meet Broken Pine. Too many soldiers with rifles marchin' at 'em might spook those fellas, and if that happened we'd have trouble all over again!"

CHAPTER 20

Jamie thought Lieutenant Tyler looked a little nervous as they approached the rise along with Preacher. That was understandable. Tyler had never dealt with the Indians, had never even seen any close up except the ones who had been killed during that battle with the Pawnee.

Tyler didn't flinch, though. He walked with Jamie on his right and Preacher on his left. Most of the Crow warriors displayed hostile expressions as the three white men came up the slope and stopped facing Broken Pine.

Preacher said, "Broken Pine, this is Lieutenant Hayden Tyler of the United States Army. Lieutenant Tyler, Chief Broken Pine of the Crow people."

Tyler nodded and said, "Chief Broken Pine, it is an honor to meet you." He glanced at Preacher as if waiting for the mountain man to translate what he had said.

"I speak your tongue," Broken Pine said. His face was impassive, as if carved from stone. "I need no one to tell me your words."

"Oh. Ah . . . Well, that's good. We can talk to each other and understand."

"What I do not understand is why you attacked a peaceful hunting party that meant you no harm."

Preacher said, "It wasn't the lieutenant who did that. It was another fella, a sergeant named O'Connor. I reckon he spotted you and the others and lost his head. He thought you were hostiles."

"Because all Indians look the same to white men," Hawk said.

"To *some* white men, maybe," Jamie responded. "But I can tell you right now, Sergeant O'Connor and I don't see eye to eye on much of anything."

"Nevertheless," said Tyler, "the sergeant is under my command, and I apologize for what he did, Chief Broken Pine."

"I am not *your* chief," Broken Pine said. "You do not have to call me that."

"Regardless, I'm sorry for what happened. Your man who was wounded . . . is he going to be all right?"

"It seems so."

"I'm glad to hear that. The soldier who was wounded isn't badly hurt, either."

266

Broken Pine just gazed coolly at the young officer, as if to indicate that he didn't care what happened to Private Jenkins.

Jamie was glad to see that Tyler was smart enough to just let that pass. Instead, Tyler went on, "My commanding officer and I have been sent here to speak with you, Broken Pine. I thought that we would have to visit your village in order to do so. Perhaps this meeting, as unfortunate as it was when it started, will prove to be a good thing after all."

"You come to ride into our village without being invited?" Broken Pine shot back at him. "That is the same thing as attacking it."

Jamie said, "We would have sent a small party and asked for permission to speak with you. Most of the soldiers would stay outside the village."

Maybe Lieutenant Davidson would have done that, and maybe he wouldn't, Jamie thought even as he spoke those reassuring words. It was entirely possible that Davidson would have just bulled in with the whole troop and started a battle that would have wrecked the whole mission and gotten a bunch of them killed. With Davidson, it was hard to say.

So in that respect, it actually *was* lucky

267

that they had run into Broken Pine and the other Crow out here on the plains. They might not even have to go to the village in the foothills if they could persuade the chief to come with them back to Fort Kearny.

Jamie went on, "Now you can speak with our commander . . . our chief" — he tried not to grimace when he referred to Davidson that way — "here instead of having to wait until we arrive at the village."

Broken Pine immediately dashed that hope. He shook his head and said, "We will not talk here. Any important talk will be in the village, where all the elders and warriors can take part."

"I'm not sure that's necessary —" Tyler began.

"If Broken Pine says that's the way it'll be, then that's the way it'll be," said Preacher. His tone made it clear there wouldn't be any argument.

"Of course," Tyler said with a quick nod. "But at least, now we can travel to your village with you when you return."

Broken Pine frowned. Jamie sensed that he didn't like the idea but didn't have any reasonable way to refuse the suggestion. After a moment, Broken Pine nodded and said to Tyler, "The soldiers will stay back. You may ride with us, and this one." He nodded toward Jamie.

"I'm not sure how Lieutenant Davidson will feel about . . ." Tyler's voice trailed off, then he nodded agreement, too. "It will be as you say, Broken Pine. But I will have to talk to my commander first and make him understand."

Broken Pine turned away, saying over his shoulder, "Do as you wish. We still must hunt buffalo. The herd will not have gone too far before stopping to graze again."

Preacher said, "I'll come with you, Broken Pine. Jamie, you'd best stay here and make sure everybody knows how things are gonna be."

Jamie regretted missing out on the buffalo hunt, but he knew Preacher was right. Lieutenant Tyler might need his help in dealing with Lieutenant Davidson.

Because if there was a way of ruining what had turned out to be an improbably lucky encounter, Edgar Davidson could probably find it.

"Absolutely not! I refuse to allow some filthy red savage to dictate terms to *me*!"

That was exactly the reaction Jamie expected when Lieutenant Davidson heard what Broken Pine had said. Davidson stood beside one of the wagons with his hands clasped behind his back, trembling slightly with what could only be outrage. His cap's strap was tight under his chin, and his mouth was a grim line turned down at the corners in disapproval.

"Lieutenant, I don't reckon we have a lot of choice in the matter," Jamie said. "Getting Broken Pine to agree to come back to the fort with us is crucial to this mission. We have to do things the way he wants."

"You have no authority here, MacCallister."

Tyler said, "I agree with Mr. MacCallister, Lieutenant. Things could have gone really badly today, but instead we have a chance to salvage the situation and even turn it to our advantage. We can't press Broken Pine too much, though."

Jamie nodded and said, "He'll get his back up and dig his heels in if we're not careful. He's used to giving the orders."

"So am I," Davidson said. "And I'm an officer of the United States Army, not some dirty primitive."

Jamie shook his head and said, "You've got to stop thinking like that, Lieutenant. It's not going to do any of us any good."

Davidson sniffed and turned his head to look at the other man who stood there beside the wagon with them.

"What do you think, Sergeant O'Connor?"

"What do I think?" O'Connor repeated. "I think we ought to clap that damn redskin in irons, drag him back to the fort, sit him down with that treaty in front of him, and tell him to sign it or we'll blow his brains out. Sir."

Davidson cocked an eyebrow at Jamie and Tyler, smirked, and said, "That does sound like an extremely effective way of accomplishing our mission, doesn't it?"

"You do that and you'll have an Indian war on your hands," Jamie told him bluntly. "And the blood of every soldier and every Crow who dies will be on your hands, too, Lieutenant."

"I believe we'd be better served by using restraint," Tyler added. "Broken Pine seemed like a reasonable man. If we treat him reasonably —"

"Riders coming, Sergeant!" one of the guards shouted to O'Connor.

The four men beside the wagon turned to look as other members of the troop responded to the warning as well. Clutching their rifles, men hurried to the side of the temporary camp where two riders on Indian ponies were approaching.

"Better order the men to hold their fire," Jamie said as his keen eyes took in the situ-

271

ation. "Those fellas look like they're bringing us some meat."

Davidson hesitated for a second, then nodded to O'Connor, who bellowed, "Hold your fire!" The sergeant looked like giving that order put a bad taste in his mouth. The troopers who had raised their rifles lowered them, although some seemed reluctant to do so.

As the riders came closer, everyone could see that they were dragging a couple of buffalo hides piled with haunches cut from the animals' carcasses. Jamie recognized one of the warriors as Hawk That Soars, Preacher's half-Absaroka son.

Hawk lifted a hand in the universal signal for peaceful intentions as he and his companion came to a stop. If being faced with dozens of well-armed soldiers who might be a little trigger-happy worried him, Hawk gave no sign of it.

"As a gesture of friendship, Chief Broken Pine of the Crow has sent us with this fresh meat, so that your men may enjoy it," Hawk said in a calm, steady voice. "Jamie MacCallister and Lieutenant Tyler will join us in the morning when we start back to the Crow village. The other soldiers will follow at a distance of no less than half a mile."

Davidson stalked forward and said, "I will

272

decide how we proceed. I am First Lieutenant Edgar Davidson, and this is my command."

Jamie eased up behind Davidson and said quietly, "Might be a good idea to thank them for those buffalo haunches, Lieutenant. That's the polite thing to do."

Davidson's head snapped around toward him. The lieutenant glared for a second, then turned back to Hawk and the other Indian.

"Tell Broken Pine that we appreciate the fresh meat. When we reach your village, I would be most happy and honored to sit down and discuss matters with your chief. Do you understand what I'm saying? Can you convey this message to your chief?"

That was a ridiculous question, thought Jamie. Hawk obviously understood and spoke English as well as any of them. Davidson was just trying to demonstrate his superiority — and his contempt for the Indians.

Hawk didn't even acknowledge the veiled insult. He just nodded and said, "I understand and will tell Broken Pine." Jamie was impressed by the young warrior's restraint and dignity.

Hawk turned his pony, as did the other warrior, and they galloped off, leaving the fresh meat on the buffalo hides lying on the ground.

Davidson snapped his fingers and then gestured toward the hides.

"Corporal Mackey, deal with that!" he ordered.

"Yes, sir!" Mackey responded as he hurried forward.

Davidson looked at Jamie and asked, "How long will it take us to reach the Crow village from here?"

Jamie considered for a moment, then said, "Might get there day after tomorrow, especially since we can follow Broken Pine's party and won't have to hunt for the village."

"Good. I'm ready to conclude this mission successfully."

Jamie hoped it turned out to be that easy . . . but he wasn't going to hold his breath waiting for that to happen.

CHAPTER 21

The Crow hunting party made camp that night about half a mile from the army camp and enjoyed fresh buffalo steaks. In the morning, Preacher swung up on Horse's back and rode to the wagons, accompanied by Dog.

He heard the sentries calling out that a rider was approaching. A couple of dragoons walked out to challenge him, but it was just a formality. One of the troopers said, "Lieutenant Tyler told us you'd probably show up this morning, sir. You're alone?"

"I reckon so," Preacher replied dryly. In this flat, open terrain, anybody else on horseback would have been spotted easily.

The guards waved him past. He saw Jamie MacCallister's tall, brawny figure standing next to one of the wagons with the two officers and headed in that direction.

Jamie raised a hand in greeting as Preacher reined in.

"I hope Hawk told Broken Pine how much we appreciate that fresh meat," Jamie said. "It was mighty good."

Preacher dismounted and said, "The Crow were happy to share. They're hospitable folks."

Lieutenant Davidson sniffed. "You talk about them almost as if they were human, sir."

Preacher's jaw tightened. He wasn't accustomed to holding back his annoyance, but he made an effort to do so now because if the fragile truce were to be shattered, some of his friends among the Crow might well die.

Dog didn't have the same sort of restraint. The big cur instinctively disliked Davidson and displayed his teeth in a snarl accompanied by a low growl.

"I don't like having a wolf in camp," snapped Davidson. "Remove it, sir, or I'll have it dealt with."

"I ain't exactly sure what you mean by that, Lieutenant, but I can do some dealin' with, too, if I'm pushed to it."

Davidson stiffened. Lieutenant Tyler stepped in and said, "Jamie and I are ready to go, Preacher. I'm looking forward to riding with the Crow and getting to know them better."

"That's fine." Preacher jerked his head in a nod. "Let's go. Time's a-wastin'."

Jamie and Tyler had their horses ready. They all mounted up, and Preacher led the way back to where the Crow hunting party was breaking camp.

Broken Pine greeted the two white men in friendly enough fashion, although some of the other warriors were clearly wary of them. Big Thunder, however, strode up to Jamie, crossed his arms over his massive chest, and regarded the frontiersman solemnly and intently. Jamie just stood there and returned the huge warrior's scrutiny.

Finally, Big Thunder said in English, "You . . . big man."

"So are you," Jamie replied.

"You fight?"

"When I have to."

Big Thunder reached out and prodded Jamie's chest with a stiff finger as he said, "In village, you fight Big Thunder."

"That would be you?"

Big Thunder didn't seem to understand the question. Preacher, holding back a grin, said, "Yeah, he's Big Thunder, all right. Don't take what he's sayin' the wrong way, though, Jamie. He ain't mad at you. He just loves to get in a tussle with somebody, and there ain't many among his people who can actually give him a good fight."

"Well, that's a relief to hear," said Jamie. "I wasn't sure I wanted a fella as big as a mountain to be mad at me." He looked at Big Thunder again and went on, "We fight . . . maybe."

Big Thunder grinned happily and thumped a ham-like hand against Jamie's arm so powerfully that Jamie lurched a little to the side.

"I reckon that's his way of sayin' he's lookin' forward to it," Preacher drawled.

"Yeah, well, I can't say as I am," Jamie muttered. "But I reckon it might be pretty good sport, at that."

A few minutes later, the men were mounted and on their way. Several of the ponies dragged buffalo hides wrapped tightly around sections of meat taken from the shaggy beasts the hunters had killed. The meat had been lightly smoked over-night, enough to preserve it until they reached the village, where most of it would be cooked and the rest made into jerky and pemmican.

A small group consisting of Preacher, Hawk, Jamie, Lieutenant Tyler, and Broken Pine led the way, with Dog trotting out in front of them. Big Thunder trailed closely behind them, and then came the other warriors, including the wounded Swift Water. The bullet had passed through his side, leaving clean wounds in and out, and luckily had not broken a rib or damaged anything internal as far as Preacher could tell. The wounds had been cleaned and packed with herbs, and although Swift Water was uncomfortable riding, he was able to manage.

Jamie looked around at the man he had shot and said quietly to Preacher, "I sure am sorry about what happened to that fella. At the time, though, I didn't have any way of knowing what was going on."

"It's Sergeant O'Connor's fault," Preacher said. "He's the one who got spooked for no good reason and started the whole thing. I made sure Swift Water knows that. He understands, and so does Broken Pine." The mountain man chuckled. "I don't reckon you and Swift Water will ever be good friends, but at least he don't want to lift your hair."

"And I'm mighty glad of that," Jamie said.

The mountains were already easily visible in the distance. They didn't really seem to draw any closer during the day, but Jamie knew better. Like any experienced frontiersman, he had a knack for knowing how far he still had to go before reaching a destination. By the time the Crow hunting party made camp that evening, Jamie was confident they would reach the foothills where their village was located the next day.

"Lieutenant Tyler and I had better ride on back to the army column and report to Lieutenant Davidson," he told Preacher.

All day long, the wagons and the mounted dragoons had been traveling half a mile behind the Crow. Jamie had checked on them several times to make sure Davidson wasn't crowding the Indians. So far, Davidson was cooperating. Jamie hoped that would continue until they reached the Crow village, but the arrogant young lieutenant was too unpredictable for Jamie to feel confident about that.

"You want me to come with you?" Preacher asked now.

Jamie shook his head and said, "I don't reckon that's necessary. Lieutenant Davidson will probably be annoyed enough to see me."

"I'm not sure why you agreed to come along in the first place with that stiff-necked little —"

"His commander's a friend of mine," Jamie explained. "He's been given the job of getting Broken Pine back to the fort so he can meet with those fellas from Washington and sign a treaty with them."

"I'm not sure Broken Pine's gonna understand all that," Preacher said with a shake of his head. "To him, givin' his word ought to be more'n enough. That piece of paper ain't gonna mean a thing."

"Maybe he'll see that it's important to our side, even if it's not to his."

"Maybe," Preacher said, shrugging.

The cooking fire Corporal Mackey had built was a large blob of orange light in the gathering darkness as Jamie and Lieutenant Tyler approached on horseback. Jamie hailed the camp as sentries moved out to meet them. The guards saluted Tyler and passed the two riders on.

Lieutenant Davidson was deep in conversation with Sergeant O'Connor as Jamie and Tyler rode up. That sight caused a faint stirring of worry inside Jamie. There was certainly nothing unusual about a commanding officer talking to one of his noncommissioned officers, but Jamie couldn't help but wonder if the two of them were hatching some new form of troublemaking.

Tyler dismounted and saluted Davidson. Jamie just swung down from the saddle.

"We're reporting in to see if you have any new orders for us," Tyler said.

"Would it matter if I did?" said Davidson.

"You seem more inclined to take orders from those painted savages than from your superior officers, Lieutenant."

Jamie said, "None of Broken Pine's bunch are wearing war paint, Lieutenant." He added pointedly, "You'd know about it if they were."

"Be that as it may . . . You've been traveling with them all day, Tyler. Do you have any sense that they're leading us into a trap?"

Tyler frowned and stared. He said, "What? Why in the world would you think that?"

O'Connor said, "It's just the sort of thing hostiles'd do, ain't it? They call 'em that for a reason, Lieutenant."

O'Connor's sneering tone seemed to rub Tyler the wrong way. Jamie didn't blame him for that. It would have had the same effect on him.

Tyler swallowed that irritation, though, and said, "I'm confident that Broken Pine isn't planning any sort of ambush. He's just heading back to his village, and he's allowing us to come with him. That's what we wanted, isn't it?"

"Perhaps," Davidson said. "But there's going to be a heavy guard tonight, just in case those redskins get the idea of trying to murder us in our sleep."

Jamie said, "You don't need to worry about that. If a Crow wants to kill you, he'll come at you straight ahead."

"No, they're sneaky devils," O'Connor insisted, shaking his head. "I've heard plenty of stories about those savages."

"And I've lived among 'em," Jamie said. "I reckon I know them better than you do, mister."

"Regardless of that," Davidson said, "I don't trust them. Keep a close eye on them, MacCallister. You, too, Tyler. I warn you, I will protect this troop to the best of my ability. In the case of a trap, if that means leaving the two of you to the dubious mercies of those savages, then so be it."

"I don't reckon I'll lose any sleep worrying about what Broken Pine and the Crow might do," Jamie said. "If there's any trouble, I figure it'll come from other sources."

Davidson flushed, obviously understanding what Jamie meant by that. Jamie didn't care. Let the lieutenant take offense if he wanted to.

Jamie went on, "I'm gonna go see what Corporal Mackey's got cooking. Smells like buffalo stew to me, and I'm ready for it."

The Crow hunting party entered the foothills by the middle of the next day and began following the stream that ran down from the mountains to join the Sweetwater. Jamie rode back and forth between the hunting party and the army troop to make sure the wagons were able to make it through the more rugged terrain. Corporal Mackey was a skillful driver and had no trouble with his team, and the trooper handling the other wagon was doing a good job, too.

While Jamie was with the hunting party, he and Lieutenant Tyler spent some of the time talking to Broken Pine about the proposed treaty. Jamie knew that Lieutenant Davidson wouldn't like that — Davidson felt like *he* was in charge of the negotiations, not them — but if they could lay the groundwork with Broken Pine, the whole affair might go much more smoothly. Sometimes when the concepts they were discussing got too complicated for Broken Pine's command of English, Preacher stepped in to translate them into Crow.

After a while, Preacher said, "Here's the thing, boys. Washington wants that treaty so the wagon trains will be protected, but there's really no reason for those immigrants to be strayin' this far north. There ain't no good passes up here, no matter what that damn fool book says."

Preacher had explained to Jamie and Tyler about the wagon train he and Hawk had helped save from renegades, as well as the fraudulent volume that had prompted the pilgrims to try to bring their wagons through this area to start with.

"Are you saying there's no real need for a treaty?" Tyler asked.

"That's the way it seems to me. The problem's gonna work itself out if folks just leave it alone."

Jamie considered that possibility for a moment and then shook his head.

"From what I've seen of government, that's not going to happen. Those politicians think that if they're not generating a lot of heat and noise about something or other, they're not doing their jobs. Worse yet, they believe the voters think that way, too."

" 'Much ado about nothin'," Preacher quoted. "I remember my little pard Audie sayin' that Shakespeare fella wrote a play called by that name, and it sums up how those varmints in Washington spend their time better'n anything I ever heard." He shrugged. "But I don't reckon it'll hurt anything to have a treaty with the Crow, even if it don't really *help* anything, either."

As the day went on, the mountain man

pointed out various landmarks to them and indicated that these meant they were getting close to the village. Late in the afternoon, the cluster of lodges alongside the little river came into view.

Preacher reined in and said to Tyler, "You head on back to the wagons and tell Lieutenant Davidson to stop where he is. The troop don't need to come any closer than that. They can make camp right there."

Broken Pine added, "Tell Lieutenant Davidson to come to my lodge this evening. We will eat together, and talk."

"All right," Tyler replied. He glanced at Jamie, who understood the look. Both of them were a little worried about how Davidson was going to handle this. Jamie couldn't imagine the stiff-necked lieutenant sitting cross-legged on a buffalo robe in a smoky Crow lodge. Maybe Davidson's ambition would overcome his attitude. He wanted to succeed in this mission, after all. It could be important for his future career.

Tyler turned back to the wagons while Jamie rode on into the village with the others. All the Crow came out to greet the returning hunting party, and although they were excited about the buffalo meat that had been brought back, they were also curious about the big white man they had never seen before. The children stared openly at Jamie while the women gave him nervous looks, and the warriors who had been left behind frowned warily at him. Broken Pine, Preacher, Hawk, and the others seemed to regard Jamie as a friend, though, so they were willing to accept him — for now.

The wounded Swift Water's wife fussed mightily over him and helped him to their lodge. Jamie watched the two of them talking as they made their way slowly through the village. The woman turned her head to look at him. He supposed Swift Water was explaining how he had gotten shot, and who did it.

Preacher came over and said, "Word'll get around the village, all right, but I don't reckon you've got too much to worry about. Now, if you'd killed ol' Swift Water, no matter what the circumstances, it'd be different. His friends would be honor-bound to try to settle that score."

"Maybe I should go back to the troop and just stay out of sight," Jamie suggested.

"I think it'd be better if you were here." Preacher chuckled. "That way I'll have help keepin' that Lieutenant Davidson from ruinin' everything." The mountain man turned and beckoned to someone. "Want you to meet Hawk's family."

Hawk came over with a woman and two children. He introduced the woman to Jamie as his wife Butterfly. She smiled demurely and murmured a greeting. The two youngsters, Eagle Feather and Bright Moon, gazed up at Jamie's towering form with awe.

When Hawk and his family had returned to their lodge, Jamie said quietly to Preacher, "I might be mistaken, but it seemed to me that Hawk's wife has got *blue* eyes."

"It's a long story," Preacher said. "Let's go find somewhere to sit down, and I'll tell you all about it . . ."

CHAPTER 22

Preacher and Jamie were waiting when Lieutenant Davidson arrived at the Crow village around dusk. Preacher had warned Lieutenant Tyler that Davidson didn't need to show up with a detachment of troops. That would just make their hosts nervous, and nobody wanted that. More than likely, it would be best if only the two lieutenants visited the village this evening.

When Davidson rode in, however, Hayden Tyler wasn't with him — but Sergeant Liam O'Connor was.

"Damn it," Jamie muttered. "Why'd he bring O'Connor with him? He's the one who's responsible for that fracas a couple of days ago, and the Crow know it."

"My guess is that Davidson wanted somebody he could count on to back his play, whatever it is," said Preacher. "From what I've seen of Tyler, he wouldn't go along with just anything Davidson says or does. He'd

289

have to believe Davidson was right."

Jamie nodded and said, "Lieutenant Tyler would follow orders . . . but only so far. He wouldn't stand by and let Davidson ruin everything, at least not without arguing."

"Reckon we'll have to make the best of it." Preacher strode forward to greet the two soldiers.

"MacCallister," Davidson greeted Jamie brusquely as he dismounted. The lieutenant looked around the village with an expression of open contempt on his face as he went on, "These people live in such filth and squalor, and yet we are forced to deal with them as if they were not subhuman savages."

"You'd better rein in that kind of talk, Lieutenant," Jamie warned. "Some of these folks speak English."

O'Connor had gotten down from his horse, too. He stepped up to Jamie, chest swollen in challenge, and said, "Ye have no right tellin' the lieutenant how to talk, MacCallister. Keep your mouth shut."

"Jamie's just tryin' to look out for the two of you," Preacher put in.

"Very well," Davidson said. He motioned O'Connor back. "Let's get this over with, shall we? Take us to whichever of these hovels the headman lives in."

Jamie jerked his head to indicate they should follow him. As they walked through the village, they were the objects of much intense scrutiny from the inhabitants. Clearly, the Crow weren't any more impressed with Lieutenant Davidson than he was with them.

"Where's Lieutenant Tyler?" Jamie asked.

"I left him in command of the camp," Davidson replied. "I didn't believe it would be wise for both officers to be away from the men at the same time."

That was a somewhat reasonable answer, at least, thought Jamie, although he would have preferred that Sergeant O'Connor not be anywhere near the Crow village. He hoped that with him and Preacher to ride herd on them, they could keep the two soldiers from stirring up any more trouble.

Hawk was waiting for them outside Broken Pine's lodge. He swept back the hide flap over the entrance and said, "We will eat first. Later the council of our people will join us."

"Are you the chief?" Davidson asked bluntly.

Preacher said, "This is my son, Hawk That Soars. I reckon Broken Pine is probably inside."

"I see no need to negotiate with anyone

291

except the chief."

"We ain't negotiatin'," Preacher said. "We're sittin' down, eatin' together, and gettin' to know each other. Then the serious talkin' can start."

Davidson's expression made it clear what a waste of time he considered that, but he sighed, nodded, and went on into the lodge, bending a little to get through the entrance. Preacher, Jamie, and O'Connor had to stoop quite a bit more.

Inside, Broken Pine stood beside the fire in the center of the lodge. His wife, Singing Woman, tended to the pot of stew simmering over the flames. Butterfly was there, too, to help serve the visitors.

"Lieutenant, this is Broken Pine, chief of the Crow," Jamie said. "Broken Pine, this is Lieutenant Edgar Davidson of the United States Army."

Broken Pine inclined his head a little and said, "Lieutenant Davidson, welcome to my home."

With a visible effort, Davidson summoned up enough graciousness to reply, "Thank you for your hospitality, Chief Broken Pine."

Well, they weren't off to too bad a start, Jamie told himself. Davidson hadn't marched in here and outright insulted anybody.

Broken Pine waved a hand toward the buffalo robes spread on the ground around the fire and went on, "Please, sit. We will eat and then talk."

Davidson cast a leery eye toward the shaggy robes but lowered himself gingerly onto one of them. Sergeant O'Connor sat to his left. Preacher was next to O'Connor, and Jamie knew the mountain man chose that spot because he figured Jamie wouldn't want to sit next to the man he had battled several times in the past. And Preacher was right about that, Jamie thought as he settled down to Preacher's left. Hawk and Broken Pine were on the other side of the fire.

Singing Woman and Butterfly filled bowls with stew from the pot and started to serve the food, which smelled mighty appetizing to Jamie. Guests were served first, so Butterfly bent down to extend the bowl in her hands to Davidson.

He took it, glanced up at her, and said, "Thank y—" Then he stopped short, set the bowl on the robe in front of him, and quickly caught hold of Butterfly's wrist as she began to straighten. "Wait just a moment!"

Across the fire, Hawk bristled at the lieutenant manhandling his wife that way. He came to his feet in a single lithe movement and reached for the knife at his waist as he said, "Let her go."

Davidson stood up, too, and ignored Hawk as he pulled Butterfly closer to him. He stared intently into her face, and Jamie had a pretty good idea what the lieutenant was going to say even before Davidson declared incredulously, "This woman has blue eyes. *She's white!*"

"Let go of my wife," Hawk said again, his voice low and dangerous now.

Jamie, Preacher, and O'Connor were also on their feet, as was Broken Pine on the other side of the fire. Singing Woman had been about to extend a bowl of stew to the sergeant when Davidson grabbed Butterfly. She moved back so she would be out of the way in case of trouble.

"Lieutenant, you're making a big mistake," Jamie said.

"I don't think so," Davidson snapped. He proved that he didn't grasp what Jamie meant by continuing, "Look at this woman's eyes. They're blue. She's white, I tell you. A captive of these savages!"

"Enough," Hawk grated. He plucked his tomahawk loose from the rawhide loop where it hung at his waist and stalked toward Davidson.

"Sergeant! We're being attacked!"

"By God, that's enough!" The bellow from Preacher's mouth filled the lodge. He drew his right-hand Colt from its holster and pressed the muzzle to O'Connor's head before the big noncom could do anything. Preacher drew the hammer back with an ominous click.

At the same time, Preacher filled his left hand as well and pointed that gun at Davidson. He cocked it, too, and said, "Lieutenant, you best turn loose of that woman right now, or else I may just let Hawk do what he wants to."

"You . . . you can't do this," Davidson blustered. "You're a white man, which means you're under my jurisdiction. You're under arrest for threatening members of the United States Army!"

"I'm about to do more'n threaten. But all you got to do, Lieutenant, is let go of Butterfly and back off."

"Her real name can't be Butterfly. That's an Indian name."

For the first time since this incident began, Butterfly spoke up. Her face was strained, maybe even a little frightened, but her voice was resolute as she said, "I *am* Indian. I am Crow. Once I was white, but no longer. Not for many, many seasons."

Davidson finally released her wrist. As her

295

arm dropped, he said in disbelief, "But my dear lady, with white blood flowing in your veins, you can't possibly believe that you're the same as these . . . these . . ."

"Savages, I think you called us," Hawk said. Jamie could tell that the warrior was keeping a tight rein on his anger, but how much longer that control would last, Jamie didn't know.

"Lieutenant . . ." O'Connor's voice had a hollow ring to it. Having a gun barrel pressed to his head would do that to a man.

"At ease, Sergeant. There's nothing you can do as long as that lunatic is holding a gun on you."

"Lunatic," Preacher repeated with a wry grin on his face. "You may think that's the first time anybody ever called me that, Lieutenant, but I can tell you right now, it ain't."

"I don't doubt that for a second."

Preacher lowered the gun he had pointed at Davidson. Butterfly scurried back around the fire to Hawk's side. He still held his tomahawk, but he put his other arm around his wife's shoulders and drew her close against him.

Preacher moved back a step, but he kept the right-hand Colt aimed at O'Connor in case the sergeant tried anything.

With all the dignity he could muster as chief, Broken Pine said, "There will be no meal. We will not talk of treaties or anything else tonight. Lieutenant Davidson, you and your sergeant will return now to the camp of the soldiers. We will see what a new day brings."

"You'd better take that deal, Lieutenant," Jamie advised. "I think it's the best one you're going to get."

Davidson glared around the lodge at all of them for a moment, then said, "Very well. But this matter of the prisoner is *not* resolved." He jerked his head toward the entrance. "Come along, Sergeant."

Preacher said, "Might be a good idea for Jamie and me to come along, too, just to make sure there's no trouble."

"Suit yourself," snapped Davidson. He pushed the hide flap aside and ducked out of the lodge.

Hawk let go of Butterfly and started to follow Davidson and O'Connor, but Preacher extended a hand, palm out, to stop him.

"I said Jamie and I will go," the mountain man told his son. "You stay here with your wife. She looks a mite upset, and I reckon she could use her husband at her side."

With some reluctance, Hawk nodded. "I

should kill that man for laying his hand on Butterfly."

"He might have it comin'," Preacher said, "but more'n likely it'd cause a war if you did, and that's somethin' none of us want."

He and Jamie left the lodge quickly and found Davidson and O'Connor outside, just getting mounted on their horses. Some young men from the tribe had been given the job of holding the mounts while the men were in Broken Pine's lodge. They had stepped back, and judging by the angry, confused expressions on their faces, Davidson must have snapped at them. They probably didn't understand what he'd said but had no trouble knowing what his tone meant.

They must have overheard some of what went on inside the lodge, too, because of a number of other Crow, men and women alike, had drifted up and a buzz of conversation was going through them. Jamie didn't understand enough of the Crow tongue to be able to follow the swift exchanges, but he guessed that word of Davidson's behavior was spreading.

"Hold on, Lieutenant," he said. "Preacher and I are riding with you."

"You don't need to accompany us like . . . like nannies or governesses," Davidson said.

Preacher chuckled and said, "I reckon you and me would be just about the ugliest governesses that ever governessed, don't you think, Jamie?"

"That's about the size of it," Jamie said as he took his horse's reins from one of the Indian boys. He swung up into the saddle while Preacher was getting mounted, as well.

The two soldiers and the two frontiersmen rode away from the Crow village. The shadows had thickened until night had almost fallen. Only a faint arch of reddish-gold light remained in the sky above the towering mountains to the west. That was enough for the riders to see where they were going as they followed the small stream south.

After a minute or two, Davidson said, "This is simply unacceptable."

"What are you talking about, Lieutenant?" Jamie asked.

"You know perfectly well what I'm talking about! The very idea of leaving that poor woman back there as a captive of those red-skinned brutes!"

"Butterfly's no captive," Preacher said. "She's right where she wants to be. In her heart and mind, she's a Crow woman."

O'Connor laughed coarsely and said, "She

probably doesn't have any choice but to feel that way after years of bein' passed around by those bucks."

"Mister," Preacher said, "you're makin' me sorry I didn't go ahead and pull the trigger when I had that gun pointed at your head a few minutes ago. You got worms crawlin' around in that brain o' yours, and they need lettin' out."

O'Connor growled and started to rein in and turn toward Preacher, but Davidson snapped, "Sergeant! You can satisfy your well-deserved resentment toward this buckskin-clad lout another time. Right now the important thing is the situation in which that unfortunate woman finds herself."

Jamie knew he was going to regret this, but he asked, "What do you think should be done about that, Lieutenant?"

"We must take her back to Fort Kearny with us and turn her over to the proper authorities so her real family can be found. We have absolutely no other choice in the matter. And once she *has* been reunited with her family, she'll thank us. You'll see."

Preacher shook his head and said grimly, "The only thing you'll see is Caroline dyin' of a broken heart if you take her away from her husband and their kids."

In the light of the rising moon, Jamie saw

Davidson turn his head to look at Preacher. The lieutenant arched an eyebrow.

"Caroline," he repeated. "So you *were* aware that she's white. You even know who she really is!"

Preacher muttered something under his breath. Jamie had already heard this story, so he knew what the mountain man was going to say.

"I know when she was little, her folks called her Caroline. Her pa was a preacher — a *real* preacher, not just somebody called that, like me — and he took his wife and daughter and headed west, probably figurin' on bringin' salvation to the Injuns or some such. Somewhere along the way, they were attacked, and Caroline's folks were killed. But she was able to get away and wandered off. She would've starved to death or got et by some wild animal if a band of friendly Crow hadn't found her."

"Broken Pine's people," Davidson guessed.

"Nope, a different bunch. Caroline, or Butterfly as they named her, grew up with them and forgot all about bein' white. As far as she knew, she was Crow and had always been Crow . . . except for a few memories locked up 'way far back in her brain. She'd grown to be a young woman,

301

gettin' up toward marryin' age, when a Blackfoot war party raided her village, killed a bunch of folks, and carried Butterfly off as a slave. But she got away from 'em, and then a bunch of fur thieves wound up gettin' hold of her, and me and Hawk and some friends of ours rescued her from them . . . and that whole business ended with her and Hawk gettin' married and settlin' down with Broken Pine and his people. That was ten years ago, and they've led a happy, peaceful life ever since." Preacher paused, then added in a flat, hard voice, "If you think I'm gonna let you ruin that, you're wrong."

Silence hung in the air for several seconds, then Davidson said, "What a dreadful story. The poor woman has never known anything except blood and death and degradation, and yet you insist that she's better off with those . . . those creatures who have inflicted such misery on her."

Preacher sighed and asked, "Were you listenin' to a word I said, Lieutenant? Except for those two times — which the Crow didn't have nothin' to do with — Butterfly has been happy all her life. She hadn't had to go through any more than plenty of other folks have."

"You expect her to live with Indians and

be happy when Indians murdered her parents?"

"But they weren't the same —" Preacher stopped short and made a disgusted sound in his throat. Jamie knew the feeling. He could have warned Preacher that arguing with Lieutenant Edgar Davidson was a waste of time, and frustrating as all hell, to boot.

After a few more moments of tense silence went by, Preacher said, "I reckon you've got a choice to make, Lieutenant. You came here to convince Broken Pine to come back to the fort with you and talk to those fellas from Washington. I promise you, if you try to take Butterfly away from the village by force, that's never gonna happen. What you'll have is a war instead of a treaty."

Davidson pondered that and then said slowly, "This situation doesn't fall within the scope of my orders . . ."

"But Lieutenant!" O'Connor protested. "You're talkin' about a white woman and a bunch of savages!"

"Nevertheless, Sergeant, a soldier must sometimes obey orders even though they go against his nature. But I haven't made up my mind yet. I have a great deal of thinking to do."

And *that* could lead to a lot more trouble for all of them, Jamie told himself.

CHAPTER 23

Jamie stayed in the soldiers' camp that night while Preacher returned to the Crow village. Lieutenant Hayden Tyler was eager to find out what had happened, but upon arrival Davidson stomped into his tent and jerked the flap closed behind him without even speaking to the junior officer. Tyler turned to Jamie with an expression that was annoyed and puzzled at the same time.

"Judging by the way Lieutenant Davidson was just acting, I'd say things didn't go well with the Crow this evening," Tyler ventured.

Jamie nodded. "You could say that."

"Broken Pine won't cooperate about the treaty?"

Jamie chuckled, but the sound didn't contain any real humor.

"Actually, they never even got around to talking about that," he said. "Something else came up. A whole different problem."

"A different problem? I don't understand."

"Lieutenant Davidson met Hawk's wife.
Preacher's daughter-in-law, I guess you
could say, although the Indians aren't that
formal about it."

In the light from the campfire, Jamie saw
Tyler's brow furrow. He went on, "She's
white, Lieutenant. Or she once was, I guess
would be a better way of putting it. She
considers herself Crow, and I sure wouldn't
want to argue the point with her."

"You mean she's a . . . a captive?"

"Not at all." Quickly, Jamie sketched in
Butterfly's history for Tyler, then said, "So
you can see why she thinks of herself as a
member of the tribe and doesn't want it any
other way."

Tyler rubbed his chin and said, "I'd be
willing to wager that Lieutenant Davidson
doesn't see eye to eye with her on the matter, however."

"He sure doesn't. As soon as he noticed
Butterfly's blue eyes, he made up his mind
that she was a prisoner and that it was up
to him to rescue her and return her to her
real family . . . even though her real family
is Hawk and those two young'uns."

"Because rescuing a white captive would
bring glory to him," mused Tyler. "You read

306

about those things from time to time, in the newspapers back east. The newspapers always fawn over someone who performs such a valiant task."

Jamie nodded and said, "I expect so. Stories like that sell papers, and that's all those folks care about." He dragged a thumbnail along his beard-stubbled jaw as he frowned in thought. "If Davidson ignores the mission that brought him here and decides that taking Butterfly away from the Crow is more important, it's liable to get him in trouble not just with Captain Croxton but with the higher-ups, as well. On the other hand, when the newspapers decide that somebody's a hero — whether he really is or not — and build him up, it's hard for the army to punish him too much or hold him back from promotion. The politicians want a fella like that to succeed."

"So Edgar has to try to weigh everything and decide which course will benefit him most in the long run."

"You've known him for a while, haven't you, Lieutenant?"

"We were at West Point together, in the same class," Tyler replied.

"Has he always been this way?"

"Ambitious? Stubborn as a mule? Con-vinced that he's always right and that everyone is conspiring against him?" Tyler laughed softly. "I'm afraid so. He comes from a long line of officers. His father is a colonel who fought in the Mexican War. His grandfather served with Andrew Jackson during the War of 1812, and his great-grandfather was a member of General Washington's staff during the revolution. There are a great many expectations he has to live up to." Tyler shrugged. "But he's made that work well for him so far. He excelled at the Point and was promoted to first lieutenant very quickly after being commissioned. Some of us are still waiting."

"I've seen plenty of good officers," Jamie told the young man. "You're going to be one of them, Hayden. Just be patient."

"I hope you're right, sir. In the meantime . . . what do we do about Lieutenant Davidson?"

"Wait for him to make up his mind," said Jamie. "And hope that he doesn't decide to raise hell and shove a chunk under the corner."

Butterfly was as proud and courageous as any Crow woman, but Preacher thought she looked a little like she wanted to cry as she stood in the lodge she shared with her husband and children.

She spoke in a low voice so as not to wake the sleeping youngsters as she said to Hawk, "You will not allow that terrible man to take me away from this place, will you?"

"Never believe that such a thing could happen, even in the worst dreams that haunt your sleep," Hawk said as he rested his hands on her shoulders. He drew her gently against his chest and circled his arms around her protectively. "This is your home and we are your family, and it will always be that way."

Preacher stood on the other side of the fire from the embracing couple. The three of them had returned here after the unpleasant encounter in Broken Pine's lodge.

He let Hawk comfort Butterfly for a few more moments, then said, "It would probably be a good idea if you didn't venture too far from the village by yourself while those soldiers are around here, Butterfly."

Hawk turned his head sharply to look at Preacher.

"You believe the white men would try to steal Butterfly away from her home?"

"I ain't been acquainted with that Lieutenant Davidson for long enough to be sure what he's capable of. I've seen enough that I sure don't trust him, though, and you shouldn't, either."

"I would never trust a man like that," Hawk declared. "And if he comes in the village again, I will —"

Preacher held up a hand to stop his son's ominous words.

"If you were about to say you'd shoot him or split his head open with a tomahawk, I understand the feelin', believe me. It just comes natural after you've spent a little time around the varmint. But you got to remember . . . he has a lot of soldiers with him, and all those soldiers have rifles. Some of 'em have pistols and sabers, too. Unless you're backed in a corner, don't start a fight unless you know you've got a good chance of winnin' it."

"And if we are backed into a corner, as you say?"

"Well, then it's root, hog, or die," Preacher replied with a grin. "But if Jamie MacCallister has anything to say about it, things won't come to that."

"MacCallister seems like a good man," Hawk admitted grudgingly as he continued holding Butterfly.

Preacher nodded and said, "He's one of the best. First time I met him, he was younger than you were when we first ran into each other. Him and this strong-minded little gal he'd married up with were

310

on their way to a place they thought they might want to settle, but they had three different batches of trouble on their trail. I helped 'em handle those scrapes, and I could tell even then that Jamie was one hell of a fightin' man, despite still bein' a kid. I've heard a lot about him since then, and he ain't ever done nothin' to make me think I was wrong about that."

Butterfly slipped out of Hawk's embrace and sank onto one of the buffalo robes. She said, "I will trust this man MacCallister, and of course the two of you, and not live in fear of the white soldiers. But I *will* be very careful."

Preacher nodded and told her, "That's a good idea."

He said his good nights and slipped out of the lodge, intending to go back to the one he was using while he was visiting the village. Instead Hawk stepped out after him and said quietly, "Preacher."

The mountain man swung around. "What is it?"

"You know that even though it means war between the Crow and those soldiers, I will not let that man take Butterfly away from me."

"Well, I can't blame you for that, boy."

"Broken Pine and the others will agree

311

with me."

Preacher nodded solemnly and said, "I know."

"If it comes to this . . . the Crow against the whites . . . on which side will you fight?"

Preacher's lips drew back from his teeth in a half-snarl.

"You ask that of me? After all we been through together?"

"You are white," Hawk said simply, as if that explained everything.

Preacher shook his head. "I didn't expect that of you. I really didn't. You and Butterfly and those young'uns are my family. The only real family I have. Damn right I'm gonna stand beside you, no matter what it takes. And you by God should'a knowed that!"

"I believed that is what you would say. But your friend MacCallister . . . if he takes the side of the soldiers, will you fight him as well?"

"I believe Jamie has more sense than that. I hope he does. But if things come down to it . . . I stand with you, Hawk, no matter who's on the other side."

Jamie was sitting on a lowered wagon tailgate and enjoying a breakfast of buffalo steak and biscuits the next morning, washed down with some of Corporal Mackey's potent coffee, when Lieutenant Hayden Tyler came up to him.

"Lieutenant Davidson sent me to find you, Mr. MacCallister. He wants to speak with both of us."

"Well, that's enough to put a bad taste in a fella's mouth, no matter how good the grub is." Jamie grinned at Mackey. "And it's mighty good, Corporal. But I reckon I've got to go see what the lieutenant wants."

He speared the last chunk of steak with his knife, chewed it thoroughly before swallowing, and then drained the last of the coffee in the cup. He could tell that Tyler was getting a little fidgety and impatient, so he smiled and added, "I didn't say just how quick I'd get around to it, though."

Tyler opened his mouth to say something, but before the words came out, Jamie slid off the tailgate and stood up, taking a half-eaten biscuit with him as he started for Davidson's tent.

"I don't suppose the lieutenant told you what's on his mind," Jamie said to Tyler as they walked side by side. He gnawed a bite off the biscuit.

"Why would he?" Tyler responded with a note of bitterness in his voice. "I'm only a junior officer, after all."

"I believe he is, too," Jamie pointed out. "Unless a first lieutenant is a whole hell of a lot more important than they used to be."

"He's the ranking officer in this detail. Out here away from the fort, he might as well be a general."

That was probably just the way Davidson looked at the situation, too, thought Jamie.

"Anyway, I don't know what he wants," continued Tyler, "but I'm sure he'll tell us."

As they approached Davidson's tent, the flap was pulled back and Sergeant Liam O'Connor stepped out. As he straightened, he caught sight of Jamie and Tyler coming toward him and stiffened. His mouth thinned down to a narrow line. Jamie was ready for some insulting comment from the sergeant, or even an attempted punch, but before he and Tyler reached the tent, O'Connor turned on his heel and stalked off without looking back.

"Can't say as I'm unhappy about that," Jamie muttered. "I just had breakfast, and looking at O'Connor wasn't going to do much for my digestion."

Tyler let that comment pass and pulled back the tent's entrance flap slightly. He said, "Lieutenant Tyler reporting with Mr. MacCallister, as ordered."

"Come in," Davidson barked from inside.

Tyler pulled back the flap and motioned for Jamie to go first. Davidson stood without his uniform shirt and jacket on, using a razor to scrape the last bits of shaving soap from his face as he peered into a small looking glass he held in his other hand. He finished and set the razor and looking glass on a small folding table, then picked up a towel to wipe his face.

"I have an assignment for the two of you," he said without any sort of greeting. "I want you to go back to that Crow village this morning and speak once more to Chief Broken Pine. Convey my apologies to him for what happened yesterday evening."

"Hold on a minute," Jamie said. His forehead creased in surprise. "You're apologizing?"

"That's correct. I was out of line, and I want to be certain that Broken Pine knows I'm aware of that. I would very much like to meet with him again to discuss matters of mutual importance to both of us."

"The treaty," Tyler said.

"Exactly." Davidson smiled faintly. "That's much more important than some Indian woman, isn't it? Or even, well, a white woman who believes herself to be a savage." He began pulling on his shirt. "After all, we *are* who we believe ourselves to be, are we not?"

"Uh, yes, sir, I suppose that's right," said Tyler, clearly taken aback by the reasonable attitude Davidson was displaying this morning.

So was Jamie. After what had happened the night before, Jamie wouldn't have been shocked if Davidson had gotten up this morning and ordered an attack on the Crow village. Instead, it seemed that he wanted to make amends for the unpleasantness.

Wonders might not ever cease, but they were welcome when they came along, Jamie thought.

"Tell Broken Pine that I would be happy to visit him again, and I promise to be on my best behavior this time," Davidson went on. "Or, if he would prefer, he would be very welcome to come here. He could bring, perhaps, a dozen or so of his warriors, if he was concerned for his safety."

That would be about the last thing Broken Pine would want to admit, thought Jamie, but to be honest, he didn't know how the chief would react to the invitation. All he and Tyler could do was deliver it.

"All right, we can do that," Tyler said. He looked over at Jamie. "Mr. MacCallister?"

Jamie's broad shoulders rose and fell.

"Sure, we'll tell him what you said, Lieutenant. Then we'll come back and tell you what he has to say in reply."

"Very well." Davidson shrugged into his jacket and began fastening its brass buttons. "I'll be waiting eagerly to hear his response. Dismissed."

Tyler saluted, then he and Jamie left the tent. Once they were outside, Jamie said quietly, "Well, if that doesn't beat all . . ."

"I suppose he decided the mission was more important than hunting for personal glory."

"Maybe so."

Jamie sounded as if he couldn't quite bring himself to believe it just yet, though.

Broken Pine had given two warriors the job of keeping watch on the soldiers' camp during the night, and this morning at dawn, two more warriors had taken their place. Preacher thought posting guards like that was a good idea. When you were dealing with someone whose actions you couldn't really predict, it was a good idea to stay as alert as possible.

So the mountain man wasn't surprised when one of those sentries raced into the village later in the morning and brought his pony to a swift halt. The drumming hoof-

317

beats as the rider approached got everyone's attention. Most of the village's inhabitants were waiting for him, including Preacher, Hawk, Butterfly, and Broken Pine.

The man slid off the pony's back and announced, "Two riders come from the soldier camp. One wears the blue coat, and the other is the white man called MacCallister."

Broken Pine looked over at Preacher and said, "Your friend returns. This is a good sign, since he seems to be a friend to the Crow, as well."

"I reckon whether it's a good sign or not depends on who the soldier is," Preacher replied. "If it's that Lieutenant Davidson, I ain't so sure, even if Jamie *is* with him."

The visitors reached the village a short time later. Preacher was relieved to see that Jamie's companion was Lieutenant Hayden Tyler, who seemed to be a decent young man even though he was sort of hamstrung by his commitment to follow military protocol.

The two men dismounted. Broken Pine told them, "Welcome."

"That's a pretty generous greeting, Chief, after what happened last night," Jamie said.

"Thank you for allowing us to visit, Chief Broken Pine," Tyler said. "I've come to apologize."

"It was not you who gave offense," Broken Pine responded with just a hint of a smile, although his voice was steady and solemn.

"I know, but I've been ordered to convey the regrets of my superior officer, Lieutenant Edgar Davidson. He's sorry for what happened and takes all the blame for the incident."

Broken Pine inclined his head a little and said, "Your chief's words are accepted. You can tell him that when you return to your camp."

Tyler fiddled with his horse's reins for a second, then said, "Actually, there's more to the message I'm supposed to deliver. Lieutenant Davidson would like to resume discussions about you accompanying us to Fort Kearny so that you can meet with the representatives from Washington."

"About that treaty?" Broken Pine shook his head. "I will not talk about this now."

"The lieutenant is willing to come back here," Tyler persisted, "but I think what he'd really like is for *you* to come to the camp and accept *our* hospitality while you talk about it."

Preacher squinted and said, "Sounds to me like that lieutenant of yours is askin' Broken Pine to waltz right into a trap."

"No, no, not at all," Tyler said hastily.

"The chief can bring some of his warriors with him. It's an open, honest invitation."

Broken Pine said, "I believe you speak the truth, Lieutenant . . . or at least what you *believe* to be the truth. But there will be no more talk of treaties, either here or in your camp. I have thought long about this matter, I have spoken with the wise men of our village, and I have prayed to the spirits. There will be no treaty because there is no need for one. The white men will go their way and leave the Crow to travel their own paths. We will not be friends, but neither will we be enemies."

That sounded fair enough to Preacher, but he saw that Jamie looked disappointed. Lieutenant Tyler seemed positively stricken.

"There's nothing I can say or do to change your mind, Chief?" the young officer asked. "I know that Lieutenant Davidson would really like to bring this mission to a satisfactory conclusion —"

"The white soldiers leaving my people alone *is* a satisfactory conclusion to me," said Broken Pine. "I can tell you nothing more."

Tyler looked like he wanted to continue arguing, but he must have been able to tell that it wasn't going to do any good. After a moment, he sighed and nodded.

"I am very sorry this did not work out, Chief, but I will take your message to Lieutenant Davidson. Thank you for speaking with me this morning."

Broken Pine just nodded grave acknowledgment. Tyler started to mount up again. Instead of swinging up into the saddle right away, though, Jamie said, "I'm willing to give you my word that it's not a trick or a trap, Broken Pine."

"I appreciate that, Jamie MacCallister, but it makes no difference. I have made up my mind."

"All right, then." Jamie put his foot in the stirrup and lifted himself onto the big horse. He and Tyler turned their mounts and rode slowly out of the Crow village, heading back toward the army camp.

Standing beside Preacher and watching them go, Hawk said, "So it is over."

Preacher shook his head a little and said, "I wish I believed that, Hawk. I surely do."

CHAPTER 24

Lieutenant Davidson was waiting for Jamie and Tyler when they got back to the army camp. He was stalking back and forth, hands clasped behind him as was his habit, but he stopped short when he saw them approaching. Jamie felt the lieutenant's intense scrutiny on them as they rode in the rest of the way.

"Well?" Davidson snapped before they even had a chance to dismount. "What did Broken Pine say?"

Jamie and Tyler swung down from their saddles and turned the mounts over to a couple of waiting troopers. Then Tyler told the increasingly impatient-looking Davidson, "I'm sorry, Lieutenant. Broken Pine refuses to meet with you again. He says there will be no treaty."

Davidson stared at him for a second and then burst out, "He wants war!"

"Nope," said Jamie. "He just wants his

322

people to be left alone. In return for that, the Crow won't bother any whites who venture into the region."

"But that's a treaty!" Davidson sounded frustrated.

Jamie shrugged. "In our eyes, maybe. But Preacher warned me about this. The Indians may agree to do something, but they don't see any point in putting it all down on paper and then signing their names to it. They just don't have any concept of such things. If they tell you they'll do something, they do it. That's the beginning *and* the end of it for them."

"Alpha and Omega," Lieutenant Tyler muttered.

Davidson's face darkened with rage. He drew in a sharp breath and said, "I won't be dictated to by ignorant savages."

"Then you can go to war against them," Jamie said. "You can attack the village and try to take Broken Pine prisoner so you can haul him back to Fort Kearny. But I don't think that's going to get anybody what they really want."

Davidson glared at him for several heartbeats, then sighed and said, "Much as it pains me to admit it, MacCallister, you appear to be correct. There's nothing we can do, then, except return to the fort and inform Captain Croxton that the mission has failed. At least it's cost only one life so far, that of poor Private Hodgson."

"You can look at it that way, all right," Jamie agreed. He was relieved that Davidson seemed willing to listen to reason. He went on, "I reckon we can go ahead and tell the men to start getting ready to pull out. We can still put half a day's travel behind us —"

"No," Davidson said with a curt shake of his head. "We'll allow the men and livestock the remainder of this day to rest, and then depart first thing in the morning."

"Are you sure about that, Lieutenant?" Jamie asked, frowning. "If you're thinking maybe Broken Pine will change his mind if you wait . . ."

"Not at all. I place no reliance at all on the intellectual capacity of a brute and a savage. If Broken Pine refuses to see the advantages of cooperating with us, I'm certain there's no way we could change his mind."

"No, I don't reckon so."

"I just prefer starting fresh in the morning, that's all." Davidson switched his gaze to Tyler. "You'll see to it that the men are aware of the plan, Lieutenant?"

"Of course," Tyler said. "For what it's

324

worth . . . I'm sorry."

Davidson waved that off and said, "We did the best we could. I shall return to the fort with a clear conscience and trust that the captain will see the mission was impossible."

The thing was, it hadn't been impossible at all, Jamie thought. Difficult, sure, but he believed that in the end, Broken Pine might have gone along with what they wanted. Preacher probably would have helped try to convince him. The mountain man wanted peace between the Crow and the whites. He had the future of his son, daughter-in-law, and two grandchildren riding on it.

But then the fuss Davidson had made about Butterfly had given Broken Pine the excuse he needed to shut everything down. After that, Broken Pine hadn't trusted Davidson, and he never would again.

Jamie and Tyler moved off and left Davidson standing there, peering off into the distance seemingly at nothing. Tyler said quietly, "It's got to be eating him up inside that he has to go back and tell the captain he failed."

"Yeah, I expect so." Jamie's eyes narrowed as he rubbed his chin. "You know, if I didn't know better, I'd say the lieutenant might be up to something."

"What could he possibly be 'up to', as you put it, Mr. MacCallister?"

"I don't know," Jamie said. "And that's what's got me worried."

It didn't take long for word to get around camp that the troop would be pulling out for Fort Kearny in the morning. Some of the dragoons seemed disappointed that they would be returning without achieving their objective, but most didn't seem to care. Their job was to follow orders, not worry about everything behind those orders.

Jamie told Lieutenant Tyler he was going to ride back over to the Crow village.

"I thought you don't believe that Broken Pine will change his mind," the lieutenant said.

"I don't. I just want to go and visit a little more with Preacher. It's been quite a while since he and I ran into each other, and who knows how many more years will go by before it happens again. If it ever does. There's no telling how long either of us will live."

"I don't know," Tyler said, smiling. "When I look at the two of you together, you seem sort of . . . I don't know. Invincible, somehow. Immortal."

"Nobody lives forever," Jamie said. "I've

heard folks say you should live each day like it's your last, and I don't think you can do *that,* either. You'd go loco pretty quick-like if you really tried to. But it doesn't hurt to keep in mind that one of these days — and nobody knows when — you're going to run out of time, so it's best to use what you've got wisely."

Tyler nodded and said, "I'll try to remember that."

Jamie laughed, clapped a hand on the lieutenant's shoulder, and said, "On the other hand, you're still young, so try to get some enjoyment in there, too." He swung up into the saddle. "Like I'm going to enjoy chewin' the fat with Preacher."

As he rode toward the Crow village, Jamie spotted two warriors on top of a nearby hill. They weren't trying to hide, exactly, but they weren't doing anything to draw attention to themselves, either. Jamie was pretty sure Broken Pine had posted them there to keep an eye on the soldiers. The Crow had been expecting him and Tyler when they rode in on the previous visit, so he'd known then there were watchers and wouldn't have expected any less.

Would they warn the village that he was headed that way now, he wondered, or did they consider him harmless since he was

Preacher's friend and didn't have any of the troops with him this time?

No one paid much attention to him when he rode in except kids and dogs, so he assumed the Crow no longer regarded him as a threat. He spotted Preacher standing near the river with a boy Jamie recognized as Hawk's son. Jamie turned his horse in that direction and rode up to them.

The youngster was practicing throwing a tomahawk at a tree. The boy wasn't bad at it, either, Jamie noted. A few of the throws landed wrong, handle-first so that the tomahawk bounced off the trunk, but most times, it revolved properly and *thunked!* into the tree with enough force for the head to lodge in the wood.

Preacher raised a hand in greeting as Jamie reined in.

"Eagle Feather's showin' me how good he is with a tomahawk," Preacher said. "And I'm givin' him a few tips, too. Nobody's ever so good at somethin' that he can't ever get any better."

"That's the truth," Jamie said as he dismounted.

Eagle Feather retrieved the tomahawk from the tree and hurried back over to the two frontiersmen. He asked in good English, "Do you know how to throw a tomahawk,

Mr. Jamie?"

"Probably not as good as your grandpa here does, but I've been known to fling a few," Jamie answered with a grin.

Eagle Feather wordlessly extended the 'hawk to him.

"All right," Jamie said. He took the tomahawk, weighed it in his hand for a moment to get the balance of it, and then faced the tree with his feet square and spread slightly. He held the tomahawk in front of him, and suddenly his arm snapped back and then forward, almost faster than the eye could follow. He didn't seem to put much effort into the throw, but after making one perfect revolution, the tomahawk struck the tree and embedded itself deeply in the trunk. The way the handle quivered slightly demonstrated just how much power really had been packed into the throw.

Eagle Feather's eyes were big as he looked at the tomahawk. He ran to the tree and grabbed the handle, but as he tried to pull it free, he failed.

"It's stuck too deep and tight!" he exclaimed. "I can't get it out!"

Preacher chuckled as he joined his grandson. He took hold of the tomahawk and wrenched it loose. Then he handed the weapon back to the boy and said, "Mr.

Jamie's a mite better'n he lets on, I reckon. I'd hate to get in a tomahawk-chunkin' contest with him."

"Me, too!" Eagle Feather said.

"Why don't you run on now and let us old fellas talk? I'll see you later."

Eagle Feather was reluctant to leave, but he was also obedient. He called, "Goodbye, Mr. Jamie," and ran off toward his family's lodge.

"Seems like a good boy," Jamie commented as he nodded after Eagle Feather.

"He is," Preacher agreed. "And his sister's a mighty fine little girl, if a bit shy. Nothin' wrong with that, though. Hawk and Butterfly have done a good job raisin' 'em, although those kids were pretty good to start with, I expect."

"They've got your blood in them."

"That they do." Preacher turned a more serious gaze on his old friend. "I hope you ain't bringin' bad news."

Jamie shook his head. "Nope. Lieutenant Davidson's going to accept Broken Pine's decision and head on back to the fort without him, first thing tomorrow morning."

Preacher was silent for several long seconds, then said, "Huh. That ain't what I was expectin'."

"Nor me, either. He looked pretty dispirited when I rode out a while ago, like he was finally forced to realize that he can't always just bull his way ahead and get what he wants in life."

"He didn't send you over here?"

"Not at all. I didn't even tell him I was coming, in fact. It's not really any of his business what I do, as long as I'm there in the morning when the troop pulls out."

Preacher nodded and said, "It's sure been good seein' you again, Jamie. We don't run into each other near often enough. Just wish we hadn't been on opposite sides, there at the first."

"How's Swift Water doing?"

"He'll be all right," said the mountain man. "Those bullet holes will probably ache a mite when it rains, but he can live with that. How about the trooper I creased?"

"Same for Private Jenkins," Jamie said. "He ought to make a full recovery."

"Then it could have been a lot worse."

"A lot," Jamie agreed.

Preacher clapped a hand on the big frontiersman's shoulder and said, "So, you just came over here to visit."

"That's right. Since we don't know when we'll see each other again."

"Then come on over to Hawk's lodge with

331

me. We'll sit down, smoke a pipe, and swap a few lies."

That sounded like a mighty good plan to Jamie.

Late that afternoon, Jamie said his farewells to Preacher before heading back to the army camp. The two men pounded each other on the back with enough force to stagger most men, if not crack a rib or two. Jamie had already shaken hands with Hawk, hugged Butterfly, and ruffled the hair of Eagle Feather and Bright Moon.

Now as he turned toward his horse, a huge figure loomed up to block his path.

"Jamie MacCallister," Big Thunder rumbled, "we did not fight!"

"I know, and I'm sorry about that, Big Thunder," Jamie replied. "But we just never got around to it, and now there's not time."

"There is time. We can still fight now." Big Thunder assumed an aggressive stance, spreading his feet and planting them, leaning forward slightly from the waist, raising his ham-like hands and crooking the fingers a little, ready to grab and throw.

Preacher stepped forward and said, "Hold on, Big Thunder. Jamie's got to leave tomorrow and head on back down to that fort where the soldiers came from. With him havin' to spend that much time in the saddle, you don't want him all bruised and banged up. That'd be plumb uncomfortable."

Big Thunder frowned. "But he is big, big enough to give Big Thunder a good fight!"

"Next time," Jamie promised as he clapped a hand on Big Thunder's upper arm. "Now that I know where to find this village where so many friends live, I'll be sure to come back."

"When?"

"Well, I don't know, Big Thunder, but I look forward to you and me having a good tussle when I do."

Big Thunder wasn't happy about it, but he nodded in grudging acceptance of Jamie's answer. He said, "Do not forget!"

"I'm not likely to ever forget anything about you, Big Thunder."

With a smile and a friendly wave for the other Crow who had gathered around, Jamie swung up into the saddle and turned his horse. Before he could ride away from the village, one of the warriors stepped forward. Jamie recognized Swift Water, the man he had wounded during the skirmish a few days earlier.

Swift Water regarded him gravely, causing Jamie to wonder if the warrior intended to start some sort of trouble. But instead, Swift Water raised his hand and held it out toward Jamie.

"Friends . . . now," Swift Water said in halting English.

Jamie leaned down and clasped the warrior's hand firmly.

"Friends," he agreed.

"Just not . . . shoot Swift Water . . . anymore."

"That's a deal," Jamie said, nodding. He was very glad to see that there were no hard feelings between them.

He rode away from the village without looking back.

It was dusk by the time he reached the army camp. A sentry challenged him but quickly waved him on. He rode to the temporary corral made from stakes and rope and turned his horse over to one of the troopers working as hostlers.

Then his long legs carried him to the cooking fire where men were starting to line up for supper. Corporal Mackey had a big pot of buffalo stew bubbling over the fire, as well as several Dutch ovens full of biscuits.

Lieutenant Tyler was sitting on the tailgate of Mackey's wagon drinking a tin cup of coffee. Jamie got a cup and filled it for himself, then joined the young officer. He propped a hip against the tailgate and sipped the strong, black brew.

"How did your visit with Preacher go?" Tyler asked.

"Mighty good. I wouldn't have minded spending more time with the old varmint. But we need to get back to the fort, and I suspect he'll be moving on pretty soon himself. A fella like him never stays in one place for very long, even when he's surrounded by friends and family."

"Like you?"

Jamie chuckled and said, "I admit, I'm pretty fiddle-footed, but back home I've got a pretty wife, a passel of fine kids, and the best ranch in the territory. I'd say Preacher and I are just the opposite. I like to roam around some, but I always come home." Jamie sipped the coffee again. "Always will."

They waited until the crowd of hungry soldiers had thinned out some, then got bowls of stew and a couple of biscuits apiece. Not much talking went on while they ate, but as Jamie was swabbing up the last of the juices in his bowl with the final piece of biscuit, he asked, "Where's Lieutenant Davidson?"

"In his tent. He usually takes his meals there. He's not much of one for eating with

335

the men."

"Yeah, I'd noticed that. Probably tonight he feels even less like fraternizing with them."

"Because of what happened with the mission?" Tyler nodded. "Yes, he has to be aware that all the men know we failed to carry out our orders. Honestly, I figure we'll see as little of him as possible on the way back."

"Yeah, he's going to be sulled up, licking his wounded pride," Jamie said. He looked around the camp. "Where's O'Connor?"

A frown creased Tyler's forehead. "I don't know. Now that I think about it, I don't believe I've seen him for the past few hours."

"Maybe he's with Davidson, both of them wallowing in their failures."

Tyler shook his head and said, "I doubt it. Edgar may appreciate the sergeant supporting him —"

"Licking his boots, you mean," said Jamie.

Without commenting on that, Tyler went on, "But he's not really the type to commiserate with a noncommissioned officer, either." He stood up from the tailgate. "It seems to me that something else isn't right."

He walked over to the fire, with Jamie trailing him curiously.

"Corporal Mackey," Tyler said, "are all

the men in camp?"

Mackey looked up, puzzled, and said, "Beg your pardon, Lieutenant? What do you mean?"

"You just fed the men. Are some of them missing?"

Mackey scratched his jaw and said, "I don't rightly know, sir. I didn't count everybody as they came through the line."

"But what's your impression? Did it seem like fewer than usual?"

"Well . . . maybe. But I'm not sure."

Jamie asked, "What about Sergeant O'Connor? Did he eat supper?"

Mackey was more animated and decisive as he replied, "No, he didn't, Mr. MacCallister. And I *am* sure of that. I noticed he wasn't here, because he always eats more than anybody else and gets mad at me when I don't want to give him even more. I thought maybe he was standing guard."

"O'Connor wouldn't do that," Tyler said. "And I'm certain he was missing before supper."

Mackey's eyes widened as he said, "Deserted, sir? Is that what you think?"

Before Tyler could answer, Jamie gripped the lieutenant's arm and asked, "Does O'Connor have any particular friends among the troops?"

337

"I'm not sure. I never paid that much attention to him, as long as he wasn't causing trouble."

"I can tell you, Mr. MacCallister," Mackey said. "There are half a dozen men Sergeant O'Connor gets along with very well. They gamble together sometimes. Berriman, Cowan, Mitchener, Page, Prentice, and Delahanty." The corporal shook his head. "And none of them were here for supper, either."

"Something's wrong, Jamie," Tyler snapped. "It's no coincidence that O'Connor and half a dozen of his friends are missing."

"It's sure not," Jamie agreed grimly.

"But where could they have gone?"

"I'm not sure," said Jamie, "but the one possibility I can think of worries the hell out of me."

CHAPTER 25

After supper that evening with Hawk, Butterfly, and the children, Preacher took a walk around the Crow village. It was a warm, pleasant night, the air full of the smells of food coming from the lodges mixed with the tang of the pines, spruce, and juniper that covered the slopes above the village. He heard children laughing. Dogs barked here and there.

A soft step behind him made him turn, not in alarm but in curiosity. His hand drifted to the butt of the Colt holstered on his right hip anyway, just out of habit.

He relaxed when he recognized the shape of the man who had come up to him.

"Shouldn't you be back in the lodge with your family, Hawk?"

"They are your family as well," Hawk pointed out. "And yet you wander the night."

That brought a chuckle from Preacher.

There was no denying what the young warrior said.

"I was just gettin' a breath of fresh air. It's a nice night."

"It is," Hawk agreed, "but I believe there is more to it than that, Preacher."

"Oh? What do you think is goin' on, then?"

"I believe the restlessness is growing inside you. Now that your old friend Jamie Mac-Callister is gone, it will grow even faster. Soon there will come a morning when you saddle your horse and ride away."

"Well, we both knew that, didn't we?" Preacher asked. "I just came for a visit. I ain't one of those old fellas who shows up at his boy's place, stakes a claim on the front porch rockin' chair, and never leaves."

"No, I cannot imagine you ever doing that. And yet . . . Butterfly and the children are happy to have you here. You have many friends in the village. Broken Pine, Big Thunder . . . all would be happy to have you stay."

"Aw, hell, I'd just be one more mouth to feed," Preacher said. "And you folks have already been havin' trouble with that, remember?"

"The meat we brought back from the hunt has helped a great deal. No one will go hungry for a time. And I believe the game has already started to return to the area in greater numbers. Besides," added Hawk, "if you stayed here, you could continue to hunt with us, and I am sure you would bring in more fresh meat for the others than you would ever consume yourself."

Preacher knew that was right. Still, he wasn't going to let Hawk's arguments sway him. He had made up his mind.

"I'll be movin' on," he said. "Not right away, since I wouldn't mind visitin' more, but it won't be too much longer, I reckon." He paused. "For another thing, I want to make sure them soldiers are long gone on their way back to Fort Kearny before I light a shuck. I just never did trust that Lieutenant Davidson."

"He is not a good man," Hawk said without hesitation. "You believe he will try to trick the Crow somehow?"

"I wouldn't put it past him. I'm just not sure what he would try . . ."

Preacher's words had just trailed off when a frightened cry suddenly shattered the peaceful night.

Preacher and Hawk both whirled toward the sound, recognizing it for what it was. The young warrior cried, "Butterfly!"

They raced toward Hawk's lodge, their familiarity with the village allowing them to dash through the darkness without tripping or running into anything. As they approached the lodge, Preacher spotted several figures just outside the dwelling. One of them exclaimed, "Look out!" and moonlight glinted on a couple of objects that rose swiftly.

Preacher didn't have to think about what was going on. He had observed enough for his keen brain to put it all together automatically. The man had cried out in English, and unaccented English, at that, which made him white. And those glints of light were the moon reflecting off rifle barrels . . .

"Down!" Preacher barked at Hawk. He grabbed his son's arm as he dived forward, throwing them both to the ground. In that same instant, the two rifles fired. Tongues of flame spurted out almost a foot from their muzzles. The lead balls passed harmlessly above Preacher and Hawk.

Preacher had filled his hands with the Colts as soon as he hit the ground. Now, stretched out on his belly, he triggered the revolvers. Their heavy boom echoed through the whole village and along the river. The two men who had tried to kill Preacher and Hawk dropped their rifles, staggered back a couple of steps, and collapsed.

Another man remained outside the lodge.

He shouted, "O'Connor, come on!"

If Preacher needed any more proof of what was going on here, that was more than enough. He scrambled to his feet and was about to drill the frantic soldier who stood at the lodge's entrance, but before that could happen, a hulking figure pushed past the flap and emerged with a struggling captive writhing in his arms.

"Better hold your fire, mister," he warned, "or this squaw will die!"

"Butterfly," Hawk rasped from where he stood beside Preacher.

"Take it easy, son," Preacher warned. He could tell that Hawk was about to dash forward. "Don't give that bastard any excuse to hurt her."

Sergeant Liam O'Connor stepped farther away from the lodge, taking Butterfly with him. He held her so her feet dangled off the ground. She kicked her legs, but the effort didn't do any good. O'Connor had one arm clamped around her waist, the other looped around her neck.

To Preacher's horror, two more troopers came out of the lodge, each with a prisoner. His grandchildren had been snatched up out of sleep and were now hostages like their mother.

The gunshots and the shouting had roused

the entire village by now. Warriors emerged from lodges holding weapons and shouting questions. Dogs barked madly.

At the center of the commotion, Preacher moved slowly forward with the pair of leveled revolvers held rock-steady in his fists.

"Back off!" O'Connor ordered. "I don't want to hurt this woman, but I'm not that worried about the kids. Nobody cares about a couple of little half-breed bastards."

"I will kill you," Hawk said, his voice low and hard as flint.

O'Connor laughed and said, "You may want to, red-skin, but I got your squaw here — and you better not forget it."

Preacher could see O'Connor's head just past Butterfly's shoulder. If the light had been better, he would have fired a shot past her ear, right into the middle of O'Connor's forehead. In these shadows, he couldn't risk that.

Preacher didn't lower his guns as he said, "Davidson sent you to kidnap Butterfly so he can take her back with him, didn't he? He's still bound and determined to *rescue* her, ain't he?"

"She's white," O'Connor snapped back at him. "No matter how long she's been here, she doesn't belong with these savages. And think how happy her real family will be once they have her back."

Preacher knew better than that. If Butterfly — Caroline — *did* have any family back east, they wouldn't be pleased to be reunited with her. They would believe that her life among the Indians had degraded her to the point that she wasn't really human anymore. They would never accept her. Preacher had seen it happen time and time again.

"I am not white!" gasped Butterfly. "I am Crow! Leave me alone! Do not hurt my chil—"

O'Connor tightened the arm around her neck, cutting off her protest.

"Shut up, squaw," he said. "Listen, mountain man, you'd better tell all your redskin friends to stay back. We're leavin', and if you don't try to stop us, we'll let the kids go once we get back to camp. Nobody has to get hurt."

"Reckon it's gone past that," Preacher said. "Somebody's *gonna* get hurt. But if you let Butterfly and the little ones go, I think maybe I can keep you from gettin' killed."

Another trooper had come out of the lodge following the men who held Eagle Feather and Bright Moon. With the two armed soldiers flanking them, O'Connor and the other two troopers began sidling away from the lodge as they held the hostages in front of them.

Preacher laughed suddenly. He said, "I can't believe Davidson thought he could send a bunch of fellas like you here to do this job. Sneakin' into a Crow village, grabbin' prisoners, and makin' off with 'em without anybody knowin' about it until it was too late . . . Good Lord, Sergeant, there ain't no way you could have done that."

"We almost did," O'Connor said, his lips twisting in a snarl as he glared over Butterfly's shoulder at Preacher. "We would have if this bitch hadn't managed to yell."

Again, Hawk snarled and leaned forward, ready to attack, but Preacher put out a hand to stop him. The way O'Connor was holding Butterfly, he could break her neck without much trouble. That would ruin Davidson's plans, of course, but O'Connor might not think that all the way through if he was pushed too hard.

"You don't really think you're gonna walk outta here with Butterfly and those young'uns, do you? Even if you do, you'll never make it all the way back to your camp. I tell you, you fellas are gonna be a lot better off if you just give up right now. That's the only way you live through this."

"If we don't live through it," said O'Connor, "then these three don't live through it. And that's a promise, you son of a —"

A huge figure loomed out of the darkness behind O'Connor like a moving mountain, and it landed on the sergeant like an avalanche. Only one person around here was that massive, Preacher realized.

Big Thunder was taking a hand.

The collision's impact was enough to slam O'Connor forward and jolt Butterfly out of his grasp. As he dropped her, she cried out and landed hard on the ground. For a second, Preacher thought O'Connor and Big Thunder were going to come down on top of her, and their combined weight might have crushed her.

She managed to roll aside just in time to avoid the two men falling like trees. Big Thunder had his arms wrapped around O'Connor, but the sergeant was strong enough to writhe around and slam his elbow into Big Thunder's face.

"Kill those kids!" O'Connor roared at the other soldiers.

The troopers hesitated instead of carrying out that command. They might be O'Connor's cronies, as well as being used to him giving them orders, but murdering children was something they couldn't do lightly. That moment of delay was enough to allow

Preacher and Hawk to reach them.

The man holding Eagle Feather cried out in fear and tried to lift the boy higher to shield himself. He was too late. The tomahawk in the young warrior's hand rose and fell with swift, deadly speed. With a loud *thunk!* followed by a crunching sound, the weapon struck the man in the head and bit deep into his brain. Spasming as he died, he let go of Eagle Feather and dropped the boy at his feet. Hawk wrenched the tomahawk free and gave the soldier a contemptuous shove away from him. The man was dead by the time he hit the ground.

A few feet away, Preacher struck with the gun he still held in his right hand. The barrel swiped across the face of the trooper holding Bright Moon, opening up a cut that welled dark blood down the man's face. Even as he was leaping forward, Preacher had holstered his left-hand gun. He used that hand now to grab his granddaughter and jerk her away from her captor. Bright Moon clutched desperately at Preacher as the mountain man pistol-whipped the soldier again and knocked him sprawling on the ground.

The prisoners were all free now, and O'Connor had his hands full with Big Thunder, but the other two armed soldiers were still a threat. One of them swung his rifle toward Preacher, but before he could pull the trigger, he grunted and arched his back. The rifle slipped from suddenly nerveless hands. The man stumbled forward and then pitched onto his face, revealing Broken Pine standing there with blood dripping from the point of the knife he had just thrust into the soldier's back.

The other trooper suddenly threw his rifle to the ground in front of him and thrust his empty hands out in front of him.

"Don't kill me!" he cried. "Please don't kill me!"

Hawk picked up Eagle Feather from the ground and hugged the boy tightly to him for a second. Then Preacher said, "Here, take the girl," and Hawk set Eagle Feather down in order to take Bright Moon from the mountain man. She wrapped her arms around his neck and her legs around his waist and clung to him as if she would never let go.

Eagle Feather wasn't neglected, though. Butterfly was back on her feet by now. She drew her son into her arms and held him with fierce determination.

Preacher turned to the battle between O'Connor and Big Thunder. The Crow had drawn back to give the two titans room. Big

Thunder, like most Indians, was primarily a wrestler. O'Connor had enough experience in that form of combat to hold his own, Preacher saw, but in addition he was a slugger. He hammered punches at Big Thunder's face, and the warrior wasn't skillful enough to block many of them. Dark blood from the cuts O'Connor's fists opened up streaked across Big Thunder's features.

Big Thunder could absorb a tremendous amount of punishment, though, before it had much effect on him. He shrugged off the blows O'Connor dealt out and continued trying to get his tree trunk arms around the sergeant. If he ever caught O'Connor in a bear hug, that would be the end of the fight.

O'Connor had to know how overwhelming the odds were against him. Even if he defeated Big Thunder, he would still be surrounded by an entire village full of Crow warriors who were angry at him. He had been caught trying to kidnap Butterfly and the two children, and nothing he could do now would change that. He would have to pay for that transgression.

But that didn't mean he was going to quit. As much as Preacher disliked the man, it was clear he didn't have any give-up in him. O'Conner kept slamming punches to Big

Thunder's head and torso and breaking free every time the huge warrior tried to grapple with him.

It was too much for Big Thunder. He began to sway and seemed to be half-unconscious even though he was still on his feet. His head jerked to the side and blood flew from his lips as O'Connor landed another roundhouse punch. O'Connor slugged him in the belly hard enough to make Big Thunder bend over. That put the huge slab of a jaw in perfect position for the uppercut that O'Connor brought whistling up from the ground. The punch landed with a sound like an ax splitting a chunk of wood. Big Thunder weighed too much for the blow to lift him off his feet, but he stood up straight with his head tilted far back.

Then, slowly, he began to topple backward, picking up speed until he crashed to the ground with such an impact that it seemed as if the whole world should have shuddered . . . even though it actually didn't, of course.

That left O'Connor standing there with his chest heaving. His fists were bruised, swollen, and bleeding from all the damage he had done by pounding them against Big Thunder. Preacher could tell that Sergeant O'Connor didn't have any fight left in him.

That didn't stop the man's lip from curling in a snarl as he peered at the Indians surrounding him. Several warriors had arrows nocked and drawn back on their bows, ready to fire. O'Connor glared at them and yelled, "Go ahead! Shoot and be damned to you! Ye can kill me, but you'll still be filthy savages and I'll still be a white man!"

"There's been enough killin'," Preacher said as he stepped forward. "I reckon the army's gonna deal with you."

"No!" Hawk protested. "He threatened my family. He must pay!"

"He will —" Preacher started to say as he turned toward his son.

But before he could go on, hoofbeats suddenly pounded close by, and riders loomed up out of the night.

CHAPTER 26

Lieutenant Hayden Tyler had to break into a trot to keep up with Jamie as the big frontiersman strode toward Lieutenant Davidson's tent.

"You don't really believe the lieutenant sent O'Connor after that woman, do you?" Tyler asked, panting a little from his efforts. "That's insane!"

"Are you saying Davidson wouldn't risk it? Broken Pine turned him down flat about the treaty. There's no way Davidson can successfully complete the mission he was sent on. The only thing he can do to maybe salvage things is bring back a white captive he rescued and hope that'll cover him with enough glory to make people forget his failure."

"But to risk war with the Crow —"

"I reckon he'd risk almost anything to get what he wants," Jamie said. "Especially if he's mostly risking other people's lives."

They reached Davidson's tent. One of the troopers stood guard outside it. He held his rifle at a slant across his chest and said quietly, "Begging your pardon, sirs, Lieutenant Davidson has already retired for the evening and doesn't wish to be disturbed unless —"

He stopped short, as if realizing that he'd been about to say too much. Jamie glared at the sentry and said, "Unless it's Sergeant O'Connor, right? Well, get out of our way, son, we're going in."

The suddenly nervous trooper looked at Tyler and said, "Lieutenant?"

"Step aside, private," Tyler said. "This is important."

The soldier still hesitated, but only for a second longer before he muttered, "Oh, well, I suppose I can't be busted down any lower than I already am."

He moved aside to allow Jamie and Tyler to reach the tent's entrance flap. Jamie grabbed hold of it and jerked it aside.

"Davidson!" His bellow filled the night.

Lieutenant Davidson jerked up from his cot as Jamie bulled into the tent. He was the only member of the troop who didn't sleep in a bedroll. But that also meant he was the only one who could fall off a cot in confusion when he was jolted out of sleep, as happened now. He landed hard on his butt and sat there blinking in confusion as Jamie snapped a lucifer to life with his thumbnail and held the flame to the wick of the candle on Davidson's small folding table.

The light from the candle revealed that Davidson was dressed only in his long underwear. His sandy hair was askew from sleep. His mouth opened and closed a couple of times as he gaped up at Jamie.

"Good Lord, you're a cool-nerved son of a bitch, I'll give you that," Jamie declared. "You send men off on a chore that'll probably get them all killed and is liable to start an Indian war, and you're still able to just turn in and go to sleep!"

"What . . . what are you talking about?" Davidson managed to say. Then his features grew taut with his habitual expression of arrogant petulance. "What the devil are you doing, MacCallister? How dare you intrude on my personal quarters this way?"

He stood up and started brushing himself off.

"I know what you're up to, Davidson," Jamie grated. He had to keep a tight rein on his temper. If he gave in to the impulses that filled him, he would pick up that little brat and shake him the way a hunting dog shakes a rat. "I know you sent O'Connor and some of the other troopers to the Crow village to try to kidnap Butterfly!"

"The woman's name is Caroline," said Davidson. "With any luck, we'll find out what her last name is when we get her back to civilization, where she belongs."

"You really think you're going to be able to do that?" Jamie waved an arm angrily and almost knocked over the candle with his hand. "I reckon the Crow are going to have something to say about that."

"Those savages are no match for a properly trained and well-armed troop of dragoons," Davidson insisted. "Once we have Miss Caroline in our custody, they'll see how futile it would be to try to steal her away from us, as they no doubt stole her to start with."

"Didn't you listen to *anything* Preacher had to say about her?"

Davidson shook his head and said, "I put no stock in anything said by a man who spends his time with those heathens by choice. He's no better than they are."

Tyler spoke up, saying, "Is what Jamie says true, Edgar? You sent men to kidnap that woman?"

"To *rescue* her. And be careful the sort of

tone you take with me, *Second* Lieutenant Tyler."

Tyler didn't seem to be worried about violating military protocol as he went on, "My God, I can't believe you'd do such a thing! You're going to get us all killed!"

"Showing your true colors, eh, Lieutenant?" Davidson's lip curled. "You're nothing but a coward."

Tyler stepped forward, clenching his fists and tensing himself to take a swing, no longer caring that Davidson held a higher rank. Jamie moved to get between the two young men, not because he was worried about Davidson but rather because he didn't want to see Tyler throw away his military career.

"I'm going to head over there and see if I can put a stop to this before everything goes to hell," he said. "If you're lucky, Davidson, O'Connor and the men with him got caught trying to sneak into the village, and the Crow are holding them now. I don't see how any other course will bring anything except grief."

"You're not going to interfere, MacCallister. That's a direct order —"

"I don't take orders from you. I never did, and I sure as hell don't now!"

Jamie swung around toward the tent's

entrance, but before he could leave, Davidson said, "Lieutenant Tyler, place MacCallister under arrest!"

Tyler's eyes got big in the candlelight. Jamie jerked back toward Davidson and said, "You can't arrest me. I'm a civilian."

"You're drawing pay from the army as a civilian scout for this mission. That means I certainly *can* arrest you. And as the only legally constituted authority in the area, that places you under my jurisdiction anyway!" Davidson glared at Tyler and went on, "Well? I gave you a direct order, Lieutenant. Do your duty!"

Tyler moved his hand toward the flap of his holster as he said, "Jamie, I . . . I'm sorry about this —"

"Lieutenant!" That was the sentry outside the tent. "Lieutenant, reports of gunfire comin' from the direction of the Indian village!"

"O'Connor got himself caught," muttered Jamie. "Anybody surprised about that? Come on, Hayden, we'd better go find out just how bad things are over there."

This time Jamie didn't stop when he turned toward the entrance. For a second, Tyler looked like he was about to step in front of him and try to block his path. But the young officer didn't do so, and Jamie strode past him and out into the night.

Behind him, in the tent, Davidson screeched, *"Lieutenant!"*

Jamie brushed by the startled sentry and headed for the corral. A moment later he heard rapid footsteps and glanced over his shoulder to see Lieutenant Tyler hurrying to catch up with him.

"I'm coming with you, Jamie," he said.

"Disobeying a direct order?"

"Edgar will calm down and cool off and realize that someone in command has to go see what's happening over there."

Jamie wasn't going to count on Davidson calming down and cooling off, but it wasn't his career at stake. He admired Tyler for standing up to the obnoxious little martinet.

"Have there been any more shots?" Tyler went on.

"Not that I've heard."

"Maybe that means the trouble is over."

Jamie wasn't going to count on *that,* either.

Everyone who had gathered in response to the gunshots and the other commotion swung sharply toward the new arrivals as they reined in. Preacher lifted the revolver he still held, then relaxed slightly as he realized the bigger of the two riders was Jamie MacCallister. Jamie's brawny figure was easy to recognize, even in bad light.

"Sergeant O'Connor!" the other man said. Preacher recognized Lieutenant Hayden Tyler's voice. "I'd ask what the devil you're doing here, but I'm afraid I already know."

"Lieutenant Tyler!" O'Connor exclaimed. "You brought the rest of the troop with you, didn't you, Lieutenant? These savages have murdered some of our men!"

Preacher said, "That's a damned lie. We defended ourselves from these varmints who were tryin' to kidnap Butterfly!"

Jamie and Tyler hadn't dismounted. Jamie leaned forward in the saddle and asked, "Any of the Crow hurt, Preacher?"

"Big Thunder took a lickin' from O'Connor, believe it or not, but I don't think anybody else was hurt."

"What about our men?" Tyler asked tightly.

Broken Pine straightened from where he had been kneeling, examining the sprawled bodies of the soldiers, and said, "Four of them are dead. Another is unconscious. I do not know how badly he is hurt. These two —" he gestured curtly at O'Connor and the trooper who had surrendered — "are unharmed."

"You see, Lieutenant," O'Connor said. "They killed soldiers! They admit it! That's

360

an act of war. Lieutenant Davidson'd be justified in wipin' out the red-skinned bastards!"

The arrival of Jamie and Lieutenant Tyler seemed to have convinced O'Connor that he was no longer in imminent danger of losing his life. He wasn't thinking about the fact that those two couldn't stop the Crow from doing anything they wanted to. If Broken Pine gave the order, O'Connor could still die in the blink of an eye.

The chief looked just about mad enough to give that order, too. Preacher holstered his gun and stepped forward to say, "Broken Pine, I think you should let Jamie and Lieutenant Tyler take O'Connor and the others back to the army camp. Let their superior officers deal with 'em. That's the best way to keep the peace."

One of the warriors spoke up, repeating in a loud, disgusted voice, "Keep the peace? The white men will not punish one of their own, no matter what they do to the Crow!"

That was Many Pelts, Preacher realized, letting his dislike for the whites cloud his thinking again.

And yet, was Many Pelts really wrong? Preacher couldn't help but wonder. If it was up to Lieutenant Tyler, O'Connor would face some sort of discipline, even though it probably wouldn't be as much as he deserved.

But it was Lieutenant Davidson who was in command, and Davidson had shown that he supported O'Connor in whatever the sergeant did. Hell, Preacher thought suddenly, stealing Butterfly away from the village could have been Davidson's idea. He might have *ordered* O'Connor to take some men and abduct her. Preacher wouldn't put that past the arrogant young officer at all.

O'Connor must have been starting to get nervous again. He said, "Lieutenant, I think you'd better get us out of here while you still —"

"No!" Broken Pine cut in. "The white soldiers will stay here. The other chief, the one called Davidson, must come and give the Crow his word that they will be punished before he can have them back."

Jamie grimaced and said, "That's actually a pretty reasonable suggestion, Broken Pine, but the problem is, I don't think you'll ever get Lieutenant Davidson to agree to it. He's going to insist that you release his men on *his* terms."

"Which will mean unconditionally," added Tyler.

Broken Pine shook his head.

"Go and tell Davidson what I have said,"

he insisted. "Until then, his men stay here."

O'Connor took a step forward and said, "Lieutenant, don't do it! You can't just leave us here. You know these savages are gonna kill us as soon as you ride off!"

Tyler looked torn about what to do. Jamie said to the lieutenant, "I'll stay here while you go talk to Davidson. I reckon that's the best thing we can do for now."

Tyler started to nod. He lifted his reins, ready to turn his horse and ride back to the army camp.

Before he could do that, O'Connor suddenly burst into action. He lunged across the distance separating him from Tyler and leaped into the air to land on the horse's back behind the young officer. Preacher and Jamie both drew their guns, but they couldn't risk shooting in this bad light while O'Connor and Tyler were so close together.

Tyler was no match for O'Connor's animal-like speed and strength. He got hold of Tyler's collar and literally flung him off the horse. Even as he was doing that, O'Connor rammed his heels into the animal's flanks and sent it leaping away. He pulled himself forward into the saddle and clung desperately to the horse.

Flame spouted from the muzzles of Preacher's and Jamie's guns before Tyler even hit the ground, but O'Connor was bent low over the horse's neck, not giving them much of a target. He didn't fall, nor did the galloping mount break stride.

Arrows whipped through the air, too, as the Crow opened fire on the fleeing sergeant. O'Connor seemed to be living a charmed life, though. In a matter of heartbeats, he was at the very edge of effective range with either bows or revolvers. Preacher's Sharps might have bought him down, but the mountain man didn't have the heavy carbine with him. It was back in the lodge he'd been using while he was here.

"Hold your fire!" Jamie said as he wheeled his horse. "I'll get him!"

Jamie raced after O'Connor as the arrows stopped flying.

The other captured trooper fell to his knees as several warriors crowded around him. He held his arms over his head and sobbed, "Don't kill me, please don't kill me!"

Broken Pine barked an order, and the men who had been raising tomahawks in a threatening manner reluctantly lowered them. While that was going on, Preacher stepped over to Lieutenant Tyler and helped the young officer to his feet.

Tyler's hand went to the scabbard buckled

at his waist. He exclaimed, "My saber! It's gone. O'Connor must have my saber!"

Preacher peered off into the darkness where Jamie and O'Connor had disappeared, wishing there was some way he could warn his old friend that O'Connor was armed.

CHAPTER 27

Lieutenant Tyler's horse was fast, but Jamie's big stallion had more speed and stamina. If this chase had been taking place during the day, Jamie would have caught up fairly quickly.

The fact that it was dark, though, make him hold back his mount to a certain extent. He couldn't let the stallion run at full speed because of the chance that the horse might stumble and hurt himself or even take a spill.

O'Connor was fueled by fear for his life, though, so he wasn't that careful. Jamie could hear the swift rataplan of hoofbeats in the distance ahead of him as O'Connor rode hell-bent for leather.

Even so, the stallion's long strides began to make a difference. Jamie could tell by the sound of the horse he was pursuing that he was cutting the gap. After several minutes, he was able to see O'Connor up ahead, in the dim light from the moon and stars.

The army camp was about half a mile away. Jamie could see the small fires burning there. He wanted to catch up to O'Connor before the sergeant reached the camp. If O'Connor got there first, Jamie wouldn't be able to take him back to the Crow village, and that would put even more of a strain on the situation.

Since they were on a flat, straight stretch now, Jamie let the stallion have his head. The big horse loved to run and practically flew over the ground. He drew up almost alongside the horse O'Connor had taken from Lieutenant Tyler.

Without warning, O'Connor twisted in the saddle and slashed at Jamie with something. Jamie saw moonlight reflect off the object and realized O'Connor had a saber in his hand. Jamie jerked back. The blade barely missed him. While O'Connor was a little off-balance from that, Jamie crowded in, hoping to get a hand on O'Connor and unseat him.

Instead, O'Connor whipped the saber at Jamie's face in a snake-quick backhand, and again, Jamie practically felt the cold steel kiss his skin.

Jamie didn't wait for O'Connor to recover and try again. He launched himself from the saddle in a diving tackle that carried him into the other man with bone-jarring force. O'Connor let out a startled yell as they both toppled from horseback and crashed to the ground.

The impact of landing broke them apart. Jamie rolled over several times before coming to a stop on his belly. He pushed himself onto hands and knees and lifted his head to look around, searching for O'Connor as the horses continued running toward the army camp.

Jamie spotted O'Connor a few yards away. The sergeant was sprawled on his back. He rolled onto his side and groaned as he shook his head groggily.

Knowing that he needed to seize the advantage, Jamie forced himself to his feet and started toward O'Connor. O'Connor was stunned, but not so much that he didn't hear Jamie coming. He rolled again and slashed upward with the saber. Somehow he had managed to hang on to it.

Jamie caught himself just in time to keep the blade from ripping through his guts. He darted to the side to come at O'Connor from a different angle, but O'Connor twisted on the ground and jabbed upward with the saber, forcing Jamie to jump back again. That gave O'Connor time to get his other hand and a knee underneath him and push himself up.

"Come on, you son of a bitch," he gasped as he stood unsteadily and waved the saber back and forth in the air in front of him. "I'll cut you to pieces, you Indian-lovin' bastard!"

Jamie's Colt was still in its holster. His fingers brushed against the weapon's grips as he stood there trying to catch his breath. He was sorely tempted to haul out the hogleg and blow a hole through O'Connor.

That would sure simplify matters.

But it might not be the best solution in the long run, the course of action that would stand the greatest chance of preserving the peace between the whites and the Crow. Preacher claimed that once folks back east realized there *wasn't* a good route for wagon trains through the mountains in this area after all, the whites wouldn't have any more reason to come this way and possibly run into problems with the Crow.

Jamie knew it wouldn't stay like that in the long run, though. He had seen how settlers were spreading out in every direction, all the time. He knew how many thousands — no, *millions* — of people there were who dreamed of making a new start and finding a new home in the West. The frontier was an irresistible lure that would always be answered, as long as people had hopes and dreams.

And that meant the whites were coming. Maybe not in great numbers, maybe not anytime soon, but they would be here, even in this wild, untamed country, and it wouldn't do anybody any good for the current inhabitants to hate them before they ever got here.

Those thoughts raced through Jamie's mind in a split second as he considered gunning down O'Connor and getting it over with. He discarded the idea. There had to be rule of law if civilization was going to get a toehold here. Might as well start establishing it now.

Jamie feinted to his right. O'Connor jerked and swung the saber that way. Jamie lunged in and got his left hand on O'Connor's wrist as the sergeant tried to recover and launch a backhand. Jamie thrust up and forced the blade away from him.

At the same time, his right hand shot out and closed around O'Connor's throat. His fingers clamped down hard to shut off the man's breath. O'Connor stumbled backward a couple of steps, Jamie going with him. If he could hold off that saber long enough, he could choke O'Connor into un-

370

consciousness . . .

O'Connor tried to hammer punches into Jamie's head with his left fist. Jamie hunched his right shoulder and took most of the force of the blows on it. He kept up the pressure on O'Connor's throat and heard the man start to make desperate little squeaking sounds as he struggled for air that couldn't get through his windpipe.

O'Connor started to sag in Jamie's grip. Jamie thought the sergeant was on the verge of passing out, but it was just a ploy. The next second, O'Connor's right foot shot between Jamie's legs, hooked behind his right ankle, and jerked hard. O'Connor threw himself forward at the same time. His chest rammed into Jamie's, and that, combined with Jamie's leg being pulled out from under him, was enough to knock Jamie over backward.

Jamie landed with O'Connor on top of him. That knocked the breath out of him and made red streaks shoot through the darkness all around them, at least in Jamie's mind. O'Connor yanked loose the hand holding the saber and raised the blade high.

"Now I'll skewer ye," he growled.

Jamie didn't have his full faculties back yet, but instincts honed during a lot of years of surviving a dangerous life pulled his head to the side just in time. The blade came down, whispering past his ear, and buried half a foot of itself in the sod. Before O'Connor could pull it free, Jamie clubbed both hands together and swung them in a sledgehammer blow to the side of O'Connor's head. The terrific impact knocked O'Connor off him. O'Conner lost his grip on the saber and rolled on the grass.

Jamie snatched the saber from the sod and went after O'Connor. He dug a knee into O'Connor's midsection, pinning him to the ground. As O'Connor gasped, Jamie put the saber's edge against his throat and pressed hard enough for the blade to cut slightly into the skin.

"It's over, O'Connor," Jamie said. "One way or another. Stop fighting or I'll slice your throat wide open."

Instead of O'Connor answering, it was a higher-pitched voice that responded to Jamie's words.

"If that man does not surrender immediately, *shoot him!*"

Jamie heard rifles being cocked all around him. It was a sound that would get a man's attention.

He lifted his head and looked around. United States Army dragoons, in various states of undress but all holding rifles, surrounded him and pointed the weapons at him. A few feet away stood Lieutenant Edgar Davidson, in his uniform now and fairly quivering with indignation.

"You might want to reconsider that order, Lieutenant," drawled Jamie. "Standing the way those boys are, if they open fire on me, some of them are liable to shoot each other. And O'Connor will wind up as full of lead as I am, I can guarantee that." He paused, then added, "Of course, he won't feel it for long, because I figure on cutting his throat before I die."

For a long, tense moment, Davidson didn't say anything. Then he told the troopers, "Step back and spread out, all of you, but keep MacCallister covered. And if he harms Sergeant O'Connor, you may fire at will."

Jamie took the saber away from O'Connor's throat. Under the circumstances, there was nothing else he could do. He pushed himself to his feet and stepped back.

"Surrender that saber," Davidson ordered.

Instead of dropping the saber as his feet, Jamie shifted his grip, drew it back, and flung it like a spear. The blade drove into the ground just in front of Davidson, making him flinch slightly. The saber swayed back and forth a little from the force of

Jamie's throw.

"Take this man into custody," Davidson went on. "You've defied the will of the United States Army long enough, MacCallister. You have to learn that you can't attack my men and get away with it."

O'Connor clambered to his feet and held a couple of fingers to his throat where the saber had nicked him. He frowned at the dark blood visible on his fingertips and then said, "You should go ahead and have him shot, Lieutenant! A court-martial would just be a waste of time. Put the bastard in front of a firing squad now!"

Davidson clasped his hands behind his back and lifted his chin.

"I understand that you're upset, Sergeant, and with good reason," he said. "But we will follow the proper protocol. In the meantime . . . ." The lieutenant's voice hardened. "I believe I gave an order. MacCallister is to be taken into custody *immediately.* I want this man in irons so he can't cause any more trouble."

With some reluctance, several of the troopers moved closer to Jamie. One of them was Corporal Mackey. He said, "I'm sorry about this, Mr. MacCallister, but I guess it'll be easier all around if you just cooperate with what the lieutenant wants."

Jamie said harshly, "Why don't you ask the lieutenant about how he ordered O'Connor to kidnap a woman from that Crow village?"

"That's a damned lie!" O'Connor exclaimed. "Lieutenant Davidson didn't do any such thing."

With his chin still jutting out defiantly, Davidson said, "Not that I have any need to answer to the likes of you, MacCallister, but I merely sent Sergeant O'Connor and a few of the men to reconnoiter the surrounding area and make certain that the savages weren't trying to sneak up on us for some sort of surprise attack. I'm aware of how craven and cowardly they are."

Rage burned brightly inside Jamie, but he realized he had no way of proving that Davidson was lying. The only ones who knew the truth about the attempt to kidnap Butterfly were back in the Crow village . . . and the soldiers might not believe them, anyway.

Surrounded by nervous, inexperienced, rifle-toting dragoons as he was, Jamie didn't see any options other than cooperating, as Corporal Mackey had asked him to do. He was about to let the troopers take him back to the camp, when Davidson said to O'Connor, "Where are the rest of the men from your detail, Sergeant?"

"Dead, sir," O'Connor answered without hesitation. "Murdered by the heathens. They attacked us, just like you thought they might."

Davidson drew in a sharp, deep breath, and said, "My God! That's the last straw. Tell the bugler to blow assembly! We're going to attack that village and wipe it off the face of the earth! Those savages will pay for their crimes!"

Horror filled Jamie. With the failure of O'Connor and the others to steal Butterfly away, Davidson's ambition had been thwarted again, and the resulting fury seemed to have tipped him over into madness.

"Lieutenant, you can't do that," Jamie said. "You've got no cause. You're talking about a massacre —"

"I'm talking about avenging the deaths of American soldiers! Don't you think that's a worthy cause, MacCallister?"

"But they were trying to kidnap an innocent woman —"

"There are no innocent Indians!" Davidson practically screamed at him. "They're all guilty! Men, women, and children! And we're going to kill them all." Davidson's head jerked from side to side as he looked around at the troopers. "Carry out my orders! Now! And if MacCallister causes any trouble, shoot to kill!"

Jamie was going to cause trouble, all right. He was through trying to find peaceful solutions. With Davidson in command of the troop, that just wasn't possible. And he sure as hell wasn't going to stand by and do nothing while the dragoons attacked the Crow village. Even though the warriors were better fighting men, the soldiers outnumbered them and were better armed. In all likelihood, such a battle would wind up being a slaughter on both sides.

Jamie turned suddenly. He grabbed a rifle barrel and thrust hard on it so the stock slammed into the midsection of the trooper holding the gun. He gasped, doubled over, and let go of the rifle. Jamie whirled, still holding the barrel. He slammed the rifle across the chests of two more men and knocked them down.

Then he darted through the gap he had created in the circle of soldiers around him. Behind him, Davidson screeched, "Shoot him! Shoot him!"

Most of the troopers hesitated when it came to pulling the trigger, though. A couple of rifles boomed, but that was all. As Jamie raced away, he heard O'Connor yell,

"Give me that rifle, damn it!"

A second later, another shot roared out, but Jamie had already put some distance between himself and the startled troopers. He heard the rifle ball hum past his head. Too close for comfort, he thought . . . but not close enough to stop him.

He whistled shrilly, knowing that his stallion would have stopped somewhere close by. Tyler's horse, the one O'Connor had grabbed, must have galloped on into the camp, alerting the soldiers that something was going on. That was why they had been able to surround him and O'Connor while they were fighting.

Shouts made him glance back over his shoulder. The troopers were giving chase, streaming over the prairie in a dark, irregular mass in the moonlight. Orange muzzle flashes began to wink. Some of the men were trying to follow Davidson's order to kill him.

Hoofbeats suddenly pounded close by. The stallion's dark shape loomed up abruptly. The horse reared up, pawed at the air, and let out a whinny of greeting. As the front hooves came down to the earth again, Jamie vaulted into the saddle.

"I knew you wouldn't let me down, old son," he said as he grabbed the reins and wheeled the horse toward the river and the Crow village. "Let's go!"

Once again, the stallion flashed over the plains as Jamie leaned forward in the saddle. Preacher, Hawk, Broken Pine, and the others must have heard the shots back there, but they wouldn't know what the gunfire meant.

They didn't know they were about to come under attack from troops commanded by a madman determined to see all of them dead.

CHAPTER 28

Hawk went into his lodge with Butterfly, Eagle Feather, and Bright Moon to comfort his family, but Preacher remained behind to talk with Broken Pine as the rest of the Crow drifted back to their lodges.

"I don't know if Davidson will try anything else tonight, but it might be a good idea to post some extra guards," Preacher suggested to the chief.

Broken Pine nodded solemnly and said, "I had already thought the same thing, Preacher."

Lieutenant Hayden Tyler and Private Berriman, the trooper who had surrendered, had been placed in an empty lodge for the night, with a guard posted just outside the entrance. Preacher knew that Tyler wasn't going to cause any trouble and figured Berriman was too scared to get up to any mischief, but the Crow felt better having them under guard. Tyler had gone along with it without complaining.

The troopers who had been killed in the kidnapping attempt still lay where they had fallen.

Broken Pine was thinking about them now as he asked, "What should we do with the bodies of the slain soldiers? I know some of our warriors believe they should be dragged out of the village and left for the scavengers."

Preacher shook his head.

"No, that would just make things worse. Treat them with respect, wrap them in blankets and put them in that lodge with Tyler and Berriman, and then in the morning we can see about returnin' them. They'll need to be buried soldier-fashion, with a flag and a bugler and military honors."

Broken Pine grunted in consternation and said, "It sounds strange, using the word *honor* when talking about the whites."

"Most of 'em are just folks who want to get along, like the Crow," said Preacher. "Davidson and O'Connor are the ones who keep causin' the trouble."

"They believe we should be wiped out." Broken Pine crossed his arms over his chest. "Can you honestly say there are not many of your people who feel the same way, Preacher?"

The mountain man's jaw tightened. He said, "No, I don't reckon I can. But that's because they don't know you. If they did, some of 'em would feel different about it."

"But not all."

"Nope, not all," Preacher admitted. "Some of 'em are like the Blackfeet. Too filled with hate to ever get over it . . ."

His voice trailed away as he lifted his head and listened to the sudden crackle of gunfire in the distance.

Broken Pine heard it, too. He said, "That came from the soldier camp."

"Yeah," Preacher said. "I wonder if Jamie caught up to O'Connor. I've been sorta worried about that since he didn't come back."

Hawk emerged from the nearby lodge and said, "I thought I heard more shots."

"You did," Preacher told him. "We'd best walk down to the river and see if we can tell what's goin' on."

He had already reloaded the chambers he had fired in his Colts. He rested his hands on the gun butts now as he turned toward the stream, as did Hawk and Broken Pine.

A groan came from Big Thunder, who still lay on the ground where he had fallen when O'Connor knocked him out. Preacher looked around and saw the massive warrior trying to sit up. He said, "Hawk, let's give Big Thunder a hand."

It took both of them to assist Big Thunder to his feet, just as Preacher expected. Big Thunder shook his head ponderously and asked, "What happened? Big Thunder was fighting with bad soldier. That is the last thing Big Thunder remembers."

"Well, I hate to say it, but he beat you, old friend. Knocked you plumb cold."

"No!" Big Thunder exclaimed. "No one defeats Big Thunder!"

"He did this time," Preacher said. "That doesn't mean he would again, if there was ever another fight between the two of you."

Big Thunder raised both giant fists and shook them.

"There will be another fight," he declared. "Big Thunder will win next time!"

Preacher didn't know if there would be another fight, but he wouldn't be surprised if that came about. Every instinct in his body told him the trouble with the soldiers was far from over.

"Come on," he said to his two companions. "Let's catch up with Broken Pine."

The chief had gone on to the outskirts of the village while Preacher and Hawk gave Big Thunder a hand as he regained consciousness. As the three of them came up to him, he turned his head and said, "There have been no more shots. But I believe I hear a horse coming in this direction."

"You're right about that," Preacher said. His keen ears had detected the approaching hoofbeats, as well. As he pulled the revolvers from their holsters, he went on, "Sounds like just one man, but we're gonna be ready if he's lookin' for trouble."

"What else could be abroad this night?" muttered Broken Pine.

Preacher didn't have an answer for that.

A moment later, he stiffened as he detected another sound in the darkness. A rumble that came from the hooves of many horses, not just one. That made alarm race through Preacher, as there could be only one cause for that rising wave of noise.

"The soldiers are coming," he said as he holstered the left-hand gun and gripped Broken Pine's arm. "They wouldn't be chargin' like that unless they planned to fight!"

Broken Pine reacted instantly to the danger. He raised his voice in a shout of warning, his powerful tone reaching to all parts of the village. Other warriors took up the cry as they scrambled out of their lodges in response to the urgent summons.

Broken Pine turned to Hawk and said,

"Get the women and children to the canyon."

"I will stay and fight!" protested Hawk.

"You will do as I say!" Broken Pine's voice didn't allow for any arguments. "The women and the young ones must be protected."

"What's this canyon?" asked Preacher. In all his visits to the Crow village, he hadn't heard about it.

"A blind canyon about a mile deeper in the foothills," Hawk explained quickly. "The women and children know to go there in case of an attack, so that they can be protected more easily. We always thought it would be the Blackfeet we might have to fight off —"

"But now it's army troops instead," Preacher said. "Broken Pine's right. Somebody's got to be in charge of gettin' those folks to safety — and keepin' 'em safe. That's a good job for you, Hawk."

Hawk didn't like it, but he didn't waste any more time objecting. Already the sound of the riders heading for the village had grown louder. Hawk hurried off to organize the retreat of the women and children to the canyon.

The hoofbeats of the single horse they had first noticed were close now. The animal splashed across the shallow stream as Jamie MacCallister hailed, "Hello, the village!"

"Jamie!" Preacher called. "Over here!"

Jamie slowed the stallion and turned toward them. He brought the horse to a halt and slipped to the ground.

"I hate to tell you this —" he began.

"You don't have to," Preacher said. "We can hear them horses. Davidson's on his way to attack the village with his whole command, ain't he?"

"I'm afraid so," Jamie answered grimly. "O'Connor told him the Crow murdered those troopers who were killed, and of course that's exactly what Davidson wants to believe. He failed at bringing back Broken Pine for those treaty negotiations, failed at rescuing a so-called white captive, and now he figures the only thing he can do to salvage any glory out of this mess is to wipe out Broken Pine and his people."

"We're not gonna let that happen," Preacher vowed.

The Crow warriors began to gather on the riverbank. Broken Pine directed their preparations to defend their home. The warriors, all with bows and full quivers of arrows, used every bit of cover they could find. They spread out along the stream, nocked arrows, and waited. An eerie silence hung over the river, broken only by the rumble of hoof-beats as the soldiers approached. The moon reflected wavily on the water's surface.

Preacher knelt behind a log with Broken Pine on his left and Jamie on his right. He glanced over at the big frontiersman and asked, "Are you plannin' to fight on our side, Jamie? If you ain't, you'd best get outta here while you still can."

"I'm not going to kill any of those troopers," Jamie replied with an obvious strain in his voice. "They're just following orders."

"The orders of a fella who's plumb loco and kill-crazy," muttered Preacher.

"You're right about that. And I don't blame Broken Pine and his people for defending their homes, no matter what it takes."

Broken Pine said, "You are a good man, Jamie MacCallister. A good man does not go against his honor. You should go to the canyon and help Hawk That Soars and the men he took with him protect the women and children, if the need to do so arises."

"I reckon I could do that, all right," Jamie said. "Protecting the women and children always comes before anything else."

"Go, my friend," Broken Pine said, and Preacher clapped a hand on Jamie's shoulder for a second. Jamie took a deep breath and then nodded.

Quickly, Broken Pine told him how to find the canyon. Jamie stood up and faded off into the shadows, moving fast. Preacher turned his attention back to the attackers. He frowned as the hoofbeats diminished and then stopped.

Broken Pine sounded equally puzzled as he said, "Why have they stopped? I thought they were going to charge across the river and attack us."

"So did —" Preacher began. Then as a possibility occurred to him, he stopped abruptly and shouted in the Crow tongue, "Everybody down!"

Preacher had barely gotten out the warning and dived to the ground, taking Broken Pine with him, when a wave of gunfire erupted from the far side of the stream. A long, continuous line of orange muzzle flashes tore the night apart. Preacher heard rifle balls whining through the air, whipping through the brush, and thudding into tree trunks.

Even worse, he heard Crow warriors cry out in pain as they were hit.

While the echoes from the volley still filled the air, men on horseback charged into the river and headed toward the Crow village. They were more than halfway across, shouting at the tops of their lungs, before the defenders recovered enough from the battering they had taken to start putting up a fight. Arrows began flashing through the air and struck a few of the soldiers. Here and there, a trooper screamed, threw up his arms, and toppled off his horse.

Nearly all of the attackers reached the shore, though. They wheeled their horses and began firing pistols at the rocks, trees, and brush where the Crow warriors had taken cover. Some of the dragoons rushed in and started hacking at their enemies with sabers.

Preacher and Broken Pine had been unharmed during the volley. They came up behind the log and opened fire on the attackers, Broken Pine with his bow and arrows, Preacher with the twin Colts roaring and bucking in his hands.

But even as he blasted away at the soldiers and saw some of them fall, Preacher felt the same unease Jamie MacCallister had professed. These young troopers weren't to blame for this situation. They were just expendable pawns in the ambitious hands of Lieutenant Edgar Davidson. Preacher couldn't stand by and allow them to massacre his friends and family, but he took no joy in the shots he fired at them.

"There are many of them!" Broken Pine cried as he nocked another arrow and let it fly.

Preacher knew the chief was right. And Davidson, despite all his faults, had made an effective move by having some of his men dismount and rake the defenders with rifle fire before the rest of the troop charged among them. The Crow would put up a good fight, but the soldiers held the advantage.

"Maybe you'd better pull back to that canyon!" he suggested. "You can hold them off better there!"

Broken Pine leaped to his feet, yipped shrilly to get his warriors' attention, then bellowed the order to retreat in the Crow tongue. All along the river, men began to break off the fighting and raced away from the stream.

It must have looked like an out-of-control rout to the soldiers. They yelled enthusiastically and started after the fleeing defenders.

Preacher raked them with revolver fire, fighting a one-man delaying action as he darted among the shadows. Broken Pine was at his side, and then suddenly Big Thunder was, too, and the three of them blunted the troopers' pursuit with a deadly flurry of gunfire and flashing arrows.

390

Since Preacher didn't know exactly where the hide-out canyon was, he let his companions lead the way. That was an unusual situation for the mountain man — he was normally in the forefront of everything — but tonight he had no choice.

They might not have made it if the soldiers hadn't fallen back to regroup. Preacher knew he and his Crow allies had inflicted quite a few casualties among the troopers, but they had suffered heavy losses of their own, too. They'd also had to leave some of the wounded warriors behind, and that was very difficult for the Crow to do.

As Jamie had said, though, the defense of families always came first.

It took a quarter of an hour for Preacher, Broken Pine, and Big Thunder to reach the canyon. The group of women and children from the village hadn't been able to move as fast, so they had barely reached the refuge before the retreating warriors caught up with them. Preacher and the other two found guards waiting just inside the canyon's entrance, which was clogged with brush and boulders. The brush was natural, shielding the opening from casual notice, and had been left in place by the Crow. They had rolled the boulders into the entrance to provide cover for defenders and make it more difficult for anyone to invade this sanctuary.

Preacher took all this in at a glance, recognizing the strategic advantages of the place — and its disadvantages. Having only one way in and out made it easy to defend, but at the same time, they were trapped here.

Jamie MacCallister stepped out from behind one of the boulders to greet them. Hawk was waiting there at the entrance, too, and Broken Pine asked him, "Are all the women and children here safely?"

"They are," Hawk replied. "They are all frightened, but not harmed. The soldiers?"

"Big Thunder and his friends killed many of them!" the massive warrior declared. "The others ran away in fear!"

Preacher scratched his beard-stubbled jaw and said, "That ain't exactly the way it was. They lost some men, sure . . . but I reckon we probably lost more. And they had us outnumbered to start with."

"They cannot get to us here," Broken Pine said. "There is a spring at the far end of the canyon for water, and we have cached enough food here to last for days. A large overhang provides shelter from the elements for the women and children, and because of it, men cannot fire down from the rim of the canyon at them."

"So you're safe for a while," Preacher said, "but if Davidson decides to lay siege to the place and outlast you . . ."

"Someone is coming!" one of the guards called softly.

Everyone swung around as a voice Preacher recognized called in English, "Don't shoot!"

"That's Lieutenant Tyler," Jamie said.

Broken Pine called out in Crow for the guards at the entrance to hold their fire. He said to Jamie, "Tell him to come in — if he is alone."

"We hear you, Lieutenant," Jamie called. "Are any of the troopers with you?"

"No," Tyler replied from the shadows. "The warrior guarding us went to join the fight when Davidson attacked. I got out of the lodge, but Berriman was too scared to come with me. He wanted to wait there for the rest of the troop to rescue him. But when I realized you were retreating in this direction, I followed."

"Come on in, then," Jamie told him. A moment later, Tyler appeared from the darkness and joined the others behind the cluster of boulders.

"I'm sort of surprised to see you here, Lieutenant," said Preacher. "You could've

393

stayed right where you were and the soldiers would've found you."

"And then Edgar Davidson would have ordered me to fight you, and I would have had to obey," Tyler said. "I didn't want to do that."

"So you've deserted to the enemy," Jamie said. "That's the way the army will see it, and they're not going to look kindly on that."

"Edgar's lost his mind! I hate to say that, I really do, but he wasn't sent out here to make war on the Crow. It was a simple diplomatic mission, but he's made things worse at every turn. Now he's out for blood, and he's wrong. He's no longer fit to be in charge."

"What do you reckon we ought to do about that?" Preacher drawled.

"There's only one thing we *can* do if we're to have any hope of ending this without a lot more bloodshed," Tyler said. He looked around at the others in the fading moon-light. "I'm going to relieve him of com-mand."

CHAPTER 29

The rest of the night dragged by without any more fighting. Jamie figured Lieutenant Davidson was using the time to assess his losses, secure any prisoners who had been taken during the battle, and plan his next step.

Inside the canyon, the Crow and their three white allies did much the same thing, except they didn't have any prisoners.

As the sun rose and flooded the mouth of the canyon with light, Jamie, Preacher, Lieutenant Hayden Tyler, Hawk, Broken Pine, and several other experienced warriors met in a council of war.

Jamie asked the young officer, "Just how confident are you that enough of those soldiers will follow your orders if you take over for Davidson?"

"I'm confident that some of them will," Tyler replied. "Corporal Mackey, for one, and I believe Corporal Briggs will, as well.

They wield some influence among the men. And don't forget, this is my troop. They've been used to taking orders from me."

"O'Connor will never cooperate. You're going to have to relieve him of command, too. And he'll fight it."

Tyler nodded and said grimly, "I know that. We'll do whatever is . . . necessary."

"You'd better be mighty sure about actually wantin' to take this step before you do," Preacher advised. "Once you do, there won't be no comin' back from it. If you make it back alive, Davidson's gonna insist you be court-martialed."

"I'll take my chances if that happens. I have to think that a board of inquiry will see I had no choice but to take command. If they decide otherwise . . ." Tyler shrugged. "I'll spend years behind bars, assuming I'm not taken out and shot. But I'd rather risk that than have this useless killing on both sides go on for any longer than it already has."

"This is an honorable thing you say," Broken Pine put in. "But it will accomplish nothing unless the soldiers do as you say."

"Only one way to find out," said Preacher. "We've got to get our hands on Davidson and O'Connor." He looked at Jamie. "That sounds like a job for you and me."

"And me," Hawk added.

"And I'll have to be there to take command," Tyler said. "Otherwise, it's all for nothing."

Before they could discuss the situation further, one of the sentries gave a birdcall that served as a warning signal. When they hurried over, the warrior slid down from the top of the boulder where he had been perched and dropped to the ground beside them.

He pointed and said in Crow, "Soldiers come."

Nature had cut the canyon into the eastern side of a long ridge that ran roughly north and south. In front of the entrance, stretching several hundred yards to a thick growth of trees that marked the course of the river, lay an area of open, mostly level ground. The dragoons had emerged from those trees and sat their horses just out in the open.

Preacher peered across at them and said, "They're too far away to get an accurate count, but I'd say there are about sixty of the varmints."

"They're not varmints," snapped Jamie. "They're members of the United States Army. And they're *not* to blame for Davidson and O'Connor being such bastards."

"You can talk all you want about 'em just

followin' orders," Preacher said with anger grating in his voice, "but that don't change the fact that they attacked my friends and family for no good reason."

Lieutenant Tyler said, "This whole thing has been a tragedy of misunderstandings from the first. My God, does it always have to be like this? Can't people of good faith on both sides find a way to get along?"

"You won't find any good faith in Davidson or O'Connor," Preacher said. "They don't care who gets hurt as long as they get what they want. What they feel like they're entitled to."

Jamie couldn't disagree with what Preacher said. He knew the mountain man was right.

"Riders," Hawk said. "They bear a white flag." He looked at Preacher. "That means they wish to talk without fighting?"

"That's what it means, all right. But it sure as hell don't mean we can trust 'em."

Four men on horseback had pushed out ahead of the main body of soldiers. One rode slightly ahead of the other three, and he held a staff with a white flag attached to it. Not much wind was blowing this morning, and as a result, the signal for truce hung limply, only flapping a little now and then.

"I'll go see what they want," Jamie said.

"Not by yourself," Preacher said. He whistled, and Dog came bounding from deeper in the canyon. The big cur had been absent during the battle the night before, out wandering and hunting somewhere, and he had seemed pretty sheepish when he showed up in the canyon at dawn, as if he were ashamed that he had missed all the action.

Broken Pine said, "I am the chief of the Crow. If there are decisions to be made for my people, I should be the one to make them."

"I will come as well," Hawk declared. "There are four of them. We should be four."

"Come on, then," Preacher told his son.

"What about me?" Tyler asked. "I think I should go —"

"Probably a better idea for you to stay here out of sight, Lieutenant," Jamie interrupted him. "That way Davidson won't find out just yet that you've changed sides. If he sees you now, he'll go back and drum the idea that you've turned traitor into everybody's head."

With obvious reluctance, Tyler nodded and said, "I suppose you're right. But be careful out there. You can't trust him."

"Reckon we figured that out a long time

ago," Preacher said as he moved his guns a little in their holsters, checking to see that they slid smoothly in the leather in case he needed them.

No horses had been brought to the canyon when the Crow fled from the attack, so the four men started out onto the flats on foot. They met the army delegation about a third of the way across the open stretch, with everyone coming to a halt when about thirty feet separated the two groups.

The rider in front holding the white flag — and looking extremely nervous about it — was Corporal Mackey. Behind him was Lieutenant Edgar Davidson, with a trooper flanking him on both sides. Davidson had left Sergeant O'Connor back with the other men, Jamie noted. Either that, or O'Connor hadn't survived the fighting the night before.

Mackey moved his horse aside so that Davidson could nudge his mount ahead and take position front and center. The strap of the lieutenant's cap was tight under his chin. He glared out from under the cap's black bill.

"I'll give you credit, Lieutenant," Preacher said. "Most commanders would'a sent somebody in their place after stirrin' up as much trouble as you have. If I was to pull these hoglegs, I don't reckon anybody could

400

stop me from blowin' you outta the saddle."

"Perhaps not," Davidson said, "but that would be a dishonorable thing to do. And despite the fact that for some ungodly reason you prefer the company of these squalid heathens, your reputation says that you're an honorable man." He sniffed. "Besides, I am the commander of this expedition. It's my responsibility to deliver the terms of surrender."

"Oh?" Preacher said with a grin. "You're surrenderin'?"

"You know very well what I meant," Davidson snapped. "Turn over to me the savages responsible for the deaths of my men, and I promise safe passage back to the village for the others, especially the women and children."

"It was a *battle,* Lieutenant," Jamie pointed out. "A lot of men were shooting on both sides. We don't have any way of knowing who did what. You can't blame those deaths on anyone in particular." Jamie paused, then added meaningfully, "Except maybe one man."

The rage that made Davidson's face turn a mottled red showed that he understood perfectly well what Jamie meant. He controlled his anger with a visible effort and went on, "Nevertheless, those are my terms.

I require, shall we say, a dozen of the savages to be put on trial for the murder of United States Army dragoons. I don't particularly care which ones are turned over to me."

"Put on trial and then executed?" asked Preacher.

"The proceedings will be fair and just. You have my word on that." Davidson smirked. "But given the circumstances, there is little doubt of the outcome."

Broken Pine slowly shook his head and said, "This evil thing you speak of will never happen. The only way to stop more killing is for you and your men to leave and never come back."

Davidson's chin jutted out arrogantly. He said, "You have my terms. I assure you, if you refuse them, I will continue to engage you and your people as the enemy until all of them have been wiped out."

"Including a bunch of innocent folks," Jamie said.

"As has been pointed out on more than one occasion . . . there are no innocents among hostiles." Davidson lifted his reins. "I'll give you one hour to comply with my terms. That's all."

He turned his horse and rode back toward the trees. The two privates followed him, casting uneasy glances over their shoulders as they did so, as if they thought the truce might not hold. Corporal Mackey, still holding the white flag, hesitated.

"It's a shame Lieutenant Davidson's the one giving the orders, Corporal," Jamie said.

"Maybe. But he's the only officer we have, Mr. MacCallister, so we don't have much choice except to follow his commands."

Mackey turned and rode slowly after the others. Jamie watched him go, then said quietly, "He was trying to tell us something."

"Maybe," said Preacher.

"If we can get our hands on Davidson, and Lieutenant Tyler officially relieves him of command, we can put an end to this."

"Problem is, Davidson made it pretty plain that he's attackin' again in an hour. That means more men are gonna die on both sides unless we can figure out a way of sneakin' into their camp and gettin' our hands on Davidson in broad daylight. To do that, we're gonna need a mighty big distraction."

Jamie said, "You sound like you've got an idea brewing in that head of yours, Preacher."

The mountain man looked back at the canyon, nodded his head, and said, "Maybe

403

I do. Just maybe I do . . ."

"You want Big Thunder to fight?" The massive warrior raised both fists and shook them in front of him. "Big Thunder is always ready to fight!"

"It'll be dangerous," Preacher told him. "You'll be runnin' quite a risk. But if you stay back outta good rifle range, I think it'll work."

Broken Pine laid a hand on Big Thunder's arm and said, "You do not have to do this."

Big Thunder shook his head. "That white man . . . that O'Connor . . . he thinks he beat Big Thunder. Not this time! This time Big Thunder will win!"

Preacher hoped that was true, but the actual outcome of the fight wasn't the most important thing. They needed to keep the soldiers watching something else, and a second showdown between those two titans ought to do it.

"All right, you know what to do," Preacher said. He looked at Broken Pine. "Give me and Jamie and Hawk and Tyler time to get where we need to be, then send Big Thunder out there. Even if O'Connor don't take up the challenge, just havin' the big fella out there hollerin' ought to garner a lot of attention."

404

"Like Goliath shouting at the Israelites," Lieutenant Tyler said with a smile. "Only in this case, it'll be more like Goliath versus Goliath."

Hawk had already said good-bye to Butterfly and their children. He and the three white men went to the far end of the canyon and began climbing out of it. Preacher told Dog to stay with the Crow, and while the big cur didn't like it and whined a little in complaint, he followed Preacher's command, sitting there and watching the four men ascending the rough stone wall. The sides of the canyon were steep but not sheer, and there were plenty of footholds and handholds to make climbing easy.

When they reached the top, the four men stayed low to decrease the chances of being spotted and began working their way south along the ridge. They traveled well out of sight of the area along the river where the soldiers were gathered before they descended from the ridge and headed for the stream. They waded across it and started back up the other side.

Preacher had told Broken Pine to allow an hour for them to get in position. Broken Pine didn't have a watch, of course, but he had a good sense of how much time was passing.

When that hour was up, Big Thunder would walk out of the canyon, stride boldly toward the troops, and start yelling for Sergeant O'Connor to come out and fight him. If O'Connor took up the challenge, that would be a battle for the ages, thought Preacher. He had tussled enough with Big Thunder himself to know that the huge warrior was actually a smart fighter. He learned from every clash, and the next time it was harder to defeat him. O'Connor probably wouldn't be expecting that.

Preacher, Jamie, Hawk, and Tyler used all the cover they could find as they approached their destination. Every tree, rock, and clump of brush came in handy.

Quietly, Jamie asked Tyler, "Do you believe Davidson will think of posting guards on the troop's rear?"

"There's a good chance he has. I've known Edgar a long time. I never liked his attitude, but he did well in his classes at West Point and has a good grasp of tactics and procedures."

"We'll keep our eyes and ears open, then," Preacher said. "We need to spot those guards before they spot us."

Jamie said, "I don't want them killed if we can avoid it. We're trying to stop the killing, not pile the bodies up higher."

"I didn't plan on killin' 'em," Preacher replied in a slightly exasperated tone. "There are other ways to put 'em out of action."

"Just so we understand each other."

A few minutes later, Preacher motioned for them to stop. He signaled silently toward some trees up ahead, then pointed at Hawk and indicated the warrior should go to the left. Preacher tapped his own chest and gestured toward the right. He made a patting gesture with both hands to indicate that Jamie and Tyler should stay where they were.

Jamie nodded. Preacher and Hawk faded off into the brush, moving with almost supernatural stealth.

Even though morning light washed over the landscape, sneaking up on a couple of inexperienced young soldiers wasn't nearly as difficult as slipping into a Blackfoot village. Preacher had done that many times as a younger man, enough so that the Blackfeet had dubbed him the Ghost Killer and halfway believed that he was some sort of phantom and not quite human.

A few moments later, Preacher found himself behind a uniformed dragoon who stood with his rifle butt resting on the ground at his feet. The trooper never had a chance to lift the weapon. Preacher looped his left arm around the soldier's neck and closed it hard enough to stifle any outcry. At the same time, he tapped the butt of his right-hand Colt against the man's head. The soldier's knees buckled, and Preacher lowered him to the ground.

It was the work of less than two minutes to cut several strips from the man's uniform shirt and use them to tie him securely, hand and foot. Preacher wadded up another strip of cloth and shoved it into the trooper's mouth, then tied it in place as a gag. The mountain man left him lying there facedown, confident that the soldier wouldn't be able to raise the alarm or cause any other trouble.

While he was doing that, he'd heard a faint rustling in the brush and wasn't surprised to see Hawk emerge and nod curtly to indicate that the other guard was taken care of, as well. The two of them went back to join Jamie and Tyler.

"There may be some more guards scattered around," Preacher whispered, "but we've got a gap in their defenses now. Let's get down in the brush right along the river's edge and have a look-see."

As they advanced, Tyler watched his companions so he could try to imitate them and move as quietly as they did. For the most part, he was successful. He stepped on a few branches, but Preacher didn't think the cracks when those branches broke were loud enough to warn the inexperienced troopers.

They crouched in the thick growth beside the river and parted it enough to study the other bank. The mounted dragoons were visible through the trees as they waited for Lieutenant Davidson's order to attack the Crow holed up in the canyon. Preacher could tell that most of the young soldiers were nervous about going into battle again. They fidgeted with their rifles, turned their heads this way and that, spoke to each other in low tones. He spotted Sergeant O'Connor stalking around and knew that the burly noncom had survived the previous night's action. Preacher had had a hunch that was the case, and the sight of O'Connor now confirmed it.

He saw Davidson as well, sitting calmly on a rock and writing in a small notebook he had propped on his knees. An inkwell was on the rock beside him.

Preacher nudged Jamie, nodded toward Davidson, and whispered, "He's gettin' all the details down so he can put 'em in his report and make himself look like a big hero."

"With any luck, he'll never get a chance to do that," replied Jamie. "I know the truth about him, and I have some friends in the army. Everything that's happened here will come out, all right, but not the way Davidson wants it to."

Hawk tapped Preacher's arm and pointed upstream. About fifty yards away, a tree had fallen so that it formed a bridge across the river, which narrowed down at that point. Preacher nodded. That would be the easiest, fastest way for them to get across and into the temporary army camp.

Suddenly, a shout came to their ears. "O'Connor!" the deep voice bellowed. "White man! Sergeant O'Connor! Come out and fight Big Thunder, you coward!"

Jamie smiled and said, "That old boy's got a pair of lungs on him, doesn't he? I can make out every word he's saying."

"So can the troopers," Preacher said. "Look."

On the other side of the river, O'Connor, who had paused to talk to Davidson, swung around sharply to glare toward the open ground between the river and the canyon. The mounted dragoons edged their horses forward a step or two. Davidson stood up quickly, snapped shut the book he had been writing in, and stowed it away inside his uniform jacket. He left the pen and inkwell on the rock as he strode forward.

O'Connor hurried along beside him, talking fast. Preacher could tell how angry the sergeant was. O'Connor waved his arms and rumbled something Preacher couldn't make out. Davidson spoke to him, and O'Conner gestured emphatically again.

All the while, Big Thunder continued shouting his challenge, spicing it with insults. Not obscenities, since Indians seldom if ever indulged in such things, but Big Thunder's descriptions of O'Connor's cowardice were certainly colorful.

Abruptly, O'Connor yanked off his cap and tossed it aside, then peeled out of his jacket. Davidson cried, "Sergeant, I forbid you to —"

O'Connor ignored him, stalked through the line of mounted men, and made his way across the prairie toward the spot where Big Thunder waited, flexing his arms and bellowing and all but pawing the ground like a maddened bull.

O'Connor was the one who was maddened. He had reached the breaking point, and as he let out an incoherent shout of rage, he broke into a run and charged toward Big Thunder. Yells of encouragement went up from the watching soldiers. "That's it," Preacher said. "Let's go!"

CHAPTER 30

Out on the flats, Big Thunder and Sergeant Liam O'Connor came together like a couple of bull moose battling for leadership of the herd. Big Thunder's legs were spread slightly, and his feet were planted solidly on the ground. He knew from the battle the previous night that O'Connor liked to punch rather than wrestle, so he was expecting the wild, roundhouse swings that O'Connor aimed at his head. He ducked under them, drove forward, and rammed his shoulder into O'Connor's stomach.

As O'Connor's momentum carried him forward over Big Thunder's back, the massive warrior wrapped his arms around O'Connor's waist and heaved upward. O'Connor yelled again, but this time in alarm rather than rage, as he found himself flying upside down through the air. He crashed down on his back with stunning force.

Big Thunder whirled, his speed surprising in such a mountain of a man. He went after O'Connor, intending to stomp him into the dirt, but O'Connor, even though the fall had knocked the air out of him, managed to get his hands up and grab Big Thunder's upraised foot as it started to come down. O'Connor twisted hard, and Big Thunder went down, too.

O'Connor gulped air and went after him. He hooked punches into Big Thunder's ribs and tried to drive his knee into the warrior's groin, but Big Thunder writhed aside and took the blow on his thigh. He smashed an open-handed right across O'Connor's face, then grabbed the sergeant by the throat and flung him to the side. That gave him time to roll the opposite direction and surge to his feet.

O'Connor came up at the same time and instantly charged at Big Thunder, again swinging powerful punches. But this time when Big Thunder tried to duck underneath O'Connor's fists, O'Connor was ready. He brought the side of his right hand down hard on the back of Big Thunder's neck. Big Thunder grunted and lost his balance, falling to one knee. He got his left hand down on the ground in time to catch himself. But as soon as he did that, O'Connor's right foot came up in a vicious kick that caught Big Thunder on the jaw.

That knocked Big Thunder sprawling on his back. O'Connor came down on top of him with both knees in Big Thunder's belly. Big Thunder couldn't breathe and couldn't get out of the way of the punches that O'Connor slammed into his face. Left, right, and then again, each blow jolting Big Thunder's head back and forth. His features were swollen and smeared with blood.

Big Thunder got his hands up, dug his fingers into the front of O'Connor's uniform shirt, and bucked up into a roll that threw O'Connor off him. Big Thunder heaved on the white man's shirt at the same time. The crushing weight went away from Big Thunder's belly. He wound up propped on his elbows with his chest heaving like a bellows.

O'Connor recovered and came at him again. Big Thunder flung up a hand and got it on O'Connor's face. He clawed at the sergeant's eyes, got a thumb in one of O'Connor's nostrils, and tried to rip the sergeant's nose right off his face. O'Connor roared in pain and punched Big Thunder in the throat. Big Thunder's hand slipped away from O'Connor's face. O'Connor hit him in the ribs again. Big Thunder swung a backhand that knocked O'Connor away from him.

Both men seized the opportunity to catch their breath as they clambered back to their feet. The pummeling they had taken left them battered, bruised, and bloody, and their movements were stiffer and slower now as brutally punished flesh rebelled. But the urge to fight was still strong in both men. O'Connor made the first move, bulling in as he swung his fists at Big Thunder.

Big Thunder didn't try to avoid the punches this time. He simply absorbed them, ignoring the damage they did as he allowed O'Connor to get closer to him. When he made his move, O'Connor couldn't get out of the way in time. Big Thunder caught O'Connor under the right arm with his left hand and used his right to reach down and grab O'Connor's left thigh. With a deafening shout of effort, he lifted O'Connor off the ground and raised the sergeant above his head. It was a jaw-dropping, awe-inspiring display of sheer brute strength the likes of which none of the men watching this battle had ever seen before. Every soldier's gaze was riveted on the scene as Big Thunder poised the struggling O'Connor above him for a second, then slammed him to the ground with incredible force.

That was when gunshots blasted behind the soldiers, closer to the river.

Preacher led the way to the log and was the first to dash nimbly across it, with Hawk right behind him, then Jamie and finally Lieutenant Hayden Tyler. When Preacher reached the opposite bank, he darted to his left and ran through the trees until he stopped next to one of them and pressed himself against the trunk.

Davidson was still out there among the mounted dragoons, watching as the battle began between Big Thunder and O'Connor. They couldn't reach Davidson while he was surrounded by the soldiers, so Preacher motioned for his companions to take cover, too. Hawk had already done so, following his father's lead, and now Jamie and Tyler did as well.

Preacher breathed shallowly as he waited. From where he was, he could see Big Thunder and O'Connor throwing each other around. It was a battle for the ages out there, and under other circumstances, Preacher would have enjoyed witnessing such an epic struggle.

Right now, though, he just wanted to get his hands on Edgar Davidson so he could put an end to all the trouble.

After several interminable minutes, Davidson turned away from the spectacle in disgust. He had ordered O'Connor not to fight the giant Crow warrior and the sergeant had disobeyed the command. Davidson clearly didn't like that, but there was nothing he could do about it now. He stalked away from the soldiers and through the trees, heading back toward the rock where he had been sitting and writing in what was probably his journal. From the looks of it, he intended to collect the pen and inkwell he had left there.

Preacher was ready for him. He moved fast, stepping up behind Davidson and sliding his left arm around the lieutenant's throat. Davidson didn't even have a chance to gasp before Preacher had him locked in a tight grip.

"It's over, Lieutenant," Preacher said quietly in Davidson's ear.

Davidson struggled briefly but soon realized the futility of it. He stiffened as Jamie, Tyler, and Hawk appeared.

"I'm sorry it's come to this, Edgar," Tyler said. "But you've exceeded your authority, caused the death of numerous soldiers, and endangered all the other troops under your command. Therefore, I am officially relieving you of that command."

"Better accept it while you still can," Preacher said as he eased off a little on the pressure of his hold on Davidson's throat.

Instead, Davidson gasped, "You . . . you traitor! I'll have you shot! You . . . you . . ."

He continued sputtering incoherently. Preacher shut that off by tightening his grip again.

"All right, Lieutenant," he said to Tyler. "I reckon you'd better go out there and let the soldiers know they'll be followin' your orders from here on out."

At that moment, a great shout rose from the troopers, then was stilled abruptly. Something must have happened in the fight they were watching. Preacher hoped Big Thunder was all right. He started to turn Davidson a little so he could look in that direction, but as he did, a cry of alarm sounded and he saw that one of the dragoons had dismounted for some reason and noticed them. The young soldier jerked his rifle toward them and fired.

The ball whined harmlessly past Preacher's head. An instant later, the Colt that had leaped into Jamie MacCallister's hand blasted, as well, the bullet kicking up dirt at the trooper's feet and making him leap backward. He lost his balance and fell, sitting down hard.

The shots had gotten all the soldiers' attention, of course. They jerked their horses around toward the river and lifted their rifles. Lieutenant Tyler stepped out of the trees and shouted, "Hold your fire! Hold your fire!"

The familiar command, coming from the familiar figure in an officer's uniform, made the men lower their weapons. They were still tense, though, and they stiffened in their saddles even more as Preacher forced Davidson out into the open and Jamie and Hawk followed them.

"All you men listen!" Tyler continued. "I have officially relieved Lieutenant Davidson of command! He is no longer in charge of this detail. Due to his willful and continued defiance of the orders given to us by Captain Croxton back at the fort, he is no longer fit for command, and I have taken his place. We came to make peace with the Crow, not to wage war on them!"

More than fifty rifles were pointing in the general direction of the small group of men just outside the trees. If the soldiers decided not to cooperate and accept Tyler taking command, there wasn't much Preacher, Jamie, and Hawk could do about it. A volley from that many rifles, at this range, would blow them to pieces.

Of course, Davidson would die in the storm of lead, too, which made the troopers hesitate.

Tyler walked forward and said in a quieter but more intense voice, "Listen, men. I know each and every one of you, and you know me. You know I believe in the mission that brought us here. Lieutenant Davidson and Sergeant O'Connor never gave that mission a chance to succeed. I don't know if we can salvage our goals or not . . . a great deal has happened, most of it bad . . . but if we continue in the same course, so will the bloodshed, until one — or both — sides are wiped out. I believe enough blood has been spilled already. That's why I'm willing to risk a court-martial and whatever fate the army wants to give me, in order to stop the killing. But that risk is mine. No one will hold you at fault for following my orders."

The long moment of silence that followed Tyler's speech stretched everyone's nerves to the breaking point. Finally, after what seemed like much longer than it really was, Corporal Mackey cleared his throat and said, "You always were a good officer, Lieutenant Tyler, and you were in charge of B Troop before Lieutenant Davidson was. I, uh . . ." Mackey looked around at the other dragoons, then squared his shoulders and went on, "I don't have a problem with following your orders, sir."

"Neither do I," said another man. Mutters of agreement came from several more.

"This ain't right!" one of the soldiers yelled. "An officer can't just take over for a superior officer!"

"Actually, one can, according to regulations," said Tyler. "An officer who is giving unlawful or improper orders can be relieved of command, and that's all I'm doing here. None of this is permanent. It'll all be sorted out once we're back at Fort Kearny, and like I said, I'll accept whatever decision is made there. But for now, and until we get back, I'm in charge of this troop." His voice was firm now, brooking no argument. "Understood?"

Again, Mackey was the first to speak up, saying, "Yes, sir!" Others followed suit. A number of the troopers wore surly expressions and didn't respond verbally, but they lowered their rifles and Preacher took that as a sign they were willing to go along with the others, at least for now.

Tyler nodded and said, "All right. Where's Sergeant O'Connor?"

"Here he comes now," a trooper called.

Everyone turned to look and saw Big Thunder walking toward the river. O'Connor was draped over his broad shoulders like a bag of grain. Preacher could tell by how limp O'Connor hung that the sergeant was out cold. Preacher hoped that was all it was and that O'Connor wasn't dead.

The ranks of dragoons parted to let Big Thunder through. He walked up to Preacher and the others, bent forward, and dumped O'Connor on the ground at his feet. O'Connor sprawled there, his chest rising and falling enough to tell Preacher that the sergeant was still alive.

"The fight is over," Big Thunder announced. "Big Thunder won!"

"You sure did," Preacher told him. The mountain man still had hold of Davidson. He asked him, "How about you, Lieutenant? Is the fight over for you? You still gonna give us trouble?"

As Preacher eased off his grip, Davidson looked like he wanted to start spewing anger and obscenities again. But then a look of despair came over the young officer's face, unlike anything Preacher had seen there before. This unexpected turn of events had knocked the arrogance out of Davidson at last.

"There won't be any more trouble," he said quietly.

Preacher looked over at Jamie. "You

423

believe him?"

"Not for one damn minute." Jamie jerked open the flap of Davidson's holster and removed the pistol from it, then pulled the saber from Davidson's scabbard. "But I feel better about it now." He turned to Tyler. "I suggest you have both of these prisoners secured and guarded at all times, Lieutenant."

"I don't know if that's necessary," said Tyler. "Lieutenant Davidson has given us his word. I accept his parole for the time being."

"Thank you, Hayden," Davidson said. "I appreciate that you still believe I'm a man of honor, despite our disagreements."

"The lieutenant may believe it," Preacher said, "but I ain't so sure. You try to cause any more trouble, Davidson, and I'll stop you myself . . . permanent-like." He let go of Davidson and stepped back, then nodded toward the still-unconscious O'Connor. "But you'd better have that one tied up while you've got the chance, Lieutenant."

"That probably would be wise," agreed Tyler. "Corporal Mackey, would you see to it?"

Mackey dismounted and said, "Of course, sir."

Tyler looked along the line of mounted

men and went on, "All of you get down from your horses. We'll make a temporary camp here —"

One of the dragoons interrupted by calling in alarmed tones, "Here come the Indians!"

CHAPTER 31

It was true that the Crow were leaving the canyon, or at least most of the warriors were. They advanced toward the river, led by Broken Pine. The soldiers started to turn toward them, bristling as if getting ready to fight again, but Tyler strode forward and called, "Hold your fire, men! Lower your rifles!"

"Are you sure about that, Lieutenant?" one of the dragoons asked.

"I'm certain," Tyler said. "Broken Pine means us no harm. Everything the Crow have done has been in defense of themselves and their families. I'll go talk to Broken Pine now."

"I'll come with you," Preacher said. "Jamie, you mind keepin' an eye on things here?"

"Nope," Jamie replied as he rested his hands on his gun butts.

Preacher and Hawk walked across the

426

open ground with Tyler. Broken Pine moved out in front of the other warriors and met them.

"Your plan has worked?" asked the Crow chief.

"It has," Tyler replied. "I've relieved Lieutenant Davidson of command and I'm in charge now."

Broken Pine nodded toward the soldiers and said, "Your warriors, they agree to follow you?"

"Some of them aren't quite as enthusiastic as others," Tyler replied with a faint smile, "but they're all following my orders. The trouble is over, Broken Pine. I give you my word on that." He paused, then said, "I was hoping that perhaps we could speak again about that treaty . . ."

Broken Pine lifted a hand to stop him. "It is too soon to speak of such things. But after we return to the village . . . I will consider it."

"Thank you. That's very generous and gracious of you. And more than I could expect, considering the circumstances and everything that's happened."

"Many things happen in life, good and bad. A stream that never flows dries up and disappears." Broken Pine looked at Preacher. "Big Thunder?"

"He's fine," the mountain man assured him. "Banged up some from that fight with O'Connor, but he won and that's all he cares about."

Broken Pine smiled and said, "Do you think that will satisfy his appetite for battle?"

"For a little while," Preacher said with a grin. "Maybe."

Broken Pine and his warriors gathered up their families and started back to the village. In order to allow them to do that without having to worry about any kind of double cross, Tyler ordered the dragoons to remain where they were for the time being. Later in the day, they would withdraw to their previous camp closer to the Crow village.

Preacher and Hawk went with the Indians, while Jamie remained with the soldiers. Jamie kept an eye on Davidson and O'Connor. The lieutenant sat on the rock where he had been earlier, but he didn't write any more in his journal. Instead he just sat with his hands clasped together between his knees, staring straight ahead as if at something no one else could see. The future of his military career, perhaps, which was very uncertain at the moment.

Sergeant O'Conner hadn't been quiet

when he regained consciousness. He had ranted and cursed until Lieutenant Tyler ordered him gagged as well as tied. O'Connor sat with his back propped against a tree, with ropes encircling his torso and binding him to the trunk. His wrists were lashed together in front of him. With the gag in his mouth, all he could do was stare daggers at Jamie and Tyler every time they moved so that he could see them. That old saying about how *if looks could kill* had never been more true, Jamie thought.

He still hoped that Broken Pine would reconsider and come to Fort Kearny with them to negotiate the treaty that Washington wanted, but one way or the other, Jamie was eager to get back to the fort so he could wash his hands of this whole ill-fated expedition and go home like he'd intended to start with. That was what a man got sometimes when he tried to help out: trouble right up to his neck . . .

He was musing about that when he heard a sudden sharp burst of gunfire in the distance, coming from somewhere downstream.

Preacher felt good, walking along with his family. Hawk was beside him, carrying the little girl Bright Moon. Butterfly strode along on Hawk's other side. The boy, Eagle Feather, ran ahead with Dog. The trouble with the soldiers was over, the hunting had improved, there wouldn't be many more wagon trains coming this direction, if any, and as far as Preacher could see, peace ought to reign over these scenic foothills, at least for a while.

He should have known better, he thought a moment later when a shot blasted somewhere to his right and one of the warriors ahead of him grunted and staggered, blood welling from the bullet hole in his side.

He'd gone and jinxed the whole damn thing.

"Down!" he shouted as more gunfire erupted. "Everybody down!"

Powdersmoke spurted from a grove of trees about fifty yards to the right. Bullets tore through the group of Crow who had been walking peacefully along the river. There was no good cover here — except for the riverbank itself. It was deep enough to provide shelter from the ambush.

Preacher's Colts filled his hands. He blazed away at the trees, knowing it would be pure luck if he hit any of the hidden riflemen. But maybe he could distract them while some of the others made it to safety.

"Head for the river!" he bellowed. "Get

down the bank to the water!"

The women and children broke into a run in that direction. Most of the warriors were still trying to put up a fight, sending arrows arching toward the trees.

Then men on horseback burst out from cover, charging the Crow and firing revolvers and single-shot flintlock pistols. More warriors fell under the onslaught, and so did some of the women and young ones.

Butterfly was one of the women who stumbled and went down. Blood ran down her leg from a bullet hole in her calf. Hawk had handed Bright Moon to her when the shooting started so that he could fight back. The girl fell when Butterfly did, but she seemed to be all right as she landed and rolled across the ground. Dog, who had gotten attached to the children, dashed up and stood over Bright Moon to protect her, snarling and growling at the attackers.

Eagle Feather started after his little sister to help her, but before he could reach her, one of the riders swooped down on him, leaning from the saddle to snatch him from the ground as he cried out in alarm. Preacher swung his guns in that direction but couldn't fire because of the danger to the boy. The rider wheeled the horse and Preacher got a good look at the person who

431

had grabbed Eagle Feather.

Shock went through him, turning his blood as cold as if he had been plunged into a freezing mountain stream.

The rider's hat hung from its chin strap, letting long, white-streaked raven hair flow down her back. Preacher instantly recognized the woman's hawklike face, even though he hadn't seen her in ten years. He hadn't known she was still alive; actually, he had assumed she was long since dead, as much of a troublemaker as she was.

But even though she was dressed like a white man now, there was no doubt about the identity of the woman who glared at him across twenty yards of bloody chaos.

Winter Wind.

"Follow me, Preacher!" she cried. "Or the boy dies!"

With that she yanked her horse around and kicked it into a run toward the trees where the killers had lurked.

The other men on horseback followed her, abandoning the assault. They were a mix of whites and Indians, and he realized suddenly that this might be the same gang of outlaws that had been preying on wagon trains, the ones he and Hawk had clashed with previously. And if Winter Wind was their leader — a ludicrous idea, unless one knew what the crazed Blackfoot woman was actually capable of — she might have spotted him and Hawk during the battle and realized she had a chance to settle her old score with them.

Hawk sent another arrow winging after the riders, then turned and shouted, "Butterfly!" at the sight of his wife lying on the ground bleeding. He ran to her and dropped to his knees beside her. Bright Moon had clung to Dog's thick fur to help her climb to her feet. She stumbled over to Butterfly from the other direction.

Preacher jammed his Colts back in their holsters and hurried over as Hawk examined Butterfly's wounded leg. The lines of strain on her face revealed the pain she was in, but she didn't say anything about that. Instead she clutched Hawk's arm and said, "Eagle Feather! Where is he?"

Hawk looked around. He must not have seen Winter Wind grab the boy, thought Preacher. Seeing that Butterfly's wound was bloody but not serious, he knelt beside his son and said, "Hawk, listen to me. One of those ambushers was Winter Wind."

Hawk seemed baffled as he looked at Preacher and repeated, "Winter Wind . . . I do not —" Then his eyes widened as the memories came back to him. "The Blackfoot! The wild woman!"

"Yeah. Looks like she's thrown in with a bunch of owlhoots. But she's after you and me. She took Eagle Feather, Hawk. She dared me to come after them. This is her vengeance on us."

"Eagle Feather!" gasped Butterfly. "Gone?"

"He was fine when she grabbed him," Preacher assured her. "She won't hurt him. He's the bait for the trap she's gonna set for me and Hawk."

"I will kill her!" Hawk raged. "We should have killed her long ago!"

"Maybe so," Preacher agreed, "but that don't change things now." He straightened to his feet and looked around. "And she sure has raised hell."

The shooting from the trees had stopped. Preacher figured the men who'd been hidden there had taken off and followed Winter Wind and the rest of the gang. But the damage had already been done, and it was extensive. Most of the Crow women and children had made it to the safety of the riverbank, but several lay bloody and motionless on the ground. A dozen warriors had fallen in the attack and now sprawled in the stillness of death.

All because of one woman's loco need for

vengeance, Preacher thought as he grimly surveyed the carnage.

He knelt again, pulled a bandanna from his pocket, and bound it around Butterfly's wounded leg. While he was doing that, she said, "Preacher, you must save Eagle Feather. You must go after him."

"Don't you worry about that," he told her. "He's gonna be fine. I'll be gettin' on their trail mighty quick-like."

"And I will go, too," Hawk said as he bent down. He kissed Butterfly's forehead. "No harm will come to our son. This is my promise to you." He put an arm around Bright Moon's shoulders and drew the sobbing little girl to him. "Do not be frightened. Your mother is all right, and your brother will be, too."

They were helping Butterfly to her feet when Broken Pine hurried over. Preacher was glad to see that the chief appeared to be unhurt.

"The soldiers come," Broken Pine said as he gestured upstream.

Preacher turned his head to look. Some of the dragoons rode toward them with Lieutenant Tyler and Jamie MacCallister at their head. They had heard the shooting, Preacher thought, and had come to see what was wrong.

Several of the warriors took the soldiers' sudden appearance as a threat and started to nock arrows. Broken Pine called out to them, telling them to hold their fire. He and Preacher and Hawk moved to meet the newcomers as a couple of the Crow women came to help Butterfly and take charge of Bright Moon.

Jamie and Lieutenant Tyler rode out in front of the others and reined in as they came up to Preacher, Hawk, and Broken Pine. Jamie looked at the bodies littering the ground along the river and said, "My God! What happened here?"

"We were ambushed," Preacher said. His face and voice were as bleak as a frozen winter day. "An old enemy of mine —"

"And mine as well," Hawk added.

"They laid a trap for us," continued Preacher. "Didn't have a blasted thing to do with all this other commotion that's been goin' on. Just pure bad luck, is all. Bad luck, and loco hate."

"But you drove them off?" asked Lieutenant Tyler.

Preacher shook his head. "They left . . . but they took Hawk's son . . . my grandson . . . with them."

"Good Lord," Jamie muttered. "We'll go after them —"

"No!" The sharp word came from Hawk. "If Winter Wind sees a large force pursuing them, she might kill Eagle Feather and flee to finish taking her revenge another day."

"I was thinkin' the same thing," Preacher said. "If we want to keep the boy safe, we have to give her what she wants . . . and that's me and Hawk comin' after her by ourselves, so she can capture us and take her time killin' us."

"Wait . . . wait a minute," Tyler said. "This person you're talking about . . . is a *woman*?"

Preacher nodded. "A Blackfoot woman, and a mighty evil one at that. She grew up wantin' to be a warrior, and she made herself into a more dangerous one than just about anybody else in the tribe. It's a long story, but what it boils down to is that she's plumb loco."

Broken Pine said, "You cannot go after those killers alone, just the two of you. There were more than a dozen of them. Perhaps twice that many."

"You'd be too outnumbered," Jamie said. "You wouldn't stand a chance." He crossed his hands on his saddlehorn and leaned forward. "At least let me come with you."

Preacher's eyes narrowed as he thought about that. He scratched his beard-stubbled jaw and then said, "Now that might be an idea. The three of us can move mighty fast, get into places a bigger bunch might not be able to, and we won't lose the trail, you can bet a coonskin cap on that." A whine came from beside him, and he looked down to see Dog sitting there. "All right, the four of us."

"You ask much," Broken Pine said. "I would go with you, and you know Big Thunder will want to, as well."

"Not this time," Preacher said flatly. "If the three of us can't do it, I don't reckon it can be done."

Broken Pine looked like he wanted to argue more, but after a second he nodded and said, "Very well. The boy is your son and grandson. You will do what is best."

Tyler said, "Broken Pine, my men and I would like to help you with your wounded and make sure nothing else happens."

The idea of such a truce clearly made Broken Pine uneasy, but he nodded and said, "If the white men want to be friends, then so do the Crow."

"That's exactly what we want. I just wish it weren't such tragic circumstances that led to this."

Preacher said, "We'll go back to the village and pick up Horse and a pony for

Hawk, and then we'll get on the trail. All right with you, Jamie?"

Jamie jerked his head in a nod. "Damn right it is. What did you say this Blackfoot woman's name is?"

"Winter Wind."

"Well, Winter Wind is going to wish she had forgotten all about trying to settle whatever grudge she's holding against you."

"I hope you're right, Jamie. I sure hope you're right."

The Crow women tended to Butterfly's wounded calf, cleaning the injury and then binding a poultice of healing moss on it. She was able to stand up long enough to hug Hawk as the three men — and Dog — got ready to leave the village.

"Bring my son back to me," she said as she rested her head against Hawk's chest for a moment.

"I give you my word."

"And you come back safely to me, as well."

"Of course." He patted her back, kissed her forehead.

A few yards away stood Preacher and Jamie, holding the horses. Dog paced back and forth, ready to get on the trail of their enemies.

Broken Pine and Big Thunder came up to

them. The giant warrior looked forlorn as he said, "Big Thunder wants to come with Preacher."

"I know, old friend, and most of the time, I'd sure be happy to take you along if I was ridin' into trouble." Preacher squeezed one of the massive arms. "But not this time. The kind of fellas we're dealin' with . . . well, they're so evil you don't need to be around 'em."

"Besides," added Jamie, "I told Lieutenant Tyler you'd give him a hand keeping an eye on the prisoners until Preacher and Hawk and I get back. You're the only one big and strong enough to handle that Sergeant O'Connor."

Big Thunder scowled and said, "O'Connor is a bad man. Big Thunder beat him."

"You sure did," Preacher said. "We couldn't have put an end to all that trouble without your help. So now, if there's gonna be peace between the whites and the Crow, Big Thunder, you were a big part of it."

That seemed to satisfy Big Thunder.

Broken Pine said his farewell. An air of mourning gripped the village, understandably so, but Preacher knew that under Broken Pine's leadership, the Crow would get through this and grow strong again. When Hawk joined them, Broken Pine

440

embraced him briefly and said, "If you need us, get word to us. Every warrior among our people will fight to help you."

"It is my fault that some of our warriors lie dead, along with our women and children," Hawk said gloomily. "Winter Wind hates me as much as Preacher."

"Then by God, it's Winter Wind's fault for carryin' around that much hate!" Preacher said. "Sure, we killed a hell of a lot of Blackfeet that year, but only because they wiped out a whole village of Absaroka first! Evil like that, you've just gotta put a stop to it, whatever it takes."

"And yet evil goes on and always will."

"Just because you can't always win don't mean the fight ain't worth fightin'."

Hawk nodded slowly and then said, "Let us go."

They swung up on their horses and rode out. As they left the village, Lieutenant Tyler rode over to intercept them.

"Are you sure you don't want any more help from us, Preacher?" the young officer asked.

"You've got your own problems to deal with," Preacher told him. "Davidson and O'Connor givin' you any trouble so far?"

Tyler shook his head. "All the fight seems to have been knocked out of Edgar. He never dreamed anyone would ever stand up to him the way we did. And O'Connor . . . well, he's just one man, and he's being well guarded."

"Better keep that up," Preacher said. "I wouldn't trust that fella any farther'n Big Thunder could throw him."

"We'll wait here, or nearby, at least, until you return, Mr. MacCallister," Tyler said to Jamie. "We left the fort with you, and I'd like to have you with us when we return."

"I appreciate that, Hayden," Jamie said. "But you do what you think is best." He grinned. "You're in command now, you know."

"Yes, thanks to your help. The help of all of you." Tyler sat straight in the saddle and saluted. "Good luck and Godspeed, gentlemen."

"We'll take it," Preacher said, and then he led his companions toward the scene of the ambush, where they would pick up the trail of Winter Wind and her gang.

CHAPTER 32

Preacher, Hawk, and Jamie peered intently at the mouth of the narrow canyon about half a mile away. They stood on top of a thickly wooded knoll, holding the reins of their horses.

"That has to be where they went," Jamie said quietly. "The trail leads straight in that direction, and they haven't gone to any trouble to try to cover it up."

"That's because Winter Wind wants us followin' 'em," said Preacher. "She can't take a chance on us losin' the trail." He snorted disgustedly. "Like that'd ever happen."

"Looks like that's the only way through that cliff without going a long way north or south, too," Jamie went on. "Have you ever been up that canyon, Preacher?"

The mountain man frowned in thought for a moment and then nodded.

"Years ago," he said. "Best I recollect, it winds around for a couple of miles through the badlands on the other side of the cliff and finally comes out at a little lake." Preacher raked a thumbnail along his jaw. "Could be that's where they've camped to wait for us."

"Only one way to find out, isn't there?"

The cliff that loomed ahead of them was sheer and rose two hundred feet above the grassy bench. Climbing it would be difficult at best, and horses could never make it. As Jamie had said, the narrow passage was the only way through. The canyon was twenty feet wide at the mouth. The towering walls appeared to lean inward, as if they were about to fall in and close up, but that was just a trick of the eyes.

Preacher mulled over the situation for another minute, then said, "I'm goin' by memory again, but I believe about five miles south of here, you'll find an old game trail that'll lead you over the cliff and across the badlands, Jamie. Is that horse of yours pretty sure-footed?"

"I'd trust him with my life," Jamie replied.

"Good, because you'll have to where that trail zigzags up the cliff."

"You're saying we should split up?"

"Hawk and me and Dog will go on through the canyon, like Winter Wind's ex-pectin' us to do," Preacher said. "But if you

444

circle around and follow that other trail, you can come up on that lake from the south. There's a ridge that overlooks it. With you sittin' up there with that Sharps of yours, you'd have a clear shot at anybody down below."

"Like Winter Wind," Jamie said heavily.

"Or anybody else who needs shootin'. I'll leave that up to you."

Jamie frowned. Preacher seemed to be trying to say something without actually saying it, but Jamie wasn't sure what it was. He felt an uneasy stirring inside him. Preacher might have a plan, but if so, Jamie figured it was one that neither of the mountain man's companions would like.

Still, the idea of them splitting up and coming at the outlaw camp from two different directions was a good one. Jamie said, "All right. I can find that game trail, I reckon. But it'll take me a while to circle around that far."

"Hawk and I will wait here until about an hour before nightfall, then start through the canyon," Preacher said. "That ought to give you long enough."

"All right." Jamie shook hands with Preacher and then Hawk. "Good luck."

"Just don't forget . . . When you see the shot you need to make . . . *take it.*"

■ ■ ■ ■

Preacher had a spare pair of Colts in his saddlebags. He gave them to Hawk, along with an extra loaded cylinder for each revolver, even though Hawk wasn't nearly as proficient with a handgun as Preacher was. Hawk was a good shot with a rifle but simply hadn't had the practice needed to become an expert with the Colts. However, that gave him considerably more firepower, and he might need it.

"There is something in your mind," Hawk said quietly as they walked through the oppressively narrow canyon with Dog just ahead of them. Preacher's Sharps was in his hands, and Hawk carried his old flintlock rifle in addition to the revolvers thrust behind his belt and the bow and quiver of arrows slung on his back. "You have a plan to save Eagle Feather."

"I damn sure do," Preacher agreed, "but it ain't time to talk about it yet. We got to find the boy first and make sure he's still all right."

"He has to be," Hawk said fervently.

"Oh, I expect he is. Winter Wind's loco, no doubt about that, but she ain't lived this long without gettin' cunning, too. She'll keep him alive until we show up." Preacher's voice hardened. "Then there's a good chance she figures to kill him right in front of us, before killin' us."

Hawk's breath hissed between his teeth. "If she harms that boy —"

"We're gonna do our damnedest to make sure she don't get the chance."

Gloomy shadows were thick inside the canyon. The sun was low enough over the mountains that none of its rays penetrated here, only the reflection of the remaining light up above. Preacher didn't anticipate running into an ambush or any other sort of trap — Winter Wind *wanted* him and Hawk to catch up to her, after all — but he kept his eyes open anyway, in case the Blackfoot woman decided to simplify matters and just kill her enemies, rather than torture them first.

The canyon never ran straight for more than a hundred yards at a time, but finally they came within sight of its western mouth. The red glow of sunset filled the jagged opening and made it look like the bloody maw of a hungry beast. The eerie sight was enough to give even the strongest man the fantods, but Preacher and Hawk never broke stride. They moved straight ahead

447

toward whatever destiny had in store for them.

They stopped just short of the canyon mouth and looked down a steep slope toward a small, deep blue lake ringed by pine trees. More cliffs and ridges surrounded it, but this was an oasis of sorts in the rugged landscape.

Preacher wasn't interested in the scenery, though. What caught his eye were the horses and men gathered on the lake shore, in a clearing in the pines. A fire burned there, and seated on a log near the flames was a familiar small figure.

"Eagle Feather!" Hawk exclaimed under his breath.

"The boy's all right," said Preacher.

That was true for the moment. But a man stood just behind Eagle Feather, a grizzled outlaw with a long, gray-streaked beard. He held a bowie knife in his hand and seemed ready to use it at a second's notice. Clearly, he had been given the job of guarding the boy . . . or killing him if Winter Wind gave the order.

As for Winter Wind herself, she paced back and forth, the poncho she wore swirling around her each time she turned, revealing her holstered guns. She had tucked her long dark hair back up into her flat-crowned hat. She reminded Preacher of a wild animal in a cage, eager to break loose and kill.

"You stay here," Preacher said to Hawk. "They won't have seen us in these shadows yet, so they won't know you're with me." He looked at the big cur. "Dog, you're gonna stay here with Hawk."

"What are you going to do?" Hawk asked.

"What Winter Wind wants me to. I'm gonna trade myself for the boy."

"No! You said she would kill Eagle Feather if we give ourselves up."

"That's why you're stayin' out of sight," said Preacher. "I'm gonna tell her you were killed in the fightin', back there at the river." He shook his head. "Chances are, she won't believe me, but she'll play along for now and pretend to let Eagle Feather go, thinkin' she can send her men after him as soon as I'm her prisoner. But it's gonna be up to you to grab the little fella and stay ahead of 'em. Get back to the village and your wife and daughter as fast as you can."

Hawk frowned darkly and said, "But that leaves you as Winter Wind's prisoner."

"That'll be worth it, as long as you and Eagle Feather get away."

"No, Preacher. I cannot abandon you to that . . . that insane woman!"

Preacher laughed and said, "You won't

449

be. That's where Jamie comes in." He nodded toward the ridge to their left. "I reckon he's up there somewhere by now with that Sharps, which is a mighty fine rifle. Jamie MacCallister's a smart fella. He'll be able to figure out what's goin' on down here. When he does, as soon as Eagle Feather is clear, he'll know what to do."

Hawk's eyes slowly widened as he stared at his father.

"You expect MacCallister to kill you!"

"One nice, clean shot cheats Winter Wind outta her revenge. And then, if Jamie can reload fast enough — and I've got a hunch he can — then he can blow *her* lights out, too, so she can't inflict more misery on anybody else. That's about the best we can hope for."

Hawk shook his head and said, "No, it cannot be this way."

"There ain't no other way open to us." Preacher put a hand on Hawk's shoulder. "The most important thing is savin' Eagle Feather's life, and then you and him gettin' away from here. Hell, if I'm certain of those two things, I'll cross the divide without ever lookin' back." He smiled. "It'll be good to see your ma again, and all the old friends I've lost over the years."

Hawk stared, shook his head, put his

hands to his temples as if in pain. But he couldn't come up with a plan that had a better chance of working than the one Preacher had just explained. Finally, with a sorrowful expression on his face, he nodded.

"You are sure of MacCallister?" he asked.

"Dead certain sure."

Hawk sighed and said, "Very well. It will be dark soon. We should go ahead, while there is still light to shoot by."

"That's just what I was thinkin'," Preacher said. He squeezed Hawk's shoulder again. "So long, son."

"Preacher . . ."

"Naw, there ain't no need for a bunch of speechifyin'. Just get that boy outta here and back home safe and sound."

Hawk nodded. Preacher turned and walked out of the canyon, into the open, without another word.

"Winter!" Appleseed Higgs said. "It's him!"

The old outlaw grabbed the boy's arm with his free hand, jerked him to his feet, and pointed with the big knife in his other hand toward the canyon mouth where a buckskin-clad figure had just strode into view. The man was coming down the slope, carrying a rifle.

Winter Wind stopped pacing and jerked around to stare at Preacher. Appleseed could tell how stiff with anticipation she was. All the other men were tense and ready for trouble, too.

But Preacher was just one man.

"Where is the young one?" Winter Wind muttered. "Where is Hawk?"

She waited until Preacher reached the base of the slope, about fifty yards away, before she called in her powerful voice, "Stop! Come no closer, Preacher!"

The mountain man halted. He said, "Howdy, Winter Wind. Never expected to run into you again."

Trembling with anger, fists clenched at her sides, the Blackfoot woman shouted, "I will not exchange pleasantries with you, white man! Murderer of my people!"

"Your people started the killin'," Preacher said coldly. "What Hawk and me did was justice, pure and simple."

"Liar!" she screeched. Appleseed had never seen Winter Wind lose control of her emotions like this. She had always been stonily stoic.

"Let's just get this over with," Preacher said. "I'll surrender, and you can do whatever the hell you want with me. Just let the boy go first."

"No! Where is Hawk?"

"Dead." Preacher's reply was flat and hard. "Killed in that ambush back along the river."

Winter Wind shook her head and said, "I do not believe you."

Preacher shrugged. "Then you should'a stayed around there a mite longer, and you could've seen it for yourself. Whether you believe it or not don't change a thing. Now, are you gonna let the boy go so you and me can get on with settlin' things between us?"

Appleseed was just as anxious to hear what Winter Wind was going to say as Preacher seemed to be. As usual, she hadn't let anybody else in on her plans. She always played her cards close to the vest.

After a long moment, Winter Wind said just loudly enough for Appleseed to hear, "No."

Fifty yards away, Preacher cocked his head to the side. "What was that?"

"I said no," Winter Wind repeated. "I no longer care whether the Absaroka is alive or dead. He is nothing without you, Preacher. He has never been important. All the death and suffering inflicted on my people . . . that is on *your* head, Preacher." She drew in a deep breath. "And so is your grandson's death." She jerked her head toward Appleseed and screamed, "Kill the boy!"

For a split second, Appleseed hesitated. He had done plenty of bad things in his life, bad enough that they might keep him awake at night if he ever allowed himself to think about them, but he had never killed a young'un in cold blood. Winter had warned him to be ready to cut Eagle Feather's throat, but for that fleeting moment, he couldn't do it.

Then his resolve hardened and he started to sweep the bowie toward the boy's throat.

Preacher's hands flashed toward the revolvers on his hips, even though he knew he was too far away and was going to be too late.

At that instant, the old outlaw's head exploded, blowing apart in a grisly pink spray of blood, brain matter, and bone shards. At the same time, the heavy boom of a high-caliber rifle filled the hole in the badlands where the lake was located.

That was a Sharps, Preacher knew. Jamie MacCallister had aimed at a different target than the one Preacher had expected.

But Jamie had made the shot.

"Eagle Feather!" Preacher shouted as he swept up the Colts. "Run!"

He was under no illusions that he could gun down fourteen or fifteen hardened outlaws without being filled full of lead himself, but if he could drill enough of them and keep the bastards busy, maybe Eagle Feather would have time to get away and reach Hawk in the canyon.

Preacher swung the Colts toward the nearest renegade, a red-bearded fellow in a black frock coat and coonskin cap who was bringing a rifle to bear, but before the mountain man could pull the triggers, one of the most amazing things he had ever seen happened.

A chunk of rock twice the size of a man's head seemed to fall out of the sky and land right on the outlaw. It smashed his skull to smithereens, sent blood and brains flying everywhere, and slammed on down to the man's shoulders, driving him to the ground like a giant hammer.

That shocked everybody into immobility, but only for a second. Then Preacher's guns began to roar and two more men went spinning off their feet as his bullets tore through them.

Another big rock landed among several of the outlaws, scattering them like ninepins. Jamie's Sharps boomed a second time and blew a fist-sized hole through one of the men as he tried to scramble back up. Preacher ventilated two more of them.

A renegade tried to draw a bead on

Preacher, but a rifle shot knocked him back into the fire. Preacher glanced around and saw Hawk drop the smoking rifle, yank out the two revolvers Preacher had given him, and bound on down the slope to join the fight. Dog was with Hawk, racing into battle alongside the warrior.

Where is Eagle Feather?

Preacher triggered another shot from each gun, the slugs pounding into an outlaw's chest and driving him off his feet. Jamie dropped another man with a long-range shot. Hawk cocked and fired as fast as he could, spraying lead among the members of Winter Wind's gang. He emptied the Colts, and the hail of bullets took down two more men. Dropping the guns, he whipped his bow off his shoulder, nocked an arrow, and let fly, burying the shaft in a man's throat. Dog had another of the renegades down, savaging the screaming man.

Another large rock plummeted down from above and crushed an outlaw's ribs. Preacher glanced up and spotted a gigantic figure standing on the rim of the canyon. It would take enormous strength to heave rocks like that, and he knew of only one man capable of such a feat.

Big Thunder had followed them despite being told not to, and taken a hand when he was most needed.

Preacher was still looking for Eagle Feather. In all the chaos and violence, he had lost track of the boy. But as he realized all the outlaws were down, either dead or badly wounded, he knew Eagle Feather still had to be around here somewhere —

"Preacher!"

The unholy screech was like that of a demon from hell. Preacher whirled toward it, guns up, and saw Winter Wind standing a few yards away, holding Eagle Feather in front of her with one arm while the other hand pointed a revolver at Preacher.

"The boy and I are leaving," she said as her face twisted in a snarl. "He is my son now! I will teach him to hate —"

Preacher's right arm snapped out straight. The gun in his hand boomed, and Winter Wind's head jerked back as the bullet drilled into her brain. She lived just long enough for her eyes to widen in shock and disbelief before she let go of Eagle Feather, dropped her gun, and crumpled to the ground.

"I've heard more'n enough outta you, you crazy bitch," Preacher said as he lowered his Colt.

Eagle Feather dashed to Hawk and was swept up in his father's arms. Preacher let them have their reunion while he walked around the renegades' camp. The few who were still alive were hurt too badly to survive. A few swift strokes of Preacher's knife put them out of their misery. He wiped the blood off the blade, sheathed it, and then looked up at the rimrock again, where Big Thunder still stood. The sun was down, but a few stray beams still slanted to that high ground and lit up the giant Crow warrior as he waved excitedly.

"Big Thunder threw rocks!" he shouted down, cupping his hands around his mouth.

Preacher returned the wave and called, "You sure did!"

"Is Preacher mad that Big Thunder followed him?"

"Not a bit, old son! You did good!"

Up on the rimrock, Big Thunder did a little jig of pure happiness at the praise.

Preacher went over to his son and grandson, ruffled Eagle Feather's hair, and asked, "Are you all right?"

The boy had been crying, but he put a brave look on his face now and said, "The bad woman told me she would hurt me. She said many mean things. But I was not scared."

"She won't hurt anybody again," Preacher said. He glanced at the sprawled shape of

Winter Wind, who lay on her back with one knee drawn up a little, her hair loose now and spread out around her head like a black cloud on the ground.

Never again.

CHAPTER 33

Fort Kearny, two weeks later

Jamie MacCallister sat at a table in the sutler's store, nursing a mug of beer.

Tom Corcoran, the sutler, stood behind the bar, clouds of acrid smoke from his cheap cigar wreathing his head as he glared at Jamie with dislike obvious in his one good eye. Corcoran and Liam O'Connor were friends, and the sergeant was going to be in the guardhouse for the foreseeable future. When he was finally released, he would probably be transferred somewhere far away from Fort Kearny, or at least that was what Captain Croxton had told Jamie.

The door opened, and a tall, broad-shouldered figure was silhouetted against the afternoon light outside. Jamie recognized the newcomer immediately and lifted a hand in greeting as the man came on inside.

"Preacher. Over here."

The mountain man walked across the room to the table, signaled to Corcoran to bring him a beer, and pulled out a chair to sit down.

"Figured you'd be headed back to Colorado already," Preacher commented as he stretched out his long legs and crossed them at the ankles.

"The post's commanding officer asked me to stay around until all the hearings were over," Jamie explained.

"Hearin's? You mean Lieutenant Tyler ain't gettin' court-martialed?"

"Nope." Jamie took a sip of the beer and set the mug back on the table. "Cap'n Croxton talked to Mackey and Briggs and a bunch of the other men, and it was pretty obvious to him that Hayden didn't have any choice but to relieve Davidson of command. He's going to say as much in the report he sends back to Washington. Hayden could still wind up in some trouble, but I sort of doubt it."

Preacher nodded his thanks as Corcoran placed the mug of beer on the table in front of him, then said to Jamie, "It'll probably help when the cap'n hears that Broken Pine will be here in a day or two, ready to talk about that treaty, which was the point behind the whole thing in the first place."

Jamie grinned and slapped the table. "He decided to trust us, did he?"

"For now. He's still more than a mite wary, though."

"And he's right to feel that way," Jamie said, nodding. "I hope the decision doesn't come back to haunt him. But all that's pretty much out of our hands, isn't it?"

Preacher drank some of the beer, then licked foam off his mustache. "Pretty much," he agreed.

"Did Hawk come with you, or is he coming with Broken Pine?"

"Neither. He's stayin' back in the village with his family. I don't think he feels like bein' apart from 'em right now, after everything that's happened."

"I can't say as I blame him. How's Butterfly?"

"Healed up just fine. I don't think she's even gonna limp any."

"I'm glad to hear it," Jamie said.

"What about Lieutenant Davidson?" Preacher asked.

Jamie shook his head. "It's just plain Edgar Davidson now. He resigned his commission and left the army."

Preacher's bushy eyebrows rose in surprise. He said, "Did he do that so they wouldn't court-martial him and give him a dishonorable discharge?"

"No. I'm not sure that would have happened, anyway. My guess is that he just couldn't stand the idea of having the stigma of being relieved of command following him around for the rest of his career. The army's like any other organization, I reckon . . . It runs on gossip and spite."

"Well, at least we won't have to worry about him causin' any more trouble for folks."

Jamie nodded slowly and said, "Yeah, that's right."

He wished he was completely convinced of that, however.

The two big men sat there in silence for a moment, then Preacher asked, "O'Connor?"

"Locked up in the guardhouse for now. The captain's waiting to hear from the higher-ups about what to do with him." Jamie drained the last of his beer. "Not my problem, though, thank goodness. I'm going home to my wife and kids."

"Lucky man."

Something in Preacher's voice made Jamie frown. He said, "You've got a family, too."

Preacher shook his head and said, "Not no more."

"What the hell are you talking about?" Jamie leaned forward. "You said Hawk and

Butterfly are fine, and I'm assuming their young'uns are, too."

"They are," Preacher confirmed, "and I want 'em to stay that way." He leaned back in his chair, and the look in his hooded eyes seemed to be a million miles away as he went on, "Think about it, Jamie. They could've all wound up dead. Some of the Crow *were* killed when Winter Wind and her gang jumped us. That only happened because she wanted vengeance on me."

"Blast it, that's her fault for hating, not your fault for being hated!"

"Maybe so," allowed Preacher, "but it don't change the fact that I've made a whole heap of enemies in my life, and some of 'em are still out there, wantin' to hurt me any way they can. I've done thought about it, and it seems to me the best way to keep Hawk and his family safe is if I never go near 'em, or even speak of 'em, again."

"But that's loco, Preacher! You're just going to turn your back on your family and go through the rest of your life alone?"

"I'm gonna keep 'em safe," Preacher said stubbornly. "Anyway, I won't be alone. I've got Dog and Horse, and friends like you who I ain't worried about bein' able to take care of yourself. Maybe I'll run into somebody else who's just as capable one of these days." The mountain man shrugged. "One way or another, I've made up my mind."

"Did you tell this to Hawk?"

Preacher pursed his lips and didn't say anything for a moment, then finally admitted, "Well . . . no. But he's a smart boy. He'll figure it out."

Jamie looked across the table and shook his head.

"I guess that's up to you, Preacher. I don't reckon I could ever make it without my family, but for all the things you and I share, we're different sorts."

"That we are," Preacher said. He pushed his still half-full mug aside. "Reckon I'll be movin' on. I'm feelin' mighty fiddlefooted. We'll run into each other again, one of these days."

"You think so?"

Preacher grinned as he got to his feet. "This ol' wilderness is a pretty small place, sometimes. And I've never knowed either of us to stay out of trouble for very long, have you?"

That was sure the truth, Jamie MacCallister thought as he watched his old friend Preacher walk out of the sutler's store and head for whatever the frontier had in store for him next. Jamie was suddenly eager to get on that trail himself.

ABOUT THE AUTHORS

William W. Johnstone has written nearly three hundred novels of western adventure, military action, chilling suspense, and survival. His bestselling books include *The Family Jensen; The Mountain Man; Flintlock; MacCallister; Savage Texas; Luke Jensen, Bounty Hunter;* and the thrillers *Black Friday, The Doomsday Bunker,* and *Trigger Warning.*

J. A. Johnstone learned to write from the master himself, Uncle William W. Johnstone, with whom J.A. has co-written numerous bestselling series including The Mountain Man; Those Jensen Boys; and Preacher, The First Mountain Man.

The employees of Thorndike Press hope you have enjoyed this Large Print book. All our Thorndike, Wheeler, and Kennebec Large Print titles are designed for easy reading, and all our books are made to last. Other Thorndike Press Large Print books are available at your library, through selected bookstores, or directly from us.

For information about titles, please call:
(800) 223-1244

or visit our website at:
gale.com/thorndike

To share your comments, please write:
Publisher
Thorndike Press
10 Water St., Suite 310
Waterville, ME 04901